WORDS OF PRAISE FOR MARY SHEEPSHANKS
PICKING UP THE PIECES

"[A] wonderfully British comedy of manners."
—*Library Journal*

"An intelligent, lighthearted romp . . . A classy comedy of manners that's also a delightfully witty commentary on those two great passions—the love of humans for each other and for their old houses."   —*Kirkus Reviews*

"[An] assured, well-crafted third novel . . . Sheepshanks draws well-shaded characters and exhibits a firm grasp of family dynamics while managing to keep the novel's romance element grounded and real."   —*Publishers Weekly*

"A fabulous relationship drama . . . The storyline is well-written as family interplay is cleverly described . . . Mary Sheepshanks . . . is clearly one of the best writers of contemporary women's fiction on the market today."
—Harriet Klausner, *Painted Rock Reviews*

A PRICE FOR EVERYTHING

"An exceptional first novel. I laughed out loud."
—Rosamunde Pilcher

"Touchingly wise and extremely funny."
—*The Times of London*

more . . .

FACING THE MUSIC

ALSO BY MARY SHEEPSHANKS

FICTION
A Price for Everything
Facing the Music

NONFICTION
The Bird of My Loving

POETRY
Patterns in the Dark
Thinning Grapes

PICKING UP THE PIECES

MARY SHEEPSHANKS

St. Martin's Paperbacks

First published in the United Kingdom by Century/Random House UK Limited.

PICKING UP THE PIECES

Library of Congress Catalog Card Number: 98-33243

ISBN: 0-312-97037-4

Printed in the United States of America

St. Martin's Press hardcover edition / January 1999
St. Martin's Paperbacks edition / October 1999

St. Martin's Paperbacks are published by St. Martin's Press, 175 Fifth Avenue, New York, N.Y. 10010.

10 9 8 7 6 5 4 3 2 1

To
my brother and sister-in-law,
David and Louise Nickson,
with love

Acknowledgments

I would like to thank all those who have kindly helped me with information in writing this story, with special mention of Dr. P.D. Hingley (Library of The Royal Astronomical Society), Alan Barker OBE, FCA, MSI, and Father John Osman MA, STL—any mistakes will be mine not theirs. Loving thanks to Kate Parkin, my editor, and Sarah Molloy, my agent, for their wonderful encouragement, and to my daughters and daughter-in-law for being such patient sounding-boards for my ideas.

Introduction
by *Rosamunde Pilcher*

Any person who has read *A Price For Everything* will be happy to pick up this enchanting novel, and be transported back to Mary Sheepshanks' Yorkshire countryside, and there encounter the delightful, and sometimes bizarre, individuals who inhabit her world.

She has the lightest, but most accurate of perceptions; touching on every kind of emotion with the wisdom of personal experience. And yet this is a funny book, too, and laughter bubbles up on nearly every page.

In *Picking Up the Pieces*, her heroine, Kate, has been a widow for a year, a period spent in coming to terms with her solitary state, keeping an eye on her elderly mother-in-law, dealing with her humorless daughter Joanna, and trying to unravel the complicated hangups of her granddaughter Harriet. In between times, she walks her dog, sees her friends, and stitches at her tapestry, referred to dismissively as Kate's *tatting,* or her *little hobby.*

But after a year of widowhood, the time has come, she knows, to become a little more assertive about her place in society. Much as she loves her grandchildren, she has no wish to become a part-time, unpaid nanny, always on hand to baby-sit, or drive them to parties. Her home, which she shared with her husband, and where she brought up her children, is now much too large. Decisions must be made, the obvious solution being to swap with her daughter, and move into Joanna's nearby cottage.

As well, there is the constant presence of Gerald Brownlow, faithful and persistent as an old spaniel, who, now that the statutory year of mourning is over, wishes to marry Kate, and so possess himself of a splendid little woman, who will load for him at pheasant shoots, and provide nourishing lunches for his masculine tweeded guests.

Kate has never been adept at making decisions, on account of being married for so long to a dynamic man who chose to make them all for her. But a catalyst comes into her life in the shape of Jack Morley, a self-made American businessman with roots in Yorkshire, returned to his home country to buy up and refurbish a large property lately come on the market. They meet by chance, and then meet again, to the consternation of the locals, and their love affair runs a gentle course, as he encourages, bombards her with bright ideas, and gradually boosts Kate's confidence in herself.

Her needlework, she discovers, is not simply a little hobby, but an expert and distinctive craft, with considerable commercial value. Her natural talent for home-making grabs Jack's attention, and he employs her as a consultant to the restoration of his newly acquired property. When she leaves her old home and moves into the Observatory, the magic little house on Jack's estate, which had always beguiled her, the county is astounded. Who is this man? They ask, but Kate is oblivious of the furor, and with joy begins to plough her own furrow.

Her tale is a little like one of her own tapestries, a montage made up of several different colored threads and varied stitches. The mystery of Harriet's father; the revelation of her own husband's infidelities; the unsatisfactory marriage of her daughter Joanna. Babies arrive and old people die. Huge meals are cooked, cocktail parties are planned, and at one point all the local ladies are gathered together for a psychic séance of mind-boggling idiocy, as the medium sweeps away antipathetic auras with an imaginary broom.

By the end of the book, it seems that Kate has sorted out everybody's troubles except her own, and she finds herself, once more, abandoned and solitary. But she is a stronger woman now, and able to accept compromise, and because of this her destiny points, if not to total happiness, then a future filled with hope.

Kate relates to any middle-aged woman, caught between the demanding needs of the generations on either side. But her understanding, patience, and life-saving sense of the ridiculous see her through, and when the book is finished, I'm pretty sure she'll have the reader on her side.

Rosamunde Pilcher

℘ ONE ℘

On the first anniversary of Oliver Rendlesham's death, his widow, Kate, went exploring, fell in love, and took a decision that was to have a profound effect on family life.

The day started badly. The moment she woke, Kate had a sense of dark clouds hanging over her. Then she remembered what day it was; but it wasn't only the significance of the date that caused her ill-ease—after all, she had woken to the realisation that Oliver was no longer there for the last three hundred and sixty-five days. What difference did one more day make? What made her want to dive under the bedclothes and pretend that she no longer existed was the realisation that in a weak moment she had allowed herself to agree to going to lunch with Netta Fanshaw.

Netta had been one of Oliver's great admirers. She had enjoyed jangling his scalp round her belt like a headhunter's trophy, together with those of other friends she considered influential—Netta didn't have insignificant friends. Kate had only qualified as an appendage to Oliver.

Kate had not heard from her since Oliver's funeral, where Netta had appeared wearing a suitably harrowed expression under a huge black hat that might have caught the lens of a television camera at Royal Ascot, but looked out of place at a family funeral in a small country church. The hat might perhaps have been useful as an umbrella in case of an unexpected shower and certainly successfully helped to obscure her husband, Miles Fanshaw, who pattered along beside her, occasionally getting bumped by the brim when Netta sorrowfully inclined her head to acknowledge an acquaintance.

Kate had been so surprised to hear Netta's voice on the telephone after twelve months of silence that she had been caught off guard.

"Sweetie, how are you?" The sugar content of the voice registered "hard-crack." "Miles and I have thought of you so often but we just seem to have been horribly hectic lately. You are dreadfully on my conscience—but there's a sad anniversary coming up for you and we want you to come over and be with us. I think Oliver would have liked that."

Despite a winded sense of outrage Kate heard herself weakly agreeing to go. Netta was so persistent you had to have a cast-iron excuse at the ready in order to resist her. Kate had been touched and amazed by the kindness and hospitality she had received during the last year, not only from close friends, but from some quite unexpected people too, but Netta, who had always showered them with invitations and claimed to adore the whole family, had not been among them.

"I can't think what possessed me—I must have been mad. I bet she's just unexpectedly short of a spare female. How dare she have me on her bloody conscience?" Kate had said crossly to her son, Nicholas, who had come up to Yorkshire for the weekend with his American wife, Robin.

"Oh come on, Mum—think how much you'll enjoy telling us all about it afterwards," said Nicholas. "It'll be worth it just for that—and when she next runs her fingers through her conscience it'll be so squeaky clean she'll be able to rinse you away for good. Luxury for both of you."

"I suppose I might quite enjoy watching her snuffling around for information and not telling her anything," admitted Kate. "I expect she wants to know what my plans are."

"Not the only one." Nick raised an eyebrow at her.

Kate had looked at him in surprise. He put his arm round her and gave her a sudden hug.

"Live dangerously, Mum," he said. "Robin and I think you ought to kick your heels up. Don't let Joanna boss you into becoming her slave—or Granny-Cis either come to that. You've earned a bit of freedom. Do what *you* want for a change."

Driving over to the Fanshaws' lunch party Kate thought about his words. It had not occurred to her that any of her family would be expecting her to make any surprise changes in her modus vivendi. Upsetting applecarts had not hitherto been her style, but during the last year she'd had time to do a great deal of thinking, and without Oliver's dynamic presence to fill her life, she had felt the pressure of living in such close contact with some of the other apples with whom she shared her cart to be increasingly oppressive—and now, suddenly, there had been unexpected developments, both nice and nasty. Kate might secretly be pondering about the future, but she didn't feel ready to discuss it with her family yet, certainly not with her daughter, Joanna, or her mother-in-law, Cecily.

The Fanshaws lived in a large stone house ten miles from Ripon. The rooms had all been decorated with stifling good taste by a London designer for whose expertise Miles had paid an exorbitant amount, though Netta would never have admitted that the ideas had not been entirely her own. The designer would have been astounded to know that Netta always spoke of him as "my little curtain man." The house often looked as if it rose romantically out of the Yorkshire mists, though in fact this was caused by the continuous arrival and departure of guests stirring up dust from the constantly renewed gravel. It would have been a bold weed that dared to poke its subversive little head through Fanshaw ground.

Kate was daunted to see several cars already parked outside the house when she arrived, although she was in very good time. Years of attending important functions with Oliver had instilled a punctuality that had now become a habit, though it was not natural to her. She had interpreted "Just a cosy little lunch, darling, so that we can really *see* something of you" with a handful of salt, but all the same her heart sank when she realised quite how many other people there would be. She knew her clothes would be wrong.

Netta greeted her effusively, with just the perfect touch of sympathetic understanding on show, as she linked her arm cosily with Kate's.

"Now who don't you know?" she asked as she led her towards the assembled company in the drawing room. It always astounded Kate how Netta constantly managed to gather new acquaintances, and she saw with a sinking heart that there were surprisingly few people that she knew.

"I want you to meet Oliver Rendlesham's widow," Netta announced in screaming headlines. "Oliver was one of our oldest, dearest friends." Netta had a way of marking priorities with her introductions that was second to none.

"Come and meet our new General," she went on, as though she had a personal stake in the regiment currently serving at Catterick, and she steered Kate towards a tall man with crinkly hair, a gleamingly clean-shaven jaw and highly polished shoes. He looked virile and youthful, but Kate had gloomily noticed lately that generals and judges, of whose acquaintance Netta boasted a large collection, were, like the proverbial policemen, getting younger all the time.

"Of course Oliver was quite unique—but Kate's a clever little thing in her own way too," said Netta, the perfect hostess, giving the obligatory conversational clue and setting Kate's teeth on edge. "She makes the most darling little cushions and things. Are you still stitching away, Kate?''

''Still stitching,'' said Kate, feeling sorry for the General. She could see that darling cushions wouldn't be his thing.

In the end of course, inevitably, they talked about Oliver.

She had just about exhausted her conversation with the General when she saw Gerald Brownlow arrive. He made a beeline towards her.

''Kate! How lovely. I didn't know you were going to be here. Why didn't you ring me and tell me you were coming? I could have given you a lift—saved you driving. We could have come together. What an independent little thing you are.'' If anyone else calls me a little thing, thought Kate, I shall throw up all over Netta's immaculate eau-de-nil carpet.

''That's very kind of you, Gerald, but I didn't know you were going to be here either—and anyway I like driving myself.''

What's the matter with me, thought Kate. I'm becoming touchy and chippy. Why can't I react normally?

Gerald Brownlow was that indispensable commodity for any aspiring hostess—a spare man. His wife had caused a huge local scandal a few years before by running off with Gerald's own farm manager, thereby causing him not only humiliation, but a double loss. There were those who said the departure of his excellent farm manager must have been the harder loss to bear. His name had been linked with other women at various times since, but so far nothing long-term had come of it. Kate was becoming uncomfortably aware that a good many people thought it would be a wonderfully tidy arrangement if she and Gerald were to find consolation together. Gerald was kind, personable and impeccably well-connected. For those that liked that kind of thing, a conversation with Gerald could be as interesting as a browse through Debrett. Kate was quite fond of him and knew he was grateful to her for all the help and hospitality she and Oliver had given him during his period of gloom and puzzlement after his wife's defection, but she did not want him to feel beholden to her, and the none-too-subtle attempts made by mutual friends to throw them together were beginning to embarrass her.

Netta however was not one of those who were hoping to nurture a possible romance, and had no intention of encouraging any possible interest Gerald Brownlow might have in Kate. He was far too useful to Netta in his single state. She swooped down on them with the speed of a vulture spotting a corpse.

"Now I can't let two such close neighbours talk shop to each other," she said. "Gerald, I want your help with one of my Lame Ducks. Come and talk to old Mrs. Northwood. She's just had her hip done, poor old poppet, and is not very mobile. I've put her on the sofa and don't want her to have to move." Neat way of tethering Gerald, thought Kate. Only the week before, she had actually seen the old poppet, who was only a few years senior to Netta herself though much less well preserved, going like the clappers on the new hip up Parliament Street in Harrogate and diving into Betty's famous tearooms for a fortifying mid-morning éclair. Kate didn't think Beryl Northwood was particularly lame—or much of a duck either, come to that. Still, you had to hand it to Netta: she was brilliant at manoeuvres. Kate gloomily supposed that she would now qualify as one of Netta's famous lame ducks herself; she certainly no longer had any other claim to fame.

Gerald smiled at Kate, and just lightly touched her arm. "See you later," he said, and dutifully went off to hear how disgraceful the food had been in the private hospital where all those with medical insurance went in from time to time, like cherished vintage cars, to have spare parts fitted.

The moment lunch was announced, Kate noticed that greedy Mrs. Northwood, her nostrils quivering in anticipation, had no trouble in nipping off her sofa unaided, and heading swiftly towards sustenance. Kate made a mental note to store up this little vignette to amuse Nick and Robin. Miles Fanshaw, who had been instructed by Netta to seat the General's wife on his right, clutched her arm all the way to the dining room in what was obviously meant to be a courtly gesture, but Kate thought it looked more as if he was terrified she might escape, and Netta would blame him if this new prize got away.

Food at the Fanshaws' was always delicious. A light fish mousse with herb mayonnaise was followed by roast lamb and new potatoes; hazelnut meringue served with a sharp blackcurrant sauce was succeeded by a wonderfully creamy Forme d'Ambert. The wine complemented the food perfectly.

Conversation at lunch centred on the sale of the Ravelstoke estate, which lay a few miles from where the Fanshaws lived. It had belonged to one family for generations, but on the death of the last owner, a reclusive bachelor, had passed to a distant cousin more interested in financing his drug habit and expensive lifestyle than in saving his ancestral acres. He had decamped to Florida and put everything, including the main house, on the market and there had been a huge advertising campaign in all the property glossies: the estate was to be sold either as a whole or in various lots. Opinion round the Fanshaws' table was divided as to which option would be best for the neighbourhood, and there was much speculation about prospective buyers. The name of a well-known pop star had been mentioned, as had the leader of a suspect-sounding religious cult. Someone had heard that a large international company intended to buy it and turn the hall into a research centre. There was even a rumour that planning permission had been granted for a leisure centre and theme park that would spoil the countryside.

Kate felt her attention wandering, her energy draining away, and longed to be out of doors. Perfect spring days are precious in Yorkshire—far too precious to spend cooped up in Netta's dining room, still eating at three in the afternoon, and struggling to make small talk while the sun shone and the birds in the garden sang invitations to less structured forms of entertainment.

It had been on just such a brilliant April day a year ago that Oliver had died after a year-long struggle against cancer. Kate still found it surprising that he had lost that battle—one of the very few campaigns in which he had been worsted. Perhaps the only one. Oliver was famous for his victories in takeover struggles, for his skill and tenacity at negotiation, and his refusal to allow defeat. As chairman of Schneiber and Pollock, he was the City's Mr. Fix-it, a man who not only knew everyone who was anyone, nationally and internationally, but was held in something akin to reverence by the financial cognoscenti. He was blue chip, cast iron: he was Oliver Rendlesham. His detractors complained that he rode roughshod over anyone who got in his way, but death had swept him inexorably away despite all efforts to fight off its hostile bid.

Kate tried to jolt herself back into the present. "On the other hand," the man on her left droned on, still clearly absorbed in the Ravelstoke estate and fooled by what her family called Kate's "listening face" into thinking she was hanging on his every word, "if they split the whole thing up there could be several quite desirable properties for sale—that quaint little observatory for one. It's years since anyone lived in it but I've often thought it a waste to leave it empty. The place has been neglected in the most disgraceful way."

He lit a cigar. "Hope you don't object to this?" he said, breathing out smoke like a fire-eating dragon. Actually Kate did mind, but it was clearly a rhetorical question and he sucked and puffed oblivious to her lack of enthusiasm. When they finally left the dining room it was nearly four o'clock and Kate insisted she had to hurry home.

"But we've hardly *seeen* you," said Netta. "I so wanted to have a chance for a cosy chat. We really must meet again *sooon.*" She had a way of stretching her words out like bubble gum. "Anyway, it's lovely to have found you again."

"I haven't moved house," said Kate dryly.

Netta looked slightly uncomfortable. "Miles and I wanted to let you lick your wounds in private, darling. We felt you needed space. Some people can be so intrusive on these occasions. Such a comfort to feel you have lovely Joanna and darling old Cecily living with you."

Kate was tempted to ask "Comfort for who?," thinking how adept Oliver's eighty-seven-year-old mother, Cecily Rendlesham, was at setting her relations at odds with each other—not to mention the sparks that sometimes flew from Kate's highly strung daughter. She resisted the temptation: Kate had no wish to see Netta's beady eyes light up with speculation about future plans or family squabbles.

Out of the corner of her eye, she was aware of Gerald Brownlow trying to attract her attention, but pretended not to see. She felt a desperate need to escape everybody. As she drove away from the Fanshaws, she decided to avoid the main road and take the longer, more scenic route home and stop to give Acer a run. She wasn't really in any hurry and the gated road across a stretch of moor would be a small price to pay in inconvenience for a taste of sunshine.

The road twisted uphill, and as she went through the small village of Wherndale, it forked. Kate would normally have taken the left fork, but the signpost pointing to the right read "Ravelstoke 3½." On an impulse Kate turned right.

The road narrowed and a notice advised "Please use passing places." She stopped the car at the first one, let Acer out and changed her tidy shoes for the old boots she always kept in the back.

"Let's go exploring," said Kate. Acer waved her fox's brush of a tail and cocked a wall eye at her mistress. Border collie was certainly predominate in her ancestry, but the farmer from whom Kate had bought her, said he reckoned there was a bit of Heinz in her make-up as well. She had certainly inherited not only brains but beauty from somewhere, with her copper-coloured coat, elegant white cravat and long white gloves; if her one blue eye did not quite match its partner, this somehow gave her an extra knowing look. She was Kate's inseparable companion.

They climbed over a stile and went along the edge of a wood. Bluebells hazed purple smoke between the trees and filled the air with hyacinth sweetness; Acer, crashing about among the tulip-like leaves and starry white flowers of wild garlic, released more pungent, oniony smells. A chiffchaff, practising its simple song, was still at the stage of making mistakes and getting the second note wrong. Curlews had come down from the moor and were bubbling to each other, marking territory, calling to mates and looking for suitable accommodation in the stone walls.

It was at this moment that Kate first saw the house.

There was another stile at the end of the wood leading into an open field where sheep were grazing peacefully; their lambs had formed into play groups and were skipping over the boulders that stuck up through the grass. Kate called Acer to heel and stopped to look at the view. To her left the ground fell away and all Yorkshire seemed to be laid out below like an unfurled map, before distant hills rose again miles away on the other side of the county. She thought that in this kind of weather it would be hard to find more beautiful countryside in which to live. Looking to the right she saw that she was nearly at the top of the field, and there above her, apparently stuck in the middle of nowhere, was an extraordinary little building—a house with a square tower out of which grew a second, circular tower surrounded by columns and topped by a cupola—a sort of cross between a temple and an old factory chimney, thought Kate. It had to be the observatory her neighbour at lunch had talked about.

She scrambled up to the top and found herself below a ha-ha which had clearly been originally intended to separate a garden from the field. Now the stones had fallen away in places and an old ewe was lying comfortably with her twin lambs in the shade of a huge clump of azaleas. As Kate and Acer approached she got up slowly, more in surprise than fright, but clearly not pleased to be disturbed by visitors. She bleated to her children to follow her and ambled off towards the back of the house.

It was easy to walk up the crumbling gap in the ha-ha that the sheep had used.

Kate felt as if the whole place might suddenly vanish like something out of *Alice in Wonderland*, as if she had unexpectedly slipped between the pages of *Lost Horizon* and stumbled on a Yorkshire Shangri-la. She would not have been surprised to discover that the walls of the enchanting little house were made of sugar or gingerbread instead of the local grey stone.

She stood gazing at the house, such wild ideas spinning in her mind that it made her legs feel quite shaky. The hollow where the old ewe had been resting looked inviting. Kate flopped down on the ground, Acer beside her. A wind-tilted beech tree, leaning out just below the ha-ha like the Tower of Pisa, was at that moment of perfection when its brilliant green leaves were still covered with the fine silver floss that would soon disappear as the leaves darkened and flattened out. She thought it surprising to find beeches growing so high up. The azaleas, a riot of yellow and apricot, smelt of honey. Even the drapes of goosegrass that were beginning to swarm over them looked beautiful at this stage. Gerard Manley Hopkins had a point, thought Kate: there is a lot to be said for weeds—providing you haven't just declared war on them and found yourself on the losing side.

Kate felt as though the straightjacket in which she had been living had suddenly loosened, and a rare feeling of peace and contentment spread through her. She folded her hands behind her head and closed her eyes, listening to the wind whispering through the leaves, hearing the occasional plaintive bleating of sheep and a distant willow warbler piping cadences from some secret place. The late afternoon sun still had warmth in it, and Kate let it soak into her bones.

Her last thought before she drifted off to sleep was, I must be in love.

❧ TWO ❧

Kate woke to the feeling that she was not alone. Acer, though still beside her, was standing up, making subdued growling noises. The sun had lost much of its warmth, and the breeze had sharpened to a light wind. For a moment Kate couldn't think where she was. She opened her eyes. The sky was still a brilliant blue, but big white clouds were now rolling over her head. She sat up.

Sitting on a tree stump a few yards away, looking down at her, was a man dressed in working clothes: frayed denim trousers, heavy black nailed brogues with tongues, and a lumberjack-type shirt with the sleeves rolled up above freckled brown arms and strong, practical hands. A shepherd's crook with a carved horn handle lay on the ground. Her immediate feeling was one of panic, and she groped in her pocket for her car keys, sticking the sharp end out between her middle fingers to make a defensive weapon, a trick Nick had taught her for emergencies; then she remembered guiltily that she was trespassing, and farmers could be tricky about dogs in the lambing season. Luckily Acer was clearly not chasing sheep.

"How long have you been there gazing at me?" she asked sharply, remembering the old fairy story of someone having a little bit of their soul stolen away while they slept and not liking the idea that she had been caught at such a disadvantage.

"Ah, so you've woken up. You were dead to the world. I was pondering about the need for a kiss to wake you up but decided it was not so much the Sleeping Beauty—more a case of Puss-in-Boots. A short-haired blue, or a silverpoint, perhaps. The Sleeping Beauty of my childhood didn't wear boots under her posh frock. Could I ask what you're doing here please?"

From his appearance, Kate had expected a Yorkshire accent, but she could not place him by his speech at all.

She decided it would be more dignified to ignore his remarks. She knew she must look strange with her old green Hunters poking out under the now somewhat muddy hem of the flowing hand-blocked cotton dress in which she always felt happy on her own ground, but which she had correctly guessed would feel all wrong at Netta's lunch party; Netta and the General's wife had been wearing snappy little suits with short, straight skirts. When she got out of the car she had taken her tights off and tied them round her waist in order to try to hitch the dress up a bit, and this improvised sash did nothing for the dignity of the ensemble. To make matters worse, she was pretty sure that if she stood up she would have a wet patch on her bottom from lying on the grass. Despite the unexpected heat wave of today, there had been heavy rain the week before and the grass was still slightly damp. The man clearly thought she looked enormously funny.

Counterattack seemed the best measure.

"What are you doing here yourself? Do you farm this land?"

"I'm not the farmer—no."

"Do you work for the Ravelstoke estate then?"

"You could say so."

"Well, do you or don't you?"

"Er—yes, I suppose I work for the estate. I'm just a caretaker really—I give an eye to the place."

"Just the person I need then," said Kate. "I very much want to look over this house."

"You interested in architecture then?"

To her own surprise, Kate heard herself answer, "It's more that I might be interested in buying the house."

The man raised an eyebrow. "What makes you think it's for sale?"

"Oh, I've heard it on the local grapevine," she said airily.

"Dangerous things, grapevines. You shouldn't believe half you hear. But yes, I'll let you look in the house now if you like. I happen to have the key on me; I was just going in myself. I don't know if the estate's going to be split up though or any of the properties sold separately."

"Has the estate actually been sold then?"

"I believe so."

"Who's bought it?"

"I'm afraid I can't tell you that."

"But it has definitely been sold?"

He looked down at her. "Oh yes," he said, "I'm pretty sure of that."

He felt in his pocket and produced an old-fashioned iron key. He offered a hand to pull her up. Kate ignored it and scrambled to her feet with as much dignity as she could muster, not helped by the tights which caught on a bramble and nearly pulled her over again.

From the garden side, the house had a bowed frontage in the centre, with tall arched Venetian windows; on either side of the central curve there were two single-storey wings. In the right-hand wing there was a door. As Kate followed him, it occurred to her that if she was going to explore a house with a strange man it might be as well to have Acer, who could be most protective, with her.

"Better call up your Rottweiler," he said, grinning, reading her mind. "You can't be too careful nowadays. Lot of sinister people about."

But Acer, clearly deciding that this particular man posed no immediate threat to her mistress, had gone off rootling after rabbits in the jungle-like garden. Kate felt round her neck for the dog whistle, but its cord had somehow become entangled both with her pearls and the diamond brooch she had worn in order to cock a snook at Netta, who was always covered in glitter, no matter what the occasion. Netta had been known to wear diamonds on a grouse moor. He watched while she struggled crossly to get the whistle to her lips before she managed to blow a couple of furious blasts, her chin almost on her chest so as not to break the string of her pearls. Acer, covered in goosegrass like the azalea bush, came bounding back, but disappointingly showed no inclination to menace the stranger.

The lock was stiff, and when the caretaker eventually got it to turn, the door was resistant too, so that he had to put his shoulder to it and push. He held it open for her. "Bit of oil needed there," he said. "I'll have to see to that. You're going to get awfully dirty—I don't think anyone's cleaned up in here for years. There are cobwebs all over the place."

"I'll risk it. It can't make me much worse than I already am."

"Do you always wear jewellery to walk your dog?"

"I've just been to a very smart lunch party."

"You must have looked a sensation."

Kate started to laugh. "Oh I did—but not the kind of sensation I would have liked. There were some very stuffy people there."

"Well, come and inspect the house. It's a rum little place. I believe it was converted about fifty years ago for some old Ravelstoke aunt as a sort of country retreat. The original Lord Ravelstoke, who built it about 1820 as his own private observatory, was supposed to be mad as a hatter, always known as Raving Ravelstoke. He discovered some crater on the surface of the moon that no one had ever spotted before and it was named after him—the Ravelstoke Crater. Not a tremendously useful discovery, but I dare say it gave him a buzz. Literally a lunatic, he must have been—only happy gazing at the moon. But then the whole family have been a sandwich short of a picnic for generations.''

There were several doors opening off the narrow passage in which they found themselves. The caretaker opened one on the left, and Kate followed him into what was obviously the main room of the house.

"Oh, how absolutely lovely! A lozenge-shaped room— I've always loved rooms with curves."

"Yes, curves can be very attractive." Kate looked at him sharply, suspecting that he was laughing at her again, being overfamiliar, but his expression appeared to be dead-pan.

"Nice moulding, too," he said. "They built with an eye for detail in those days. See what the theme is?"

Kate looked up. "Oh," she said, enchanted, "it's all the signs of the zodiac. How suitable."

"Want to come up the tower?"

"Oh yes, please—have you time?"

He looked at his watch. "I'm all right for a bit." He led the way back through the door into the passage and then into another room at the back, a square one this time, along one side of which rose a stone staircase with a delicate ironwork balustrade topped by a narrow mahogany hand-rail.

"I believe old Miss Ravelstoke used this as a dining room. The kitchen's in the right-hand wing of the house, where we came in, and there are three bedrooms and a bathroom in the left-hand wing—but she slept up above here. Quite a climb for an elderly lady, but one can see why she thought it worth it."

The stairs led up to a little landing off which there were two doors. "Bathroom," he said, opening one of them. "And the bedroom." They went into another square room, at the end of which a small spiral staircase twisted up towards a large trap door in the ceiling. The view from the windows was breathtaking.

"Now you're in the tower. As you see, you can walk all round the outside, but I'm not sure I could get the window open at the moment. Through the trap door is the observatory proper, which you may remember is round. You can see it from miles away—it's a great landmark." He grinned. "It's known locally as the phallic symbol."

It had been on the tip of Kate's tongue to suggest this idea herself, but she had refrained. She decided to ignore his remark.

"It's an extraordinary building. I've never seen anywhere like it—and yet it looks right." She looked around her. "It's as if a large grand house had given birth to a little baby one; only it's actually bigger inside than you'd think from the outside."

"That's because the proportions are so good. It was all designed by old Raving Ravelstoke himself, down to the last detail. Presumably he could have been an architect as well as an astronomer—a talented chap, even if he was barmy. All the building and plasterwork was done by the estate workers of the day. Pretty good, they must have been too. See the shell motive up here? Look at the architraves over the doors and the swags of shells round the little fireplace."

"Oh, and scallop shells round the windows instead of egg and dart," she said in delight. "I think this is the most magical house I've ever been in."

Ideas for new embroidery designs based on the seashore were immediately buzzing in her head. She went and sat in the window seat and traced the outline of one of the plaster shells with her finger. He came and sat beside her, a big man, who moved lightly and easily and had an outdoor look about him.

"You know a lot about the house," she said, "but you don't sound as if you come from this part of the world. Have you had the job long?"

"I spent part of my childhood round here, but I've knocked around the world a good bit since then. I've had a lot of jobs in my time. I gather jobs are hard to come by here now."

"Yes indeed." Kate looked at him with quick sympathy. "You have to take what's going." She wondered if he'd fallen on hard times. He seemed an educated type.

"Have you been house-hunting for long?" he asked.

"I only really started this afternoon," she said with careful accuracy, but seeing no reason to be extravagant with the truth either.

He gave her a curious look. "And what sort of thing are you really looking for?"

"I suppose," said Kate slowly, more to herself than to him, as if she were making and inspecting a discovery, "I suppose that what I'm really looking for is my own identity."

"Not a very usual request to a house agent."

"No. But a place like this might help me find it."

"I hope you won't set your heart on this particular one." His face wore a troubled expression. She wondered if he knew more about the new owner's intentions for the whole estate than he was letting on.

He said: "It's rather a unique house and I believe it's unlikely to be put on the market."

"If it's got my label on it then it will be," Kate said, dreamily drawing a shell on the dusty windowpane, and then adding a starfish. "Do you think that we can sometimes stumble on things—as if by accident—that are really meant for us? Do you believe in serendipity?"

He considered. "I used not to think that. I used to think one was either solely responsible for what happened in one's life—or else that it was all pure chance. A spin of the roulette wheel, and no pattern. But, yes, I think on the whole I now believe that sometimes things or people are put in one's path for a reason. What action we take then is up to us.''

"Exactly," said Kate, beaming at him. "Just what I think. So tell me what I should do now."

"Ah, that's cheating. I can't tell you what to do."

"But you could perhaps tell me which agent is acting for the new owner?"

"Cooper and Wilkinson."

"Thank you," said Kate. "Thank you very much." She looked at her watch and shot to her feet. "Oh my God! It can't be that late! I'm going to be in trouble. I must fly."

"Not even time for just a quick look at the observatory?"

"I'd love to but I really can't. Another time. I shall have to make a proper appointment and come again. I know Graham Cooper who runs the York office. Are you likely to be talking to anyone from the firm?"

"I may see Mr. Cooper, yes."

"If you do, will you put in a good word for me? Tell him someone is seriously interested?"

He hesitated. "It'll be up to the new owner, not Cooper and Wilkinson what happens, but I could tell him, I suppose. Shall I give a name?"

"Rendlesham. It's Kate Rendlesham." Then a thought struck her. "Oh, but please don't mention it to anyone else who comes round, and please ask him not to either. That's important. It could be awkward for me if rumours got round."

"On the local grapevine for instance?" he suggested.

"Touché." She laughed and held out her hand. "You've been most kind. A real bit of luck that you were here. When I talk to Cooper and Wilkinson I'll tell them how helpful you've been."

"Thank you," he said gravely, "that would be very kind."

"What's your name?" she asked.

"Jack," he said.

"Nothing else—just Jack?"

He hesitated as if he were considering saying something else, but then changed his mind.

"That'll do," he said. "Just Jack."

❧ THREE ❧

Joanna Maitland had cooked furiously most of the day. This was partly because she had set herself a huge amount to do, and partly because she was feeling furious anyway: with her children who had driven her mad all week, with her husband for not being there, a state of affairs—both the fury and the absence—which was in danger of becoming a habit for both of them, and to add to her misery, today she was also furious with her mother. Secretly, she knew this was unfair, but such an admission didn't help her feelings one bit. Her relationship with her mother often teetered between love and resentment, and at the end of a long wearing day, resentment was winning by several lengths.

Tomorrow was the day of The Great Food Fair which Joanna had organised as part of the Save Granby Abbey Appeal. Having recently taken over as chairman of the Friends of the Abbey, she had not only arranged the event but felt that as it had been her idea in the first place, her own contributions of delicious home-made food ought to outshine everyone else's. Joanna liked outshining and was very good at it. No one had ever accused her of slacking—though one or two people might have found her easier company if they could have felt justified in doing so. Also, because she was a professional cookery writer, there would inevitably be critical eyes and taste buds assessing anything she had produced. Joanna was on her mettle—but she nearly always was.

Today of all days she thought her mother should have been at her side, not just to help—and goodness knows, Joanna could have used some practical help—but because on this first anniversary of her father's death, she felt it would have been the appropriate thing for her mother, her grandmother and herself to have spent the day together. The fact that they all saw each other most days anyway, and that it was entirely by her own arrangement that she happened to be so particularly busy herself, was neither here nor there. She thought it insensitive of her mother to have gone jaunting off to a lunch party, even if it was one—as Kate claimed—to which she hadn't wanted to go. Since she loved the social round herself, Joanna found this hard to credit.

She doubted if her mother had even made a special pilgrimage to the nearby church where Oliver was buried. Joanna had gone at seven o'clock that morning after she'd exercised her horse. *"Visit grave"* she had written at the top of the list of things-to-do that she made for herself each day, and had felt relieved to tick it off before breakfast, though somehow it had not been a satisfactory expedition.

Joanna missed her father dreadfully. She had longed to pluck some comfort out of this act of remembrance, to find some peace. She wanted to feel both sorrowful and uplifted, to have a sense of closeness to her father, instead of which she just felt empty, lonely and hungry with a sort of dull ordinariness that was deeply distressing. She had nearly given in to a wild urge to kneel at the grave-side, even to prostrate herself on top of it—but then suppose someone saw her? So she had just stood awkwardly in the late April sunlight, her throat constricting so painfully that she could hardly breathe, but quite unable to shed the tears that might have brought release, gazing at the headstone with her father's name carved on it. It had only recently been erected, after the ground had been allowed the required interval of time in which to settle. It would have been unthinkable to let Oliver Rendlesham have a lop-sided gravestone. He had been sixty when he died—still at the height of his powers; still with everything to live for.

Joanna wondered if she missed Oliver more than Kate did, and both wanted this to be so, and yet felt uncomfortably shocked at herself for feeling competitive about bereavement. Her father would have understood. He was the only person who had ever completely understood her, she decided. They had thought each other just about perfect—which could certainly not be said about her present relationship with her husband, Michael. No one seemed to be finding her perfect at the moment, she thought sadly, and despite her successful career, unfailing competence, good looks and assured dress-sense, Joanna had a secret hunger to know she was approved of and admired.

Kate had in fact produced a contribution for the food fair, consisting of some rather curiously shaped buns, a chocolate mousse, and two large, dented foil containers of fish pâté which would probably taste good—there was nothing wrong with the gastronomic quality of Kate's cooking—but which, in Joanna's view, was a bad choice for the occasion. It might well go off, unless it was snapped up early in the sale, which seemed unlikely, given its unappetising beige colour and complete lack of enticing garnish. She had no doubt that the foil containers had seen the inside of Kate's deepfreeze during previous incarnations, and that the buns had collapsed because they had been taken out of the oven too soon when her mother got bored with waiting for them to cook. It amazed Joanna that Kate, who could embroider so beautifully and meticulously, who was clever about colour and design when these concerned needlework, seemed incapable of the proper presentation of either food or herself. Joanna frequently thought her mother looked a mess. Although Kate's clothes were often unconventional, she could occasionally look wonderful, but no one, least of all Kate herself, knew when she was going to manage to pull this off. Joanna, always suitably dressed and incapable of looking untidy even in a force nine gale, simply couldn't understand it.

There was a good deal about Kate that her daughter found difficult. It was as though their roles were reversed, with Joanna trying to improve her mother, giving her sensible advice and hoping that one day Kate might suddenly change for the better. As for Kate's effect on Joanna's elder daughter, Harriet, Joanna could feel herself tensing up at the very thought of it. When Kate and Harriet were together, they managed to make Joanna feel as though she was left outside a charmed magic circle. It was a hurtful sensation. Joanna thought Kate indulged Harriet and let her get away with being tiresome and silly. Given the fact that Kate had more or less brought Harriet up for the first six years of her life, the triangular relationship between grandmother, mother and child—not to mention a resident, cauldron-stirring great-grandmother—had been a difficulty waiting to happen. And it had happened.

Before her marriage to Mike, during Harriet's early years, people were always telling Joanna how lucky she was to have such an understanding mother to help in her single-parent role, but gratitude, difficult enough for anyone to handle, was not an emotion that came easily to Jo, who was well aware that Harriet loved Kate best.

It would have been fair to say that Kate usually tried not to exacerbate this problem—but Joanna didn't want to be fair at the moment. She just wanted someone to appreciate her own worth and tell her so, often. She wanted her father back.

By half past five she had finished cooking. The kitchen—Kate's kitchen in fact, which was larger than Joanna's and therefore more convenient for mass onslaughts—was immaculate; trays of appetising-looking food covered the tables and the whole thing looked like an advertisement in a glossy magazine. She hoped it would help Kate to see how important it was that they should swap accommodation soon. It was ridiculous that Kate should rattle about in the main house while Joanna and the children—and Mike when he was at home—squeezed up in the stable cottage. The cottage had been fine as an occasional weekend retreat, but now that they had decided—or rather Joanna had decided—to live in the country, it was far too small. It was tight during the week, but seemed to shrink if Mike came home on a Friday night, so that the Maitland family tended to spend most of their time in the bigger house anyway, which made it all the more ridiculous not to be permanently in residence there. Joanna thought her brother, Nicholas, had an awful nerve to suggest that she imposed on Kate. Nick and Robin swanned home and filled the house with their friends whenever it suited their plans, and Kate was always enchanted to see them.

Joanna looked at the clock. She hoped Kate would be home in time to fetch Rupert and Tilly from their tea-party. Where was Kate anyway? At that moment the front doorbell rang. She had better go and see who it was. It would be quite in character for her mother to have forgotten her keys and locked herself out, she thought, automatically checking her hair in the mirror before going through the door that divided the back of the house from the front, and out into the hall.

When she opened the front door, Gerald Brownlow was standing on the doorstep with a pot plant in his hand.

"Oh Gerald, how nice." Joanna was genuinely glad to see him. "Have you come to see Ma? I'm afraid she's not here. She went to lunch with the Fanshaws."

"I know. I saw her there. Netta invited me as well, and I accepted, so I was there too," said Gerald, who had a double talent both for repetition and for stating the obvious, which Kate always found hilarious.

"Well, do come in." Joanna smiled at him. "Would you like a cup of tea or is it too early for something stronger? I was expecting Ma back much sooner. It must have been a great party if you're only just on your way home now."

"Oh I've been home already. I'm surprised Kate's not back because she left well before I did. In fact I think Netta was rather put out that your mother broke the party up by making a move as soon as we all left the dining room, but apparently she said she was in a hurry to get back, so naturally I assumed I'd find her here already. Most of us stayed on to look round the Fanshaws' garden—which I must say was perfection. Their daffodils are sensational and all the cherries are out. I tried to have a word with Kate before she left but I couldn't catch her eye. I thought she might like this cineraria from my green house." Gerald, a keen racing man, considered Joanna to be a damn fine-looking filly, though a bit highly strung, perhaps—might need to run in blinkers. She was too brainy for his taste, but easy on the eye and made a chap feel welcome. "Yes please, Jo. Never too early for a drink," he said. "You're looking very fetching—but then you always do."

"Well thank you. Actually I've been slaving in the kitchen all day so I feel a perfect mess." Joanna was pleased that Gerald was coming in. As an old friend of her father's, he slotted neatly into one of her approved-of boxes.

"Thing is, I know today's a bad day for you all. Anniversary and all that," said Gerald. "Didn't like to say anything to your mother before lunch in front of everyone else, but that's why I wanted to catch her afterwards. Thought I might ask her out to dinner. Cheer her up a bit. Brought her this plant."

Joanna led the way into the drawing room. "You are thoughtful," she said, genuinely touched. "Make yourself at home, Gerald. I'll just go and get some ice and ring the cottage to ask Jenny if she'll fetch Rupert and Tilly for me. I'd told her she could go off early this evening because I thought Ma might actually like to collect the children, but I don't suppose Jenny'll mind changing." Jenny, an adaptable New Zealander, was the latest in a long line of au pairs and mother's helps. She had already lasted six months, which was almost a record. Luckily, she combined a capacity for hard work with a relaxed attitude to life and a good sense of humour. The children loved her and behaved far better with her than with their disciplinarian mother.

"That's fine," said Joanna, coming back with the ice. "Jenny'd rather have tomorrow night off anyway. She'll put the little monsters to bed too." She poured out hefty gin and tonics for herself and Gerald, and they settled themselves comfortably on Kate's drawing-room sofa.

They decided that as it was already so late, instead of taking Kate out to dinner, Gerald should stay to supper at Longthorpe. Joanna had saved some delicacies from her cooking orgy and had been intending to feed her mother and grandmother anyway—not that she'd consulted them. She said: "Honestly, Gerald, there's oceans of food and one more will make no difference. Cheer us all up to have you." The combined effect of gin and some male company was having a mellowing effect on her.

"You don't think Kate might mind? Oughtn't we to ask her first?" Gerald suggested.

"Heavens, no. She'll be thrilled," said Joanna firmly, thinking her mother was very lucky to have someone to bring her flowers and be so concerned about her. "But I can't think where she can have got to."

"Perhaps she looked in on someone on the way home. Or might she have—you know—dropped into the, er, church?" Gerald sounded slightly embarrassed. Anything to do with death, sex or religion was not part of his repertoire of social small talk. Joanna, conscious of feeling put out that she hadn't considered this possibility herself, was also uncomfortably aware that though she felt this was exactly what her mother ought to be doing, she didn't really want her to do it. She couldn't explain it to herself.

By half past seven Joanna was getting fidgety.

"You don't think she could have had an accident? Do you think I ought to ring the police?"

"Oh, I think we should wait a bit longer." Gerald felt far less confident than Joanna that Kate would be all that pleased to find her house invaded and her evening all mapped out for her when she did get back from whatever she was doing.

They were finishing their second drinks, and it was nearly eight o'clock when Harriet, bare-footed, sauntered into the room munching one of the cheese vol-au-vents destined for the food fair.

"*Where. Are. Your. Shoes?*" asked Joanna automatically. "And please don't help yourself to those. They're for tomorrow—you really are the limit."

"Sorry. Just testing. These are yummy," said Harriet. "Hi, Colonel Brownlow. Does Gran know you're here?"

"Hello, Harriet. No, your grandmother doesn't know I'm here because she's not here herself—she hasn't come back yet."

"Oh but she has." Harriet draped herself over the sofa and brushed crumbs off the front of her fluorescent lime-green top on to the carpet; she shot a triumphant look at her mother from under her spectacular eyelashes. "She's been in for ages. She's upstairs with Granny-Cis."

Kate and Acer had panted back to the car after their tour of the unexpected little house. All the way home Kate's mind had been racing with ideas. She felt charged with new energy as though several volts had been shot through her battery. Possible solutions to hitherto seemingly impossible situations seethed through her mind. Funny how easy it was to talk to strangers. The sense of identity, which she had told that nice caretaker chap that she was searching for, was important to her, though it was not something she had voiced to anyone before. The thought of buying and living in that delightful observatory just might make the realisation of a private ambition into a possibility. Kate had told no one about the interesting proposition that had recently been put to her. There were also other, less pleasant, things which had recently come to her attention about which she had only told one person—so far. She wondered for how much longer this would be feasible. She thought she might just be able to tell Nicholas, if it became necessary, but the idea of telling Joanna made her blood run cold.

It was seven o'clock when Kate turned into the drive of Longthorpe House, the house Oliver had bought and which had been renovated and altered over the years as their bank balance grew and their lifestyle changed. Her heart sank as she saw that there was a car parked outside her front door. Hell, I can't cope with visitors now, she thought—and she drove straight round to the back yard. A glance into the kitchen showed her that Joanna had obviously commandeered it, and spent an exceedingly busy and fruitful day. There were times when even the thought of her daughter's restless energy made Kate feel tired; times too when she found herself resenting the assumption that her house and her affairs were equally Joanna's territory and concern. Clearly the kitchen was no place for Acer at the moment, who would have had no compunction at demolishing a whole day's culinary work in a couple of minutes. After Kate had fed her with some less exotic fare, she decided to shut her in the old playroom, which Kate now used for her sewing—when it wasn't taken over by her grandchildren. Harriet was in there now, watching "EastEnders" on the television. She was a boarder at a school near York, but this was an exeat weekend and the girls had been collected at twelve in order to accommodate those who lived some distance away, an arrangement that had not suited Joanna at all.

"Oh darling, how lovely to see you," said Kate, warmed by Harriet's welcoming hug. "Don't let me interrupt the crucial goings-on in The Square—you can bring me up to date with it later—but have you any idea whose car is at the front?"

"Probably one of Mum's Granby Abbey slaves. Mum's bossometre's gone over the top—she's in her element. Peo-

ple have been turning up all afternoon prostrating themselves before her with twee little offerings on paper doilies.
I sneaked in here so as not to get caught. Mum's been
drizzling balsamic vinegar over meringues and piping little
blobs of cream on things all day. She's in a filthy mood.
She's really stressing out,'' Harriet rolled her eyes. ''You
want to steer clear.''

''I expect she's feeling low today,'' said Kate. ''I'll go
and see her as soon as whoever's visiting her has gone.
Meanwhile I think I'd better pop up and sit with Granny-
Cis for a bit. I know she had people in for bridge this
afternoon, but she'll be feeling the draught today too—not
that she'd admit it. I'll say one thing for your great-
grandmother: she may be infuriating but she's never sorry
for herself. You might go and suss out that car situation,
darling, and come and tell me when the coast's clear.''

Cecily Rendlesham was sitting in the upright wing chair
from which it was easiest to heave her large frame. She
had a pair of powerful binoculars round her neck, a tumbler
of chilled Fino sherry at her side, and her walking stick
hooked over the arm of her chair. The sherry was only there
for one purpose: to fortify the inner woman—not that anyone who knew her thought Cecily needed much fortifica-
tion. The stick and the binoculars were dual purpose. The
first was partly a walking aid, but its real purpose, according to its owner, was so that she could give an intruder
what she called ''a good thwack'' should she consider it
necessary; it never crossed her mind that she might not be
the one to get in the first blow. The binoculars were for
studying birds, which were her passion, but were also invaluable for studying the activities of all who came and
went at Longthorpe House. Through them she could watch
Joanna and Harriet exercising the horses and practising over
the jumps in the paddock; she could keep an eye on croquet
or tennis, check up on Rupert and Tilly playing in the garden; if Kate took her sewing out on the terrace, she always

swore that her mother-in-law could spot a wrong stitch at thirty yards; above all Cecily could be informed before anyone else about the arrival of visitors. Kate had no doubt that her beady eye would have identified the owner of the car outside the front door.

All those years ago, Cecily Rendlesham had been astonished at her son's choice of bride. She would have expected her brilliant Oliver, who was always surrounded by a flock of clever, beautiful young women when he was up at Cambridge, to have picked someone far more dashing than Kate. She had thought Kate a quaint little thing, mousey and lacking in sparkle, when she first met her, and had not imagined that the relationship could last. Kate didn't even seem particularly intellectual. When they announced their engagement, Cecily had been extremely disappointed that Oliver should throw himself away on this nonentity, and had done her best to put a stop to the romance. Of that terrifying time when Oliver had first taken her to stay with his alarming parents, Kate remembered only a numbing shyness and sense of inadequacy. Had she not been so wildly, desperately in love with Oliver, nothing would have induced her to set foot through their doorway again. Oliver's father, a high court judge with a whip-cracking wit and darkly threatening eyebrows, out of which long hairs sprouted like sinister antennae, completely paralysed Kate's powers of speech—and she thought her future mother-in-law a horror.

They had both been wrong. Cecily was to learn that there was more to Kate than met the eye, and Kate was to appreciate Cecily's courage and backbone, and come to be amused by her ruthless ability to ride roughshod over others, and her breath-taking outspokenness.

"Hello, Kate. How was your lunch?"

"Awful. Netta in full cry and I wished I hadn't gone. What about your bridge?"

"Roz and I had a very profitable afternoon. She really has the devil's own luck—she always holds the most amazing cards." Lady Rosamund Campion, though years younger than Cecily, was her bridge partner whenever she was in Yorkshire. Together they made a formidable combination: two wilful and occasionally outrageous women, both accustomed to getting their own way, by fair means or foul, though their style could hardly have been more different. Lady Rosamund's son, Sir Archibald Duntan, was a local landowner, and she had a charming Queen Anne house on his estate, to which she repaired from time to time in order to scandalise the Yorkshire locals and recharge her own batteries from her international jet-set life.

"Not that we had much competition today," Cecily went on. "Cynthia never knows how the cards lie and Babs Mallory is getting awfully ga-ga, poor old thing. Roz thinks it's all due to her hormones, but I told her I don't think our generation ever had those, and we got on splendidly without them. Rosamund always puts everything down to hormones, but I think it's much more likely to be this other newfangled Alkaseltzer thing, from cooking in aluminium pans. I've read about it in *The Times*."

Kate gave her mother-in-law a fond look. She thought she looked unusually drawn.

"Anyway, today will be a good day for us both to have behind us," she said gently.

"Yes." Cecily took a hefty swig of sherry, and Kate thought her hand shook just a little.

"Kate," Cecily's voice was especially gruff. "Do you think about Oliver a lot?"

"Every day," said Kate. "And you?"

"Oh yes. All the time. You can't think how unnatural it seems at my age to survive your child, even if that child was past middle age himself. I would have given anything for it to have been me and not Oliver that had to die—anything."

They sat together in silence for a bit, their thoughts following two very different tracks. Then Cecily gave herself a little shake.

"A year today—but it certainly hasn't taken you long to acquire a stalker," she said sharply.

"A *stalker?*" asked Kate. "Do you mean a follower? Whoever are you thinking of?"

"That Gerald Brownlow—sniffing around again. I watched his car coming up the drive an hour ago. I was quite surprised that you bothered to come up to see me at all. What have you done with him?" Cecily always leapt into attack mode if emotion threatened to undermine her guard.

"Oh really!" Kate was caught between amusement and annoyance. "So that's whose car it is. I knew you'd know. Harriet thought it was one of Joanna's helpers. Wonder what he wants. I dodged him after Netta's lunch."

Cecily gave a sniff which managed to convey a whole range of conflicting innuendos, and then suddenly surged to her feet and banged angrily on the window with her stick. Kate wondered if she was speeding a departing Gerald Brownlow on his way, but a flock of assorted birds flew off with a great flurry of wings. Cecily's windowsills were always hung with coconut shells, bird tables and nut holders. The droppings on the terrace below had been a source of irritation to Oliver.

"That damn spotted woodpecker again. I give it its own supply but it pinches all my little birds' nuts and frightens the bluetits away." There was a flash of black and white and a glimpse of red as the thief streaked off. Even spotted woodpeckers, with their gimlet beaks, didn't tangle with Cecily Rendlesham.

At this moment the door flew open to reveal Joanna, her face like a thunderclap.

"Well really, Ma! You might have let me know you were back. I've been entertaining Gerald Brownlow for you for the last hour and I gather from Harriet that you've been here all the time."

"Jo, darling, don't look so cross—I had no idea that Gerald was here. I hadn't invited him."

"I've been extremely worried about you. Where've you been? Gerald said you left the Fanshaws really early."

"Certainly wasn't early; I thought we were never going to leave the dining room—but I suppose I was the first to leave. I thought I'd stifle if I stayed a minute longer."

"Whatever took you so long after that?"

"I took Acer for a lovely walk and then I fell asleep in a field."

"Ma! That's completely irresponsible. You shouldn't do that sort of thing."

"I really don't see why not." Kate looked at Joanna's tense, cross face, but then, as she so often did, saw the vulnerability behind the furious expression. She felt like pointing out that this was actually her house, in which Joanna—without asking—appeared to have cooked all day, that it was not for Joanna to invite people into it, and what was more, that she herself was now a free agent and did not have to account for her movements to anyone; but today of all days did not seem the right moment to have all this out with her daughter, especially as a much bigger confrontation might be pending.

"Oh well, I'm back safe and sound now," she said lightly. "I'm sorry if you got stuck with Gerald, but I trust he's gone now?"

"No, he's still here—he was anxious about you too. He'd come to ask you out to dinner."

Cecily shot her daughter-in-law a triumphant look.

"Well, it's very kind of him but I'm certainly not going out to dinner with him," said Kate. "I've had enough socialising for one day, but it was a kind thought, so I suppose I'd better come and tell him so myself."

"You don't need to. I've asked him to stay to dinner here with the three of us. Don't look like that, Ma. I've done all the cooking. You won't have to do a thing."

"Oh darling, I do so wish you hadn't."

"I thought you might have been pleased," said Joanna huffily. "I was only trying to give you a nice evening. I thought we could have spent at least the last bit of today together—the three of us.''

''I agree. But not with Gerald too.''

''Oh Ma, he's only doing it for Dad—he wants to return some of the kindness you both showed him when Nancy took off. He remembered about today and came specially. How could I turn him away?''

''Well, I shall enjoy the company even if your mother doesn't,'' said Cecily, much entertained by the undercurrents between mother and daughter. ''I shall go and change my frock and come down in exactly quarter of an hour.''

Kate followed Joanna out of Cecily's flat, and on to the landing. She could see Joanna was at bursting point.

''I never get anything right for anybody,'' Joanna said in a strangled voice.

Kate put a conciliatory hand on her daughter's shoulder. Joanna felt as stiff as a coiled spring.

''I'm sorry, darling, of course it will be lovely,'' Kate said. ''I was just tired and perhaps a bit het-up too.'' How could she tell her thin-skinned daughter that she wanted to be on her own; wanted to think about her day and mull over new ideas? ''Tell you what—let's see if we can wrench Harriet away from the television and perhaps she'll come and join us too. It is her long weekend after all.'' But even as she spoke Kate knew she had made a mistake.

''Harriet!'' said Joanna. ''She's all you really mind about. You'd always rather be with her than me.'' She stalked off downstairs, every inch of her conveying wounded feelings.

❧ FOUR ❧

The evening had turned out to be more successful than Kate expected. Harriet, primed by Kate not to be confrontational, was on her best behaviour—and her best behaviour could be as beguiling as her worst behaviour could be shattering. Cecily had decided not to snipe at anyone, and Gerald had somehow succeeded in mollifying Joanna and making them feel quite festive. He really is a nice man, thought Kate, so why is it I always end up laughing at him?

Cecily had kept them entertained with accounts of Rosamund Campion's latest exploits. Apparently she was having a flirtation with alternative therapies and was thinking of running day courses from her house.

"I'll have to go if she does," said Kate. "I couldn't possibly miss out on that."

"She's a very good advertisement for them," said Gerald. "I don't know how old she is exactly, must be well over sixty, but she always looks pretty terrific by any standard."

"Ah, but you never know which parts of her are real," said Cecily darkly. "She's always having bits chopped off, or inserted. She's into tattooing now, she tells me."

"Surely not." Kate couldn't quite envisage the glamorous Lady Rosamund decorated with hearts and snakes. "You mean she may have a red anchor on her bottom like a bit of Chelsea china?"

"We didn't discuss her nether regions, but I know she's had her lips and eyebrows permanently done, and little dots at the root of each eyelash. What rubbish!" Cecily snorted scornfully, her own wonderful complexion a tribute to soap and water, plenty of bracing fresh air, long walks and wet picnics. "She says it saves time—not that she's ever been short of that. I wouldn't put it past her to have had one of those little chemotherapy bags fitted just to save her the trouble of going to the lavatory."

"What can you mean? Surely not a colostomy? Nobody could have that done for fun."

"Rosamund would try anything—besides, I believe nowadays you can have it all put back if you don't like it." Cecily, who had hardly known a day's illness in her life, regarded other people's preoccupation with their health as a self-indulgent little hobby.

"It's true though," said Harriet, through a mouthful of chicken pancake. "Polly says Lady Rosamund has some sort of special gunge squeezed into her wrinkles to fill them out." Harriet gave an exaggerated shudder. "Polly and I thought it might actually be Polyfilla—don't you think that's brilliantly witty? We got hysterics when we thought of it." Polly Duntan, Rosamund's granddaughter, was one of Harriet's school friends. "Polly says you can sometimes tell when she's just had it done because if they put too much in, it all sticks up like a ploughed field—then the furrows sort of flatten out a bit and she looks really brill again till the next time. Think of having it done though. Rank. Perhaps you should try it, Gran?"

"Thanks," said Kate. "I think I'll stick to the ploughed field I know."

After supper Cecily went back upstairs to her own flat, and Joanna said she was exhausted and must have an early night before the food fair the following day.

"That was so thoughtful of you to come and cheer us all up, Gerald," said Kate, standing outside the front door and watching her daughter and granddaughter walk across the lawn together to the cottage. She had tried to give Joanna an extra loving hug, but it was like clutching an unpadded coat hanger: Joanna had never been at ease with physical expressions of affection, whereas Harriet, twining her arms round Kate and almost lifting her off the ground, had whispered, "Love you, Gran" into Kate's neck. Harriet, at fifteen, was taller then Kate, nearly as tall as her mother and just as slender, though they were not alike in any other way—Joanna so sleek and dark, and Harriet with her extraordinary mop of wild blonde curls which were totally resistant to brush or comb. Harriet was saving up to have her hair straightened. Kate often wondered who Harriet's father was, but secretive Joanna had always refused to say. Even Oliver had not been able to get that out of her.

Gerald hovered hopefully. Kate knew he would have accepted an invitation to come back in and have another drink, but she did not ask him. She had an awful feeling that he might want to discuss things with her that she had no intention of talking about yet.

After he kissed her goodnight, once on each cheek, and a third kiss for good measure, he held her away from him and looked down at her. "Now a year has gone by, Kate, you must put the past behind you and start a new life— that's what you and Oliver told me after Nancy departed. I know that was a bit different, but I'm sure Oliver wouldn't want you to go on mourning for him. It's time to consider yourself."

"Thank you, Gerald. I mean to try and do just that," said Kate, gently disengaging herself. She didn't think that what they each had in mind by this was at all the same thing.

"I'll give you a ring soon, then, shall I? Shall I telephone you?"

"Yes, do. Lovely." Kate, resisting the temptation to say that she had understood the question perfectly well the first time, blew him another kiss and shut the front door before he got to his car. She stood in the hall listening until she heard him start the engine, but it was some time before he actually drove away. She wondered if he had hoped she might change her mind and come back out again. A small part of her had been tempted to do so, as the emptiness of the house seemed to close round her, and she felt imprisoned in it with her uncertainties and her memories of Oliver. Oliver's absence hung like a fog in every room.

The following morning Kate telephoned Cooper and Wilkinson, not sure whether there would be anyone there on a Saturday morning. Mr. Cooper was not in, the receptionist said, but would she like to speak to his assistant? Kate said she would.

"I would like to make an appointment to look over the Observatory on the Ravelstoke estate."

"I'm sorry, Mrs. Rendlesham, I'm afraid it's not on view. If you'd asked us a few weeks ago we could have show it to you, but it's no longer on the market."

Kate hesitated. She didn't want to get her caretaker friend into trouble by disclosing that he had let her in the day before, in case he had, perhaps, been exceeding his orders, especially as he had obviously known about the sale.

"I really do want to look at it. Am I to understand that it has sold separately?" she asked, feigning ignorance.

There was a hesitation the other end of the line too. Then: "Look, I don't suppose it matters telling you as you're a friend of Mr. Cooper's. It will all be in the papers soon anyway, but the whole estate's been sold and we've been instructed to take all the individual properties off our lists."

Kate was conscious of a surge of disappointment.

"Perhaps the new owner might still consider an offer for that particular house?"

"I can't comment on that, I'm afraid."

"Who has bought it?"

"Well, it probably won't mean anything to you, though I gather he's quite well known in business circles. He's an American property tycoon called Franklin J. Morley. I don't think he lives over here. I really can't tell you anything further, I'm afraid."

"Well, will you tell Mr. Cooper—in confidence please—that I rang, and that I'd still like to talk to him about it?"

"Yes, of course, Mrs. Rendlesham. I'll be pleased to do that for you. Mr. Cooper is away all next week, but I'll get him to call you when he returns. Can we send you the brochures of any other properties? We've got some very desirable houses on our books at the moment. Do you want to tell me what your requirements are?"

"No thank you," said Kate. "It was just that particular house I was interested in—for a friend," and as she put the telephone down she felt as if she might cry.

The letter from Jane Pulborough was in Kate's desk in the playroom. She had been careful not to leave it lying about.

She had met Jane the previous autumn at a charity sale at Duntan, the local stately home, owned by Lady Rosamund Campion's son, which was open to the public. Kate had made a batch of needlepoint cushions for the Duntan House Shop stall, and had also produced an embroidered silk waistcoat, which she had based on an eighteenth-century design. Jane Pulborough, a friend of Sonia and Archie Duntan's, had a shop in the Cotswolds, at Chipping Marston, specialising in unusual luxury items of clothing and exclusive knick-knacks for the house. She traded under the name Midas and often held sales in private houses round the country. She had been greatly taken with Kate's work.

"This is fantastic," she had said to Kate, on being introduced by Sonia. "I know this waistcoat is meant for a man, but a smaller size would be heaven for women too. Could you make some more?"

"I should think so." Kate had been flattered and pleased. "This one took me quite a time because it was a new idea and I wasn't sure how it would work out, but I loved doing it. I'd meant it as a Christmas present for my son, but stupidly got the size wrong. I've promised to do another for him, so I gave this to Sonia for a raffle. In fact she's decided to auction it. I'm quite chuffed she thinks it would be worth it." The waistcoat had sold for three hundred and fifty pounds. Even though she knew the bidding had been extra high because everyone was trying to support the Macmillan nurses for whom the proceeds were destined, Kate had been stunned. She had agreed to make two more for Midas, and had worked away at them after Christmas.

Kate had always been prone to attacks of gloom in January and February, and this year, surrounded by uncertainty, with the driving force of her life removed, she had felt especially vulnerable. It was good therapy in the dreary dark days after the New Year to have a project which she had to finish to a deadline. Sitting in the playroom, stitching away in fine silk, while the snow fell outside her window, Kate had felt like the Tailor of Gloucester. She had been reading it aloud to Rupert and Tilly one evening and had been enchanted when Tilly, putting her finger on the picture of the waistcoat to which the little mice had pinned their note saying "No more twist," had exclaimed in astonishment: "Just like yours, Granny."

Now Jane Pulborough had written to Kate with a proposition: "The waistcoats were snapped up immediately, as I knew they would be, and I've had masses of enquiries about commissioning more. I think your work is exceptional and I'm amazed you've never done it professionally before. How about going into business together? You could have your own design label and make whatever you like— though definitely more waistcoats please—and I would have the exclusive right to market your stuff for Midas. You would certainly need some outworkers because I'm sure you wouldn't have time to make all the stuff yourself given the likely level of demand. Would this be a problem? We'd have to get a proper contract drawn up, and you will want to look at all our accounts. I have to say we're doing very well! At the moment I have no working partner, though my husband, Christopher, owns half the shares and audits the books. If you like the idea—and I do hope you will—perhaps we could meet and talk about it? Give me a ring when you've had time to think."

Kate had received this letter a couple of days before Netta's lunch. It had done wonders for her morale. None of her family had ever taken her skill with a needle seriously, certainly never regarded it as something she might take up as a career. It had been approved of as a nice little hobby, "Mum's tatting"—not to be allowed to interfere with more important things, of course—and her cushions and chair seats had been in demand as Christmas presents. She had made clothes for herself and Joanna, smocked enchanting little dresses for Harriet and Tilly and occasionally for the children or grandchildren of friends, but it had never occurred to anyone that Kate might branch out into business and make money—Kate who was so unbusinesslike. Oliver always joked that she had to count on her fingers. It had been a shock to discover that Oliver had left so little money. She would be glad of extra income.

Kate was also well aware how badly Joanna wanted to exchange houses, and was quite prepared to let her move into Longthorpe—always provided that this was what Mike wanted too. Mike was well off and the Maitlands would be able to afford it, which was no longer true of Kate herself. Nick and Robin couldn't have afforded it either and in any case they had the London house. It wasn't the idea of handing over Longthorpe that bothered Kate, so much as Joanna's vision of her, conveniently installed in the cottage and constantly to hand in Granny role as a back-up baby-sitter, children's chauffeur and indispensable aid to Joanna's own career. Joanna had it all planned out: the big kitchen would be perfect for cookery demonstrations, she could take over Oliver's study for her writing, and there would be heaps of room for all the children and a nanny, as well as plenty of scope for entertaining friends. The thought of leading this second-hand family and domestic life made Kate's heart sink—much as she loved her grandchildren. Of course she loved Joanna too, difficult though they often found each other, but was guiltily aware that her relationship with Nick was a different matter altogether. He and Kate had always shared a wavelength, as indeed Oliver and Jo had done. Oliver's pride when his precious, beautiful daughter had won an exhibition to Oxford had known no bounds. Poor Jo, thought Kate, so used to being the star of the family and feeling left out in the cold for the first time, what would she feel about me pursuing a career of my own?

If they simply exchanged houses and lived at such close quarters, Kate was afraid she might find it impossible to stick to her new resolutions. Am I terribly selfish to want my independence? she asked herself, but in her heart of hearts she didn't really think so. She had given up her inner longings and submerged herself in the lives of Oliver and their children, and in return, she supposed, received much cushioning from the leaner side of life. Surely now was the time to try to be a little more adventurous and strike out in a wider sea?

She had been brooding about all this when she had seen the Observatory, and a whole new vision of how she might transform her life had suddenly danced before her imagination. What had Nick so surprisingly said to her? "Live dangerously, Mum. Robin and I think you ought to kick your heels up. Do what *you* want."

I can't have had this unexpected offer from Jane, and then seen and fallen in love with that perfect house at exactly this moment, just to have it all snatched away again, she told herself. I shall beard that American and *make* him sell it to me. I am going to start a new life. Perhaps, like the Tailor of Gloucester, I shall even grow quite stout and rich.

❧ FIVE ❧

Breakfast in the Maitland family on Saturday morning was an acrimonious affair.

Harriet was having a sulk. She had promised to help Joanna on her stall at the food fair, but Polly had rung up to ask her to go over to Duntan for the day to ride.

"Surely you don't really need me. You've got hundreds of bossy old bats longing to help. You told Gran you'd got too many people and wouldn't need her there."

"I don't need her because I've got you."

"But Granny offered. I heard her. Why can't she do it instead of me? She might like to."

"Because a promise is a promise."

"But if I rang Gran and she said she wouldn't mind, surely you could let me off. It would be great for Star to have a really long hack and it's so blissful riding in the park at Duntan. Please, please Mum. I'll come and help clear up after," Harriet tried a wheedling tone.

"I said *no*." Joanna's short fuse was beginning to smoulder. As so often happened between her and Harriet, positions were becoming entrenched too quickly, and then neither liked to lose face. Harriet's expression became mutinous.

"Why not? Give me one good reason why not. Everyone else's mothers are doing things with them for the exeat weekend and you didn't need to have your stupid old sale this Saturday."

"Enough!" shouted Joanna, her permanently festering guilt complex over Harriet already throbbing. "You'll come because I say so, and you promised. There doesn't need to be any other reason."

Six-year-old Rupert started to bite his thumb. The nail was well below the quick and the skin round it was permanently sore and soggy. Sometimes Rupert made it bleed.

"It'll be your fault if Star gets laminitis through lack of exercise and I give everyone the wrong change all day," flashed Harriet before she slammed out of the kitchen muttering audibly about megalomaniacs.

Joanna was feeling extremely brittle. Michael had arrived late the night before. He was devoted to his children, was infinitely better with Harriet, who was not his child, than Joanna was, and hated being parted from the family during the week. He was no countryman, and the idea of gardening or shooting—let alone having anything to do with any portion of a horse, an animal he considered dangerous and revolting at both ends and unreliable in the middle—was no compensation for a long, exhausting flog up the M1 at the end of his hard-working week. Michael's idea of a pleasant Saturday would have been to potter about in his dressing gown most of the morning, take his children to a museum in the afternoon, and then settle down in the evening with a bottle of Chateau Margaux to listen to late Beethoven piano sonatas played by Alfred Brendel. He had tried to stop Joanna moving from London, had opposed the idea as strongly as he could, but as usual she had got her way. It had been a case of the thin end of the wedge. When Oliver had become too ill to carry on working, he and Kate had retreated to Yorkshire, and Joanna, desperate about her adored father's failing health, and wishing to see as much of him as possible before it was too late, had decided to stay on at Longthorpe after the family's sad last Christmas together. Michael had felt this to be entirely understandable and had readily acquiesced to it as a temporary measure. Rupert had been sent to the village school and Harriet to board at Essendale Hall. But that had been eighteen months ago, and Joanna no longer pretended that the move was anything but permanent, as far as she was concerned.

After Oliver died she had been quite unable to make herself return to London and take up the reins of her former life. By staying in the country she had felt she could hang on to some sense of her father's presence. She said she could write her regular cookery column just as easily, if not better, from Yorkshire, and—which was increasingly important, she told everyone—would be able to give it a greener, more organic slant if she lived in the country; she said it was better for the children to be brought up away from the toxic fumes of the city. She had always hunted with her father on Saturdays in the winter; now she would be able to look after the horses and keep up with the riding which had been such an important part of her youth, a passion she had shared with Oliver. She also said—though no one was deceived—that she wanted to give Kate companionship and support. What she didn't say was what possible advantage there could be for Michael in this arrangement, nor had she admitted, even to herself, that it was a relief to be away from him for a bit.

Oliver had made the cottage at Longthorpe over to Joanna and Michael when they first got married, and to start with this had been fun for occasional weekends and holidays. Michael was a solicitor specialising in company law, and Oliver thought extremely highly of him—indeed it had been Oliver who had introduced them, which had naturally predisposed Joanna in Mike's favour from the start. He was good-looking in a romantic, slightly effeminate way with a long, sensitive face and wavy hair which flopped over one eye. Joanna had been attracted by his polished manners and found his air of slightly deferential diffidence flattering: after nine years of marriage it had come to grate on her nerves and set her teeth on edge like a broken fingernail running down a silk shirt.

The Maitlands had been reasonably happy at first. Oliver was in London during the week, though Kate usually left for the country on Thursdays in order to have everything ready and perfect for him at Longthorpe, where he liked to entertain friends and business associates at the weekend: he expected a high standard of comfort and hospitality for his guests, and this required preparation. The four of them dined together regularly in London, but Oliver often came to supper by himself with Mike and Joanna on Thursday nights. If Mike was away or working late, father and daughter dined *à deux*, and these evenings, when she had her father to herself, were always a highlight for Joanna.

After university, Joanna had started out as a freelance journalist with a special interest in food, but soon her career as a cookery writer began to take off. Michael enjoyed escorting her to esoteric little restaurants and basked in the admiration that her cool elegance aroused in his friends; she liked cooking experimental dishes for dinner parties and was proud of his discriminating palate and knowledge of wine; she also liked going with him to first nights at the opera and to private views of art exhibitions. The gap between their other tastes and inclinations had only added interest to the relationship, at this stage, and had not yet widened into the chasm which now yawned between them. Lately the pleasure of the social round had begun to pall for Mike, who worked extremely long hours and lacked his wife's physical stamina; as for the hyperactive Joanna, evenings spent at home listening to music were not at all to her taste. She said she needed to have her music live: it was the cut and thrust of the crush-bar in the interval, the other people present at a concert, the discussions about a performance or a production afterwards that appealed to her. The idea of lying back in her own armchair and drifting off in a private cloud of Bach was quite foreign to her nature.

When Michael and Joanna had announced their engagement, Kate, with much secret anguish, had suggested that six-year-old Harriet, and Lindy, the nanny who had helped Kate since Harriet was born, should go to live with the newlyweds. She had been torn between relief and dismay when Joanna had emphatically turned the idea down.

From the start, Joanna was hopeless with Harriet. At twenty, in her second year at Oxford, she had prepared for the birth with the brisk efficiency she brought to every project she undertook. Because she was such an outstanding student, her college had agreed to hold her place while she took time out to have the baby, provided she could arrange to have it cared for afterwards. Everyone had been astonished when Joanna had suddenly announced that she was four months pregnant, some were surprised that she had not considered an abortion, but they were even more puzzled when she resolutely refused to discuss the situation, name the father, or explain what had led her to decide to have a child—if indeed it had been a deliberate decision at all. She simply said it was not a subject she was prepared to talk about to anyone. She had then studied every conceivable book on child rearing, and had no doubts that with good organisation—and her mother's help, that went without saying—she would cope with the situation. She would certainly have got a first in the theory of babycare by the time the baby was due: it was the practical which defeated her.

"Shut up, shut up, *shut up!*" Three days after Harriet's arrival, Joanna had almost flung the screaming infant down on the bed, and sat shaking and huddled with her hands over her ears.

"Oh darling, poor little baby! She just hasn't read the same instruction books as you," Kate had said, shattered by her daughter's hostile reaction to the baby. But to Joanna it seemed as if her squalling, desperate child had activated her private nightmare of being out of control. What was worse, the baby revolted her. Attempts to breast-feed had lasted for two terrible weeks before Joanna gave it up, but Harriet seemed to cry continually for the first three months of her life whatever anyone did. Kate, pacing the floor with the baby night after night, had ached with anguish for mother and child. Joanna had gone back to Oxford with huge inner relief—and a real taste of failure.

It wasn't until Joanna was pregnant with Rupert, and Kate and Oliver had to go to Australia for three months, that Harriet and the devoted Lindy had gone to live with Joanna and Michael on a permanent basis. Kate had dreaded what effect another baby might have on Joanna, but in fact Rupert's arrival had gone better than she feared. This time there was a fully trained monthly nurse ready to take over the care of the baby, there was never any question of Joanna trying to feed him herself, and he was, of course, from Joanna's point of view, the right sex—she had no doubt that her son would take after his grandfather. Lindy had remained to act as nanny after the monthly nurse had left, but Lindy's own marriage, eighteen months later, had been devastating for both Joanna and Harriet. Luckily, in contrast to his wife, Michael had taken to family life with ease and enthusiasm and somehow a modus vivendi had been achieved.

"That's it then. Positively no more children ever," Joanna had announced after the arrival of Tilly three years later. "I only had another to please you, and you can jolly well do your share of looking after her."

Michael, already besotted with Rupert, and now looking entranced at his miraculous, perfect, newborn daughter, had been fully prepared to comply with this request and had got up uncomplainingly to give Tilly her nighttime bottle for the first three months of her life. Joanna had been profoundly thankful to her husband for this—and at the same time had quite unfairly despised him for it.

Including Harriet, which unfailingly Michael always did, the Maitlands had become a three-child family, but since Joanna had moved up to Yorkshire they were so seldom all together that it often seemed to Michael that they were hardly a family at all.

Joanna was well aware that Mike had made a special effort to come home this weekend, and had been full of good intentions to try and be more conciliatory than usual. They had got off to a bad start.

It was after midnight, and Joanna was dead to the world, when Michael had eventually staggered into the cottage after a nightmare hold-up on the motorway. She always hated being woken up once she had gone to sleep, and her welcome was hardly encouraging. Michael had crashed out almost immediately, utterly exhausted, but Joanna had then been unable to go back to sleep till the small hours and had heard the church clock strike four before oblivion claimed her.

Michael, who had been hoping for a long lie-in in the morning, had forgotten about the food fair—if he had ever known about it—but Joanna's alarm clock had woken him early, and he had decided he had better start as he meant to go on this weekend and come down to breakfast. His wife did not appreciate the charm of the relaxed approach to a new day. He suggested that they should all go out for the day and take the children for a picnic. As Mike hated eating out of doors, unless it was a proper meal eaten at a table on the terrace of some civilised villa in Tuscany, this had been intended as an olive branch to Joanna, who, like her grandmother Cecily, always rose sickeningly above whatever weather the northern climate could throw at her. Despite the welcome April sunshine outside, the climate inside Longthorpe Stable Cottage was already too chilly for olive branches to flourish, and this one shrivelled as soon as it was presented.

"Are you mad? You're welcome to take Rupert and Tilly if you like, but I shall be far too busy." As soon as the words were spoken, Joanna could have bitten her tongue out. Michael looked at her in silence, and then stooped to kiss the anxious upturned face of his son, and the calculating, eggy one of his daughter without comment, but there was something in his expression that gave Joanna an unexpected frisson of unease.

Kate woke early, despite the fact that she had not slept well either. Her mind had been too full of ideas to switch into neutral, and she had tossed and turned, read her book, listened to the World Service, and made herself tea. However, when she woke it was to a vague feeling of pleasure. She reviewed the day ahead. Nick and Robin were coming for the weekend. Their relaxed attitude was always a welcome relief after the undercurrents and intensity of the Maitland household.

"We'll drive up on Saturday morning, and we may or may not get to you for lunch, but don't go and bother about food," Robin had said. "It's you we want to see—company before calories."

"Lovely," said Kate. "I'll stock up on goodies from Joanna's food fair and that'll kill three birds with one stone: it'll please Jo, I'll do my bit for Granby Abbey, and we won't have to cook all weekend." She looked forward to seeing them.

Before she went downstairs to let Acer out, she opened the door which led to Cecily's flat and knocked on her bedroom door. Cecily was sitting up in bed gazing out of the window through her binoculars, her thick white hair, which would later be piled up on top of her head, lying in a long plait over one shoulder. She was counting the swallows on the telegraph wires. Kate wouldn't have put it past her to be organising their nesting sites, arranging which pair was to be allocated which site, according to her own individual whim, as she had once organised the housing of evacuees during the war in her WVS days.

"There are some very late arrivals this year," said Cecily disapprovingly, and Kate got the impression that Cecily considered such tardiness entirely due to fecklessness and lack of planning. "They should have arrived by the nineteenth of April and got well settled in by now."

Kate knew better than to ask her mother-in-law how she was, and always thought up some reason for her habitual morning visit other than a wish to check up on Cecily's health and welfare—which would have been greatly resented—though Cecily would have not at all appreciated any failure of duty on Kate's part. It was a game they both played to preserve the illusion of Cecily's complete independence, and each knew the rules.

"I came to see if you would like a lift into Blaydale to Jo's food sale this morning?" asked Kate.

"No thank you. I'm still perfectly capable of driving myself. I may give old Babs a lift—she's getting very feeble. Says she doesn't like roundabouts any more, if you please! Ridiculous. I've never had any trouble with them myself." Cecily's expression was withering. Her driving was a source of constant anxiety to her family, not that it was really all that much worse than it ever had been, though some of her idiosyncrasies were becoming more exaggerated: her use of the horn, for instance, which she regarded as a perfectly legitimate signal to other road users that she claimed priority under all circumstances. She was always outraged when other petrified drivers tooted back at her.

Joanna had recently tried—and failed—to extract a promise from her grandmother that she would no longer drive the children, and it had now become a point of honour with Cecily to inveigle Rupert and Tilly into her battle-scarred old Metro as often as possible with promises of little trips to buy sweets at the village post office. Since Joanna, as far as her children were concerned, though not perhaps the readers of her cookery column, was a fanatical card-carrying member of the anti-sugar brigade, this was not difficult to achieve; apart from the thrill of the journey, with the violent accelerations and sudden jamming on of brakes which made trips with Cecily such a memorable experience, there was all the excitement afterwards of smuggling toffees and jelly babies past their mother. Tilly's knickers were a favourite hiding place, but since she was never willing to give Rupert his share of the loot once she was safely through the customs, the ensuing scene between the two of them usually gave the game away.

Kate had long since given up entering into this particular battle between her daughter and her mother-in-law, considering Joanna and Cecily pretty evenly matched in will-power, though Cecily was certainly more prepared to play dirty than Joanna. After breakfast Kate rang Mike and offered to take Tilly with her to the sale, and let Mike have a peaceful morning with Rupert, which she felt would be good for both father and son. It was clear that Tilly, age three, had already inherited much of her mother's competitive spirit, and had a talent for hogging the limelight that often left her elder brother lurking nervously in the wings.

By the time they reached Blaydale Kate never wanted to hear the song of "Puff the Magic Dragon," which Tilly insisted on listening to repeatedly, again, and the food fair was in full swing at the Old Mill Art Gallery, which Zara

Bennet, the owner, had lent for the occasion. The walls were hung with dark and threatening charcoal drawings by a promising young artist whose work Zara was currently promoting. As the subject matter was mostly of death and decay, largely featuring piles of human skeletons or hollow trees, Kate couldn't help wondering if they were the ideal complement for the dainty little plates of fairy cakes and the cream-filled Pavlovas that were laid out on trestle tables below them. The Bishop of Granby, looking particularly well fed, was hovering about at the entrance extending a genial Christian welcome to all comers, and telling anyone who cared to enquire how well the appeal fund for the Abbey was going. A tricky assignment, thought Kate: nobody likes a failing cause, on the other hand over-enthusiasm about the state of the Abbey coffers might result in the loss of a sale of rock buns. The bishop, who preferred to dress informally whenever possible, was wearing sandals over purple socks. His wife stood gloomily beside him clutching a polythene bag of disintegrating scones. Years of living with her husband's glowing enthusiasm for his fellow men (a little too glowing, some people thought—there had been rumours recently that the bishop greatly preferred ordaining homosexual men to female candidates for the priesthood) had long since sapped any joie de vivre she might once have had herself.

"Well, hello there, Tilly," said the Bishop, who suffered little children to come unto him with all the enthusiasm of one determined to wear a hair shirt and look as if he liked it. He considered himself at his best with teenagers, and always made a point of expressing a passion for the latest pop group, much to the embarrassment and disbelief of his audience. "And what is your dolly called?" he asked.

"She is not a dolly," said Tilly coldly, "she is a girl. Her name is Cleareye."

"Oh, how silly of me—well, that is nice," said the Bishop, smile still fixed with super-glue. "Cleareye Maitland—what a lovely name."

"She is not called Maitland. Her name is Cleareye Clikes." Tilly, at her most crushing and inscrutable, felt no call to return the Bishop's friendly overtures with any reciprocal effort. Kate hurried her past the episcopal party, before Cleareye Clikes, who favoured nudism and whose cloth body was an unappetising shade of grey, could exhibit any particularly outrageous behaviour. Cleareye was Tilly's alter ego.

A sunburst of yellow at the door proclaimed the presence of Mrs. Barlow, one of Joanna's helpers, who was taking the entrance money and selling raffle tickets. Mrs. Barlow invariably wore yellow—"such a pleasant shade, I always think"—and today she was a vision in primrose Crimplene and amber beads. Kate had always liked Gloria Barlow; they had both attended classes in crewel work a few years ago and Kate greatly admired her skill and perfectionism as a needlewoman. When the teacher of their particular class had been taken ill and had to have an emergency operation, Kate and Gloria had taken over the class for her and carried on teaching in order to keep it going till the end of term. However, after Oliver's illness prevented Kate from following any pursuit that took her away from home, they had lost touch with each other, though Gloria had sent Kate a touching card when Oliver died.

"Oh Gloria, how lovely to see you. How are you?" Kate bought a batch of raffle tickets, and fervently hoped she wouldn't win the mustard velvet cushion, Gloria's own contribution, which was embroidered with a picture of two chimpanzees, dressed in poke bonnets and smocks, sitting on a see-saw.

"Oh Kate, love—long time no see, as I said to Joanna only the other day. I felt sure you'd be here. I'm a bit housebound nowadays as no doubt Joanna told you."

"No," said Kate. "No, she didn't. What's happened?"

"My Jim's got that motor neurone disease. Our Alan's taken over the farm but Jim's had to give up his milk round of course, so life's a bit tricky. I don't like to leave him for too long, but his sister's stopping over today, so I felt I could come. Still, nothing I can tell you about sick husbands. As I said to Joanna, I always admired the way you kept so cheerful.''

"Oh Gloria, I'm just so sorry. I know how isolating it can be. I can't think why Jo didn't tell me. I would have come to see you." Kate felt mortified that Joanna had not passed this information on to her.

"Jim's ever so good. Never complains, but he hates not working and worries about the money. Of course we get the benefit, which helps, and there's loads of folk worse off.''

Kate was suddenly struck by an idea.

"Look," she said, "I might have a proposition to put to you. I don't want to talk about it here. Could I come over and see you sometime?''

"Oh, that would be pleasant. Just give me a ring, any time. I'd love to see you. I miss the classes—though it was never so much fun after you left. We did have some laughs, didn't we? It was ever so sad about your husband.''

"I'll be in touch soon," said Kate. "I'd better go and buy lots of food now or Joanna will kill me.''

So, that's another little prod I've been given to pursue certain possibilities, she thought.

Their progress round the hall was complicated by the fact that Cleareye Clikes became overcome by kleptomania whenever they passed a stall with anything sweet placed too near the edge.

"Cleareye is being very, very naughty this morning," said Tilly self-righteously through a mouthful of illicit chocolate cake, cream oozing down her chin.

"Yes, well you can tell Cleareye that if she doesn't behave herself she'll be going straight to bed—with you— the minute we get home, and no sweeties after lunch either," said Kate firmly, regretting the altruistic impulse that had made her bring them both along.

When she got to Joanna's stall, Harriet, who was temporarily in sole charge while Joanna went the rounds checking on everyone else, appeared to be enjoying herself enormously, martyrdom forgotten.

"Hi, Gran. Guess what? A brilliant career in marketing may lie ahead of me: I've just managed to flog your fish pâté to the Bishop's wife. Perhaps they'll get ptomaine poisoning—another little step up Jacob's ladder or wherever priests have to go to qualify for heaven—mortifying their vile flesh, you know."

"Well, that is a cheering thought," said Kate. "Now find me something really scrummy cooked by your mother for Uncle Nick and Aunt Robin to eat over the weekend."

❧ SIX ❧

Kate did not mention the Observatory to Nicholas and Robin, but she showed them the letter from Jane Pulborough. They had been most enthusiastic.

"That's a fantastic idea!" said Robin. "Midas is brilliant. I've bought a whole load of things from them. Jane's a friend of my decorator cousin, Ellie Hadleigh, and Ellie always lets Jane hold a Christmas sale in her London house. That's how I know about it. Just what you need—something of your own that you really enjoy—and I've always said you're far too modest. The things you make are to die for. All my friends would come and buy your stuff. Go for it, Kate."

No one could have called Robin Rendlesham pretty—her mouth was far too wide for one thing, her nose too snub, her freckles too abundant, her hair too wild, but she had a quality of vivacity and enjoyment that was so engaging that you always felt better for being in her company. Unlike Joanna's restless energy, which so often left her companions feeling drained and inadequate, Robin's company inspired an instant recharging—like jump leads on cars with flat batteries, Kate thought.

"Let's face it, Mum," said Nicholas, "you're not exactly on the bread line, but a bit of extra cash for spending wouldn't come amiss, would it? Did you ever discover why Dad withdrew all that money or what on earth happened to it?"

This was the question that Kate had been dreading. After his death, they had all been astonished to discover that Oliver, who was generally supposed to be a wealthy man, had made enormous and inexplicable inroads into his capital during his last year of life, selling stocks and shares and then withdrawing extraordinary amounts of money in cash. There was certainly very little in his current account at the time of his death. Now Kate knew what had happened to that money, but she did not at all want to tell her children.

"Umm—bit odd, wasn't it?" she said evasively. "Perhaps one day we'll find out about it." Nick shot her a speculative look. Her surprise about the financial situation at the time of Oliver's death had obviously been genuine, but Nick was fairly sure she had made another discovery recently that was causing her no small amount of anguish. He decided not to press her. If she felt able to tell him what was troubling her, no doubt she would do so in her own time.

Nick, like Joanna, had inherited his father's height and dark colouring, but it was from Kate that he got his quirky, original face, and amused expression. "Oh well, if anything suddenly comes up, don't be afraid to discuss it if you feel like it," he said lightly. The look of reprieve on his mother's face when he did not pursue the matter, told him more clearly than words that he had hit the mark.

Later when he and Robin were discussing the new possibility of Kate becoming a partner in Midas, Nick said: "I just hope my precious sister won't go and wreck the whole thing for Mum if it comes off. Do you think I should have a go at Jo?"

"*No!*" shrieked Robin. Nick always felt protective towards his mother, but Robin knew he still nursed a good many childhood grudges against his sister, and was not above trying to pay off old scores. "You're only looking for an excuse to bait Jo. You know you always make her worse."

Nick flicked at Robin's nose with his finger. "It's your unswerving loyalty to me that I love so much," he said.

Robin pulled a half-guilty face. She had mixed feelings about her sister-in-law. She thought Joanna spoilt and selfish, but at the same time was intrigued by her and couldn't quite resist her glamour. Jo could spring surprises: just when you most wanted to kill her, she might suddenly become good company, or have an unexpected moment of real generosity. There was also the mystery of Harriet.

"I think Jo's pretty unhappy, and not only about your father, either," she said.

"Lucky she's married to a saint—or a wimp," said Nick. "I can never quite make up my mind. What Mike puts up with is beyond me. I sometimes long for him to sock her one."

"I don't think Mike's a wimp. Anyway, I've a feeling it's all about to change," said Robin. Privately she also thought that Kate was far more capable of standing up for herself than either of her children realised.

"You just keep out of all your family's complications, Nick Rendlesham," she said to her husband. "Concentrate on me instead."

After the weekend, Kate rang Jane Pulborough to express enthusiasm about her suggestion concerning Midas, but also to voice considerable anxiety about whether she was really up to such a commitment. "Of course you are," said Jane breezily. "I wouldn't have asked you if I didn't think you'd be the most amazing asset. Christopher could tell you that plenty of chums have wanted to come in with me, but I've always said no. This is the first time I've ever wanted a working partner—and I know we could work together. I may have the drive, but you have a special talent. You need to look at yourself with new eyes.''

Kate couldn't help being thrilled by this tribute. Jane Pulborough, who possessed enormous confidence herself, also had the knack of inspiring it in other people. When she was actually talking to Jane, Kate felt she might be capable of all sorts of things; it was when she was no longer in her enthusiastic presence that the doubts started to creep in again and she thought she must need her head examined for even considering Jane's suggestions. Robin and Nick were sworn to secrecy, but Kate wished she felt able to share the idea and excitement with Joanna too; she hated the feeling that she was being devious by keeping it to herself. The very thought of Joanna's reaction made her sick with apprehension.

She made a date to go down to Gloucestershire to spend a night with the Pulboroughs to thrash out ideas. She also rang Gloria Barlow and arranged to go over for coffee one morning the following week. Provided she could be steered away from any hand in the design side of things, Gloria would be ideal as an outworker, and might well be glad of the money and the occupation too. Kate decided to send Gloria a letter outlining her plans, to give Gloria a chance to think it over before they met. The more Kate thought of it, the more the idea of starting a new life and trying to make a career for herself appealed to her—but in her imagination this also now involved a vision of herself living and working in the Observatory.

The sale of the Ravelstoke estate had been announced in the press, and the identity of the purchaser had been confirmed. ''Mystery of Ravelstoke purchaser unravelled'' ran a headline in the local paper. A representative for Franklin J. Morley Inc. had declined to divulge Mr. Morley's plans beyond saying that he intended to be personally involved in the future running of the estate. ''Mr. Morley has many divergent interests,'' his spokeswoman had told the *Yorkshire Post*. "He will be considering a number of options for the future." She would not be drawn further.

Kate awaited the promised call from Graham Cooper, of Cooper and Wilkinson, with impatience, convinced that he would be more optimistic about her chance of seeing the house again than his assistant had suggested, but it was over a week before he rang. It was a discouraging call. No, said Graham Cooper, he was sure the new owner didn't intend to sell the Observatory. In fact, he went on to say, he rather thought Mr. Morley might be intending to live in it himself on a temporary basis, until he had decided what alterations he wanted to make to the big house itself.

"So he is really going to come and settle in Yorkshire?"

"Oh, I don't suppose he'd live here much of the time—too many business interests in the States—but yes, I believe he intends to spend part of the year over here."

"But there must be lots of other houses on the estate. Surely he doesn't have to have this particular one. Specially not just as a stopgap." Kate could already feel a passionate dislike of Mr. Franklin J. Morley building up inside her. How dare he decide to live in what she now thought of as her house?

"Couldn't you tell him how badly I want it?" she asked, knowing she must sound absurd, not really understanding herself why she had developed this curious obsession. Mr. Cooper said he would certainly mention that someone was interested, but it really was no longer anything to do with him now that the firm had sold the estate.

"Look, I'm really sorry, Kate; but if you'll take my advice, I think you should forget about the Observatory." Graham Cooper privately thought that Kate Rendlesham sounded thoroughly unhinged and wondered if she was heading for a breakdown. She'd always seemed such a sensible person before, but widows were notoriously unpredictable, and losing someone as outstanding as Oliver must have knocked her for six. Mr. Cooper felt uneasy with emotional women; the whole topic of bereavement embarrassed him acutely: the less said about these things the better, in his opinion. He must get his wife to ask Kate to one of her women's lunches, on a day when he was in London. He made a memo in his neat little leather pocket-book to this effect.

"Couldn't you introduce me to Mr. Morley and let me ask him myself?" asked Kate.

Mr. Copper began to feel irritated, but if Kate might turn out to be a potential client it would be foolish to alienate her. In his opinion, she seemed very well set up where she was, at Longthorpe, especially with old Lady Rendlesham in the flat to keep her company, not to mention that competent and attractive daughter living so close. It would be surprising if Oliver Rendlesham had not left Kate well provided for, but there had been a few rumours that all had not been quite as expected, so you never knew. Also, if there was one thing Graham Cooper had discovered in his years as an estate agent, it was that people had the most unreliable ideas about what they wanted when they were house-hunting: they might tell you they wanted a small convenient bungalow but you could bet your life they'd then fall for a crumbling old Stately. "Nowt as queer as folks" as the Yorkshire expression had it, and Graham Cooper had plenty of reason to agree with this dictum.

"I'd be delighted to try and help you over any other house, or in any other way I can, but I really can't help you over Franklin Morley," he said firmly. Mr. Morley had not struck him as the sort of man who would relish interference in his affairs. Unlike most clients, the new owner of the Ravelstoke estate had seemed to be a man who not only knew exactly what he wanted, but was used to getting it.

"Are you putting Longthorpe House on the market then?" he enquired. "I hope you'll let us act for you if so. It would be very easy to sell. There's a shortage of that kind of house up here—the ideal size for a biggish family but still very manageable and in excellent condition. I'd willingly come over and discuss that with you if you'd like.''

But that was the last thing Kate wanted. ''No, no. Forget it. I'm a bit unsettled at the moment,'' she said hastily, and added with some truth: ''I suppose it was really just a sudden whim,'' correctly guessing that Graham Cooper would find this explanation completely acceptable as evidence of her frail and manless condition, even if such folly was incomprehensible to him personally. His own wife had never had a whim in her life.

All the same, Kate made up her mind to try and meet the American millionaire if a chance came up.

Soon after this Kate was surprised to receive another invitation written in Netta's twirly handwriting.

''Mrs. Miles Fanshaw'' it read, ''At Home—to meet Mr. Franklin Morley. Drinks 6:30–8:30 p.m. RSVP.''

''Well, what do you think about that?'' Kate said to Cecily, who had received a similar envelope in her post. ''Netta certainly hasn't wasted much time, has she?''

''I don't suppose she's even met him herself yet. Perhaps he won't turn up.''

Kate laughed. ''It reminds me of that bit in *Henry IV* Part 1 that I always think's so funny, when Glendower boasts that he can conjure spirits from the vasty deep, and Hotspur says, 'Why, so can I, or so can any man; *But will they come* when you do call for them?' I suppose you or I could have bunged off an invitation to him too if we'd wanted to. Poor Netta—wouldn't it be too awful for her if she'd conjured away like mad and he didn't even put in an appearance. I bet she's asked the whole county. I shall certainly accept.''

Kate thought it might prove tricky, with her mother-in-law and Joanna both probably breathing down her neck, to explain to the new landowner why she absolutely had to live in one of his properties. Still, at least I will manage to meet him, she thought, and then I might have to do a bit of conjuring myself.

She had a mental vision of herself greasing up to a stocky and lecherous-looking dwarf with a huge stomach and massive calves—a sort of cross between the late Aristotle Onassis and the famous statue of Morgante in the Boboli Gardens in Florence, though presumably the tycoon would not be able to arrive at Netta's cocktail party riding on either a yacht or a turtle. A stretch limo perhaps? She visualised this powerful character wearing Bermuda shorts patterned with palm trees and chewing on a vast cigar. His body would be covered with impregnated plaster patches, to ward off every conceivable medical emergency, and a retinue of effete young aides, recording his instructions into dictaphones, would follow his every move. Or perhaps he might look like Clint Eastwood—that would be nice—and gaze speculatively at Kate across a crowded room through narrowed lids? He would beg Netta for an introduction: "Who is that interesting-looking woman by the window? I have to meet her"—even Kate's imagination didn't run to calling herself glamorous. She was so enthralled with these two scenarios that she was only recalled to reality by the most appalling smell of hot metal and burnt vegetables, and realised that she had allowed the saucepan of soup she was making to boil dry. The blackened pan had to be rushed out into the yard smoking like a volcano, and Kate knew quite well that when it had cooled down, she would furtively throw it away rather than bother to fight it with Brillo pads.

Another black mark for Mr. Morley as well for the pan.

Across the lawn, in the stable cottage, Joanna sat at her desk tapping cookery magic on to her word processor. Mike was not coming home this Friday. Nor had he done so the one before, but a letter from him had arrived yesterday. Mike, kind, gentle, civilised Mike—or wet, irritating, feeble Mike—had given her an ultimatum. Bring the family back to live in London by the end of the summer, he had written, or else I've had enough. Or rather, I shall consider you to have left the matrimonial home, and taken our children away. I hope you come back: it's your choice.

Joanna had been absolutely stunned, but she had no idea what to answer. She had gone into the kitchen, her usual refuge in times of trouble, to shut her husband and the state of her marriage out of her head.

She had experimented with a new stuffing for duck, and been pleased with the result. It listed amongst its ingredients: onions, oatmeal, garlic, honey, young rhubarb, grated ginger, toasted pine kernels and dried apricots soaked in brandy—all to be bound together with egg yolks and fresh breadcrumbs; Joanna had then deftly boned the duck ("the less adventurous amongst you might want to ask your butcher to do this for you," Joanna typed scornfully to her band of devoted readers), after which she had carefully eased the duck skin so that the stuffing could form a layer between skin and flesh. "This may seem rather a fiddle to prepare," she wrote, "but the fun you will have doing it and the exquisite flavour of the finished dish will more than compensate you for your trouble."

What is more, she actually believed it.

"Yuk, yuk, yuk. Rhubarb and duck!" rhymed Harriet, who had sauntered in smelling strongly of horse, and peered over her mother's shoulder. "That sounds absolutely rank."

Joanna's article was headed "Surprise Your Friends With a Treat This Week."

"Surprise! I should think they'd die of shock with that lot. Certainly get the squitters."

Joanna swung round on her swivel chair and glared at her daughter.

"How many times do I have to tell you not to come in here in your riding boots, and how dare you read my writing without asking?"

"Can't be very private if it's going to be published," said Harriet provocatively. "I just feel sorry for the poor people who are going to be conned into trying it out. Actually I came to tell you that I've exercised Flame for you. Thought you might even be pleased—but I suppose that's too much to hope for. Oh and by the way, Tilly's just bitten Rupert on the arm so he's thrown her smelly doll out of the window, and now she's having a mega wobbly on the stairs and says he's killed Cleareye Clikes. Thought you ought to know. Had you forgotten Jenny's away?"

Joanna buried her face in her hands, but not before Harriet had seen tears welling up in her eyes. Joanna, who never cried. Harriet, horrified, looked at her mother uncertainly. "Mum?" she said, stretching out a tentative hand and placing it on her mother's arm: "Oh Mum. Sorry, really sorry. I didn't mean to knock your cooking. We all know you're brill. What's the matter? Please tell."

But Joanna had disastrously shaken Harriet's hand off before she could stop herself. "Nothing's the matter, except that you children drive me crazy and I'm tired. Just go and get yourself cleaned up before lunch for God's sake."

There was a charged silence. Then: "Don't worry, I'm going. But I won't be in for lunch. I'm going over to Gran. At least there's one person in my life who loves me."

The door slammed, and Joanna watched her daughter storm off up the path, her shoulders hunched as though there was a hostile wind cutting through her instead of the warm, honey-laden May breeze that riffled the yellow cascades of laburnum outside the cottage.

Difficult, unfamiliar tears coursed down Joanna's face as she sat staring unseeingly at the screen of her word processor, hearing her younger daughter's furious yells and drumming feet outside the door, but unable to make herself go to cope with the tantrum. She had snatched her arm away from Harriet's spontaneously conciliatory gesture:

now she would have given a great deal to be able to snatch the moment back—and play it differently.

Inexorably, the painful memories bubbled up, memories of another time when she had felt rejected and hopeless.

֍ SEVEN ֎

Kate was stitching away at an experimental design in the playroom and listening to Liszt's orchestral arrangement of Schubert's Fantasia in C, ''The Wanderer,'' and musing about whether she would have the courage to do a bit of wandering herself, when Harriet burst in and threw herself dramatically on to the squashy old sofa. Kate's heart sank. One look at her granddaughter told her there was trouble.

''Hello, darling, lovely to see you,'' she said, refusing to react. ''Could you possibly *not* lie on that new roll of canvas?''

Harriet obligingly shifted her position, but: ''Please can I come and live with you again? I feel like killing myself.''

''Well, it might be a bit difficult to kill yourself *and* come and live with me.'' Kate bit off a piece of silk and started to rethread her needle. ''It depends which you're contemplating first. I love having you to stay any time— you know that—but I'd be rather miffed if I'd just made up the bed, put flowers in your bedroom and then found you drifting soggily in the burn like Ophelia.'' Then, seeing Harriet's white, anguished face and desperate, twisting fingers, Kate decided this emergency just might be real.

''What is it, Hattie?'' she asked gently. ''Think you'd better tell me?''

For answer Harriet came and buried her head in Kate's lap, drenching the piece of scarlet silk that had been destined for an evening coat as she sobbed uncontrollably, her thin frame racked by great shudders. Kate stroked the electric mop of unruly curls and said nothing. Harriet's muffled torrent of words was quite inaudible. Kate let her cry, unrestrained, for a few minutes, and then said, "Now stop it, darling. I can't hear a word you're saying, and if I'm going to help, you must calm down. Mop up your face, and try to tell me properly."

Harriet leant back on her heels and blew her nose on the proffered tissues. After a long pause and several attempts to get words out, she managed: "Mum's always hated me. Why does she hate me so much?"

"She doesn't hate you. She may be difficult and short-tempered, you may not find each other easy, but she really does love you." Kate had said this many times before; it was ancient territory, but it was quite a long time since they'd been over it, and she'd hoped it was better. This time something in Harriet's expression rang alarm bells in Kate's head.

Harriet looked at her: "Please tell me the truth, Gran. Did she absolutely hate my father too?" she asked. "Is that what it is?"

Kate had often wondered this herself. She opened her mouth to deny it, to take the easy way out, and make bland, comforting assertions. A black hole of uncertainty as to how to deal with the situation opened up before her. It had been one thing to take a stormy six-year-old on her knee and soothe her wounded feelings, hug her better and distract her, but Harriet was now an intelligent fifteen-year-old, only a few years younger than Jo had been when Harriet was born. Kate had often felt like an interpreter between Joanna and Harriet, but nowadays, she felt like one who did not have a very firm grip of the language herself.

"Darling, there are questions I can't answer for you," she said quietly. "Only Mum herself can do that. But I'm certain she doesn't hate you. Sometimes I think she hates herself, and that's tough to live with, but deep down I'm sure she loves you."

"But who was my father? Why haven't I ever been told? You must know."

"No, darling, I don't know. I don't think Mum ever told anyone, certainly not us—we never knew why, but she wouldn't tell us anything, and there wasn't much we could do about it. Have you asked her yourself recently?"

"Yes."

"And what did she say?"

Harriet's voice shook. "When I was little she used to say she might tell me when I was grown-up—though she always got very cross when I asked, and I was so frightened of her then, I used to have to work myself up to asking. Sometimes I still am frightened of her, though I'd die rather than let her see. It drives me mad to watch Rupert looking like a scared rabbit whenever Mum shouts at him. Last time I asked her, she told me to mind my own business. My own business! She said I was never to mention it again. She said that if I nag again she'll never tell me—ever."

"Hattie," Kate said, "be truthful about this: I bet last time you asked her it was when you were both in a rage. One of the reasons you get on so badly, is that you try to say important things to each other when you're both in a temper—and that never works. And you really do goad your mother sometimes, don't you?"

"I suppose so. I don't always mean to, though—but she just makes such a big deal out of everything. Sometimes it starts as a joke, but she never thinks anything funny like you do."

Kate couldn't help feeling that Harriet had put her finger on a crucial difficulty. She was always astonished herself that she had managed to produce a daughter with so little sense of the ridiculous as Joanna. She sighed. Nothing was going to change that.

She said: "You know, darling, I think Mum is really very unhappy at the moment. She misses Grandpa terribly. She always adored him and relied on him, and she's finding it extremely hard to get over his death. I do see that this is a question you need to have answered, and I think you have a right to know too—but I don't think this is the best moment for you to tackle Mum again. Not just yet.''

Harriet pounced: "So it's all right for Mum to be hooked up on her father," she said passionately. "She can behave more like a widow than you do. She can be bloody to Mike, and make us all move, and everyone has to pussyfoot round her because she's lost her precious Daddy and can't cope—but she won't even let me know if I have one. Was he a murderer or something?''

It was clear that Harriet was in a worse state than Kate had first thought.

"Your mother knows I've always thought she should talk to you about this," she said. "You think she doesn't love you, but has it ever occurred to you that it's because she loves you that she gets so jealous when you and I get on so well? Have you ever thought that she'd love to be close to you too but doesn't know how? She's never found children easy—some people don't. You can't tell me she isn't difficult with Rupert and Tilly too.''

"No—but that's still different from how she is with me. I see about when she was at university, but if she loved me so jolly much why wouldn't she have me to live with them when she and Mike first got married? Tell me that. She's always resented me. Always.''

Kate was miserably aware that this was all too true. She tried another tack: "But Mike loves you—really loves you for yourself, and he's done his best to be a father to you.''

Harriet looked at her sadly. "I know. Mike's smashing. I love him too—but he's not my dad, and now I think he may go away too." Kate's heart sank still further.

"Look, it may not do any good," she said. "And Mum doesn't like it if I interfere, but I will try to talk to her again if you want. But I might make things worse for you, darling. You must realize that.''

"They couldn't be much worse than they are already between Mum and me," said Harriet, but she had calmed down. "I'll risk it, Gran. Please try. You don't know how often I think about it. I used to dream about my father when I was little. I imagined he was a romantic hero and made up stories about him. I used to pretend he was searching for me—but he can't have made much effort after fifteen years. Now I'm afraid of what I'll find out. But I still need to know." She looked at Kate with tear-stained, troubled eyes and Kate felt as if her heart was wrenched in two.

"I'll do a deal," said Kate. "You go home now, tell Mum you're sorry if you were rude—and I bet you were, Harriet—and then you keep out of range and don't provoke her for the rest of the weekend—and I'll pick my moment, sometime when you're at school, and tell her that though nobody else need know who your father is, sometime soon I really think she should tell you."

"I've already tried to apologise to her once today," said Harriet bleakly. "She wouldn't accept it. Can't I just come back and live with you? Then we could all be happy. Please, Gran. I feel as if I belong when I'm with you, and I'd be really helpful. I swear it."

"No, darling. It wouldn't be right," said Kate firmly. But though she genuinely felt this to be true, she was shaken to find that she suddenly felt quite threatened at the idea. "You try the sorry bit again, and I'll see what I can do. Bargain, Hattie?"

"OK, bargain—but I bet it won't work."

They both stood up. Harriet leant against Kate for a moment. "Oh Gran," she said. "Isn't life complicated? It must be so sad for you now. I do know that. I'm sorry to be such a pain too. I'd die without you."

Watching Harriet go, Kate thought that Oliver would have been the only person who could have coped with Joanna at the moment—but then if Oliver hadn't died things wouldn't be so bad for her anyway. She thought how alike father and daughter were. Joanna had Oliver's brains, his restless drive and enterprise, his wonderful good looks—but there was an ingredient missing in Joanna that Oliver had had in abundance; she lacked his special brand of charm: Oliver's dark, devastating, dangerous charm.

Kate sent up a fervent prayer that Joanna would accept Harriet's apology; but she wasn't very optimistic.

ᚷ EIGHT ᚨ

On the morning of Netta's party Kate woke with a vague feeling of pleasure. So often she slept badly, and woke to a sense of exhaustion and anxiety; it seemed as though she could not shake off the shadow which the long months of Oliver's final illness had cast across her view, as though their echo constantly reverberated in her ears; but last night she had slept better than she had done for ages and this morning she felt rested. The night before Robin had rung up for one of her long gossips: Kate loved the way Robin treated her more as a friend than a mother-in-law. Robin said she and Nick were agog to hear what the mystery millionaire was like, and how Netta had managed to acquire him so swiftly on her social list—though of course Robin could have no idea just how important the meeting was to Kate.

"Mind you store up any special Netta-isms to tell us. I just love hearing all the local gossip," said Robin, in her deep husky voice. "I'm so glad you're going to meet my compatriot. I meant to ask my father to do some research on Mr. Franklin J. Morley last time we had a call, but I forgot. We were afraid you might chicken out of the party, after your ghastly lunch with the Fanshaws, and Jo never tells us any of the titbits we die to know—she's no good at dressing up the dolly like you are."

"What rubbish! You know you always get the plain unvarnished truth from me," said Kate, laughing. "By the way—what shall I wear to stun a millionaire and get up Netta's nose?"

"How about one of your own waistcoats? That would look terrific, Netta'd turn green, and it would be a great advertisement for Midas. Have you got one finished?"

"As a matter of fact I have, though it's a bit more ambitious than a waistcoat. It's a gentian-blue silk jacket, embroidered with shells and starfish in pink and buff shelly sort of colours, and I have to admit I'm quite in love with it myself. I was intending to take it down to show Jane Pulborough when I go to stay with her, but I don't see why I shouldn't wear it if I'm careful not to slop drink down my front. Better not stand too close to old Beryl Northwood either: she always sprays out crumbs at a party like a gritting lorry after a frost warning. Wouldn't do to show Jane something covered in gobs of garlic dip, would it? But you are clever, Robin! Why didn't I think of it myself?"

"Because you're too darn modest—but all that's going to change. Good practice for the new confident Kate—super-model and businesswoman of the year. Wear it with your black silk trousers—that'd look real neat. You can experiment with your sexy image on worthy old Gerald Brownlow. Have you told Jo about Midas yet?"

"I keep putting it off. Perhaps I'll go and see Jane first. I'd hate to upset Jo at the moment and then find the deal with Midas was off and it had all been for nothing."

Kate didn't tell Robin that she was now facing a double confrontation with Joanna. She had not seen Harriet again before she went back to school on Sunday evening, and Joanna had not referred to the incident. At least Harriet had not come hurtling straight back across the garden, as Kate had half expected, so she presumed an apology had been offered and accepted, and some sort of temporary cease-fire achieved. She had not yet found a suitable moment to tackle Joanna about the identity of Harriet's father. Probably there never would be an easy time, she thought gloomily, and she would have to force the issue. Perhaps it would be better to have one huge, horrendous session and tackle the paternity question, her own career and a possible move

of house, all together? By inclination Kate always preferred
to divert trouble. Nick called her "Peacemaker Mum" and
teased her about her love of compromise, but this time she
knew she must stiffen her sinews and summon up her
blood—or fail Harriet, and despise herself. When it came
to imitating tigers, Kate knew that on past performances
Joanna had an infinitely better track record than she had
herself, but lately she had felt a new resolution strengthen
within her.

It was to be tested, in a minor way, almost immediately.

By five o'clock, Kate had put away her sewing, taken
Acer for a walk, looked in on Cecily, and was just about
to go and have a leisurely bath and change, when the telephone rang. It was Joanna.

"Ma? I've got a favour to ask. Jenny's got a sick bug
and can't baby-sit this evening. Could you possibly come
to my rescue?"

"Oh darling, I can't. It's Netta's party. Had you forgotten?"

"No, of course not—that's where I'm going too, and
then on out to dinner with the Duntans afterwards. But I
thought you mightn't mind skipping it?"

A vision of what would be expected of her if she moved
into the stable cottage and remained living so conveniently
close to the Maitlands, rose before Kate. She had cancelled
several engagements of her own to suit Joanna during the
last year, and up to now she had never wanted to go anywhere enough to mind—but she wasn't missing this chance
to meet the new owner of the Observatory.

"I'm so sorry, Jo, but for once I actually want to go to
the party myself, but I'll willingly leave a bit early and
come and take on from you after that, if you like. At least
you can still dine with Archie and Sonia then."

"But you don't like drinks parties and you can't give a
hoot about meeting the billionaire anyway."

"I'm just as curious as everyone else. I want to meet
him too."

"Oh come on, Mum," Joanna's voice started to sharpen. "You've never gone willingly to a drinks party in your life." There was a pregnant pause, then: "Is Gerald Brownlow giving you a lift by any chance?" she asked. Kate envisaged her pointing like a setter who has unexpectedly scented a hidden bird.

"As it happens, yes. I thought it would be a good way of keeping Granny-Cis off the road. I guessed she'd be bound to refuse to be driven by me, as a matter of principle, so he's kindly taking us both."

"You didn't seem all that pleased to see Gerald after Netta's last party. And you can see him any old time if you're so keen."

"Gerald's got nothing to do with it. I just want to go to Netta's party." But as she spoke, it occurred to Kate that it might suit her rather well if Joanna imagined that she was dying to be chauffeured by Gerald, rather than intent on meeting the American tycoon for her own private reasons.

"Look, I'll ring Gerald and explain that I've asked you not to go, if you like," said Joanna graciously. "I'm sure he'll understand—you can ask him to supper here afterwards when he drops Granny-Cis back, if you're that keen, and I promise I won't stay late at the Duntans."

"Jo, the answer is no," said Kate quietly.

She felt she could almost touch the silence at the other end of the line.

"But I think Tilly may be sickening too, and Jenny's literally being sick every few minutes. I really don't think I should leave her to cope alone." Joanna sounded rattled. What she really meant was that she was terrified at the thought of having to cope alone with a sickly child herself.

"Quite right, darling," said Kate. "I'm sure you shouldn't."

"And you'd prefer to go to a cocktail party and jaunt off with Gerald rather than help me out?" Joanna sounded outraged.

"I'm afraid so. Sorry, darling, but I expect you'll find someone else. Try Mrs. Stokes." Mrs. Stokes was Kate and Cecily's daily help.

"Damn and blast Gerald Brownlow," shrieked Joanna. "I think you're unbelievably selfish," and she banged down the telephone.

Kate went to run her bath feeling some very mixed emotions which included pity, irritation, guilt, and a rare, but not unpleasant, sense of triumph that she had, for once, not given in.

Gerald arrived to pick up the two Rendlesham ladies on the dot of six-fifteen, as arranged. He spent a lot of time on dots, and felt very uncomfortable if anything prevented him from being in the middle of one.

Kate and Cecily were ready waiting in the hall.

"The invitation said six-thirty, so I reckoned we ought to arrive about ten to seven, and as it takes half an hour from here, I thought quarter past would be about right," he explained. Kate resisted the impulse to say "Oh well done, Gerald." One of the charms of Gerald's company was his ability to jump so consistently through the expected hoop. Kate never failed to enjoy it, though she thought it might become irritating if one allowed oneself too much exposure to his undoubted kindness. Perhaps the ex-Mrs. Brownlow and the former farm manager had both been victims of fallout.

Cecily shot him a scornful look. "Well, I hope you're not going to kerb-crawl all the way there just for the sake of getting the time right," she said. "I can't stand kerb crawlers myself."

Gerald looked startled, and Kate tried not to laugh as she locked the front door and set the burglar alarm, while Gerald solicitously installed Cecily in the front seat of his ultra clean and dog-hairless Mercedes. Gerald owned two field-trial champion springer spaniels to whom he claimed to be devoted, but they only travelled by Range Rover, strictly on business, and were not the companions of his heart. Kate had a feeling he would loathe a trip in her own car with its scattering of peppermints, torn map books, tapes, tissues and Rupert and Tilly's left-behind toys—not to mention a muddy Acer in the back.

The Fanshaws' invitation had obviously acted on the Yorkshire county set like a three-line whip at a crucial vote in Parliament. Everyone had turned out, and despite the potential danger of being seen to arrive too early at a party, there were already a lot of cars assembled in the field which the Fanshaws used as a car park for their larger gatherings.

"I'll drop you both off at the house first, and join you later," said Gerald, adding: "When I've parked the car," in case they hadn't quite grasped the situation.

The first people Cecily and Kate encountered on arrival were the contingent from Duntan. Kate liked both Archie and Sonia Duntan very much. It had been common knowledge that their marriage had hit a dangerously rough patch a few years previously, and come very near to capsizing, and Kate admired the way they had somehow managed to keep it afloat. At any rate, they now appeared to be sailing in calmer waters. Cecily made a beeline for Archie's mother, Rosamund, in order to arrange another bridge afternoon, and have a restoring chat about the failing state of poor Babs Mallory's mental powers.

"Oh Kate, how wonderful you look. I could snatch that jacket off your back," said Sonia Duntan. "Janey Pulborough tells me she's made you a proposition, all due to my Christmas sale last year. She's dying for you to say yes. Do tell me you're going to accept." Kate was disconcerted. It hadn't occurred to her that Jane would have told anyone else.

"I'm brooding about it still. Very flattered, but nothing fixed. I haven't even discussed it with the family yet," she said cautiously.

Sonia, no fool, shot her a shrewd look, "Oh well, I won't mention it to Joanna then," she said easily. "She's dining with us tonight—so sad Mike couldn't come. I'm hoping to persuade Jo to let Harriet come and stay with Polly next weekend. I dote on Harriet—she's my favourite out of all the children's friends; one I really find congenial."

Kate wondered how much the Duntans guessed, or perhaps knew via Polly, about Harriet's stormy relationship with her mother, though she knew they both liked Joanna. She would have liked to talk to Sonia about Harriet, but this didn't seem the time or place, and anyway Sonia, who was always engulfed at a party, immediately got waylaid by other friends.

It sounds as if Joanna had found a baby-sitter after all, thought Kate, not at all surprised, but unworthily not feeling all that pleased either. If Joanna was about to descend on the party she had better try for an introduction to Mr. Franklin Morley straight away.

Netta was over at the far side of the drawing room standing in the open French windows, trying to encourage people to go out into the garden. As always she looked immaculate, if slightly overdressed, her beautifully coiffed hair even more blonde than on the day she had married Miles some forty years previously, her perma-tan owing as much to a sun-bed in Harrogate as the huge villa in Ibiza that she and Miles owned, which she usually referred to coyly as "our little hideaway." Beside her stood a large man in a dark suit with his back to the room. He was deep in conversation with Lady Rosamund Campion, his head tilted attentively towards her. So, not the dwarf image, obviously, thought Kate. Judging by the gleam in Rosamund's eye it was more likely to be the Clint scenario, though this was a heavier-built model with silver hair. Kate's heart sank: she felt any charm she might try to switch on would be a pathetic little flicker beside the laser beam variety that Lady Rosamund had at her disposal, but she bravely made her way over towards them.

Netta would not have bothered with Kate—she had bigger fish to fry—had Kate not deliberately presented herself so that acknowledgement was unavoidable.

"Why hello, Kate, dear," she said, not looking at all pleased to see her. Dear, in Netta parlance, was an endearment reserved for the lame ducks, a clear signal that Kate had now been downgraded in the pecking order from the sweeties and the darlings. Netta kissed the air about nine inches from Kate's cheek, pursing her lips up as if she was trying to blow out smoke rings. She was already turning away, clearly not about to waste an introduction on someone so unimportant, when Rosamund caught sight of Kate.

"Kate! What heaven! I've just been talking to Cecily, and she said you were here." Rosamund's amazing blue eyes—their colour, according to Cecily, enhanced by tinted contact lenses—sparkled with malice: she couldn't stand the Fanshaws, considering Miles boring—possibly the worst crime in her book—and Netta pretentious: worth cultivating for amusement value, but to be put down on every possible occasion, of which she usually found plenty. Sonia said her mother-in-law was so fond of the act of putting-down that she should have been a vet.

"Let me introduce you to our new neighbour, Mr. Morley. This is Kate Rendlesham," said Lady Rosamund, deliberately pinching Netta's rights. The guest of honour turned round.

"Hello, Puss-in-Boots," said Franklin J. Morley.

Kate gazed at him, stunned.

"Hello, Just Jack," she said.

To say that their hostess was surprised too would have been the understatement of the year. She also looked incandescent with fury, as if sparks might fizz out from her well-manicured nails; Kate thought that if she touched Netta accidentally at the moment, she would probably get electrocuted.

"You never told me that you knew each other," she hissed accusingly at Kate.

"You never asked me," said Kate.

Rosamund Campion looked as if she'd been given a saucer of cream. Netta made a quick recovery: "But how stupid of me!" she tinkled, with a laugh that might shatter at any moment, like ice-cubes in a crusher. "Of course I might have guessed that you'd have come across each other before—darling Oliver knew absolutely everyone."

"Everyone except me perhaps," said the new owner of the Ravelstoke estate, his eyes alight with amusement. "I knew of Oliver Rendlesham's business reputation, of course, but it's Kate that I know," and he held out his arms and enfolded Kate in the sort of hug that great old friends might exchange after a long absence from each other's company. "So good to see you again," he said when he had kissed her on both cheeks. He held her away from him for a moment, laughing down at her, before he released her, and Kate emerged from his embrace, breathless—but not only from suppressed mirth.

A number of people were looking extremely interested in this exchange, not least Gerald Brownlow, who had presumably parked the car, and come in search of Kate to tell her how he'd done it—power steering and army training: nothing like it. He stood gawping at Kate in astonishment.

"Well, isn't this lovely?" said Netta, always socially quick on her stiletto sandals, her gold bangles jingling like temple bells, smile back in place but claws unfurled: "But as there's obviously no point in introducing you two, I'm going to whisk my guest away to meet some new friends," and she put a predatory hand on Mr. Morley's arm.

"Fine," he said easily. "I appreciate that; you're most kind. See you then, Kate. I'll be in touch," and he allowed himself to be led away.

"Well done, Kate," said Rosamund, in her hot-chocolate-sauce voice. "You do play your cards close to your chest.

Who'd have guessed you were holding a Royal Flush while all poor old Netta's got is a Full House?'' Kate had the feeling that a number of people whom she had known for years were suddenly going to see her for the first time. ''I must give you a ring soon,'' went on Rosamund. ''I've got a world famous trance channeller coming over from the States for a weekend later in the summer, and I thought I'd ask a few selected friends to come and experience her amazing powers and have a reading. I had a sitting with her last time I was in New York, and it was quite fascinating. You may care to bring Cecily over and perhaps you might both be able to have a little chat with Oliver if the reception's good enough.'' Rosamund might have been talking about a special offer on a mobile telephone or a new transformer in the area; she aimed a scented kiss in Kate's direction. Kate managed to have a quick scan for telltale tattoo marks so that she could report back to Harriet, but Rosamund's complexion appeared disappointingly flawless: not a scar or furrow to be seen. Rosamund wafted off in a haze of Madame Rochas, managing a slide skilfully past Mrs. Northwood, who had cornered one of the catering team in the doorway, and was downing smoked-salmon canapés as if her salvation depended on it.

Kate felt as if she was sleep-walking for the rest of the party, apparently making the right social responses, to outward appearances moving and talking normally, but with her mind elsewhere. She took great care to avoid Graham Cooper, of Cooper and Wilkinson, who tried to attract her attention, and gave her an inquisitive look. Now that she knew the identity of her caretaker acquaintance, she wondered if she had been incredibly dim not to have guessed it before, but she didn't really think so.

Gerald, with Cecily on his arm, came to find her. ''I think your mother-in-law is getting tired,'' he said. ''Perhaps we should head for home?''

"I'm not in the least bit tired," said Cecily, adding loudly, "it's just that there are far too many people here that I don't in the least want to see, and they will mutter so. Can't hear a word anyone says. Young people nowadays have no diction."

Joanna was arriving, as Kate, Gerald and Cecily made their way out.

"Oh good, darling, so you managed to find someone to help?"

"Well, yes—thank you—Mrs. Stokes stepped in." But Joanna's expression made it clear that a black mark against Kate had not yet been rubbed out. Mrs. Stokes, a charmless but reliable lady with a striking resemblance to a bullfrog, was much in demand for babysitting, though not for much else. Cecily was the only person capable of shutting her up, and ruthlessly stemming her tidal wave of conversation. However, with children in bed and parents out, Mrs. Stokes was unable to indulge her passion for filling in an audience with intimate detail of the Stokes family lives—and some of the details could be very intimate indeed. Fathers were always amazingly eager to offer to drive Mrs. Strokes home after an evening spent guarding their children, watching their televisions and gobbling up their biscuits: anything to get her off the premises.

"You're leaving early," said Joanna. "Wasn't it worth coming after all?"

"It turned out that Mr. Morley was an old friend of your mother's." Gerald Brownlow looked like a petulant small boy.

Joanna looked at her mother in astonishment.

"Such a nice surprise," said Kate airily. "I simply hadn't made the link so I'd no idea. I've always known him as Jack, not Franklin." She felt pleased with herself for producing this truthful explanation so easily. "Have a lovely evening, darling. I'll ring Mrs. Stokes and check that all is well as soon as I get back, so don't worry about the children.'' Joanna gave her a dark look, still feeling resentful of her mother—but disliking herself even more.

"I'm not sure that I take to your friend, Kate," said Gerald as he drove the Rendlesham ladies home. "I went and had another word with him—just to be neighbourly, you know—but he wasn't very forthcoming. Can't quite make him out. One, er, wonders what his background is—if you know what I mean."

"Oh, I know what you mean all right," said Kate, enjoying herself enormously. "You mean What School Did He Go To and Are His Family People We Know."

"Quite," said Gerald.

"Oh well, he's knocked around the world a good bit," said Kate, which was about the only thing she knew about Mr. Morley herself. "I'd describe him as pretty cosmopolitan really."

"I don't usually care for foreigners," said Cecily sweepingly, "but actually I thought he looked quite distinguished—though of course one does tend to mistrust men with a tan. Still, some Americans do go in for them." Men, in Cecily's opinion, should be English—Scots were permissible provided they came out of a particular drawer—and should always have a wholesome antipathy to direct sunlight.

"Oh come on," said Kate, "Oliver only had to look at the sun and he went as brown as a nut."

"And look where it got him," said his mother triumphantly. "If you hadn't had all those unhealthy holidays abroad he'd probably be with us now—Indians and Australians are riddled with disease entirely due to sun spots. I heard it on the wireless." Cecily had great faith in any information which she gathered from the BBC, though what she gathered was usually slightly different from that obtained by other listeners.

"Personally I shall reserve judgment on Mr. Morley," she went on. "We don't yet know what his plans are for the estate, but until we do I shall give him the benefit of the doubt.''

From the way the corners of Gerald's mouth turned down, it was clear he was not disposed to be so magnanimous. "I'd never be able to trust a chap who could wear such a vulgar tie," he said disparagingly. "One can't be too careful with the nouveaux riches."

When they got back to Longthorpe House, Kate felt the least she could do was offer hospitality to their driver, so she made omelettes and salad for the three of them in the big kitchen that Joanna coveted so much. Gerald would clearly have liked to settle down for the evening, and was obviously itching to pump Kate for more information, but however useful his military training might have been for parking cars he was no match for Cecily at social manoeuvres.

"Thank you, Gerald, for your kindness," she said, rising majestically to her feet with less than her usual agility, after they had finished off their supper with cheese and fruit, "but I really am tired now. I can no longer drink coffee at night and I shall have to ask Kate to help get me to bed, I'm afraid—but I'm sure you won't mind seeing yourself out.''

"You are a wicked old woman," said Kate severely, after Gerald had beaten a reluctant retreat.

"I know," said Cecily, glinting at her, and looking particularly spry. "But there have to be some compensations to old age. There certainly aren't many."

She added over her shoulder as she walked briskly off, ramrod straight and unaided, to her flat: "And you, Kate Rendlesham, are more devious than I thought," and they both laughed.

Kate was in bed when the telephone rang after eleven o'clock.

"Am I too late to ring? It's Jack Morley here." She hadn't needed to be told who it would be.

"No, of course not. I was still reading. You have some explaining to do."

"Ah, I know. I'm sorry. I behaved very badly at the party, but I couldn't resist it. I hope you don't have too much trouble explaining our long-standing friendship to your flabbergasted friends! Our hostess doesn't seem too fond of you. What a dame—she looked as if she wanted first to eat you up and then to spit you out."

"Well, I'm old currency now," said Kate. "Without my husband I no longer have any purchasing power."

"I wouldn't be too sure of that."

"And what about this Franklin bit, Mr. Just-Jack-Only-The-Caretaker?"

"Both true. Franklin's truly my first name, though no one outside the States has ever called me that. My mother was a fanatical admirer of President Roosevelt way back in the thirties when America was in the grip of the depression. I've always been Jack to my family and friends—and I do indeed feel like a sort of caretaker to the estate. You don't know how near I came to telling you who I really was when we first met, but the contract hadn't been signed by both parties, and I've never in my life taken a deal for granted until it's finally in the bag. Am I forgiven?"

"Of course. You had absolutely no reason to tell me anything—why should you?"

"Well anyway, I want to make amends. I've rung to ask if you'd like to have lunch with me."

"How very kind, thank you. Yes, I'd love to. When?"

"Anything wrong with tomorrow?"

"Nothing," said Kate. "Nothing at all."

"Right, I know where you live. I'll come and pick you up at about half past eleven. Would that suit?" Kate hesitated for a moment, thinking of Cecily's binoculars, and wondering if a different meeting place might not be preferable; then she gave herself a stern mental shake. What about all this resolution to try and make a life of her own? If she allowed her habitual anxiety to please—or appease—

her family, to rule every decision, she would always be on the run from their strong but varied opinions.

"Fine," she said.

"Great. Come dressed for a picnic, not in your posh clothes, or you might have to tie your tights round your skirt again—and we'll take your Rottweiler for a good walk, so bring her along too. See you tomorrow then—goodnight, Puss-in-Boots, sleep well," and he rang off.

But Kate lay awake for some time, with her mind in a whirl.

❧ NINE ❧

With a prospective picnic in mind, Kate listened to the weather forecast at five to seven, but she didn't really need this official confirmation to tell her that the settled weather was going to continue. From her first glance out of the window it was clear that it was going to be a fabulous day.

She went downstairs in her dressing gown to let Acer out and stood on the doorstep enjoying the fresh, early morning smells and the heady scent of the wisteria that climbed up the side of the house.

Kate hoped that Acer would not discover and dismantle the long-tailed tits' nest that Cecily had pointed out to her in the honeysuckle bush in the hedge bordering the sunken garden. It was a work of art, so carefully and intricately built from lichens and cobwebs, so luxuriously lined with thousands of tiny, downy feathers, that it seemed a much more amazing construction than the Observatory. She thought the nest was like a little observation tower itself, with its long shape and opening at the top: not for nothing did local people call the elegant little birds "bottle-tits," because of their elongated dwellings. Acer, who practised her innate herding skills so patiently and gently on Harriet's Pecin bantams, without harming a feather of their absurd plus-four breeches, and who would never have considered robbing the hen house, was sadly addicted to eating small birds' eggs and wrecking nests. As Cecily was keeping a close eye on the family life of the long-tailed tits through her binoculars, Kate was well aware that any delinquency on Acer's part would not go undetected. Swallows and swifts were giving spectacular aerobatic displays in pursuit of invisible flies, slicing the sky as if they wielded the curved blades of Samurai warriors. Kate went reluctantly back into the house to eat her own breakfast in a less dramatic fashion.

She wished Graham Cooper hadn't told her that Jack Morley intended to live in the Observatory himself. It was one thing to try to bully or persuade an unknown owner, especially one against whom she had managed to work up a highly satisfactory prejudice, to part with a property he wanted to keep for himself; it would be quite another to attempt the same tactics now that the owner turned out to be someone to whom—and she had to admit this to herself—she felt so drawn, and who had clearly fallen under the magic spell of the strange little house as strongly as she had herself. Perhaps—unwelcome thought—it was purely for the sake of the Observatory that he had actually bought the Ravelstoke estate? On reflection this seemed unlikely: millionaire tycoons don't buy whole country estates for the sake of one decaying little property on them, no matter how charming and unusual. He could have put in an outsize bid for the one lot and bought it separately. What did he want it all for anyway? The image of the hard-nosed and immensely wealthy businessman from across the Atlantic didn't tally with the humorous and gentle-seeming caretaker she had first met. There was a lot Kate Rendlesham needed to find out about Mr. Franklin Jack Morley. He might even be a crook for all she knew about him.

Stop this nonsense, she scolded herself. You are the fifty-six-year-old widow of a well-known man, a mother and a grandmother—not a green girl on a first date, even if you have fallen romantically in love with a house. Her chances of being able to purchase the house were now even more remote than they had been before—but she still wanted to go on a picnic with its owner.

She shampooed her short hair when she showered, even though it didn't really need it. Kate had found the first silver thread when she was only twenty-five, and Joanna and Nick were little. By the time she was in her early thirties, and several miscarriages had put an end to her hopes of a large brood of children, it was completely grey. Other people told her she was lucky that her hair had gone such a pretty colour and that it looked very attractive set against such a young face, but she had minded at the time. Oliver had refused to let her tint it, and no one could imagine now what she had looked like with hair any other colour.

When she went up to pay her usual morning visit to Cecily, she had still not made up her mind whether to tell her mother-in-law about her late-night invitation after Netta's party. Not to disclose it, would make it seem so much more significant afterwards; to tell her would arouse her instant curiosity—and the same of course applied to Joanna.

As it happened, Cecily's interest had been diverted by Rosamund Campion's involvement with the paranormal, and the promise of a famous medium descending on the Dial House, Rosamund's English base, which she had recently made so charming with the help of Robin's clever cousin, Ellie Hadleigh. Unlike Netta, Rosamund had quite enough self-confidence to give professional interior decorators the credit that was due to them, secure in the knowledge that she had wonderful taste and plenty of good ideas herself.

"I'm going to have lunch with Roz today," Cecily announced. "I think she's got her charming Arab lover staying, though I gather he may be on the way out—she's had him for four years so I expect she needs a change." She might have been talking about chair covers. "Anyway, she's going to fill me in on this transatlantic woman—or whatever it's called. I thought I'd go a bit early and look in on Babs on the way and tell her all about last night's party. Poor old thing—such a shame she was too ga-ga to make herself come. I've told her she ought to pull herself together; managing old age is only a question of mind over matter. 'If you're not careful you won't *have* any mind left,' I said to her. 'Stop mollycoddling yourself.' Would you believe it—the other day she thought she was playing the hand in no-trumps when she'd actually made the four spades game-bid herself! And she'd no idea where the ace lay.''

''No!'' said Kate with mock horror. She had never been able to sustain sufficient interest to master the intricacies of bridge herself, so her sympathies lay entirely with the delightfully vague but gentle Babs, who struck Kate as still being perfectly on the ball, though not always perhaps on the one that Cecily required. ''Oh well, you've got a nice day ahead of you, then,'' she said. ''I'm so pleased. I'm out to lunch myself too. Have a good time, and tell Roz nothing will keep me from attending a seance when the time comes.''

She went downstairs feeling relieved to have been truthful without attracting attention. She rang up the cottage to enquire after the invalids and was further relieved when Jenny, not Joanna, answered the telephone. Kate had no doubt that Joanna would put her through an inquisition about her so-called friendship with the new owner of Ravelstoke. She wondered whether Rosamund had been dining at Duntan too, after the party, and if so what on earth she would have told Joanna about Kate's meeting with him, and Netta's furious reaction.

Jenny said she was miles better, now, thank you.

''It was kill or cure last night,'' she said cheerfully. ''I felt like death for a bit, but Mrs. Stokes is strong medicine: anyone who has her standing at the end of their bed for an hour telling them every intestinal detail of the Stokes family

ailments is going to be fully operational pretty damn quick
rather than risk that again, I can tell you. I think I must
have eaten a bad prawn or something because no one else
has got the lurgy. Tilly wasn't sick at all—there's nothing
whatever the matter with her. She was just playing her mum
up. Did you know Jo's gone off to do a cookery demo for
some Red Cross do over at Scarborough for the day? She
left really early—before seven.''

''I think she may have mentioned it ages ago, but I'd
forgotten. I'm out myself today, but I just thought I'd check
that all was well first.''

How like Joanna, she thought, torn between relief and
mild annoyance, to have made such a fuss about everything
last night and then gone off this morning without even
thinking to send a message to say that all was well.

She had meant to get some ideas for needlepoint cushions sketched out on paper to show Jane. She thought that
some of her designs might sell well if they came as a kit
with wool and silk provided, and one corner of a repeating
pattern already started, but somehow she couldn't concentrate. She flitted about from job to job, and achieved nothing. She went upstairs to put on a clean pair of cotton
trousers and a fresh T-shirt.

From her bedroom window, Kate saw a big green four-
wheel-drive car arriving. Quite into the English country-
landowner style already, thought Kate wryly, and was
thankful that Cecily was not there to turn espionage technique from birds to humans. Kate was full of curiosity herself, but she also felt suddenly anxious, and almost wished
she had refused the invitation. He has to be a financial high-
flyer at least, she thought, perhaps another exceptional man,
like Oliver. What if we have nothing to say to each other?
What if the day is a disaster?

She need not have worried. From the moment she answered the front doorbell and found Jack Morley standing
on the step reassuringly dressed in old country clothes, as

he had been when she first met him, constraint fell away and they might indeed have known each other for years.

"I'm not going to presume on our old friendship again, Mrs. Rendlesham," he grinned, holding out his hand to her with mock formality.

"I should think not," said Kate severely, but Acer gave him a warm welcome, and jumped happily into the back of his obviously new Range Rover with its (rather ostentatious, Kate thought) number plate of FJM 2. Kate chucked a dog towel in after Acer, knowing her fondness for lying down in streams and practising total immersion just before a return journey.

"Where are we going?" she asked.

"Where do you think?"

"I'd rather not guess. You tell me."

"Coward," he said. "Well, I thought we might finish our tour of the Observatory, which if you remember was cut short so suddenly when you took flight. I thought we'd eat our lunch there, and then, if it would amuse you, I thought you might like to come and look at Ravelstoke with me. We could walk your dog in the park. Have you ever been in the big house?"

"No, never, but I adore poking round houses. What a lovely idea—just my kind of day."

"Good," he said. "I rather hoped it might be. You'll be my very first guest."

He drove expertly, never causing Kate to flatten any imaginary brakes in the floorboards, but not hanging about either. She told him Cecily's Mrs. Malapropism about kerb crawlers on their way to the Fanshaws', and he was hugely amused by her verbal snapshot portraits of all the people he had met there. She thought he must have a phenomenal memory to have taken in so many of them.

"I can see you're a very dangerous lady. I'm not sure I'm safe with you," he said.

When they reached the village of Ravelstoke he turned left and just out of the village they passed the lichen-covered grey stone gateway to the Hall. It looked in a pretty crumbly condition, thought Kate—dark and rather threatening: not the kind of entrance that opened its arms to you. The finals were missing from the top of the columns on either side of the arch. Wrought-iron gates, with curly back-to-back Rs in the centre of each, were heavily chained and padlocked, but an avenue of very old yew trees could be glimpsed through them. Jack slowed down so that Kate could look, but he didn't stop the car.

"We'll go in the back way later on. There used to be two rather splendid unicorns holding shields on either side of the gates, but I gather they got nicked or vandalised some time ago. Anyway, they're not there now."

"That's sad: unicorns are symbols of magic. Shall you try to replace them?"

"I don't know. I hardly know where to begin with lots of things—and magic is notoriously hard to reproduce. I shall welcome your advice; there are so many imponderables I have to think about. Perhaps I'll bore you with some of them over lunch."

Kate thought that the last thing she might feel in his company would be boredom.

A mile further down the road, Jack slowed down as they came to another set of gates on the left—less ornate ones, but beautifully crafted all the same, and with the same double Rs; these ones were open. He drove through them.

"Oh," said Kate. "We're *here*. I didn't realise we'd arrived yet, but of course last time I walked up from below."

"Last time you were trespassing. This time you're here by special invitation."

Kate looked at him rather anxiously. She couldn't help wondering if he had brought her here only to break it to her that the house was not for sale; she knew she must brace herself for disappointment. He had after all warned her at their first meeting not to set her heart on buying the house, and Graham Cooper had now told her why. The house lay a little below them. Trees had grown up, so it was hardly noticeable from the road, and though the observation tower was visible above these, the house did not exert the magic pull from the back as it did when viewed against the skyline from below. Kate felt glad that it kept itself secret in this way.

On either side of the gates there were stable buildings: she supposed Raving Ravelstoke would have arrived for stargazing sessions on horseback or in his carriage. She could imagine the stables converting wonderfully into workshops and a studio. There was a little walled courtyard outside the front door. She noticed that the windows in the tower were now open, and that the grass all round the house had been roughly cut. Someone had been busy with a Hayter or a Flymo.

Jack smiled at her. "Don't look so bothered," he said. "I know you have a lot of questions to ask—but so do I. We need to talk, but let's just enjoy lunch first, shall we? Unlike most people I don't like doing business over meals—and never over picnics." A spark of hope fluttered inside Kate.

"I think you can read my thoughts," she said. "But of course let's enjoy lunch. You're so kind to bring me here and I'm starving anyway."

The front door opened on to a little hall. "Go straight ahead." Jack held the door open for her, and they went through the room at the base of the tower, where the staircase was, and then on into the curved drawing room. All the cobwebs and dust had disappeared: it was bare but spotless, and the French windows which led on to the garden, where she had slept so soundly only a few weeks earlier, were open. It seemed ages ago. There was a garden table and two chairs on the little terrace.

"Not quite worthy of Raving Ravelstoke's Regency designs, I'm afraid," said Jack. "But the best the local garden centre could produce at short notice. Shall we eat outside?"

"Oh yes please. I can never bear to waste a day like this. It was a longing to be outside that had set me exploring when we first met. I'd actually been lunching with the Fanshaws that day, and I suddenly felt so claustrophobic that I bolted."

"And imagined you were 'guided' to come here?" he teased. "I quite see you were ripe for a discovery. What did you ask me that day? Did I believe in serendipity?" He roared with laughter. "What a question to ask an unknown local yokel caretaker! Now you go and sit out there while I fetch our picnic."

"Can't I come and help?"

"You can come and carry a bottle out of the refrigerator if you like."

"*A fridge?*" asked Kate. "Surely Raving Ravelstoke didn't have a fridge?"

"I've lived too much of my life in the States to go without ice for long: I've lost the taste for warm beer. But there was an ice-box here already. You forget that the house has been converted since his day; after old Miss Ravelstoke died, I believe it was used for holiday lets for a time, so there are all the basics here. Now that it's clean, it's quite civilised."

"I noticed someone had been busy—inside and out," said Kate.

She followed him back into the house.

They hadn't been into any of the rooms in the two wings of the house on her last visit. The kitchen wasn't exactly like an advertisement from a glossy magazine but it looked serviceable enough. There was an electric oven that had seen better days, a white porcelain sink of the kind currently enjoying a fashionable renaissance, and an old scrubbed wooden table in the centre of the room which would now be considered the height of country chic by Joanna's readers. On it were a couple of baskets obviously containing the picnic.

Jack opened the fridge and handed Kate a bottle of Sauvignon Blanc and a bottle of sparkling mineral water. "This all right?" he asked. "I don't know what you like yet, so I've had to guess. There's gin and tonic if you'd rather?"

"This is just perfect," said Kate. The "yet" was not lost on her.

He produced melon and Parma ham, a quiche and salad, and strawberries and cream.

"A feast!" said Kate. "All my favourite things. You are clever." She wondered how much he had done himself, or whether hosts of hidden minions lurked behind the bushes.

"When I was at university I used to earn pocket money as a waiter, and twice I worked in the long vacation for an American shipping magnate on his luxury yacht. I can turn my hand to most things—even cooking if I choose—but it's not very difficult to buy an instant picnic." He shot her an amused look; again showing an unnerving knack of reading her thoughts. Kate told him about all the local speculation that had been humming about his identity and of her own alternative visions of him as Aristotle or Clint.

"How disappointing to find I was just Jack the caretaker."

"Not at all," she said, laughing back at him. "It was such a relief because I was nerving myself to tackle you, and I'm easily intimidated."

"Oh I don't think so," he said. "You strike me as quite persistent in your own quiet way. I knew you'd be at that party." Kate wasn't sure how to take this.

"How could you know?"

"Graham Cooper duly reported to me that there was a woman who was obsessed—his words—with buying the Observatory, though for reasons of confidentiality he could naturally not disclose the name of the client in question." Jack Morley had got Graham Cooper's wah-wah voice to perfection. "I didn't have to be a genius at sums to add that one up. If I hadn't felt sure you'd be at the party, I wouldn't have gone." He filled her glass up with more wine.

"Tell me your life story," said Kate, unwilling to pursue this line of conversation. "What on earth made you want to buy the Ravelstoke estate? Are you English or American? I'm sitting comfortably—you begin."

So they sat in the half-shade of the great beech tree and he told her how he had been born the son of a miner, in a back-to-back terrace house, in an area which was entirely populated by people who worked down the pit. "A wonderful community," he said. "Tight-knit and close, but tough as hell, and narrow in a way too because you didn't rub shoulders with outsiders much. I'm a Geordie really, but my mum was a Yorkshire lass, and came from here. Her father was head gamekeeper to Lord Ravelstoke, and her mother, my gran, had worked first as a housemaid and then as lady's maid to Lady Ravelstoke before she married my grandfather. My grandfather was a very handsome man, even when I knew him. It used to be said that half the children in the village were either dead ringers for him or for Lord Ravelstoke, though my mother and her sister were his only children born in wedlock." He laughed. "There were those who said my grandfather and the old Lord had a striking similarity to each other too—were half-brothers the wrong side of the blanket—but one will never know. My father loathed it here. He disapproved of the whole feudal set-up on principle, and hated the effect it had on my mother. I think he blamed it for the fact that she never really settled in her new environment—but that had more to do with her longing for the countryside than anything to do with a sycophantic view of the English class system, as he liked to assume. She just pined in an urban environment and I don't think she ever felt entirely accepted by her neighbors. She was always homesick for Ravelstoke."

"And your father?" asked Kate. "What was he like?"

"Oh, he was a brilliant man—if he'd had my sort of education I don't know what he might have become. He had a burning passion for knowledge, and was about as far to the left politically as you can get. I don't know what he'd think of my lifestyle now—probably spinning in his grave with disapproval—but he's left me with a few ideals he might not be too ashamed of."

"But you love this place, don't you?"

"Yes," he said. "I've been all over the world, but nowhere pulls me quite like this bit of Yorkshire. My grandfather taught me every bit of country lore you can think of, and I was brought up on stories about Ravelstoke. We used to come here to visit, and when war broke out and the bombing over Newcastle got bad I was evacuated here to my grandparents. My father never really forgave my mother for that. It was the one time she overruled him."

"Were you an only child?"

"I had a sister who died of pneumonia. That changed my mother. By the time I was at university my father had made a name for himself in the Union. Funny thing was, though he was very ambitious for me, wanted me to have the education he hadn't had and drove me on to sit for scholarships, a part of him resented it when I won them. I admired him tremendously in some ways—but from a very early age I knew my life was going to be different from his. My parents didn't have a happy marriage, and I'd seen the longing in my mother's eyes for wider skies."

"So you flew to America to try your wings in them?"

"More or less. I got a scholarship first to grammar school and then to Oxford. Oxford was a culture shock, I can tell you—but of course you need luck in this life as well as application. And I was lucky: chances fell my way and I took them." He looked at Kate. "Success is about recognising opportunities—and then seizing them."

"My serendipity?" suggested Kate.

Something in his expression made her look quickly away. "As you say—your serendipity. If that ever comes your way you mustn't mess with it.'' They drank their wine and ate their picnic and it occurred to Kate that she felt carefree in a way she had not done for a very long time. I am happy, she thought in wonderment. I had forgotten what it felt like. Not just enjoying myself, which is different, but wonderfully, completely happy. I must never forget this moment.

"Go on," she said, eventually.

"Not much more to tell. The freedom and opportunity in the States went to my head. I'd spent so much of my growing-up studying and being serious and I went wild— still worked hard, but played hard and drank hard, and tried just about everything going. I started to make serious money. Heady stuff. Then I made a disastrous marriage to the ambitious, socialite daughter of my boss. I was crazy about her, but after a few years she ran off with someone she thought would get rich quicker than me.'' He pulled a wry face. "As it happened she made the wrong choice in that respect," he said.

"And did you never feel the need to marry again?"

"I didn't live like a celibate monk, if that's what you're asking."

"No," said Kate, hurt and surprised by a sudden change in his tone. "Of course that's not what I meant."

"Yes, I married again. A car crash dealt with that marriage."

"Oh, I'm *so* sorry." Kate looked at him with quick sympathy and waited for him to tell her more, but he said nothing.

"Do you have children?" she asked, to break the silence.

"One daughter."

"And are you close to her?"

"Close? Well, no. I'm mostly based in New York, and she's married to a Canadian and lives in Toronto." He looked as if he was about to say something else, something important, but had changed his mind, and Kate instinctively knew he had deliberately misinterpreted her use of the word close.

"Any grandchildren yet?"

"No."

"A treat in store then perhaps," said Kate smiling.

He didn't answer. An awkward little silence fell. She had felt so at home with him they might have known each other for years, but suddenly it was as if a cold wind had drifted a cloud across the sun. Kate found herself giving a shiver, and had the oddest sensation as if she had been caught trying to peer through a keyhole at something he did not want her to see.

"Did you keep up with your family over here?" she asked, after a pause, feeling that the topic of his early life was somehow safer territory than his present one in the States.

"Of course. After old Lord Ravelstoke died the whole estate fell into decay. The only son was an eccentric recluse—the family always had a tendency to mislay marbles—and my grandparents were not well treated in retirement. I always resented that. Then disaster struck my parents. My father was involved in an accident down the mine, and was paralysed from the chest down. My mother was chained to him for the rest of their lives. I could have made things much easier for my mother, but my father would never let her accept any help or take a penny from me when I came over—even though he knew by then that I would hardly have noticed it. Perhaps because of that. I often think that if I'd had less, he'd have taken more. Wealth does unpredictable things to people: both having it and not having it. You can do marvellous things with money, but it can erect barriers too. I used to send regular amounts directly to my mother but she never used it—it all came back to me after their death. That hurt. My father was a proud, bitter man and he couldn't forgive my mother for his dependence and her unselfishness. He was awful to her. I found it hard to forgive him for a long time, but now I can see things through his eyes too. That helps. She lived for six months after he died and I got her over to the States for one visit. It's a very precious memory.''

He suddenly smiled at her again, and whatever had caused the cloud was gone. But it left Kate slightly puzzled all the same. She would have liked to sympathise with him, and wondered if he still found the death of his second wife too hard to talk about. He hadn't struck her as someone who would find emotion a taboo subject.

''So have you bought all this because you loved it or resented it, out of gratitude or revenge?''

''Both, I suppose, though I hadn't quite thought of it like that,'' he said. ''Anyway, enough about me. It's your turn for the inquisition next, Mrs. Oliver Rendlesham—but would you like to come up to the observatory first?''

''Oh yes, please.''

This time, when they climbed up the stone staircase, the windows of the first room were open and he led her out on to a narrow balcony that ran all round the square tower, protected by a stone balustrade.

''There would have been transit telescopes here, on stands which could be moved,'' Jack told her, ''so that people could come and stargaze, but the serious stuff went on upstairs in the observatory proper. That telescope would have been fixed to the floor and weighed tons. Actually you can't see much up there, but come and inspect it.'' They went back inside and she followed him up the narrow spiral staircase at the end of the room. He had already opened a trap door at the top, surrounded with railings.

''Careful,'' he said, giving her a hand.

''But it's quite dark,'' said Kate, surprised. ''There aren't any windows. How did Raving Ravelstoke see out?''

Jack flicked a switch and turned on a single electric bulb. ''There wouldn't have been any light then. You could only see through a refracting telescope via four slits in the dome—one at each point of the compass. Three of them have been nailed up because of problems with damp, but you can still open the shutters on one of them—with difficulty. I won't try it now, we might not be able to shut it again.'' He pointed to the centre of the bare, round room, where there was a large, dilapidated old day-bed in buttoned black leather with horsehair stuffing cascading out of it: "Only used by mice now," said Jack. "But that's where he would have lain to stargaze. It's called a Wield observing couch.''

"Goodness," said Kate. "Perhaps it wasn't only for stars, but for the 'hurly-burly of the chaise longue' that the old raver came here?''

Jack laughed. "No, no, he had ten children by his wife—a termagant by all accounts—so, unlike Mrs. Patrick Campbell, his hurly-burly must have been in the marriage bed, and I think this is where he came for his 'deep peace.' Perhaps he needed a rest. He would have spent hours up here taking copious notes, checking on the exact positions of stars and noting the exact time against special clocks with a very loud tick so that he could mark every second—lost in a world of his own.''

"I hope he was happy here anyway," said Kate. "I think he was—it's got a good feel to it. I knew that when I first came here.''

"Yes," he said, "I think so too. I used to come to tea with old Miss Ravelstoke when I was a little boy. I never told my grandparents—it was a secret between the old lady and me, which made it special. If my grandmother had known she'd have made me smarten up and brush my hair and told me to mind my manners, which would have spoilt it all and made me tongue-tied. It was from here that I learnt so much about the house and the family. I've always loved it here.''

They went downstairs and Kate blinked in the brilliant sunlight. He showed her the other wing of the house. It was unfurnished except for one bedroom. Though very spartan, this was clearly occupied. The bed was made, a dressing gown hung on the door and a jacket was flung on the only chair; there were towels and soap and shaving things in the bathroom. She looked at him in dismay.

"You are living here already," she said. "That's why you brought me here, isn't it? Because you aren't going to sell me the house, are you? You want it for yourself. I quite understand, but oh, I wish you'd told me straight away and hadn't brought me back here."

∿ TEN ∾

Kate brushed past Jack and went out and stood on the terrace, gazing at the view, but not really seeing it, because, to her shame, she found she was fighting tears, and her throat felt as if it had been squeezed. She was aware that her acute disappointment was absurd and quite out of proportion.

He came and stood behind her. Then he put his hands very gently on her shoulders. She gave a fierce little shrug, but he did not take his hands away.

"Kate," he said, "Kate—you don't half take a flying leap at conclusions. Give a chap a chance."

"Don't play with me," she said. "Is the house for sale or isn't it?"

"The house is not for sale—and I'm not playing."

He wondered what was behind such a strong reaction. Was it the grief of losing her husband? But he thought that was not quite sufficient explanation for her fixation with this particular house. Widows are more inclined to hang on desperately to a home where they have been happy, and her own house seemed highly covetable by most standards. Was it to run away from something? He felt that if he made a wrong move she might take wing like a frightened bird and be lost to him. The thought suddenly seemed unbearable. They stood in silence while Kate battled to control her unwelcome, untidy emotions.

"You must think me extraordinary silly," she said at last, in a tight voice. "I do apologise. I don't know what came over me. There's no reason in the world why you should sell—I wouldn't if I were you. It was nice of you to ask me out to lunch and I really have enjoyed it. Please forget this stupid outburst—perhaps I ought to be getting home."

"I don't think you silly—except to imagine I could want to tantalise you over it. I'm not selling the house for a load of reasons, but there are other options I hoped we might discuss—some sort of lease, for instance. We haven't even started to explore the possibilities, and our day has only just begun. I'm certainly not taking you home yet—unless my company has become unbearably tedious to you and you can't stand any more of it?"

"No," she said. "Oh no."

He turned her round to face him, and just touched her cheek with one finger, tracing the course of a tear. "We have a lot to discover about each other," he said. "Don't let's rush. I want to take you to Ravelstoke and tell you my ideas for that, but before we go there, let's sit on the grass and drink mugs of coffee and you can tell me what you would like to do with this funny little house of mine if you lived in it. You told me when we first met that you were searching for your own identity. It seemed a funny thing to say to a stranger. Tell me: 'If there were dreams to sell, What would you buy?'"

Kate looked up at him: "'Some cost a passing bell, Some a light sigh,'" she quoted. "I love that poem too. Yes, I'll tell you, Jack."

So they made themselves coffee and stretched out in the dappled sunshine, and she told him about Midas and Jane Pulborough's suggestion, and how much she wanted to make a new life for herself. "I couldn't do it from Longthorpe," she said. "The house is too full of Oliver and all my memories. Oliver is in every bit of that house and garden, which he made so beautiful. Oliver found the house, and it was always Oliver who chose things for it and arranged them; he had wonderful taste. Now I see his absence everywhere.'' Jack felt a rush of envy against this departed husband who obviously affected Kate so profoundly.

"Do you ever do jigsaw puzzles?" Kate asked suddenly.

"Not for years, but when I was a boy I loved them. Why?"

"Well, you know how if there's one bit missing when you've finished the puzzle, your eye is always drawn to the dark hole of the bit that isn't there—and it completely ruins the whole picture?" Jack nodded.

"Well, Longthorpe is like that for me now. All I can see is the hole left by Oliver. If I'm to make a new life it has to be somewhere different. My son has got our flat in Fulham—and I'm a country bumpkin now. I'd stifle in London. My daughter, Joanna, would like to exchange houses with me and live in Longthorpe, and it's the obvious solution, I suppose. But I know that if I stayed on in Jo's cottage at the end of the garden I'd never have the resolution to do my own thing and stick to it—and I'd still be left looking at the gap in the jigsaw. When I saw this house by chance I suddenly thought I might be able to be myself in it—to find myself, instead of being only the wife, mother and grandmother I've been for so long. I know it sounds silly, but I suppose I fell in love with this magic little place. Can you understand that?"

"Oh, yes," said Jack. "I believe in love at first sight too. Tell me more." So Kate explained about her ideas of having a studio and outworkers to help with some of the sewing while she concentrated on her own designs.

"Did you make that jacket you were wearing last night?" he asked.

"Yes," she said, surprised and flattered that he had noticed.

"Then you will succeed. You looked wonderful."

"Oh, thank you so much." Kate beamed at him, and he thought how unaware she was of her own attraction.

"I've never been much good at anything," she said. "But I do have this talent for stitching." She held her hands out in front of her and frowned at them as though assessing them and finding them wanting—small, practical hands with short, unvarnished nails. "Oliver used to say that I could only think with my fingers."

Something in her voice made him ask: "And was that a compliment?"

"No," said Kate. "Not a compliment in any way at all."

"I wasn't quite truthful with Netta Fanshaw," said Jack, watching her face as she lay looking up at the leaves of the beech tree, the offending hands now linked behind her head. "Though I couldn't say I really knew him, I did actually meet your husband once, through a business deal. We were on opposite sides over a takeover."

"And did you get on well together?" asked Kate.

Jack juggled with the fear of offending Kate and an instinct to be truthful. Truth won.

"I have to say that I disliked him intensely," he said at last, not daring to watch her reaction, "and that's rare for me—but I guess it was mutual. I got what I wanted in that particular case so my feelings had nothing to do with the outcome. Tell me, Kate, this brilliant man that you were married to, a sort of legend for charm—even I could see he had plenty of that if he chose to switch it on—was it a good marriage? Did you love each other? Did he make you happy?"

There was a long silence, and when she turned to look at him he could hardly bear the pain in her face.

"Oliver made me about as unhappy as one person can make another," she said. "He was a sadist and a bully—but not many people knew it."

"But you loved him?"

"Oh, I loved him. For a long time I was besotted. He was such a star—always surrounded by glittering people, and he could make you feel wonderful. I couldn't believe it when he noticed me, let alone wanted to marry me. To start with he was my yardstick for perfection, and when I measured myself against him I always felt totally deficient; soon I was also terrified of him. He never hurt me physically—that wouldn't have been his style at all—but he was a calculated and meticulous puller off of metaphorical butterfly wings. No one could undermine your confidence like Oliver, or make you more afraid to express an opinion. Later, I couldn't bear to watch him do it to other people too—always to small unimportant people, never to the grand important ones, and seldom in front of anyone else. He had his whipping boy at home, you see—I think it's why he married me." She started to plait three pieces of grass together with great concentration. "He needed that outlet: no competition—just an adoring slave who would go on loving him however awful it was."

"And one day did you stop adoring?"

Kate nodded. "Yes, I stopped. One day I decided I wouldn't be a victim any more. I couldn't change him— that was his problem—but I could stop my fear of his mockery spoiling my life. The day I ceased to worship him was a day of great release for me; and the day he realised he couldn't hurt me any more—or not in the way he'd been used to—drove him wild: like all bullies he was afraid of being outfaced. It's a miracle our son Nick has survived as well as he has, because Oliver bullied him too, though I could often stand up to Oliver over that. Even cowards like me can sometimes be brave for their children."

"You don't sound very cowardly to me," he said gently.

Kate threw the grass plait away, sat up and clasped her knees, gazing into the distance, but seeing the past.

"I once witnessed a hen partridge killed by a mower," she said. "I've never forgotten it. She had nested on a bank, though no one knew she was there, and when the long grass was being cut after the daffodils had finished seeding, the machine went right over her. She was killed, of course, but all the eggs were untouched because she'd stayed put. I put them under a broody bantam and they all hatched. She must have heard that machine coming for ages, getting nearer and nearer, as she crouched over her nest with wings stretched out. I could imagine her terror, and how her heart must have thumped under her feathers, and yet somehow she resisted the impulse to fly. Amazing. I still think of it. At the time I was near the end of my tether and contemplating running out on Oliver, but I thought if that mother bird could do that for her eggs, I can stick it out for my children as well.'' She gave a little self-mocking laugh and shrugged, but Jack could see she was deadly serious. ''I suppose I could have left him after the children grew up. I don't know if it was laudable endurance or despicable feebleness that kept me from going. And partridges mate for life, you know. Hen partridges are unspectacular, drab little birds too,''

''Did Oliver love you?''

''I don't know. He needed me—but he didn't really know anything about love. To him love was about ownership and control; about buying, but not about giving. But I had to admire his courage over his last year. I'm grateful for that—it gives me one memory I can respect.''

''And your daughter? How was she affected?''

''Oliver idolised Joanna, but funnily enough Jo, not Nick, is the person Oliver has really damaged. He brought her up to believe that she could have and do anything she wanted. But life doesn't work like that, and she can't cope when things don't go her way. Jo's clever and forceful and intolerant; she has all her father's ambition, but she's not cruel like him—she doesn't *enjoy* hurting people. Unlike Oliver, all Jo's faults are on the outside. She can give people a really hard time—steamroller over them—and then be upset and puzzled when they don't like her. She's absolutely hopeless with her children and she never understands why they're difficult. Sometimes I tremble for her. She's taken his death terribly hard." She hesitated, and then said, almost in a whisper, "There are things that may come out about Oliver which would absolutely slay Jo. I so pray I can keep them hushed up. Only one other person really knows." She gave herself a little shake. "I've said too much," she said. "I don't usually talk like this. I'm sorry."

Jack got up. "Don't regret it—sometimes it's easier to talk to strangers. I'm honoured you trusted me, and anything you say is safe with me. Promise me something?"

"What?"

"I won't press you with questions now, but if there's anything you need to unburden yourself about, or if I can ever help, in any way, I'd like to feel you could come to me. I've learnt a thing or two about human nature in my itinerant life—and also how to deal with some of its less attractive manifestations. I would be there for you."

"Thank you," she said, much touched. "I won't forget."

"Come on," he said, feeling a change of key was needed. "That hound of yours is getting restless. We don't need to get in the car to go to the house. Feel like a walk?" He held out his hand to pull her to her feet and, unlike the day they had first met, this time she took it.

They scrambled down the ha-ha and walked together across the field from which Kate had first seen the Observatory. Acer bounded joyfully ahead, stopping occasionally to check that Kate was coming, or to pick up some particularly exciting message left in the grass by a hare or a pheasant. The sweet smell of cow parsley had taken on from the bluebells, and sunbursts of buttercups, scattered through the grass, were waiting to ask their yellow questions under children's chins.

"If cow parsley was rare and hard to grow I always think it would be in the collectable class of flower," said Kate.

"Like kippers to caviar," suggested Jack. "Now look to your left and you can see the house."

Below them Ravelstoke Hall crouched in a hallow, like some grim grey dinosaur that had got left behind after the rest of its species had died out.

"Oh dear," said Kate. "It doesn't look very inviting. Do you really want to live there?"

"I've no intention of living in it at all. For one thing I shall still have to spend a good deal of time in the States, but anyway I have other plans for the Hall. Come and look round and I'll tell you." He led her down a path and round the side of the house to the great oak front door which opened on to a forecourt surrounded by stone walls; beyond it, the drive disappeared through the park; on either side, the yew trees which they had glimpsed through the main gates before lunch, formed a mournful guard of honour.

"No lovely view from here." Kate looked across the park while Jack opened the door. "You can see why Raving Ravelstoke liked to escape to the Observatory. This wouldn't have been nearly so good for stargazing. Does it feel funny to you to come back here as the owner after all these years?"

"Very funny," Jack held the door open for her, and laughed. "Funniest of all to be coming in through the front door. If my grandmother every brought me here we went round to the back. I didn't buy the estate because I had grand ideas of playing Lord of the Manor and living in the big house. I love the land, and I'd like to put all the farms in first-class order and get the whole estate really well run, but I want to turn this house into a holiday home for seriously disabled or handicapped people—to make it possible for their day-to-day carers to have proper breaks, and I want to set up an endowment to fund the whole scheme."

"That sounds a wonderful idea. Is it because of what your mother went through?"

"Partly that, but also for another reason. I'll tell you about it sometime. I've learnt a lot about people who need a break from caring—but many can't afford one."

Kate looked at him questioningly but he did not elaborate, and she had the feeling he was holding something back.

She followed him through the stone-flagged hall with its dark panelling, above which glum-looking portraits of long deceased Ravelstokes gazed down. The pictures were dark and badly in need of restoration; some actually had water marks and patches of mildew where there should have been a face or hand. It was hard to tell whether they would once have been fine examples of portrait painting or not. Most of the women had puffy faces and full, pouting lips; one clearly had an incipient goitre, her bulging neck and bulging eyes giving the unnerving impression that she had just encountered something particularly unpleasant: none of them looked as if she had got any pleasure from her stiff dress or the pearls twined in her crimped, centre-parted hair. A few early portraits showed men in sweeping hats, their long locks touching fine lace collars, but in later ones the men wore wigs, and posed lounging against stone pillars, often with one hand resting on the head of a large, unloved-looking dog. Kate made a mental note that a study of their embroidered coats could prove useful for ideas of her own designs, but she also thought it was one of the gloomiest houses she had ever been in.

The ringing of a telephone was a surprise.

"Damn." Jack felt in his pocket and took out a mobile. "Yes?" He sounded brusque. "I thought I said I didn't want to be disturbed today." Kate thought he looked very forbidding while he listened to whoever was on the other end of the line. She didn't envy them. Then he said: "I see. Yes. Well all right, I suppose so—but tell him to bloody well get on with it. Fast." He snapped down the aerial and put the telephone back in his pocket. "Sorry about that," he said smiling at her, all grimness gone.

"Quite the big tycoon, Mr. Franklin J. Morley—the other side of Caretaker Jack," she said lightly, but there was a little edge to her voice that didn't escape Jack, and a small silence fell between them.

"Is there a picture of Raving Ravelstoke?" she asked after a moment, partly to change the subject but genuinely curious to see a likeness of the man who had designed and loved the house she already loved so much herself.

"Yes—miraculously in better condition than most." Jack opened the door of what had obviously once been a billiard room, though the table lay in pieces on the floor, the green baize, rotted and torn, exposing cracked slate slabs; six vast legs, standing in the middle of the room, looked strangely lost without anything to support.

"Oh how horrid," said Kate. "They remind me of that terrifying fairy story about the girl who wished for company, and this awful giant appeared bit by bit from the feet up before he gobbled her up."

"You really don't like this place, do you? But look over the fireplace," said Jack, pointing. "There's our friend. See his telescope in the picture?"

"Oh I like him," said Kate. "Actually he looks a lot less batty than the rest of them. Where is that telescope now?"

"I don't know. Perhaps we'll come across it when we start turning things out. I've got Sotheby's coming to do a valuation and look through everything. Of course it may have been sold, but it would be of interest. There was a famous maker of astronomical instruments in York called Cook, so it was probably made there."

"Who is the portrait by?"

"Owen, I believe—he did a lot of portraits in the north of England. He painted another Yorkshire astronomer, Richard Sheepshanks, who was a Fellow of the Royal Society too."

"Were they friends?"

"Richard Sheepshanks was more famous for his litigation and quarrels than friendship."

Kate looked at Jack curiously, thinking what a mixture he was. "What a lot you know."

"I read history at Oxford. I would like to have been an art historian." He grinned ruefully: "But I wanted to make money even more. Now that I've done that, I can afford to play at the other as a hobby. I'm exceedingly lucky."

He whisked her round the rest of the ground floor, flinging open doors, and showing her other large rooms, from a vast dining hall with a timber ceiling and a long refectory table, to a drawing room where beautiful early plaster work was in an appalling state of repair. The rooms were still partly furnished with what she imagined were valuable pieces of Tudor or Elizabethan oak furniture. Heavy brocade curtains, much frayed, hung at the latticed windows. Even on such a hot day the house struck chill.

The grand staircase was also of oak and as they went up it Kate felt as if she was sliding to one side.

"I feel giddy," she said. "As if my feet don't belong to me. Did I have too much wine for lunch or are the stairs on the slope?"

"It's the stairs—they've subsided away from the wall and are on a slant. We won't go all over the house. I'll just show you the State Bedroom—one of the many Queen Elizabeth is said to have slept in on one of her 'progresses'—and the Long Gallery—you have to see that. It's famous. Pevsner waxed lyrical about it. Then I promise we'll go out into the garden. I think you're finding the house oppressive; some people think it has a strange atmosphere and you wouldn't be the first person to be affected by it."

"Is it supposed to be haunted?"

"It's said to have the statutory grey lady like so many old houses, but my grandmother also had an unpleasant story of one of the spare rooms where an ice-cold baby could sometimes be felt trying to snuggle up in bed to female visitors. To be honest I hardly ever came here so I've not yet encountered any spooks first-hand. Doubt if I would anyway."

Acer followed them upstairs, her nose pressed close to Kate's side, her ears flattened back and the hair round her neck standing up like a ruff. Kate felt a desperate urge to run—anything to get out of the house. She had an inexplicable sense of panic, and her heart started to thump. Jack glanced down at her and suddenly took her hand in his own comforting warm clasp and they went on up the stairs hand in hand. It seemed the most natural thing in the world.

All the same it was a relief to get back into the sunshine. They sat on the wall of the courtyard, and Kate found herself taking deep breaths as though her lungs had been choked up.

Jack looked at her with concern. "Oh Kate, I'm so sorry—what an unthinking clot I am. That was too much for you. I shouldn't have made you walk here in this heat."

"Rubbish," she said. "I walk for miles with Acer and I love the heat. Living in Yorkshire, sunshine is a treat. I do apologise. I don't know what came over me, but I think it's the house. Jack . . ." she hesitated.

"Yes?"

"I'm glad you don't intend to take this house over for yourself. I think you may have to get something done about it—have it exorcised or something. Otherwise I don't think your patients are going to have very happy holidays here. It gives me a bad feeling—threatening. Promise me something?"

"What is that?"

"Promise me that you won't come and live here yourself, even temporarily," she said.

"Why do you feel so strongly about it?"

Kate flushed. "I don't really know, but I just do. Don't ask me why, but I feel the house might bring bad luck."

"Where I decide to live, when I'm up here, might partly depend on you." Jack was stroking Acer, who had come and leant her head against him. "Look, Kate—I don't want to put pressure of any sort on you, so I'll bowl some ideas at you; but you must be free to say what you feel about them. I'm open to suggestions, but I want to do up the Observatory and make it really lovely—worthy of its atmosphere and charm. I couldn't do it myself. I wouldn't have time for one thing, but I don't just want to hand it over to a decorator who might not understand the special something that you and I both see in it. You're right that I've been camping out there lately, and until I met you it had occurred to me that I might go on doing so and make it my Yorkshire base. I still have to be in the States for much of the time. I hate hotels and have a flat over my London office which I use when I'm there on business, but I'd like somewhere up here where I can come on the spur of the moment while I'm setting things up on the estate.''

Kate knew that something important was about to be suggested and hoped she would be up to providing an answer and making a decision.

''I have it in mind to offer you a free hand to do up the house for me in exchange for you living there and starting your business in the stable block. How many bedrooms would you want?''

''I hadn't really thought. Three or four, I suppose. I'd like to be able to have my son and daughter-in-law to stay—and I'd love a room for Harriet, my eldest granddaughter, to come to sometimes. But the whole idea is so new I haven't really worked it out. But I would have to pay you a proper rent. I don't want charity.''

''And I wouldn't offer it to you. Later we might think of rent, if that's what suited us both, but not to start with. I'm not making this up—I'd like you to redecorate it and supervise alterations, and I wouldn't dream of charging anything while you were doing that for me. It would work in my favour just as much as in yours—I'd have to pay someone else to do it. I'd willingly pay you too, but I have a feeling you might not like that. Nothing you did to turn the stables into a studio would wasted, whatever the future holds for either you or me—or the house itself. But how would you react to living in the house if I still kept one bedroom here myself?'' He laughed. ''You wouldn't have to look after me, or do anything you didn't want to do. I'm making you a proposition, Kate—but I'm not propositioning you. You met me as the caretaker. How would you like to be the caretaker for the Observatory yourself?''

''I don't know,'' said Kate, outwardly cautious—though inwardly her heart was singing and she knew her answer quite well. ''I'd need to think about that. How would I know that you wouldn't sling me out just when I'd got my business going and really transferred my affection here and made it into my home?''

''We could make an arrangement for, say, two years. After that it's a risk you'd have to take. We can neither of us look into the future that far. I think we're both going to have to take risks of various kinds. I may be more used to that than you, though. I've never got anything that's really important to me without taking a calculated chance.''

''And what do you think my neighbours would think of me sort of sharing a house with you?''

''I've no idea. Does their opinion matter to you so much?''

''No,'' said Kate, light-heartedly puffing caution to the entrancing new breeze she felt blowing round her, and thinking in particular of the Fanshaws and Gerald Brownlow. ''I don't think I really give a damn.''

''What about your family?''

''Ah—more tricky,'' said Kate. ''But if I'm to do this at all, I also know I have to make my own mind up, because their opinions will all be different, and some of my family aren't going to approve whatever I do. How soon do you want to know? I'm due to go and stay with Jane Pulborough next week, and also try and get my stitching ladies organised. Then I must somehow let Joanna have a decision about Longthorpe.''

"I go to the States at the end of next week for a few weeks," said Jack. "But you can let me know any time. I'll leave you with a key, so that you can come and potter about here on your own while I'm away and come up with some ideas to tell me when you're ready. Any building alterations, carpentry or decorating could be done by the estate workers, some of whom are extremely skilled. That would be in keeping with how the original building was done." He smiled. "I was at school with several of them. How would that be?"

"Wonderful," said Kate. "Just wonderful."

"Good," said Jack. "That's settled then. Now let's enjoy the rest of our day together. Let's walk back to the Observatory and get the car because I want to take you out to tea with someone important to me—and I hope you're hungry, because you're certain to be offered a vast amount of food and it'll cause great offence if you don't eat anything. Will you come with me?"

Kate knew she would have gone anywhere with him— but she also felt conscious that while she had opened a very private window on to her own life for him to look through, he had not really done the same for her. She couldn't help wondering why.

For his part, Jack was aware that he had missed a perfect chance to tell Kate something. He was unsure what her reaction might be, but the moment had gone now. He swore to himself that he would wait until the right opportunity cropped up again before he told her. It was too vital a matter to risk getting it wrong.

ᔑ ELEVEN ᖰ

Kate got home to find a message on her answering machine from Joanna: "Mum—ten-thirty on Monday evening. Tried you earlier but no reply so I suppose you're out to dinner. I've had a marathon day so I'm going to bed now, but I badly need to talk to you. Can I come up tomorrow morning? Will you ring me first thing if you're not going to be there?''

It struck Kate immediately that the message was less peremptory and more conciliatory than usual, and also that Joanna's voice sounded strained. She knew that whatever it was that Jo wanted to say to her, it must also be her own chance to say several things to Jo that she had been putting off but which had to be faced. Her own plans had taken a leap forward today, and it was time to put her daughter in the picture; she hoped that the sop she would be able to offer in the way of the promise to let the Maitland family have Longthorpe, might soften the effect of the bombshell she was about to burst about her own impending move and new career plans. Last but by no means least, she knew she must tackle Joanna about Harriet. She had no idea what to say about Jack Morley.

The important person to whom Jack had taken her for tea had turned out to be his one remaining Yorkshire relation—his mother's sister, Hannah. At nearly ninety, she still lived alone on a smallholding, almost up on the moor, on the edge of the Ravelstoke estate. She had carried on running the little farm single-handed after her husband died ten years earlier and still had a few sheep, a couple of cows and some chickens. The neighbouring farmer helped her at lambing time and gave a hand if there was a crisis, but Jack said that for the last year she had been locked in conflict with the firm of land agents who had managed the estate for the Ravelstoke family, and who had been trying to force her to move to sheltered accommodation in the nearby small town of Winterbridge.

"At least that's something I can do," said Jack. "I can keep the vultures away and make sure she can stay on in the home she's lived in and loved for sixty years."

Kate had been well aware that she herself was under intense scrutiny from the old lady, whose beady blue eyes looked shrewdly out from behind the kind of round spectacles which were now mysteriously considered flattering by those of the young with ethnic leanings. Kate guessed that very little would go unobserved by Jack's Aunt Hannah.

A white embroidered tablecloth, which looked as if it had been lovingly kept for special occasions, was spread with the vast tea about which Jack had warned her, and she and Jack had dutifully munched their way through ham and egg sandwiches, scones with home-made jam, fruit cake, shortbread biscuits and Victoria sponge cake, all washed down with strong tea from a big brown teapot. Despite the effort that had obviously been made, it was clear that Jack Morley's position in the world as a wealthy tycoon of some international renown, meant nothing to his aunt—or nothing that she was prepared to let on about in front of him.

"Hello, our Jack," she had greeted him, permitting a respectful peck on the cheek. "I don't know where your manners have got to, or what you're thinking of, bringing a visitor in through the yard. I unlocked the front specially."

"I'm sorry, Aunt Hannah," said Jack meekly. "But I thought we ought to leave the car in the shade because of Kate's dog. This is Kate Rendlesham. She's going to help me do up the Observatory. Kate, this is my aunt—Hannah Hartley."

Kate had exchanged a handshake, feeling the work-roughened skin and bony hardness of Hannah Hartley's fingers. Veins stood out on the backs of her hands like a three-dimensional drawing of the circulatory system; though the wide gold band of her wedding ring was loose, there was no way that she would now be able to get it off over the lumpy knuckles that were swollen with arthritis. In the hands of the old, we see our skeletons, thought Kate: an unwelcome reminder of things to come. She had a vision of Oliver's hands, once so strong and elegant, as they had looked during his last weeks of life: the skin appearing so transparent, that it seemed as if the whiteness of the sheet on which they lay was showing through them. Unlike Hannah Hartley's ring, latterly Oliver had been unable to prevent the heavy gold signet ring which he had always worn on his little finger, from slipping off; it had to be placed beside him on the bedside table. After Oliver's death Kate had given the ring to Nick. The hesitation with which Nick had put it on his own finger said more about his feelings for his father than any words, and Kate guessed he had worn it to prevent any hurt to her own feelings rather than because he had admired—or even loved—Oliver. It was almost as if he had been afraid of being in some way contaminated by that ring. She had realised too late that she should have given it to Joanna.

During tea, they had discussed the Observatory.

"You always did have a fancy for yon house," said Hannah Hartley with a disparaging sniff. "I knew all about your visits to old Miss Violet Ravelstoke when you were a little lad—though I never let on to your gran. Beats me what the old tartar saw in you—but you was always a harum-scarum child with a brain full of moonshine, and she was daft as a brush like all her kin. Nowt as queer as folk, as they say."

"The moonshine must still be knocking about my head because I have a fancy for the house now," said Jack, laughing. "Kate's going to transform it for me, and make it lovely again, aren't you, Kate? She'll probably move into it to supervise the work, and carry on her business from there, meanwhile. I hope you'll keep an eye on her for me, Aunt Hannah, and introduce her to the neighbours. Tell Aunt Hannah about your embroidery, Kate."

He had listened, well satisfied, while the two women had discussed drawn-thread work, long-and-short stitch, French knots, satin stitch and the rival merits of different brands of embroidery silks and cottons, or Appleton's wools for crewel work. Kate admired the tablecloth, which she rightly guessed had been made by her hostess for her bottom drawer before her marriage, and correctly identified all the stitches that had been worked into it.

"How many of the hassocks for Ravelstoke church did you make yourself, Aunt Hannah?" prompted Jack.

"Since when have you been interested in hassocks, I should like to know, Jack Morley?" she replied sharply, but was not displeased all the same to tell Kate that she had done the long altar kneeler and all the hassocks for the first four rows of pews, and soon she and Kate were exchanging opinions about long-legged Gobelin, Smyrna stitch and the best gauge of canvas for working needlepoint on church hassocks.

"You've just given me an idea," said Kate. "I'm going to try and get together some designs for cushions with lots of different stitches in, which could be sold as kits. It would be fun to do some designs for church hassocks too—something a bit different. Perhaps you'd advise me?"

Jack listened to them both, well pleased with his stratagem. When they also discovered a mutual passion for Border collies, Hannah Hartley went to the cupboard and brought out a bottle and three glasses.

"My last year's parsnip," she announced. Kate took a cautious sip: the golden wine had a kick like a mule, and a disconcerting aftertaste of mouldy vegetables.

"So now you're going to work for our Jack, are you?" the old lady said to Kate as they were leaving, having declined all offers to help her clear away the tea things.

"Er, yes—part time anyway." Kate found the question disconcerting and studiously avoided catching Jack's amused eye.

"Well, you can come and visit me if you've a mind to," said Hannah Hartley. "I'll take you into the church. I keep the key."

"Thank you. I'd love that—and thank you for such a wonderful tea too."

*   *   *

As they drove away, Kate waved to the hairpin-bent figure standing in the doorway.

"Goodness, I feel like a Strasbourg goose after all that tea. I wouldn't like to run up that sloping staircase now. What a lovely lady, though."

"Well, you certainly made a hit," said Jack.

"Did I really?" Kate was pleased. "How nice: but hard to tell—she's so wonderfully inscrutable."

"Not hard if you can read the signals. No one gets Aunt Hannah's lethal parsnip unless she takes to them. It's a mark of great favour—and the penalty you pay for earning it."

"And I'm supposed to be working for you now, am I? I hope you don't fire people as quickly and unexpectedly as you appear to hire them, Mr. Franklin J. Morley."

"Ah," he said. "Are you cross? Please don't be. I just thought it would make things easier for you round here if we made your occupation of the house sound official. If Aunt Hannah likes someone, it carries a lot of clout in the village, and I just want you to have all the help you can get when I'm not here. Not that anyone could resist you anyway. I don't think I'm likely to fire you, Kate. The boot's more likely to be on the other foot."

"Of course I'm not cross." Kate suddenly started to laugh. "Flattered, but not cross. It is quite funny though— one minute I'm trying desperately to know what to do with my life, and the next I've got not just one career, but two. It seems I'm an interior decorator now as well! I shall be busy." She added after a pause, "I'm very grateful, you know. Thank you, Jack."

"I don't want your gratitude," he said. "That isn't what I want at all."

"What do you want?"

"I just want you to be happy," he had said simply.

Joanna's telephone message had not been the only one. There was one from Jane Pulborough, confirming Kate's proposed visit to Gloucestershire; one from Rosamund Campion giving the date of the visit of what Cecily still called the transatlantic channeller and asking anyone who wanted to hear her to go over to the Dial House for lunch; and there was one from Gerald Brownlow announcing that he would drop in the following day. He too had things he wanted to discuss with Kate. As she rewound the tape on the answering machine, Kate's mind was also rerunning every moment of her day.

It had been seven o'clock by the time she and Jack had got back to the Observatory. They had spent a happy evening discussing ideas for renovating it. Because the house was listed, planning permission would be needed for anything major, but luckily neither of them thought anything structural was required. The partitions in the stables, at the moment so piled to the rafters with junk that it was hardly possible to move, would have to be knocked down to make one big room, but Jack did not think this would present any problem. He wanted the kitchen to be completely redone from scratch:

"Get the kitchen right, the heart of the house, and everything else follows," he said. Installing central heating was high on both their lists of priorities, and to Kate's relief Jack was insistent that this must include the stables too. "You can't work in there if you're freezing—and you certainly wouldn't get anyone else to work for you either. It's all got to be properly done. I can't stand half-measures."

Kate wondered if this included relationships. She felt she could talk to him about anything, as though they had known each other for years. She supposed it was odd to be planning a house with a stranger, but it did not feel like that. She confided some of her worries about Harriet to him. He was a wonderful listener.

After such a huge tea they had neither of them felt hungry, and when they had finished poking about in the stables, they had sat on the little terrace with a bottle of wine, listening to the swifts screeching and watching the sun set.

Before it got dark, Jack had made them both an omelette which they had eaten with the leftover salad from lunch. Then he had driven to her home.

As they turned into the drive at Longthorpe, Kate wondered whether to ask him in, and wondered if she did, what the repercussions might be, but with his knack of guessing her thoughts, he forestalled her.

"I'll see you safely inside, and then I'm off," he said, as he got out and opened her door for her. He stood watching while Kate grovelled in her bag for the key and then punched in the number on the burglar alarm and switched on the hall light. She started to thank him, but he stopped her, putting his hand gently over her lips.

"Don't say anything. It's me that's had a perfect day with you," he said. "One day, I hope we won't be parting like this, but for now I'll do the thanking," and he kissed her, very softly and quickly, on the mouth, and again just touched her face with one finger, as he had earlier in the day.

"Goodnight, Kate," he said. "I'll ring you tomorrow," and he had driven away.

But the brief contact had gone through Kate like an electric current.

❧ TWELVE ❧

Kate rang Joanna first thing the following morning, hoping to catch her before she exercised the horses.

"Jo, darling? It's me. I got your message last night but just too late to ring you. I want to see you too. Why don't you come and have breakfast with me—then we can talk peacefully without the children?"

Like her grandmother, Cecily, Joanna tended to turn down any suggestion made by anyone else before she'd even considered it, but this morning, after a slight pause, she agreed—a sign, Kate felt, that she must be rather desperate.

"All right. Thanks, Mum. Jenny can do the school run. I'll be over about quarter past eight."

Kate put some bread rolls in the oven and laid the round table in the bay window in the kitchen. I am planning to leave all this, she thought—this beautiful house where I have lived for so long. I wonder if I'm mad? But mad or not, she had no intention of changing her mind.

Joanna arrived looking as elegant as usual. She had the knack of making whatever she wore look exactly right for the occasion. Kate thought that if Joanna chose to wear jeans to a formal dinner party, everyone else would automatically feel overdressed. She poured them both big cups of coffee and put a jug of freshly squeezed orange juice on the table.

"Now, darling," she said, feeling she needed to get her oar in the water first, "I have come to some big decisions, so you've come at exactly the right moment. I would have rung you if you hadn't got in first. I have at last decided to move out and let you and Mike have this house. I do hope you'll be pleased."

She had not expected Joanna to be surprised at this part of her decision—it was, after all, what she thought her bossy daughter had been taking too much for granted all along, but she had certainly not expected Joanna to burst into tears.

"Jo! I thought you'd be so thrilled. What is it?"

"Everything. Nothing has gone right since Dad died. Yes, it's what I've always wanted, so badly, but now I'm not sure Mike will come here. He says if we don't all move back to London by the autumn, then he wants out. He might even mean it. Rupert's started wetting his bed and Harriet's impossible. I don't know what to do with her—read this." Joanna shoved a letter across the table to Kate. It was from Miss Ellis, the headmistress of Essendale Hall. Harriet had announced that she had become a vegetarian and the school required Joanna's permission before they could accept this. Miss Ellis went on to say that they were worried about Harriet's eating habits generally: Sister had weighed her and found she had indeed lost weight since the beginning of term; not serious yet, but disturbing, and they were concerned. Had Joanna noticed anything when Harriet was at home?

"Oh dear," said Kate, full of foreboding. "We don't want anorexia."

"It's rubbish, of course," said Joanna. "Harriet's always eaten like a horse and she loves meat. She's only doing this to bait me. I won't give in to her."

"Darling—don't let positions get too entrenched. And for God's sake don't rise—if she wants to be vegetarian then let her. If it's genuine, well so be it. Lots of people feel that way. If it's just a try-on then she'll soon get tired of it, provided you play it cool. I agree this may be aimed at you, but I don't think it's just to bait you. I think it's a scream for help. I wanted to talk to you about Hattie anyway." Kate hesitated, very much afraid that what she had to say might make things worse. "If I tell you what I really think, will you listen to me before jumping down my throat?"

"I'll try," said Joanna, resting her head on her hands and massaging her temples with her fingers. Kate thought she looked exhausted.

"I know this is a highly sensitive point. You don't need to tell me anything, but Jo—darling Jo—you really should reconsider talking to Harriet about her father. She's very disturbed—she's at an age when identity is extremely important, and I promised her when she had that last outburst that I would talk to you about it again myself." Kate pulled a wry face. "I've been putting it off because I dreaded how you might react," she said, "but if I'm honest I think Harriet has every right to know who her father is."

There was a long silence, then: "I can't," said Joanna.

"You mean you don't know?" Kate was taken back. All those years ago, she had always imagined Joanna would have a love affair while she was up at Oxford, but she had also thought it would be out of character for her to be promiscuous: she was too fastidious.

"Oh I know all right—but I made a vow that I wouldn't tell anyone."

"He had no right to ask that of you."

"He didn't ask me. He doesn't know himself."

"You mean Harriet's father has no idea she even exists?"

"That's right."

Joanna had never tried to conceal her pregnancy from her friends. It had always amazed Kate that none of them seemed to have the faintest idea who the father was either, but she had always assumed that just one of them—the one who was responsible—must have known.

"But you really are sure yourself—without doubt?"

"Of course. But there was—is—a very good reason why no one else should know, including . . ." Joanna's eyes widened: for a moment she had almost mentioned a name. "Including the man himself," she finished. She looked very distressed. In sixteen years she had never vouchsafed as much information as this.

"Who did you make the promise to, then?" asked Kate.

"To myself." Joanna sounded fierce. "I never discussed it with anyone. But I don't go back on vows, even private ones."

Joanna suddenly longed to tell her mother the whole story, but she hadn't kept her difficult silence for all these years only to break down now. She looked at her most uncompromising, and Kate's heart sank. She got up to get the rolls out of the oven, glad of a chance to hide the anxiety in her face. After a pause, while they helped themselves to butter and honeycomb, she said:

"I can't make you tell Harriet, Jo, but please think about it—even if it's just talking to her: explaining a bit. The fact that your relationship with Dad was so important to you, adds considerably to her grievance. Had you ever thought about this?''

''No.'' Joanna, never perceptive about other people, was genuinely surprised.

Kate knew it would be counter-productive to press her any more at the moment, so she switched problems.

''This is very upsetting about Mike—so unlike him too. Does he really mean it? He loves the children so much. Perhaps when he knows about my move, and when you have so much more space and are not all so on top of one another he'll think again? Maybe I should have made up my mind about Longthorpe sooner, but some unexpected chances have just come my way that suddenly made it seem right.''

''Like what?''

So Kate told Joanna about Jane Pulborough's offer— and then, more evasively, about the Observatory.

''I saw it by chance and got on to Cooper and Wilkinson's about it at once. Such a coincidence that it turned out that I knew the owner without realising it.'' Although she was being truthful, Kate felt devious.

Joanna looked astonished.

''Well, I can see that's marvellous about Jane—in a way—but you don't want to get too embroiled, Mum. You want time for family life. You need to ease up, not take on new things.'' The words ''at your age'' hung unspoken in the air, and Kate thought with amused irritation how typical it was of Joanna to be so unaware that new things, at any age, can be far more rejuvenating than any amount of easing up; in any case, what Joanna would list under the heading ''family life'' was hardly likely to include a rest cure. ''And there's no need to go somewhere completely different—let alone rent a house. That seems crazy,'' Joanna continued. ''I've always imagined you retiring to the cottage.''

"I know you have," said Kate dryly. "But you see that's not what I want—and I hope I still have a few years left before the Zimmer and the fleecy slippers beckon."

"Surely you couldn't bear to leave Longthorpe altogether?" Joanna was clearly bewildered, her mother's irony quite lost on her.

"It will be a wrench in some ways, but I have to make a fresh life." Kate weighed her words carefully: "Your father was a remarkable man, darling. I've lived in his shadow for years—and in many ways was content to do so. I had a role to play and it seemed natural. But don't you see that now he's gone, I must be brave and find some sunshine of my own?"

"It never occurred to me that you wanted a career."

"I didn't. But I do now. Jo, you of all people ought to understand. Your work is so important to you—important enough for you already to be tossing up in your own mind between that and your marriage," said Kate shrewdly. From the way Joanna winced Kate could see that she had scored a hit, though she felt guiltily that it was slightly below the belt. "You have so many talents, darling," she went on, "but I only have this one small gift. Now that a chance has presented itself, I want to use it before it's too late. Can't you see that?"

"I suppose so. But you are a dark horse—it's just not how I think of you." Joanna looked at her mother as though she were seeing a stranger. She felt as if cold winds of uncertainty were blowing round her.

"Oh Mum," she said, a rare wobble in her voice, "I feel as if my whole life is falling to bits. What do you do when everything falls apart?"

"You pick up the pieces."

"But supposing the most important bits are missing?"

"Then you pick up what's left, reshape it, and make something new out of it—like a patchwork quilt," said seamstress Kate.

She refilled their coffee cups. "I'm going to stay with Jane Pulborough at Chipping Marston next week to discuss business." Kate gave a rueful laugh at the expression on her daughter's face. "Yes, all right, I know that's funny. I'm not exactly anyone's idea of businesswoman of the year—but luckily Janey is. Then I thought I'd seize the chance to go to London. I want to look in Liberty's to see what new silks they may have, and stock up with more materials. I suppose I'll need to find a wholesaler now. I was going to stay with Nick and Robin, but perhaps Mike could give me a bed for the night? It would give me a chance to talk to him and tell him my decision about Longthorpe. Might that help? Could I be a sort of intermediary?"

Joanna opened her mouth to refuse, and then stopped. She shrugged her shoulders despairingly. "I suppose it might be worth a try. We don't seem to be able to communicate without rowing. Or rather," she added honestly, "I shout and Mike walks away, or puts down the telephone. It drives me crazy. He won't come home this weekend so he's insisted Jenny takes the children down to London—I can't go because I'm doing another demo. Yes, please, Mum. Mike's always been fond of you. You might be able to get more out of him than I can. The spare bed's always made up. I'll tell him. You talk sense into him."

"And what if he wants me to talk some sense into you?"

"I don't know. I just don't know—but I'm not passing up the chance to live at Longthorpe." Joanna set her mouth and stuck her chin out, and the old inflexible look was back in her face. "By the way, have you mentioned anything about your plans to Nick and Robin yet?"

This was the question that Kate had hoped Joanna would not ask. "I think I did mention Janey's idea about Midas when they were last here, because it cropped up in conversation—but they don't know anything about the Observatory yet," she said, thankful she'd had the foresight not to say anything about that, and thereby send a spark too near the detonating fuse of Joanna's inflammable jealousy. "I hope you'll all come and look at it with me."

"I think you're mad. What would you do about furniture?"

"Take what I want and let you and Nick divide the rest, probably, but I haven't got that far yet. I don't even know whether Jack Morley may want to let it part furnished—but I'd certainly want some of my own things round me, even so." She realised there was a great deal about her new venture that she had not yet thought out, but she had no intention of being pinned down to details by her daughter at this stage.

"By the way, how did your Red Cross do go?" she asked, to change the subject.

"Great success. Lots of people were asking me to do catering for their parties. I may well think about that, as a way of expanding. This kitchen would be ideal. Well, thanks for breakfast, Mum." Joanna got up and gave her mother one of her cool kisses, and Kate realised that any moment of near intimacy had passed: Joanna had got herself back in hand. But that the emotions which simmered below the clamped down lid of Joanna's personal pressure cooker were very powerful, her mother had no doubt. She guessed that whatever had once passed between Joanna and Harriet's unknown, and unknowing, father, must surely have been a very strong brew indeed. It seemed strange that nobody had known about it at the time.

Joanna walked back to the cottage, a queue of thoughts jockeying for position in her head, and an old pain gimleting away in her heart. She made two telephone calls: one to Mike, who seemed perfectly agreeable to the idea of having his mother-in-law for the night, but wanted to know when his wife was next considering coming home herself. He had been disappointed that she had refused to bring Rupert and Tilly to London herself. Joanna was evasive.

The other call was to Sonia Duntan to accept her offer to have Harriet to stay with Polly for the weekend. Joanna greatly admired Sonia, and saw in her skilful juggling of her own burgeoning career as a successful artist with the running of a family life and the demands of a house open to the public, the epitome of how she would like her own life to be. Of the heartache and compromise that had gone on behind the scenes before this facade was achieved, she had no idea.

"Oh, great. Polly will be thrilled," said Sonia. "Archie can bring the trailer over and pick up Harriet's pony on his way to collect them both on Saturday morning, then they can ride in the afternoon." The girls at Essendale Hall were allowed to go home to lunch on Saturday provided they were not involved in any school activity over the weekend. "How's your darling mum?" went on Sonia. "I thought she looked a million dollars the other night. How riveting that she should have known our new local wonder-man all the time, when we've all been speculating about him like mad. I quite expected Netta Fanshaw to slip a drop of arsenic in your ma's champagne cocktail. You must tell me all about him sometime."

It occurred to Joanna, that during her conversation with her mother, so full of surprises already, this was one thing that Kate had not discussed. She was relieved that Harriet would be at Duntan for the weekend. She did not feel up to a confrontation with her daughter just yet. She wondered whether to tell Sonia anything about Harriet's eating problems, and decided not to. It would be more enlightening to enquire afterwards if there had been any apparent problem over the weekend.

Joanna was more bothered than she liked to admit by the idea of anorexia—even though she felt fairly certain that Harriet was using food as a weapon because she knew it was a subject about which her mother would be particularly vulnerable. She had also been shattered to discover how vulnerable the idea of Kate's move made her feel. All her life she had thought of her father as the driving force in her life, and Kate merely as a background figure whose presence she had taken for granted. Now the idea that she might no longer be permanently on call made Joanna feel unexpectedly panicky. Despite her strong and confident words about Longthorpe, she did not really know how she would feel about a split from Mike, and this uncertainly was very foreign to Joanna. Up to now she had always known exactly what she wanted from life, and—with one notable and painful exception—always got it, too.

She found herself mooning about the kitchen unable to concentrate. It was not a feeling she had experienced before.

ઝ THIRTEEN ૬

Kate combined an overwhelming sense of relief that she had managed to talk to Joanna, with an almost equal sense of foreboding about the Maitland family's future. It struck her that Joanna, though so outwardly soignée, was a case of arrested development, and that if she was about to go through a belated crash course in maturity, it was bound to be painful for all concerned.

The sound of a heavy tread on the stairs heralded the arrival of Mrs. Stokes, en route from Cecily's flat to do her stint of trailing a broom round the passages of Kate's part of the house. Kate usually tried to be out when she came, because Mrs. Stokes had perfected the technique of trapping a potential audience in a doorway and holding them to ransom to her unstoppable flow of chat while she leant on her mop with all the unbudgeableness of thirteen stone. The doctor had once persuaded Mrs. Stokes to attend a slimming clinic, but, according to her, Mr. Stokes had soon put a stop to that. " 'E likes summat to grab hold of, does my Herbert,'' she had told Kate smugly. "Doesn't fancy

scrawny types.'' This titillating little vignette of the Sto-
keses' sex life had nearly caused Harriet to have apoplexy
from suppressed giggles.

"He probably has to grab hold because he's afraid of
falling off,'' she had said to Kate later, wailing with laughter, "like clinging to the wreckage of an upturned boat.''
Mr. Stokes, a narrow little whippet of a man, was the
shorter partner by several inches.

"Good morning, Mrs. Stokes,'' said Kate now, trying
to look purposefully on the move, and edge her way past
the massive obstruction in her path. "Forgive me if I don't
stop but I'm just off upstairs to see Lady Rendlesham.''

Mrs. Stokes barred her way with an ominous yellow
envelope. "I've brought the snaps,'' she said, pinning Kate
with her basilisk eye.

"Snaps?'' Kate's heart sank.

"The ones you wanted to see,'' said Mrs. Stokes, ruthlessly sinking her conversational teeth into Kate's will-
power with the tenacity of a bulldog. "The ones of our
Sharon being a maid of honour at Herbert's sister-in-law's
cousin's daughter's wedding. I brought them specially—
you being so interested in making clothes,'' she added.
"The bride wore silk-finished polyester with lace insertions
and a sweetheart neckline.'' Mrs. Stokes lowered her voice.
"She couldn't wear white,'' she said, looking suspiciously
round as though an ill-intentioned eavesdropper might be
lurking behind a curtain, "so it had to be cream.''

The significance of this announcement was not lost on
Kate, though she would have been surprised if many brides
in the 1990s would have been entitled to wear white in
Mrs. Stokes' view.

"Our Sharon made a lovely bridesmaid, though, as
you'll see.'' Mrs. Stokes firmly opened the envelope. "She
was all in sweet-pea shades of mauve worn with a coral
shoe.''

"How . . . how lovely,'' said Kate, an absurd vision of
the well-endowed and top-heavy Sharon Stokes hopping

perilously up the aisle on one foot floating before her inner eye.

"Do let me have a quick look at the photographs then," she said, despising herself for her weakness. She knew when she was beaten.

Twenty minutes later, visually exhausted, she tottered up to see her mother-in-law. At least her mind had been able to override the sartorial saga of the Stokes family's nuptials, and follow its own course.

I'd better tell Cecily my plans, she thought, as she opened the door of her mother-in-law's sitting room; it would be too awful if she heard about impending changes from Joanna rather than me.

Cecily had listened in silence to Kate's sometimes faltering words.

"Of course you must stay on in this flat," finished Kate, when she had disclosed her plans. "There'd be no question of you having to move: I'd make that a condition, but Jo would want you anyway. How would you feel about that?"

"Not surprised," said Cecily—surprisingly. "Sad, but not shocked. I never thought you'd stay here long after Oliver died—and I've always known you were never happy in this house."

"Oh Cecily," said Kate, a lump like a large marble forming in her throat. "How did you know?"

"I know a lot more than you think," said Cecily, adding gruffly: "You go all out for what you want, Kate—but I shall miss you here."

Kate went and put her arms round the old lady, tears prickling behind her eyes, and laid her own cheek against Cecily's soft, wrinkled one that always smelt of violets. She wondered, not for the first time, just how much Oliver's mother knew, perhaps had always known, about the shadow side of the son she had adored so much.

Kate went into the old playroom to sort out the designs she wanted to take down to Gloucestershire, aware that while she worked, she was also hoping the telephone would ring.

She was sitting on the floor, surrounded by silk and velvet and immersed in the notebook in which she jotted down new ideas, when there was a tap on the door. "Come in," said Kate, her heart doing funny things. The door opened to reveal Gerald Brownlow.

"Oh, hello, Gerald." Kate didn't sound any more thrilled to see him than she felt, and her heart settled back into a boringly steady rhythm.

"I walked in," said Gerald, giving one of his illuminating little explanations. "The front door was open, and Mrs. Stokes said you were in here. Hope you don't mind, but I want to talk to you." Having said this, he then proceeded to prowl round the room, putting things straight but saying nothing.

"Well here I am," said Kate, wanting to scream.

"I know. I know. Perhaps you might like to have lunch with me, or dinner tonight—we could talk then? I never seem to catch you on your own."

"I'm afraid I can't tonight, and I've got a busy few days ahead." Kate felt she must at all costs keep the next few days free, and preempt any Brownlow invitations. "Shall I get you a cup of coffee and you can talk now while I go on sorting these patterns out?" she offered.

"No coffee, thank you." Gerald considered mid-morning breaks to be an exclusively female pastime. He looked rather nonplussed. "What on earth are you so busy about?"

"Well, you won't have heard, because it's all fairly new, but I'm going into business with Jane Pulborough."

"Kate! There's no need for that."

"What do you mean—no need? I'm thrilled to bits. It's what I really want to do."

"But I want to marry you." Gerald sounded outraged.

"Oh Gerald—you are so kind—such a good friend. I'm very touched that you should even think of it, and I'm truly fond of you but it wouldn't work for either of us."

"But it would work. I've thought about it very carefully, and considered all the pros and cons." Gerald had obviously not attended evening classes on how to conduct a whirlwind romance: "And I think it would work wonderfully well for us both. Of course I know I couldn't measure up to Oliver—wouldn't want to try, marvellous chap and all that; one of my heroes; brilliant shot—a joy to watch—but never poached one's birds either. I always liked drawing the stand next to him—but you and I could have a lot to offer each other. I didn't want to rush you, but after a year I thought the time might be ripe." He put his hands in his pockets and stood looking down at Kate as she sat on the floor covered with bits of material.

Kate felt she could see Gerald's vision of married bliss floating over the top of his head like a cartoon bubble: a doting little woman who would be loading for him on a freezing cold December pheasant shoot, naturally not distracting him with chatter, apart from the occasional breathless "Oh good shot, darling" as she plunged her numb fingers into the pocket of her Barbour to pop another cartridge down the barrels of his gun. Doubtless this paragon would already have cooked a delicious shooting lunch for twenty-five guests (Gerald, who liked feminine company— or thought he did—would want the wives invited provided they didn't actually shoot), before coming out with homemade sloe gin to join the men for a couple of drives. Kate felt sure this vision included someone who unquestioningly voted Tory, knew a special recipe for gingerbread, and was a dab hand at filling baps before settling down on the river banks to watch Gerald play a fish and . . . there was silence while Kate ran this absorbing little documentary through her head.

"I can see I've taken you by surprise," said Gerald, noticing the glazed look in her eye and feeling rather pleased.

Kate didn't like to say that she'd been trying to avoid him making a declaration for weeks.

"I'm so sorry, Gerald, but—no. I really want to go for this new career."

"Well, but you could go on sewing in my house. I wouldn't dream of trying to stop you," said Gerald magnanimously. "It would be nice for you—and I've lots of room as you know. Cheer my house up a lot to have some nice new cushions and things about. You could even have a sewing room if you wanted." He smiled at her indulgently. "Such a clever little thing you are, Kate—always thought you were underrated—and I want to look after you now."

"Gerald—thank you so much. Don't think I don't appreciate your kindness. But no."

"There isn't anyone else, is there?"

"No," said Kate, lying through her teeth.

"Well then? Look, this is all a shock, my dear; you haven't had time to think it over. Perhaps I shouldn't have spoken yet, but I shall ask you again." Kate half expected him to get out his diary and make a note. Part of her wanted to hit him for being so condescending and taking her acceptance for granted, though at the same time she knew he was capable of being very hurt and her heart smote her. She supposed a good many people would think she was a fool at her age not to leap at such an offer. Gerald Brownlow was kind and very comfortably off, and, since widows outnumber widowers and are supposed to have an earlier "best-before" date stamped on them, he was much sought after in certain quarters.

At that moment the telephone rang. Kate answered at the second ring. Gerald watched her pick up the receiver.

"Hello?" she said, and something in her face and voice set his not very quickly activated alarm bells ringing.

"Yes," he heard her say, "Yes—how lovely. Of course I would—yes, I did too. See you later then. Bye."

He couldn't stop himself asking: "Who was that?"

"Someone I'm going to be working with."

Kate couldn't wait for Gerald to leave. She stood up and walked towards the door, and he had little option but to follow her into the hall.

"You're a dear person, Gerald," she said, giving him a swift peck on the cheek, and darting quickly out of range. "You could make someone so happy, and I'm sure you'll find that person—but it won't be me."

Gerald stood on the doorstep looking like a disconsolate small boy who would like to make a scene, but can't make up his mind which scene to make. An awful suspicion was forming in the back of his mind. Clearly reconnaissance was required before action could be taken. After that, counterintelligence, possibly followed by guerilla warfare might be necessary. Gerald squared his shoulders and strode towards his car. He thought he should recruit a volunteer force. Netta Fanshaw might possibly sign on.

As he was about to get into his car he was waylaid by Cecily, on her way in from replenishing her bird table with nuts, bacon rind and crumbs, as edible provisions for busy parents, and dog hairs gathered from Acer's brush in case more building materials were required by those who had not yet nested.

"Hello, Gerald. What an early visitor you were this morning! But I don't suppose you've caught your worm." Gerald looked blank. Naturally, his arrival had not gone unnoticed by Cecily, who would have stood in splendidly for Miss Marple; her presence in the drive now was far from accidental: she thought a little conversational prompting might bring interesting revelations.

"You look as if you were just about to leave," she went on, longing to know what had passed between him and her daughter-in-law. "But if you'd like to come upstairs I'll give you a glass of sherry—I never bother about that yard-arm nonsense—and then you can sit and look at my tits through binoculars." This unusual invitation had the effect of making Gerald Brownlow, not normally a fast mover, metaphorically lay back his ears and bolt into the car. "Funny man," said Cecily to Kate later. "I thought as a countryman he would be interested in birds, but he looked quite panic-stricken."

꒓ FOURTEEN ꒓

Later in the day, on her way to the Observatory to meet Jack again, Kate went to visit Gloria Barlow.

Mr. Barlow was sitting in an armchair in the kitchen, and despite the warm weather was wearing a thick dressing gown and had a rug over his knees. He looked so blue he might have been suffering from hypothermia. Kate took his frail hand in hers, and thought sadly what a big, strong rubicund man he had been when she last saw him. Now she had to stoop low to catch what he said.

"You try and get my Gloria out a bit more, Mrs. Rendlesham," he whispered, between lips that had become almost immobile. "I can't bear for her to be so tied to me. I'm nobbut a nuisance to anyone now, and I can't do ought for myself. But my Gloria, she never complains. Proper ray of sunshine she is," and he looked fondly at his wife who was indeed dazzling to behold. She had just had a new rinse and her hair, yellow as a duckling a few weeks before, was now a striking shade of burnt sienna.

She gave Kate a great hug. "Well, this is pleasant," she said. "Thanks ever so much for your letter. I made the coffee when I heard your car. We'll take our drink through to the front, and then we can talk while Jim looks at the racing on telly."

Kate followed her through into the front room. The walls were hung with Gloria's framed embroideries; their workmanship was as wonderful as their subject matter was whimsical. Fairies flew, elves danced and small animals carried parasols and pushed prams. Kate thought they represented Gloria's defiantly optimistic view of life.

"You are brave, Gloria," said Kate. "It's so sad to see Jim like that. How are you coping?"

"You have to cope, don't you? No choice—you know that. But thanks for asking. My neighbours are wonderful, but sometimes they're afraid to talk to Jim and he feels it. Nothing wrong with his brain."

"What do you think of my idea? Would it appeal?"

Gloria's eyes filled with tears. "Oh Kate! It would just about save my life. I'd love it. I'll not pretend the pennies won't be a help too—but it's having something to occupy my mind that'll be the best. My Jim's ever so pleased too."

"Would . . . would you mind that it would have to be all my designs?" Kate asked tentatively. "You see, Jane Pulborough wants very specific things." She couldn't bear the thought of Gloria's feelings being hurt.

Gloria laughed. "You don't need to look so worried, love," she said comfortably. "I know what you're saying. You don't really like my 'little friends' as I call them, and if I'm honest I sometimes think your ideas are a bit too sober for my liking, but 'shackern arson goo' as they say. I'd be happy to do anything you like."

Gloria was full of practical suggestions, and had far more idea than Kate about how many other helpers they might need. "Were you planning on making the jackets and waistcoats yourself?" she asked. "Because I think I know just the person who could do it."

"Wonderful. No, I thought I'd make a prototype, and then get someone else to copy it—and the same with the embroidery."

"I'll mention it to Jessie Worsencroft. She's a young mum in the village—such a pleasant person—who takes in dressmaking and does alterations; but her youngest is starting school and she'd like a bit of regular income. She's good."

"Anyone you approve of would be all right with me, Gloria. You're a perfectionist."

* * *

Kate felt very cheered by her talk with Gloria, and full of ideas to bowl at Jane Pulborough on Monday. She suddenly felt enormously confident that the venture could succeed.

"Fancy working in the Observatory! I've always been fascinated by the place—and it will be near enough for me to pop over easily to collect work to bring back home. I remember Jack Morley from way back. His aunt Hannah still lives hereabouts—everyone knows old Mrs. Hartley. I do think it's romantic, him getting so rich and buying the estate and that—like a fairy tale. He used to come and stay with his gran and granddad when I was a schoolgirl. He wouldn't remember me, but my older sisters didn't half fancy him. They used to ogle him in church. He was ever so handsome as a lad."

"He's not bad now," said Kate, laughing—which caused Gloria to tell her Jim afterwards that if he wanted her opinion, she wouldn't be surprised if Kate Rendlesham didn't take a shine to Jack Morley.

Jack's car was already at the Observatory. Kate tooted her horn, and he emerged from the stables as she got out of the car. This time he just stood there and held his arms open, and Kate walked straight into them.

"Oh Kate," he murmured into the top of her hair. "I only saw you last night and all of today it has felt far, far too long ago."

"For me too," she said softly.

She leant against him, and it seemed so natural to do so, that she felt as if she had just tried on a tailor-made garment that was exactly right and completely comfortable.

"I don't believe this is happening," she said. Then she started to laugh. "Wouldn't my grandchildren be surprised if they could see me? Harriet would have a fit!"

"Thanks," said Jack, laughing too. "I shall have to meet Harriet. I can see she's important."

"Do you realise this is only the fourth time you and I've met," said Kate in wonder.

"Ah," he said, stroking her face, "but I knew I'd stumbled across something very special when I first saw you asleep, Puss-in-Boots. I stole a march on you then."

"Perhaps you stole a bit of my soul," she said. "I remember thinking so at the time."

His arms tightened around her, and what she read in his face made her heart turn somersaults, and something long dormant, deep inside her, started to clutch and tighten.

He bent his head to kiss her. "Yes?" he asked just before his mouth met hers. "Yes," she whispered.

The sound of a car made them separate, hastily. "Damn and blast," said Jack. "It'll be Frank. I asked him to meet us here—but I didn't expect them for at least another couple of hours. He's too bloody punctual by half. Oh Kate—and I might have inveigled you up to Raving Ravelstoke's hide-out!"

A green van was turning in, with three men inside. "Frank's the estate Clerk of Works," explained Jack. "We were at school together when I was evacuated here—and he's brought the head mason and carpenter with him. Hi, Frank," he said. "Good of you to come. Afternoon, Walter, hello, Josh. Meet Kate Rendlesham."

Kate shook hands with the three men, wondering if she appeared as breathless and dishevelled as she felt. Frank was a burly little man with bandy legs, a bald head and handshake like a rat trap.

"Pleased to meet you," he said to Kate. "Glad to find you here, Jack—we're a bit early, but we finished that job at the farm sooner than expected, so I says to the lads, we'll go up to that there Observatory, and 'ave a look-see."

"Fine," said Jack. "Frank's a genius about buildings," he told Kate. "But get him in the pub after a pint or two and you'll realise he could have been on the music halls. Best mimic I know—people, animals, birds, machines. He missed his vocation."

Frank grinned: "Can't all be millionaires."

He produced a grubby notebook out of his pocket and took the stub of a pencil from behind his ear. "Right, Jack," he said. "Let's be having your ideas then, and we'll see if there's owt we can do—if it's not too yankified I dare say we'll manage."

Kate was very impressed at Frank's expertise. He made everything sound simple. "No problem," seemed to be his favorite phrase. They decided that the stables should be made into one big room, a studio workshop, with masses of cupboards, and trestle tables as work surfaces, which would be easy to move if necessary. Excellent overhead lighting was essential. Frank suggested that the feed store would easily convert into a small cloakroom. They decided to use part of the building on the other side of the gates, where the carriage would once have been kept, as storage for all the fabrics and materials Kate would need to keep in stock, and part of it as a toolshed for the garden.

"You can't commandeer the whole thing for your business," teased Jack.

The house itself needed remarkably little structural alteration.

"Kate's going to be in charge of all the decorating for me," said Jack easily. "She'll move in as soon as the tower bedroom's habitable so that she can keep an eye on things, and she can tell you what's wanted for the kitchen and the bathrooms." If Frank or the other men thought this arrangement in any way surprising, they didn't show it, and Kate could sense that they were well disposed towards her. She thought it must be odd for Frank to have Jack as the new owner of the estate, but there didn't seem to be the slightest feeling of ill-ease between them.

"What are you going to do about those slits in the dome for the telescope to go through?" she asked as they finally went up the spiral staircase to the observatory proper.

"Good point," said Jack. Frank examined the shutters: "No wonder there's been so much damp in here over the years," he said. He dragged the Wield observing couch under the one slit where the shutters had not been nailed up, and stood on it. "This wood's all rotten. You could put your fist through it," he said, and proceeded to do so.

"We could put in proper windows with glass easy enough, couldn't we, Josh? Make a frame inside the copper dome and double glaze them, make 'em so they'd open, and renew the shutters as well, for extra warmth? It needn't change the look of the place from the outside at all."

"Aye." Josh, a man of few words, got out his slide rule and did some measuring.

"Can we take the old shutters out now to see how light it would be?" asked Kate.

"Why not?" said Jack. So Josh went to his tool box for a big screwdriver, prised the nailed-up shutters open, and he and Walter managed to remove them. The sunlight filtered in from the four corners of the dome, giving the room criss-cross beams of light that met in a point in the middle.

"Not enough natural light to do owt much by. What you going to use this room for?" asked Frank.

"We haven't discussed it yet," said Jack, looking at Kate with eyes alight with amusement. "No doubt we shall find a use for it." Kate caught his glance and looked hastily away.

After the three men had accepted a glass of beer and they had discussed a few minor points, they told Jack they'd make a start on Monday morning.

"I won't see you for three weeks, Frank," said Jack. "I have to be in London at the beginning of the week, and then off to the States for a fortnight."

"What about you, Mrs. Rendlesham?" asked Frank.

"Oh, please call me Kate. Well, I'm going to Gloucestershire on Sunday night, and then to London on Tuesday. I shall be back at Longthorpe on Wednesday or Thursday.

Shall I give you a ring when I get back, Frank? I might have some wallpaper patterns by then and I'd like to bring my family over to have a look.''

"Right then. If you ring the estate office, they'll put you through on my mobile wherever I am—oh, and I take it you'll be wanting two separate telephone lines installed to the house and the stables?'' Jack nodded. "So long then,'' said Frank. "Thanks for the drink.'' They piled into the van and drove off.

"What lovely chaps,'' said Kate. "You're lucky to have them, Jack.''

"Yes,'' he said, "and what's more, this morning I think I found someone to advise me about what will be needed from a medical point of view to convert the Hall into a holiday home for invalids. Stroke of luck, really. Aunt Hannah suggested her: someone called Anne Piper who used to be Matron of Blaydale Hospital—before it was done away with, more's the pity. Anne had to give up nursing to look after an old mother, but now she's free again. But don't let's talk about that now. Let's give Acer a run.''

As they walked round the field, stopping occasionally to look up at the house, and bounce new ideas off each other, Kate thought she had never felt more companionable with anyone, but at the same time her feelings about the timing of the arrival of Frank and his team were ambivalent: regret at the interruption of a moment when her inclination was giving a clear signal, was coupled with relief that she had been unable to give way to an impulse she might later have regretted. After Oliver had died, she had sworn to herself that she would never again let anyone hurt her, as he had hurt her over the years, nor yet allow loneliness to drive her into a relationship that was not right.

"Pleased with everything?'' Jack asked as they climbed back up the ha-ha and went to sit on the terrace.

"Oh, yes,'' she said. "This is fun. I am lucky.''

"You weren't alone when I rang this morning, were you?'' he asked suddenly. "I could tell by your voice.''

"No. I had a visitation from Gerald Brownlow. You met him at Netta's party."

"Ah, the gallant Colonel. Somehow I don't think he approved of me much. He looked like a gamekeeper who thought he might have encountered a potential poacher."

"And had he?"

"Of course," he said, laughing at her. "Of course."

"Gerald asked me to marry him this morning."

"And what did you say?"

"I said no."

"Why?"

"Lots of reasons. Because I can't see myself getting married again. Because I don't just want to be anyone's hostess and housekeeper, or warm their slippers and nurse them through their prostate operations. And because," said Kate slowly, "though he would never hurt me, and is a good, kind, dull man, I don't love Gerald Brownlow."

"So you want love—and safety? They don't always go together."

"No," said Kate. "I of all people am well aware of that." They sat in silence for a bit, and whereas before their silences had been so easy, this one was a razor's edge.

"What about you?" asked Kate after a bit. "Would you ever want to marry again?"

"No," said Jack, and his face had the sudden withdrawn look she had noticed briefly the day before. "No, I'm not likely to marry again."

Each of them felt relieved to have made a point—and yet each somehow felt dissatisfied with what they had said.

ᛞ FIFTEEN ᛞ

Harriet and Polly Duntan lay under a huge old rhododendron bush at the top of the school grounds. It was an ideal hide-out: the dark leaves made it impossible for anyone to see in from the outside, but from the inside they had a

perfect view of anyone who might be climbing up the steep
path below them; this gave them plenty of time to disappear
round the back, and hide the supplies which they kept hidden in an improvised store under the roots. As an emergency alibi they had copies of *King Lear*, the set book they
were supposed to be revising—and in reality they had just
indulged in a highly dramatic rendering, swapping parts
with scrupulous fairness, each secretly thinking her own
interpretation greatly superior to that of the other. They had
been especially moved at the idea of the poor mad king's
own dogs shrinking away from him.

"I do think Tray, Blanch, and Sweet-heart are divine
names for dogs," said Polly. "I think I'll suggest them to
Mum for the new shihtzu puppies. Shambles is going to
have another litter and Mum says if I get a better report
this term, I can keep one for my own."

"Fat chance of that if they catch us with this lot," said
Harriet. "But, God, you're so lucky. My boring old bat of
a mother won't let me have a puppy. Granny said she'd
look after one for me, too—so it's pure spite. Has my
mother got problems!" She rolled her eyes. "She really
needs counselling, of course: she stresses for England—it's
pathetic."

Joanna would have been extremely surprised at having
this particular adjective applied to her.

The two girls drew, not very deeply, on their cigarettes.
The packet of Marlboros which they kept in their lair had
got rather damp, as had the matches, and they'd had trouble
lighting up. Neither of them really enjoyed smoking,
though each would have died rather than admit it; there
was a lot of nonchalant blowing out of smoke through
flared nostrils after cautious puffing. Inhaling properly
made them choke, which spoiled the effect of dissipated
worldliness they wished to impart. Cans of Coke, on the
other hand, which had been fortified with the remains of a
bottle of vodka Polly had succeeded in nicking off the
drinks tray at Duntan, were another matter and made them

feel extremely witty. Soon they were helpless with giggles—not that it needed alcohol to reduce them to this state, but it was always good to be able to tell one's friends that one had been pissed out of one's tiny mind.

"I'm starving," moaned Harriet. "My tummy's rumbling like Vesuvius—not sure how long I'm going to be able to keep this veggie lark up for. Would you believe it, my mother rang up Miss Ellis and *gave her permission*. I could hardly believe it; I'd never have asked if I hadn't thought she'd just stress out at the very idea. I was given tofu-burgers for lunch, can you imagine? Luckily I managed to stuff up my cheeks like a hamster and then spit most of it out in my hanky. God! They were filthy." Harriet waved her cigarette in the air, and tapped ash off with what she hoped was an expert flick, that would have done justice to a performance in Noël Coward's *Private Lives*. "Actually I pine for rare roast beef and mad cows' disease. By the way, where are the KitKats?"

Polly scrupulously divided one in half, and then in an unusual fit of magnanimity said Harriet could have her share too. "Your need is greater than mine," she quoted dramatically.

"Thanks, Poll, you're a star."

"Any news on the father front?"

"Nope." Harriet took a swig of neat vodka straight from the bottle. "I rang Granny last night and she said she'd talked to Mum as she promised—but she didn't sound hopeful. Said I'd got to be patient and tactful. Patient! I'm still waiting, of course."

Polly looked enviously at her friend. "It's so cool. Your father might be someone really thrilling. I wish I didn't know who my boring old farther was—he's so predictable; it's a real drag. Surely you could find out for yourself?"

"How can I? It's not on my birth certificate, and I've asked everyone who could possibly know."

"But there must be some evidence somewhere." Polly looked thoughtful. "We might ask Martha to help—she always has amazing ideas." Martha Campion, though only five years older than Polly, was her father's half-sister, daughter of the unpredictable Lady Rosamund by the last of her string of husbands, a charming American banker who had died a few years earlier. After his death, Martha had made her home at Duntan, and was more like a sister than an aunt to the four Duntan children. She was now up at Oxford. "It's always wild when Martha's home," said Polly.

"Why does she live with you more than her own mother?"

"Oh Granny Rosamund likes a free hand to have her lovers all over the place. Martha says she feels like a gooseberry at the Dial House."

"Don't be silly—your grandmother can't have lovers. Not properly, I mean. She's far too old."

"She does too. The last one was an Arab prince. He was really sweet, but Mum says she thinks he's on his way out. Mum says it's a sure sign that Granny Roz is getting bored of a lover when she takes up a new ploy. She's into mediums now—lovely seances and things. You must come—it's wicked." Polly put on a deep growly voice and what was intended to be the accent of a Red Indian—not that she had ever met one: "I Tawny Eagle. I bring news of Loved One from other side. Is there anyone in this room whose name begins with H who wants message from dead father?" she asked thrillingly.

"But your grandmother's even older than mine," objected Harriet, reverting to the ever absorbing topic of sex. "Granny'd certainly be past it. I think that's revolting, Polly. Think of their withered old bodies writhing on the bed. Yuk!"

"Granny Roz probably isn't all that withered—plastic surgeons are always taking darts in her—as the actress told the bishop," said Polly, draining the last dregs of vodka. They rolled about with laughter.

A bell sounded in the distance. Hastily they shoved their ill-gotten booty down the hole they had made in the roots of the bush.

"I feel awfully peculiar," said Harriet, crawling out through the leaves and cautiously standing up. "My head hurts and I think I'm going to be sick."

This prophecy was soon fulfilled.

"You're as bad as my sister Birdie. She's always being sick," said Polly, looking on with a mixture of concern and scorn, while Harriet heaved and retched. Polly's own constitution was made of sterner stuff: her stomach had all the robustness of a concrete mixer.

"Never mind, Hat," she said consolingly. "At least you look green—everyone will think it's the veg starting to act. I'll take you up to Sister and then you can miss maths with the dreaded Miss Noakes—it'll all help with the bug-your-mother campaign anyway."

As they wove their way back down the path, respectively groaning and giggling, Polly suddenly said, "If your mother doesn't cough up the information within the next few weeks, we'll hatch an amazing plot, because I think I've just had the most brill idea. Lucky you're staying with us next weekend."

When Archie Duntan turned up, horsebox in tow, to collect the two girls on Saturday, he was waylaid in the hall by the headmistress's secretary.

"Could Miss Ellis have a little word, Sir Archibald?" Archie's heart sank. Little words with those in authority were never good news, and he had been put through a good deal of drama by his mother and half-sister over the years. The idea of the rogue genes that might have passed from Lady Rosamund to his own daughters filled him with doom, but, not an ex-soldier for nothing, he bravely prepared to face fire.

Miss Ellis was a good-looking woman, well dressed without being fashionable, who had a crisp handshake, a sense of humour, and the wisdom not to pretend to be trendy to her pupils. She also had a formidable brain, and had done great things for the school's academic reputation since she had taken over five years previously. Most of the girls secretly both liked and respected her—though naturally one had to be cautious to whom one admitted such weakness. Archie and Sonia had asked her to dinner several times and found her a congenial guest.

She was standing by her desk when Archie came in. On it were several empty cigarette packets, a lot of scrunched up biscuit wrappers and an earth-covered empty vodka bottle.

"Good morning, Archie—sorry to delay you, but we have a little problem I'd like to nip in the bud." She indicated the vodka bottle. "Our head groundsman has seen Polly and Harriet Rendlesham emerging from the bushes at the top of the grounds several times, and this morning he went to investigate. This is what he's just brought me."

"Oh hell," said Archie, wishing it was Sonia who had come for the girls. "Have you seen them yet?"

"No. If you're agreeable I thought we might confront them together now. I'd rather hoped Mrs. Maitland, or her mother, would be coming for Harriet, but I gather she's spending the weekend with you?"

"Yes, that's right."

"I tried to ring both of them, but there's no reply from either house. I believe the Maitlands are friends of yours?" Miss Ellis was clearly feeling her way with caution.

"Yes. We've known Joanna's family for years, but we like both the Maitlands. Michael Maitland's a very nice chap—damn good lawyer too. Don't think things are very easy there at the moment, though."

"No," said Miss Ellis. "So I gather. Are you aware of Harriet's somewhat unusual circumstances?"

"Yes," said Archie, adding, "Sonia's particularly fond of Harriet. Like to do anything to help if we can."

"Good," said Miss Ellis. "That's what I thought, because it's Harriet I'm worried about—handled wrongly, Harriet might have real problems. Polly's just being a typical teenager—this is standard rebellion and a bit of showing off. Polly is thoughtless and might do something silly, but Harriet thinks and thinks, and is capable of doing something really destructive. She could go either way. She was very unwell the other day, and Sister suspected drink—she also thinks Harriet might easily become anorexic. We know she's disturbed at the moment—she's extremely bright, but her work is frightful and all the staff who teach her are complaining."

Miss Ellis did not tell Archie how much difficulty she'd had in persuading Joanna to follow Kate's advice to agree to Harriet's vegetarian diet without comment. Miss Ellis felt thankful now that she had won the day, but she dreaded to think how Joanna might overreact to this escapade.

"So what line are you going to take?" asked Archie.

"Oh, nothing too dramatic—I don't want martyrs. It's lucky they're both going home anyway, because all the girls know that if they're caught with drink they get sent home immediately. A little bit of threatening, and perhaps some parental sanctions too?"

"Fine. I'll talk to Sonia about that. Might be an idea for you to try and get her on the telephone before we get home?"

Miss Ellis pressed a buzzer on her desk and spoke into an intercom. "Would you ask Polly Duntan and Harriet Rendlesham to come in please?"

At the combined sight of Archie and the loot from their hideout, Polly went crimson and Harriet went white.

"I don't think I need ask if you know about these." Miss Ellis thought it would be a mistake to give them a chance to lie. "In any case you have both been seen several times by a member of staff coming out from the bush where these were found. What have you to say?"

"Sorry," they both muttered. Polly cast a glance at her father. Archie had a court martial face on and looked impassive.

"Very juvenile and stupid," said Miss Ellis, coolly. "I had thought better of you both. You realise, of course, that drinking, smoking or drugs are all offences which can mean expulsion?"

They nodded.

"And I don't care much for stealing, either," put in Archie. They both looked horrified.

"Does my mother have to know?" Harriet blurted out.

She looked so pale and distraught that Miss Ellis felt her heart turn over, but she said firmly: "Of course she does."

"You couldn't just tell my grandmother—and not tell Mum?"

"You were very anxious for your mother to know all about your new diet, Harriet—which suggests to me that if you imagine you can lay excuses for tiresome behaviour at your mother's door then you want her to know, but if you are ashamed of yourself and know you're in the wrong, then you don't want her to hear about it." Harriet's gaze burnt a hole in the floor.

"It was me that took the vodka, not Harriet," said Polly.

"But I knew she was going to do it," said Harriet in a small voice.

"Well," said Miss Ellis, "I think you've both been equally silly." She let them stew for a long silent minute and then said, "There's not long left to the end of term now. You will both lose all fifth-form privileges till the end of term. Next term you will be on approval, but if I hear that either of you has been boasting about this episode to your friends I shall reconsider what I do with you. If there's any more trouble with smoking or drinking, then next time I would have no option but to take the matter extremely seriously. I shall be ringing your mother, Harriet. You may go now."

"Go and get in the car, both of you. I'll be out in a minute," said Archie. "Can't help feeling rather sorry for that child. She looks a wreck," he said as the girls closed the door behind them.

"I know. I wish I didn't have to tell her mother—but of course I must."

"Tell you what—you talk to Joanna, of course, but how would it be if I got Sonia to ring her too? Make up something about wanting to take the same parental line. Joanna rather admires Sonia," said Archie shrewdly. "It might help."

"That's a very good idea. Thank you, Archie. Wish all parents were as easy and cooperative as you two."

Archie went out thanking his stars that he and Sonia had narrowly escaped a matrimonial breakdown four years before that would certainly have precluded Miss Ellis from regarding them as such model parents.

When they got to Duntan, and had put Star in the stables, Archie sent the two girls in to find Sonia. "I'll give you ten minutes to tell her what's happened yourselves before I get in for lunch," he said sternly. "I don't advise you to hide anything."

Sonia was taking a chicken casserole out of the oven when they came in, and even if Miss Ellis had not managed to forewarn her of their peccadillos, one look at their faces would have told her they were in trouble.

"Oh, darlings, how could you be so silly?" Sonia managed to look suitably shocked as they blurted out their sorry tale, vivid memories of similar exploits in her own past springing up before her. "That is just so disappointing."

"It all seemed so funny at the time," said Polly mournfully.

"Yes, well, these things do. Of course we'll have to stop your allowance for this month—and you will have to pay Daddy back for the bottle of vodka."

"Oh Mum! It wasn't even full. You know I'm saving up for those 501s," wailed Polly, who was always saving up for something.

"Well, tough. You know I think it's ridiculous to spend so much money on jeans, and if you can afford to smoke—or did you nick the cigarettes too?"

"No, no. Promise."

"And then of course going to Melissa's party in London must hang in the balance," went on Sonia remorselessly. "How do we know we can trust you now?" The girls exchanged anguished looks. Not to go to that would indeed be a terrible sanction. They had plans for Melissa's party. Besides, that divine Alexander Rivers was going to be there, with whom they were both deeply in love. At a party in the Easter holidays, he had actually asked Harriet when she was going to have her train-tracks taken off—a tremendously encouraging sign, in Harriet's view. This life-enhancing event having recently taken place, when Harriet smiled now, her mouth displayed perfectly even teeth and was temptingly free of stray wires. It would be catastrophic not to be able to put this new advantage to the test.

Sonia tried not to laugh at their gloomy faces and watched with amusement as Harriet devoured the chicken casserole without any apparent symptoms of being a conscience-stricken vegetarian or suffering from anorexia.

The girls were thankful when lunch was over and they could escape to their ponies and spend the rest of the afternoon hacking through the woods, deep in gossip, having successfully managed to choke off the dire threat of being accompanied by Polly's younger sisters.

After dinner that night, during which Polly and Harriet, to their great annoyance, had not been allowed to have theirs in front of the television, with a gory session of "Casualty" to titillate their appetites, but had been made to go to bed at the same ridiculous hour as Polly's sisters, Sonia decided that chilly disapproval can only be kept going successfully for a short time, and went to kiss them both goodnight. She curled up on the end of Polly's bed, kicking off her shoes and tucking her toes under the duvet.

"I've had an idea," she said. "Seeing as you both say you're so broke, how would you like a holiday job for a few weeks in August? If you take a pull on yourselves, I might—repeat might—let you work part-time in the caff." The caff was the restaurant for the house-opening, and August was the busiest month.

"Brill!"

"Amazing!"

Polly and Harriet brightened up at once.

"Bet Mum wouldn't agree, though." Harriet started to bite her nails.

"Oh yes she would," said Sonia, "because I've talked to her. She's as upset as we are about what you've done— and that's up to you to sort out when you next go home, Hattie—but she likes the idea of you having a holiday job. You'd have to stay with us, of course," Sonia went on smoothly, "because you'd need to be on the spot." She didn't add that Joanna had said she was absolutely dreading the thought of the long summer holidays with Harriet at home for so long. Sonia had thought this statement profoundly sad. Joanna had jumped at the idea of having her daughter taken off her hands for a bit.

"Wonderful. Wicked." Harriet's eyes looked enormous in her white face, her mop of pale hair a cloud of silky corkscrews round her head.

"There'd be a condition." Sonia hoped desperately that she could pull this off.

"Anything," said Harriet.

"Well, you'd both have to behave, of course, but you, Harriet, would have to promise to give up all this nonsense about not eating and having special diets—and I mean at home as well as here. Your choice. Agreed or not agreed?"

"Agreed." Harriet twined her arms round Sonia and nearly throttled her with a hug.

"What about Melissa's party?" asked Polly hopefully.

"That," said Sonia, getting up and snapping off the light, "depends entirely on both of you. No promises at all. Night, my loves. Sleep tight."

Long after Polly was asleep Harriet wept silently and desperately into her pillow. She would have given a great deal to have a mother who was as easy to talk to as Sonia. She would have given anything to have had a father like Archie—even when he had looked so grim and strict at school before lunch that Harriet had felt genuinely scared of him. She would have given anything to have a father at all.

Where are you? Who are you? Why don't you look for me? Harriet asked her own father, before, drenched and exhausted, she finally fell asleep too.

◄ SIXTEEN ►

As Kate drove down to Gloucestershire late on Sunday afternoon, she was glad of the prospect of three hours alone in the car, a chance to do a lot of hard thinking without fear of interruption.

The spell of hot weather had broken: more changeable weather patterns, with a chance of storms, was forecast, especially in the north. All day it had been oppressively grey and overcast, and felt cold. Kate thought this seemed symbolic. She had always been affected by the climate, not so much by heat, though she loved that too, as by light; the greyness and lack of sparkle that often hung like a pall over the north-east of England was one of the few things she didn't like about living in Yorkshire. The lightness of the Observatory was one of the things that attracted her to the house.

She had not seen Jack today, thought they had spent most of Saturday together. After their moment of awkwardness on Friday evening, they had sat in silence for some time, each afraid that they might have damaged something precious.

Jack had taken her hand. "Kate," he said, "I think I'm getting a message not to rush things. Am I right?" She had nodded, afraid to speak or look at him. "I think we both know we might have something big starting between us," he went on, stroking her hand with his thumb, "but you've obviously been through a very traumatic time and must be coming to terms with some complicated feelings. We might have had a moment, earlier this afternoon, when things could have happened quite easily and spontaneously between us—but it was not to be. I don't want to spoil something so important by forcing the pace at the wrong moment. I believe it will come again, and I so much want it to be right for you when it does. You must know how much I want to make love to you, but would you feel happier just to build on our new friendship together and let things take their course gradually?"

"Yes," she had whispered. "Yes please, Jack." He watched her face, thinking how expressive it was; how much pain was only just below the surface of her cheerful veneer. "I hadn't expected or looked for love or new relationships at this stage in my life," she said, the words coming with difficulty. She gave a bleak little smile. "I would be very out of practice too. It might not work—and oh Jack, you may think me cowardly and selfish, but I'm so afraid of being hurt again. That side of life, well, sex if you like, is so tied up with torment in my mind. I'd known for a long time that Oliver had always taken his pleasure elsewhere as well as with me, even in our earliest married days. Sometimes it amused him to tell me about it, and that was torture—though I learnt to hide what I felt. He could make sex wonderful, if he chose, but he was a master of taking one to the edge of bliss—and then—then just stopping and laughing at one. In the end I took a vow never to let him do that to me any more. I banked those fires down long ago. I would be scared of lighting them again. There might be no spark left.''

Jack thought wryly that it was just as well that Oliver Rendlesham was dead already, because right now he felt like killing him. He looked at Kate's troubled face—not a conventionally pretty face—Jack had known many women far more beautiful and glamorous than Kate, but never one whose face had moved him so much. He longed to bring back the look that had been there earlier in the afternoon, to see her eyes crinkle in the corners as they did when she was just about to laugh. It didn't seem the moment to tell her more about his own life. He was afraid that if it went wrong in the telling, he might lose her beyond recall. And that, thought Jack, I couldn't bear. So they had worked their way back to their former ease; they had discussed furniture and measured windows, because Kate wanted to look at materials while she was in London, and they'd had supper at a pub which had a reputation for simple but excellent food. Jack had told her tales about his exploits as a young man on the make in America and Kate had told him about some of the local people who would be his new neighbors when he was in Yorkshire. They had made each other laugh inordinately.

He had kissed her goodnight, and then held her in his arms, his cheek on her hair, rocking her gently to and fro, before opening her car door and then waving her and Acer off as they drove out of the gates.

They had not gone to the Observatory the following day. Instead Jack had come over to Longthorpe and had a simple kitchen lunch with Kate, smoked-haddock kedgeree and salad, followed by cheese. She had been guiltily aware that had Joanna not been away doing a demonstration, Rupert and Tilly down in London with Mike, and Harriet staying at Duntan, she might not have suggested this plan. By a stroke of luck, Cecily had gone over to bully poor Babs Mallory for the day. Kate knew, because Babs had once told her, that Babs always had to resort to the valium bottle after Cecily's visits. In fact Kate was half sorry that her mother-in-law wasn't at home, because were it not for her being Oliver's mother, Kate thought Cecily and Jack would get along very well and amuse each other greatly.

Going round Longthorpe, looking at its beautifully manicured garden, and the impeccable taste with which the house was furnished and decorated, underlined for Jack just how unhappy Kate must always have been there, in order to be so keen to leave it. At first glance it seemed so highly desirable, though he could see that, apart from the old playroom at the back, it was not imbued with any particularly personal stamp. He thought a house that bore Kate's own individual flavour would have had some unexpected and original touches. This house gave no clue to the tastes or lives of its owners. It was too perfect, as if it had been done up specially for a photographic visitation by a glossy magazine, or built as a stage set: as though, like its deceased owner, thought Jack, it was too perfect to be true.

Jack had wanted Kate to have dinner with him on Tuesday night, when they would both be in London, but she had been adamant that she must have supper with Mike, which she now regarded as the most important part of her visit to London, so they had compromised with a plan to meet for a quick lunch on Wednesday, in the middle of a busy day of meetings for Jack, and before Kate drove home to Yorkshire.

Jack gave her a card. It was engraved with the London and New York addresses of Franklin J. Morley Inc., his holding company—though he had numerous subsidiaries as well. He underlined one telephone number. "You can always get hold of me through this one, night or day, wherever I am." His London office was in South Audley Street. "If only I'd got more time we might have had a leisurely lunch at the Connaught, but it's a bad day for me and I have a meeting at two-fifteen. If fish is all right with you—and after that sensational kedgeree, I guess it must be—let's lunch at Scott's in Mount Street," he suggested.

"I'll try to be there at a quarter to one. Drive very carefully, darling Kate, and good luck with Jane Pulborough. At least you can now tell her you've got a definite base for your work with Midas."

Kate went over all her conversations with Jack in her mind. Am I just having the famous mid-life crisis? she wondered; am I just flattered to have anyone paying me attention after so long? But then she thought of her reaction to Gerald, and knew this was not so. What would I feel if I never saw Jack Morley again, she asked herself—and realised it would feel intolerable. She had been absolutely truthful in telling him that she did not want to marry again, and knew she ought to have felt relieved to discover he felt the same, but she had to admit that she most unfairly wished that Jack wanted to marry her. He had seemed so cosy, so unassuming, whenever they had been together, so quick to laugh at all the things that amused her, so intuitive, above all so kind—but somehow seeing his business card had made her realise that there must be another side to Jack that she knew nothing about. Gamekeepers' country-loving grandsons of his generation didn't get to own several international companies by being soft touches.

She was so deep in her own thoughts that she nearly missed the turning off the M1 for the M42 and had to cut in to the left-hand lane rather too sharply, to get on to the slip road. A lorry hooted at her. I must concentrate on driving, she told herself sternly, furious because, while she needed to turn her mind to Midas and all the details she had to ask Jane, she kept thinking about Jack, which was far more distracting. Harriet also wove in and out of Kate's head. Kate had dropped in to say goodbye to Joanna and pick up a key to 19 Oxton Road, as Mike wouldn't be back by the time she arrived on Tuesday, and of course had heard Joanna's version of the two girls' exploits.

"I suppose I shall have to have it out with Harriet next weekend," Joanna had said, looking fraught. "Lucky for her she was with the Duntans. I would have murdered her."

"Would it help at all for me to talk to her?" asked Kate diffidently. You never knew how Joanna was going to react.

"No thank you, Mum. Do please, for once, try not to interfere over Harriet."

"And am I still to try and interfere over Mike?" asked Kate, raising an eyebrow.

Joanna had the grace to look a little abashed. "Sorry," she said, with difficulty. "But, yes please—I do want you to tackle Mike. He's on at me to go down and talk things over too, and I suppose I shall have to—though when I'm going to find time I can't think. This latest effort of Harriet's is all I need. Sonia seems to think the silly little fools won't do it again and have had a fright. I hope she's right, that's all." Kate also thought it was lucky that Harriet had been at Duntan, and sent grateful thoughts winging in the direction of Sonia and Archie. As had so often happened in the past, part of Kate wished desperately that Harriet still lived under her own loving day-to-day care, and yet, and yet . . . what would her feelings be now if she were to find herself providing a home for Harriet again?

The Pulboroughs lived in a charming old house in mellow Cotswold stone a mile outside the pretty village of Chipping Marston. Kate hadn't been there before, but competent Jane had sent her a printed postcard with excellent instructions.

Kate had so far only met Jane Pulborough in her professional capacity in the glamorous setting of Duntan Hall, and though she had liked her, she had also thought her formidably elegant and somewhat alarming. It was a relief when Jane opened the door, to see that she was wearing faded jeans, her hair was tied back in a ponytail and her face was free of make-up. She was desperately hanging on to the collar of a young labrador, who had clearly not yet learnt that it is possible to give a warm welcome to guests without first knocking them flat on the floor.

"Kate, how lovely, you have done well. Down, Jasper!
Get down! Just let me shut this hellhound in the boot room,
and then I shall make sense," and she yelled back over her
shoulder: "Christopher! Kate's here—for God's sake come
and remove your dog."

Christopher Pulborough came up behind his wife and
smiled at Kate. "How do you do, Kate. Heard lots about
you. Back in a moment," and he hauled the panting Jasper
out of sight.

"Thank God for that! Come on in—Chris will get your
case in a minute. He promised me he'd have the monster
out of the way before you arrived, but you know what
husbands are!" Jane rolled her eyes, but whereas with
Joanna this would have signalled the arrival of a lengthy
spell of matrimonial frost of arctic temperature, to Kate's
relief Jane looked quite unconcerned.

"Oh how lovely," said Kate as they went through the
hall and into a room on the right. "How warm and welcoming. I love that soft terracotta colour."

"Oh good. You've said just the right thing. We've only
just had it done and I wasn't sure if I'd made it too dark.
I hope you don't mind if we don't use the drawing room
tonight, but it's turned so unexpectedly cold I lit a fire in
here earlier on." "Here" was a cosy sitting room, strewn
with books and Sunday papers, with a television set in one
corner and big squashy armchairs, their covers faded and
wearing a little thin on the arms.

"You said you'd have eaten, Kate, but it would be very
easy to scramble an egg?"

"No, thank you. I stopped on the motorway. Couldn't
eat a thing."

"Tea? Coffee? Herby bag?"

"Coffee would be lovely."

Kate very much enjoyed her evening with the Pulboroughs. Christopher, a chartered accountant, was a large,
shambling man with a shrewd mind well hidden behind his
jovial exterior. He and Jane were obviously devoted to each

other, and to their three teenage children, and Kate thought
sadly that this was how she longed for Mike and Joanna to
be together—each following their own line, yet with a
happy meeting place in the centre of their marriage.

She told them about the Observatory and made a funny
story about her chance meeting with the so-called caretaker.
She would have been surprised to know that Jane had said
to Christopher afterwards, "Kate pretends there's nothing
between them, but it glows out of her like an aura. Bet
Joanna hates his guts." And Christopher had said, "You
know, Janey, it must be *the* Jack Morley. Goodness me.
He's a very well-known name in the property world—specially in the States. Wonder what she's getting herself into?
He's seriously rich, but he has a good reputation, and people who've met him seem to like him—tough but straight.
I wonder how much she knows about him."

The following morning Kate and Jane got down to business.

"How about these?" Jane produced a bundle of labels
for stitching inside clothes: "Kate Rendlesham for Midas."

"Wow!" said Kate. "Very grown-up! I like the letter-
ing—plain but elegant. That really does look terrific."

"Yes, well, your work is terrific."

Kate showed her the things she'd brought with her, and
they made plans and lists and exchanged ideas. Jane was
delighted with all that Kate had done so far.

"Do you want to sell things from the Observatory?"
she asked.

"I don't really know. I hadn't thought. What do you
think?"

"Well, it's quite time-consuming," said Jane. "On the
other hand, it's a good way of getting known. I'm always
havering about whether the shop's worth it, because the rent
is so huge in Chipping Marston; but it's very profitable
when the American visitors hit the Cotswolds in the summer. We don't open the shop on Mondays, but I thought

I'd take you over to look this afternoon. Why don't you just open on request and only sell your own things to start with? I thought we'd have new cards and bill headings done with 'Midas' in the middle, and then our two names and addresses in each corner. I take it you'd want to put 'The Stables' rather than just 'The Observatory' if you're going to live there? I never let anyone come here.''

"How about 'Midas at the Coach House, The Observatory, Ravelstoke'?'' suggested Kate.

"Sounds great to me.''

As they drove over to Chipping Marston after lunch, Jane told Kate what hard work she found all the sales round the country.

"It's frightfully difficult deciding what to take, and then packing everything up, and you've no idea how bitchy people can be at these charity sales, real claws-out stuff—fiercely competitive. If you find the wheels of your clothes rack overlap someone else's space by a centimetre, all hell's let loose. When it's only me and, say, just a couple of others in a private house—like Sonia's at Duntan—then that's great fun, but the really big Christmas sales are a nightmare.''

"What about individual commissions?'' asked Kate. "One or two people have started asking me to make things for them specially.''

"Entirely up to you. If the idea appeals to you—go for it. I'd like it always to be under our label though.''

"Of course,'' said Kate, flattered to death.

"Anyway, I don't think you should ever make too many things exactly the same. We want them to be pretty exclusive.''

Kate was very impressed with Jane's shop, which had a prime position just off the main street, with a yard behind for parking. "Parking's vital,'' said Jane. Kate thought everything in the shop was highly desirable, from beautiful handmade silk flowers to wonderfully tempting Spanish leather belts and handbags; there were some brilliantly colourful painted wooden boxes from India, unusual hand-made jerseys and a stand of enchanting cards.

"It's so hard to know where to draw the line," said Jane. "I adore the buying trips, especially abroad, and Christopher is always warning me about not diversifying too much, but I have to tell you that when he saw that first waistcoat we auctioned at Duntan, he agreed that anything of yours would be a brilliant addition."

"I feel quite overcome," said Kate. "Goodness, he is nice, your husband."

"Not bad, is he?" Jane gave her a brilliant smile. "Now look, Kate, I want you to make me a really stunning evening jacket, as soon as you can, because I think I'd get lots of interest every time I wore it—like you obviously have with that lovely shelly one you made for yourself."

"What colour?" asked Kate. "Any special theme?"

"I don't know really. Any ideas?"

Kate thought for a moment. "Well," she said, "as the Observatory is going to be on the address card, how about midnight-blue velvet with the moon and stars on the front, and a great big sun on the back in real gold thread? Gold for Midas."

"Brilliant," said Jane. "A Midas jacket. Why don't you make a few—one-off, exclusive and not repeatable, as a sort of launch thing, and I'll wear mine as an advertisement? Oh Kate, this is going to be fun. You might like to come to a trade fair with me sometime. I think you'll breathe new life into the business. Where do you get your wonderful ideas?"

"Well anywhere, really," said Kate. "Once you're beamed on to it, you get ideas everywhere. For instance," she went on, "I was given a marvellous book for Christmas called *Mrs. Delany and her Flower Collages*. It's a real inspiration. She was an amazing lady who lived in the eighteenth century and not only painted, but did these stunning paper mosaics of flowers which are actually in the British Museum now. I thought I might drop in and look tomorrow—but she was a wonderful stitcher too, and there are gorgeous details in the book of the embroidery on her court dress. I'm not at all original,'' she added. ''I'm always copying things.''

But Jane thought that Kate, as a person, was highly original—and wonderfully unaware of it.

The following morning Kate was quite sorry to say goodbye to the Pulboroughs, but the whole venture had suddenly become very exciting. She kissed them both goodbye with real affection, thinking how deceptive outward appearances can be. Janey was a much softer character than she appeared on first acquaintance, and her genuine enthusiasm had managed to give Kate the confidence to feel that she really might be bringing something of value to the business itself.

She thought ahead to her evening with Mike and felt considerable trepidation, dreading what she might discover about the state of his and Joanna's marriage, very afraid of being asked for advice which she felt quite unqualified to give.

But the prospect of lunch with Jack drew her like a pin to a magnet.

❧ SEVENTEEN ❧

Kate was not the only one to be uneasy about her meeting with her son-in-law. Michael Maitland felt agonised about the future. He had adored having his son and daughter to himself for the weekend and it had been touching to witness Rupert's pleasure at being back in his London home, though Mike thought Rupert's all too obvious and permanent state of anxiety extremely worrying. Tilly was made of sterner stuff; besides, she was three years younger and her roots had not been so firmly planted in Number Nineteen Oxton Road at the time of their move to the cottage. Occasional visits to London over the last year had not made it into her home.

Rupert had rushed round the house having a passionate reunion with everything, from his sandpit in the tiny garden, now rather grubby and full of earwigs, to the plastic toys that had sat forlornly in the nursery bathroom, unloved and unplayed with for too long.

"I like being in my own bed again," Rupert said to his father on Friday night as he snuggled under his duvet. "When are we coming home properly?"

"I don't know, old chap. Mummy and I will have to talk about it. But you love Longthorpe and being in the country, don't you?"

"Ye-es," said Rupert doubtfully, picking at his sore thumb. "But I like home more."

Because he had missed Friday morning at school, Rupert had been set some homework to do. He had to write one sentence describing himself, and Mike was dismayed at what a terrible state his son had got into over this task.

"I don't know what to say," Rupert whispered miserably, as tears oozed slowly down his cheeks.

"Come on—you think of one thing and I'll help you write it."

"I can write but I can't think—and what I say might be wrong."

"Just think about something you like or don't like."

Mournfully, and with great anxiety—an altercation with his mother, who had lost her temper with him for picking "slimy bits" out of a chicken fricassee, still painfully fresh in his mind—Rupert had eventually written: "I am a boy who duzent like mushroms."

"Is he always as nervous as this?" Mike asked Jenny.

"He is now," said Jenny, who deeply disapproved of Joanna's ways of dealing with her son.

"Hattie sometimes calls him Droopy Rupey," announced Tilly smugly. Rupert let out a wail of misery.

*   *   *

Mike had driven Jenny and the children to King's Cross on Sunday evening to put them on the train for York. Rupert had clung to him desperately, winding himself round his father's leg like an elastic bandage, tears squeezing painfully out of his eyes, the scared rabbit look that so irritated his mother, making him look as if he was being hypnotised by a stoat.

Tilly looked on with interest. "Cleareye Clikes thinks Rupert is a very silly boy," she announced.

"Well tell Cleareye that I think that's very unkind of her," said Mike sternly. "Tell her I don't like it when she's horrid." Tilly gave him a speculative look, and then, deciding she might be losing out on a leading role in a rattling good melodrama, started to bawl at the top of her lungs, her brand of tears, which she kept constantly at the ready for emergencies, coursing effortlessly down her rosy cheeks.

Jenny picked her up and bundled her unceremoniously on to one of their reserved seats in the train, before coming back to receive Rupert. Mike managed to disentangle his quivering little son, mopped his face, gave him a quick hug and handed him up to Jenny, feeling horribly like a traitor. As he stood on the platform watching the train pull out, physically and emotionally shattered, he wondered whether he could put his children through the trauma of shuttling between him and Joanna on a more permanent basis. But he also knew that he was not prepared to give them up. What made him so angry was the knowledge that whereas he genuinely enjoyed their company, to Joanna they were often an ill-disguised irritation, and lately, he thought, in danger of becoming pawns in a complicated game of emotional chess. He stayed rooted to the spot long after the train was out of sight.

What was he going to do about his marriage? He had no reason to suppose that Joanna had been unfaithful to him—so far—though as a beautiful woman living apart from her husband, the probability that temptation would come her way sometime was strong. There was no other woman in Michael's life at the moment, but recently he had become aware that there could be—just possibly—a man.

At the beginning of the summer he had agreed to have as a lodger, and strictly on a temporary basis, a young barrister who had recently joined the firm in which Michael was a partner. Joanna had agreed without a thought—they had a spare room, and Mike had made it plain that if the family were at home, or he needed the spare room for a guest, then Nigel Harrington must move out.

The arrangement had worked well. Nigel's presence made the house feel less empty to Mike, besides which Nigel was a self-effacing, well-mannered young man: intelligent and pleasant company if invited, but always careful not to intrude if Michael had other friends round. They discovered that they shared many tastes. Lately they had started listening to music and going to concerts together; gradually Nigel's efforts at flat hunting had ceased. Soon Mike became aware that the younger man greatly admired him—and not just as a senior member of his firm either. It had been a shock when he first realised this. Nothing had developed between them, but Mike was uneasily aware that if he wanted it to do so, then the possibility was there. This was a side of himself that Mike had wondered about in his university days, but had not thought about for years. Marriage had laid it to rest. Though he was not seriously tempted down that road now, it did occur to him that a little admiration was a very pleasant change, and Nigel's companionship underlined for him how very lonely his life without his family had become.

He wondered if Kate would be coming with definite proposals from Joanna, though he thought this would be out of character for both of them. He was fond of Kate and had felt deeply sorry for her. He had started off by admiring Oliver Rendlesham almost to the point of idolatry, and ended by disliking him intensely. Apart from the fact that he had come to suspect the cruel side of Oliver, it is hard to find yourself constantly compared by your wife to your father-in-law—always unfavourably—and not resent it. Michael Maitland was a very troubled man.

Kate went to have lunch with Robin, who had promised to come shopping for materials with her. It was lovely to have someone to talk to about her plans.

"Oh, Robin," she said, "what a good daughter-in-law you are. Thank you for listening. I always feel I can bore you and Nick with my vacillations and my doings. If you live alone one of the difficulties is not having anyone to tell things to, and it's always such fun being with you two."

"Might be us three soon," said Robin.

"No! You're having a baby! Oh darling, how wonderful."

"Pretty good, isn't it? Not for ages, though. Another six months."

Kate hugged her ecstatically. "Where will you have it?"

"Oh, I expect I'll just go squat in a corner," said Robin breezily.

"No, silly. I mean London, Yorkshire, or back in the States with your mum?" Soon they were deep in baby-talk. It was agreed that Robin and Nick would come up to Yorkshire for the weekend and Kate would take the whole family over to inspect the Observatory. In a way it was good that Jack was going to be away for the next few weeks, she thought. It would not only be a kind of test about what she really felt about him, but she could get her move organised, and sort out a few questions in her own mind.

"I know what we ought to do while you're here," said Robin. "Let's go visit my cousin Ellie Hadleigh—the decorator one. She's got all these amazing patterns in her house—paint, materials, wallpaper, the lot—and she's always full of wonderful ideas." Kate looked doubtful. She was well aware that Ellie's glamorous husband, Simon

Hadleigh, and Sonia Duntan had almost been swept away by a passionate love affair a few years earlier, and though both marriages had been painstakingly and brilliantly patched up, the stitches that held the patches together might not stand up to anything but the most careful treatment.

"I don't think your cousin Ellie has very happy associations with our part of the world," she said. "Besides, I don't want to make the Observatory all grand and pretentious. I don't think Jack Morley would like that either, though he's given me carte blanche to do whatever I like." Robin looked at her mother-in-law with carefully concealed curiosity, simultaneously smelling rats and sensing rainbows. She couldn't wait to meet Jack.

"No, no," she said reassuringly, "that's just where Ellie's so clever. She has a great feeling for what a house needs. I've often heard her say that the house itself should dictate the style, but that it should always reflect the owner's personality too. And she'd never push anything on you—that's part of her gift. She's good at keeping within a client's means too. As for coming to Yorkshire—well, I don't think she'd mind that. She'd just make sure Simon didn't come too! Are you on a particular budget for decorating?"

"Well, no." Kate flushed slightly. Money no object, Jack had said. Make it as you think it ought to be. Go wild.

"Let me call her," said Robin, who couldn't wait to relay all this to Nick. She made a date for them to go round to the Hadleighs late that afternoon. "It'll be a breeze, you'll see. It's just so easy to have everything under one roof and not trail round from place to place trying to match things up. We might look for nursery ideas too. You'll adore Ellie."

Kate and Robin spent a happy day together. Kate found lots of new ideas both for materials and designs, and the visit to Ellie was a great success. She was one of those rare people who are prepared to listen carefully to the other person, before tossing out their own ideas. She also gave

Kate lots of addresses of suppliers and introductions to wholesalers. Her own house was both ravishing and unusual.

"I have to go up to Scotland in the next few weeks. Would you like me to take a little detour and come round by you?" Ellie had asked—and added, pulling a rueful face: "Just so long as you promise I don't have to bump into Sonia Duntan."

"I promise," said Kate. "I'm very fond of Sonia, but I'll make sure to have a great neon sign saying 'Duntans Keep Out' if you come."

Kate's evening with Mike was less easy: not that he was anything other than charming to her, as he always was, but she sensed a wariness about him, and all her antennae told her that his and Joanna's marriage was in more serious trouble than she had already guessed. Until this meeting, it had not occurred to Kate that Mike might not want Joanna back. She had assumed that his letter demanding his wife and children's return to London by the autumn term—or else—had been an attempt to call Joanna's bluff. Now she wondered if Mike did really want Joanna, or if it was only his children he minded about.

Mike had produced a delicious and simple supper. He had always enjoyed cooking but Joanna hardly ever let him near the kitchen, marking it clearly as her territory. He and Kate had eaten kidneys Tobago with new potatoes and salad, with which Mike had opened a bottle of Clos du Marquis, Saint-Julien 1989; there was a really ripe brie which was almost, but not quite, running out of the house, and for pudding there was hot lemon soufflé.

"Goodness, you have taken a lot of trouble for me, Mike," said Kate. While they were eating she had outlined her own plans and told him about her ideas for Longthorpe. "I'm not making it over to Jo yet. I have told her this, though I don't think she's quite taken it in; you know how she hears what she wants to hear. Jack Morley won't sell me the Observatory, and though I shan't have to pay him rent until I've finished doing it up for him, if the whole thing doesn't work out I don't want to find myself without any property.'' She did not say that this had actually been Jack's suggestion, for her own protection. ''You know, better than anyone, how I'm placed, but if it does work out, then you and Jo can rent Longthorpe—which Nick and Robin don't want—from me, and I'll rent the Observatory from Jack.'' She hoped she sounded both more businesslike and yet more casual than she felt, but had a nasty feeling she sounded neither.

''Hope you know what you're getting into,'' said Mike. ''Isn't it all rather sudden?''

''No, no,'' said Kate airily. ''I've been thinking of doing something of the sort for some time.''

''The business side isn't what I meant,'' said Mike dryly.

''What would your reaction be to living in Longthorpe?'' asked Kate, hastily turning the attention back to the Maitland family. Mike got up and walked to the window. ''At the moment,'' he said, ''I'm rather worse off than if we were divorced. I only see my family if I go to Yorkshire. I had a fight to make Jo send them down to London this weekend, and I'm very worried by Rupert. I can't live there because of my job—and I don't want to flog up there every weekend. Perhaps we can reach some sort of compromise, but compromise isn't Joanna's best thing, and I'm tired of always being the one who gives way.''

''Do you still love Joanna?'' Kate asked.

''I don't know,'' said Mike, sadly. ''I know I love my children, but Joanna? I wish I could say yes and be sure it was true. I don't enjoy being shouted at, and I can't think it's good for the children to live in the acrimonious atmosphere we seem to develop when we're together. Jo must make her mind up. If she wants everything her way as usual—Longthorpe full time, and the children all the time too—then I want to divorce and I'll fight for equal custody of our children.''

Kate had never heard Mike sound so decisive.

''And where does Harriet come in?'' she asked. ''I've always thought you were a wonderful stepfather to her, Mike, but she seems to be left out of everyone's calculations.''

''I know, and I'm sorry. I'm really fond of Harriet, and she could come and stay here whenever she wanted, and I'd always do anything I could for her, but if you remember, when Joanna and I married, I wanted to adopt her. Jo refused. She's not my child, Kate. Rupert and Tilly are. She's at boarding school—and she's got you too.'' Kate's heart sank. Harriet seemed to be like a superfluous suitcase stuck in a left luggage office.

At that moment there was a tentative tap on the door, and Nigel Harrington put his head round the door.

''Sorry to interrupt, but just to let you know I'm in, Mike,'' he said. Mike introduced him to Kate. ''Nigel's our lodger. You'll have heard about him from Joanna,'' he said. Actually Kate hadn't. Nigel made polite conversation for a minute or two, but withdrew almost immediately. Kate was quite unable to put a finger on what aroused in her a sense of disquiet: something guarded about the atmosphere perhaps. Mike reminded her of an animal that has sensed possible danger, and frozen into stillness so as not to attract attention. She had a horrible feeling that the Maitland marriage might be on an irreversible decline.

❧ EIGHTEEN ❧

Kate was late for her date with Jack at Scott's. She had pondered whether to leave the car at Mike's house and fetch it later, but as she intended to drive north immediately after lunch, it seemed silly to have to go so far back on her tracks, and she felt confident of finding a Pay and Display space in Grosvenor Square, which would allow her all the time Jack had free between meetings. She thought she had allowed plenty of leeway, but everything conspired against her. When she tried to start her car, the battery was flat, and she realised that she had not only left her car unlocked all night, but left it with the lights switched on. She supposed she was incredibly lucky the car was still there at all. She kept a set of jump leads in the boot, and eventually the driver of a passing delivery van took pity on her, resulting in a queue of angrily hooting cars trying to get past, while her own car and the van were joined together as though they were mating in the middle of the road. Precious time had ticked away by the time she was en route for her assignation.

What is the matter with me? she thought. She tried to blame her scattiness on her anxieties about the Maitlands, but in her heart she knew it wasn't due to that at all. Every set of lights was against her, and the traffic seemed even heavier than usual. When she got to Grosvenor Square, it was already five to one, and all the spaces were occupied. Kate drove round and round, feeling more and more desperate, and had just decided to cut her losses and make for the nearest multistorey car park, when she saw a large Volvo preparing to leave. Her heart was thumping as she drove into the newly vacated space, blowing a heartfelt kiss of gratitude at the surprised driver of the departing car. She almost forgot to get a ticket, and her hands were shaking as she pushed the coins in the machine. She had thought very carefully about what to wear that morning, wishing to present a more sophisticated version of herself to Jack, but as she ran down South Audley Street towards Mount Street she realised with mortification that she had neither changed into her tidy shoes nor put on the jacket that went with her dress; to make matters worse it started to spit with rain. It was a wild and dishevelled-looking Kate that burst into Scott's, breathlessly asking for Mr. Morley.

One look at her appearance told Jack the tale. He roared with laughter. "What, no tights tied round your waist?" he asked, as he kissed her. "I am disappointed." He looked extremely smooth himself, not at all the caretaker figure of their first meeting.

"Oh, Jack! I'm so sorry." Kate was almost in tears, and she felt weak with relief that he seemed so unfazed: memories of how Oliver would have reacted in similar circumstances made her wince. "I wanted to be punctual, and look smart and collected—I know you haven't got much time, and I can't bear to have wasted it."

Many women had set their caps at Jack Morley over the years, and used many different stratagems in their pursuit of him. He thought he had never met a woman with less guile than Kate and his heart turned over at the sight of her.

"Shush," he said, "you're here. Nothing else matters—relax." He grinned: "Since I'm in the chair, no meeting can start without me. I hope you don't mind, but I've ordered fish cakes for us both—may sound rather dull but they're so very good here and I thought it would save time. I'll give you the lobster treatment another time."

"Wonderful. I love fish cakes. Goodness, it's got very smart and modern since I was last here. Somehow I think I preferred all that dingy old red plush to this pale and gleaming look, though."

She had wondered how it would be to meet Jack in such a different setting, and whether the magic between them would have melted away. She thought of Elizabeth Barrett Browning's words:

> "Yes," I answered you last night,
> "No," this morning, sir, I say.
> Colours seen by candle-light
> Will not look the same by day.

But Jack's colour seemed just as bright to Kate as when she had first met him, though there was no mistaking the gloss which only serious money can produce, and which her years with Oliver had caused her to regard with caution. Clearly Jack Morley liked everything, including his city clothes, to be the very best. The deference with which he was treated and the speed with which they were served in the restaurant were not lost on her either.

"I've been busy on Ravelstoke Hall affairs," Jack told her, after he'd enquired about how she'd got on with Jane Pulborough, and expressed pleasure at her news. "My company solicitor is setting up a charitable trust for me, and Sylvia is organising an office in the billiard room which will be up and running next week."

"Who is Sylvia?" asked Kate. "And do all the swains adore her?"

"Sylvia is my long-standing and totally indispensable PA over here. By the way, she's under instructions to give you any help you need over the Observatory. All the young men in the company are absolutely terrified of her—don't think she has much time for swains. She's too busy smoothing my path." He grinned at her: "You must meet sometime."

Kate decided she might well take one of her rare dislikes to Sylvia. Jack laughed at her expression. "Don't look so suspicious and disapproving. I think you might actually get on rather well together," he said. "You share a sense of humour and you're both capable of putting me in my place. Now, will you put your mind to something while I'm away? Could you be thinking of one or two Yorkshire worthies who would be really good on a governing body to run the Ravelstoke Hall Centre Trust?"

"Why do you want a governing body?" asked Kate, who loathed committees herself. "I thought you were going to endow the whole thing out of your vast riches?"

"Well, I am going to endow it, and I do propose to put a great deal of money into it—but it would be the kiss of death to the enterprise if I gave too much."

"Really?" said Kate. "How very peculiar. Why?"

"Because to succeed it will need local backing and publicity, and unless some dedicated Yorkshire people are
committed to the enterprise, and prepared to give up their
time and energy to running it—do some fund-raising too—
the project will wither and die before it's even started. It's
one of the quirks of human nature that if something is made
too easy, no one values it. I hope we shall draw patients
from all over the place, but local interest is vital."

"What sort of people do you want? How many?"

"Not too many. We'll need an architect, and a finan-
cier—someone with building connections would be good
too, and a solicitor of course. We could provide all those
from Franklin J. Morley Inc., but we must have people on
the spot too. I think I told you that I've got my eye on an
ex-hospital matron, didn't I, because we must have medical
advice. Someone who has experience of what it's like to
be a long-term carer would be good, and someone who's
good at getting other people to do things. Think about it,
will you?"

Kate pulled a face: "There's always grotty Netta, I suppose. You have to hand it to her—she's an ace fundraiser.
Her steamroller factor is off the thermometer, and she's so
upwardly mobile she gives me a crick in the neck, but she
positively adores all those prestige charity events that fill
me with such doom, and she knows absolutely everybody."

"What a sociable little thing you are! Netta sounds just
what's wanted, and she's a very attractive lady," Jack
teased. "Anyway, have a little battle with your prejudices,
and see who you can come up with. And go flat out for
Midas and all the alterations needed at the Observatory. I
shall expect great progress when I get back." He looked at
his watch.

"I wish you weren't going away," said Kate, though
she had vowed this was exactly what she wouldn't say to
him. "When will you be back?"

"As soon as I can. In about three weeks with luck, but
I shall be ringing you up. Don't think you're going to be

free of me." He signed the bill. "Now, darling Kate, I must go. I'll walk you to your car."

An immensely glossy black Cadillac pulled up outside the restaurant as though by telepathy, and a uniformed chauffeur jumped out and opened the door.

"All right, thank you, Leslie—pick me up at the office in five minutes, will you?" said Jack.

"I'm not sure I feel comfortable with your public persona," said Kate, as they walked towards her car. "I've developed an acute allergy to the trappings of power over the years. The old saw about power corrupting can be terrifying true."

He took her in his arms and kissed her. "We all have our different sides," he said gently. "If I hadn't got this other achieving, business side to me I'd never have met you in the first place. Leslie's my driver, but I'll always be Just Jack for you, I promise."

He looked down at her: "I love you, Kate," he said—and then he was gone. Kate watched him walk away till he turned the corner and was out of sight. She wondered if he would look back and wave, but he didn't.

Then she started her car, and headed towards the M1 for the long drive north.

❧ NINETEEN ❧

Kate went over to the Observatory on Thursday afternoon. It was amazing how much work had gone on during the few days she had been away. The stables were cleared and the partitions knocked down; there were wires and pipes everywhere in the house and radiators were propped against walls. The old fittings had been ripped out of the kitchen.

"Goodness, Frank, you have been going it," she said.

"Ah well, Jack doesn't like the grass to grow. He told me to crack on—wants everything finished yesterday, does

Jack. Got a lot of new Yanky notions. We've taken on extra staff. Says he's keen to give work to as many lads as possible—got a thing about helping the unemployed, seemingly.'' Frank sniffed as though he had very little time for this eccentricity on the part of his new boss and old school mate. ''Now you come and tell me where you want these rads fixed.''

There had been a message from Gloria on Kate's answering machine to say that she had already started work on the designs Kate had left with her, and that Jessie Worsencroft was thrilled at the idea of helping with the tailoring and dressmaking, and had a copy of the sample waistcoat Kate had sent her ready for inspection.

Kate decided that she would take all the family, including Cecily, over to Ravelstoke on Saturday afternoon. She had the bright idea of asking Joanna to advise on the kitchen, knowing she wouldn't be able to resist the challenge, and hoping it might make her feel sufficiently included to break down some of her resistance to the idea of Kate's move. Joanna was going over to collect Harriet on Saturday morning, and Kate hoped that they might have achieved some communication before they got home. So often a car journey provides the ideal conditions for intimate but difficult discussions: there is no escape, and yet the protagonists do not have to look at each other.

Cecily gave her a touching welcome. ''Thank goodness you're back. I can't stand having to let your silly dog out,'' she said. As Cecily much missed having a dog of her own, adored Acer—except when she raided birds' nests—and was always trying to inveigle her up to her flat by means of tempting titbits, Kate correctly interpreted this as an admission that Cecily was pleased to see her home. Her heart smote her at the thought of leaving the old lady.

''I've got a very profitable commission for you,'' Cecily went on. ''From Roz Campion—you could charge her the earth.''

"Wonderful," said Kate. "I'd be flattered to do something for her. I know all her clothes are usually from top designers and she always looks amazingly elegant. What does she want me to make for her?"

"A shroud."

"A *shroud?* Don't be ridiculous, Cecily!"

"I'm not. When I went over the other day Roz was standing admiring herself in front of her looking-glass draped in this marvellous length of white cashmere material she's bought on one of her trips. She wants you to embroider it with all the themes of her life."

Kate shrieked with laughter. "I'd better brush up on erotica then—the Kama Sutra with a few cats and broomsticks thrown in."

"I assure you she's perfectly serious. She's busy planning her funeral arrangements and getting all the service sheets done—rubrics in red, and no over-familiarity with God."

"I thought Roz was on tremendously matey terms with God," Kate objected. "She always gives the impression she's got a direct line through to him. In fact, I would have thought it would be the other way round and she'd be very put out if the Recording Angel got her title wrong."

"Funerals are public occasions," said Cecily reprovingly, giving the impression that God might be allowed his little intimate moments with Lady Rosamund in private, but woe betide him if he overstepped the mark in front of other people. "And by the way, I said you'd want your Midas label, and Roz says she'd have no objection to you sewing it in the shroud—on the inside, of course."

"Well, that would be really great for publicity—sealed in a coffin, or smoking up the chimney at the crem."

"Roz intends to be frozen. It's the latest thing."

"Oh terrific. You mean in two thousand years someone may thaw her out and reconstitute her. That'll be great for business."

"You may laugh," said Cecily severely, "but I think it would be very profitable for you. Don't say I'm not trying to help get your business launched. By the way, Wednesday next week is the day for her transatlantic lunch."

"Can't wait," said Kate. "I wouldn't miss it for the world."

Joanna had secretly been pinning her hopes on Kate's visit to Mike to get their marital problems sorted out. She was disappointed with her mother's guarded and not very optimistic report about Mike's reactions.

"But didn't you spell out all the advantages of Longthorpe?"

"Advantages for who?"

"Well—for the children certainly." Joanna had sounded more certain than she felt.

"Oh darling," said Kate sadly, "I'm really sorry, but you will have to sort it out between you. I did tell him how much living at Longthorpe means to you—but he knows that already. I think he might try to come to a compromise, but you would have to do a lot of compromising yourself. If not I'm terribly afraid he may want a divorce, or anyway a legal separation."

Joanna felt a sense of rising panic. Rupert had wet his bed every night since he'd been back, and kept complaining that his chest felt funny and he couldn't breathe. He had also developed a persistent cough. Joanna took him to the surgery and was dismayed when the doctor said it was an asthmatic cough. He had prescribed a Ventolin inhaler to be used while the cough was bad, and a Becotide inhaler twice a day on a regular basis. He had asked if Rupert was under any special stress. Joanna tried to tell herself that it was all Mike's fault for dragging the children to London, but her own innate honesty and the fact that both the bed-wetting and the cough had started before they went, but got worse since they had come back, made this unconvincing.

She had often been wildly irritated by Mike, always taken his love for her for granted, but now that he suddenly didn't seem to value her as she had assumed he did, she found herself wanting him more than she would have believed possible. She determined she must go man-hunting for herself, if only to tantalise Mike and bring him back to heel.

At Miss Ellis's request, Joanna had been to see her before collecting Harriet.

"Normally I would be dealing with Harriet and Polly's behaviour far more severely, Mrs. Maitland, but I think we might be wise to deal with Harriet with great sensitivity at the moment: she's very . . ." Miss Ellis paused for the right word, one she hoped would not antagonise Joanna. "Very vulnerable and unsure of herself. I think she and Polly have had a fright. Both girls have been most subdued all week; Harriet's work reports have improved, and she's been eating normally. I think Archie and Sonia dealt very well with the situation, but I would treat Harriet with kid gloves if I were you."

Joanna had never even tried on a pair of kid gloves, let alone worn them, but she agreed doubtfully to try.

When Harriet got in the car, Joanna, who would normally have leapt straight into the attack, wasn't sure what to say to her—another novel experience. It was Harriet who broke the silence. "Sorry about the booze, Mum," she said, not looking at Joanna, but gazing down at the enormous, clumpy boots that made her feel so elegant, and which were an essential item in the wardrobe of any pupil at Essendale Hall with aspirations to be fashionable.

"Well, like the Duntans, I was extremely upset. Miss Ellis seems prepared to give you another chance, but how do I know you can be trusted over anything now?"

"Oh Mum, it just seemed fun at the time. I promise we won't do it again and we're going to pay Archie back for the vodka out of our earnings at the Duntan caff in the hols."

"Well, it was thoroughly dishonest, and you might have got sacked. How could you be so stupid? Drink can lead people to do extremely irresponsible things."

"I know, I know. I've said I'm really sorry." Harriet, who had also received advice from Miss Ellis on not over-reacting, tried not to rise. "But didn't you ever do anything stupid when you were young?"

"Yes, of course I did. If I'm strict it's to try to stop you making the same disastrous mistakes that I did," said Joanna primly, not seeing the pit she had just opened up and that now yawned before her.

There was complete silence. Then: "I suppose I'm your disastrous mistake?" asked Harriet. "Well thanks very much—it's great to know one was loved and wanted. Was I a deliberate mistake which turned into a disaster or just a careless accidental one that you've had to live with ever since? It would just be nice to know."

"Don't be ridiculous, Hattie. That's not what I meant to say at all."

"No, but it's what you actually *meant*," said Harriet. "It's what you've always felt about me. And as for my father—" Harriet's voice shook "—whoever he is, he's obviously never cared two pins about me. At least you've put up with me. He's rejected me completely."

"Oh Harriet, don't be so melodramatic. Your father hasn't rejected you at all. He doesn't even know you exist."

The moment the words were out, Joanna felt she had taken a disastrously wrong turn, but had no idea how to right herself. Her hands trembled on the steering wheel; normally an expert driver, she cornered too fast, nearly collided with a tractor coming from the opposite direction and swerved on to the grass verge. The car crunched to a halt up against the hedge, the hawthorn spikes covering the paintwork on the passenger side with long scratches. Both Joanna and Harriet were jerked into their seat belts, and the tractor driver gave a two-finger sign. When Joanna tried to drive on again, the wheels spun in the long grass which was sodden after three days of rain.

"Damn and blast." Joanna felt thoroughly shaken. "Are you all right? You'll have to get out and push."

Harriet had to climb into the back of the car in order to get out of the driver's side. Eventually, with a mud-spattering jolt, Joanna got the car moving again. She halted on the road for Harriet to get in again. Mother and daughter were both relieved to have had an interruption in their conversation, and they drove the remaining miles in stony silence—but a hitherto half-formed idea hardened inside Harriet to an ironclad resolve.

It was agreed that Joanna should drive Cecily, Rupert and Tilly to the Observatory, and that Kate should go on ahead with Nick and Robin and Harriet. She wanted them to see the house from below, so that the full impact of the surprising little building, with its tower and dome standing against the skyline, should strike them as it had struck her the first time she had seen it. She parked the car where she had done after Netta's lunch party, which now seemed an age ago, and they walked along the path by the wood and then up the field.

"Now look," said Kate.

"That's magic!" said Robin.

"Oh Granny, it's really cool—like something out of a fairy tale." Harriet was gratifyingly impressed too: "Rasputin, Rasputin, let down your hair," she declaimed, striking a suitably dramatic pose with a hand on her heart.

"I think you mean Rapunzel, darling. Rasputin would have had a long straggly beard. Not quite so romantic."

They were still laughing as they got to the ha-ha. Walter, the Ravelstoke mason, had been at work with his team, doing some skilled dry-stone walling, and it was no longer necessary to scramble up into the garden over loose stones. The steps in the centre had been repaired too, and Josh had made a little wooden gate at the top.

"What a view!" said Nick. "I do see this is a really special place, Mum. Funny we've lived in Yorkshire all these years and never noticed it before."

"It's a landmark from above and below, but you don't actually notice it from the road itself—which is why I wanted you to come this way. I wanted you to understand how I fell in love with it." Kate told them the local nickname for the house.

"Better be careful about your landlord then," said Nick lightheartedly, and then said, "Ow! What did you do that for?" as Robin kicked him on the shin. Kate pretended not to notice, but was rather unnerved that Robin had obviously seen straight through her carefully casual references to Jack. Perhaps there wasn't much point in trying to hide her feelings, but she felt she needed to hug her privacy to her for a bit longer. Luckily at that moment Joanna's car turned in at the gates, and they all trooped round to the front. They heaved Cecily out of the front seat of the car, and the children spilled out of the back, and were soon whooping round the garden with Acer.

"Hi, Jo," said Nick, greeting his sister with a kiss. "Who's been dragging their nails along your car then?"

"Bloody stupid tractor hogging the middle of the road, forced me into a hedge," said Joanna shortly, not looking at Harriet.

"Rather him than me. I bet you gave him a real earful, didn't you?" teased Nick, earning another kick from his wife, who hissed at him: "Do shut up, Nick—don't goad her. I want this afternoon to go well for your mother, and I can't stand the strain of you two bickering. It's too hot."

In fact Joanna, wretchedly aware that she had started the day disastrously, had vowed to herself to avoid any more pitfalls, and managed not to reply, though Nick could usually wind her up and then jerk her up and down the string of his teasing like a yo-yo.

"Where shall we start?" asked Kate, brightly; she was anxiously aware of the undercurrents dragging away at

Joanna and Harriet. "Come and look in what will be my workrooms first, and then I'll take you round the house and we'll have our picnic."

On the whole, the visit proved a success. Joanna had known immediately what should be done to improve the kitchen and make it both practical and pleasant, and had agreed to come over again with Kate the following week and talk to Frank, though she still thought it extraordinarily selfish of Kate to want to decamp. Nick and Robin had been extremely enthusiastic and the children, who were enchanted with the place, had immediately established a secret camp underneath a weeping pear tree, and played without quarrelling for a record amount of time.

Later they all climbed to the top of the house and Cecily, who had puffed ominously on the stairs but refused to allow herself a halt, had pronounced the tower ideal for bird-watching; her afternoon was made by sighting a merlin which had obviously strayed a few miles from its usual moorland habitat. Kate felt it was a lucky omen.

"Are you sure it's not just a kestrel, Granny-Cis?" teased Nick. The look Cecily gave him would have sizzled bacon.

The only nerve-wracking moment came when Cleareye Clikes, true to form, sailed over the parapet and got caught in the branches of the beech tree. Tilly, initially entranced at having so successfully staged this act of Clikes' derring-do, then became distraught at the possibility that her alter ego might be forever stuck up a tree, and started to scream. Luckily Nick managed to shake the offending branch with a window pole, and Tilly and Cleareye were reunited to everyone's considerable relief.

They had a picnic tea on the terrace, and Kate felt that her bold move towards independence and a new life might yet be given the seal of family approval. However, they would obviously need time to adjust. Looking at the three downstairs bedrooms, Harriet had asked who else was living there.

"Oh, Jack Morley has been camping out here himself. Perhaps he's left some of his things." Kate hoped she sounded unruffled and off-hand, but had the impression of a pack of hounds—suddenly alerted by a whiff on the breeze—simultaneously scenting a fox, which must, at all costs, be hunted down.

Joanna thought that with three spare bedrooms, Kate would at least still be able to do some Granny duty when required, even if it was less convenient than having her right next door.

Cecily wondered if it might be nice to install herself—and her binoculars—in the tower bedroom, and move with Kate. She wasn't sure how easily she and Joanna would share Longthorpe. As she had always relished power struggles before, she wondered if this could possibly be an unwelcome sign of old age—more worthy of Babs Mallory than herself, perhaps?

Harriet thought that if she could only live with Kate in this fairy-tale little house, then she might be really happy.

After Joanna had driven off with the oldest and youngest family members, Nick and Robin, holding hands, pottered off with Acer for a walk. Harriet followed Kate back through the house on to the terrace. Kate went round checking that all the windows were shut, and that nothing had been left unlocked, and then went and flopped down beside Harriet, who was sitting on the grass, in characteristic position with her elbows on her knees and her chin in her hands. Looking up at the tower, she said to Kate with great urgency: "Granny, I love this place—it's brilliant. Please, please let me come and live with you here. I could be company for you." And she added forlornly, "You might even be glad to have me."

Kate looked at the white face of this specially loved granddaughter, and suddenly saw her as half woman, half child, precariously balanced between past and future, both of which were full of uncertainties. She felt a terrible anguish for her.

"Oh, Hattie," she said, "as far as I'm concerned, you can always come and *stay* with me—whenever you like, for as long as you like. You are as dear to me as anyone in the world, and one of the things I told Jack Morley when he asked me how many bedrooms I required was that I would want a room where you could always come. But I can't take you away from your mother on a permanent basis. We've been over this before. You know I can't."

Harriet chewed a stalk of grass. "Mum told me today that my father doesn't even know about me."

"Yes, she told me that too." Kate felt terribly afraid of saying the wrong thing. "It's the first time she's ever said as much. Does that make things better or worse for you?"

"I don't know. I feel so angry, Gran. Have you ever felt unwanted?"

"Unvalued, perhaps, yes," said Kate slowly. "Oh goodness me, yes. But I'm not sure if that's exactly the same."

"By . . . by Grandpa, you mean?"

"Well, yes—not always, but perhaps often enough to understand a little of what you feel."

"I was scared stiff of him. I hated him. Did you know that? I once heard him refer to me as 'Jo's inconvenient little bastard'—and I knew he meant me to hear. Mum's hero worship of him has always been a real turn-off. I was glad when he died. Really glad," she said fiercely. "I've never told anyone before, and I suppose I specially shouldn't tell you, because I still feel dreadfully sinful about it."

"We can't help what we feel. We can help what we *do* about it, but everyone has feelings they'd rather not own to. It's all right to tell me anything, darling. Better out than in."

"Do you miss him, Gran?"

Kate sighed. "In some ways I do—it's difficult being on my own, after years of being part of a pair and knowing exactly what my role was. All the motivation for everything I do now has to come from myself, and I find that hard. That's why this new venture is so important to me. I need to find out what I'm capable of doing myself—but if I'm truthful I wish I missed him, as a person, more.''

"It's not a good feeling, is it—being unwanted or un-valued?'' said Harriet sadly.

"No, darling—but nor is it entirely true for either of us either,'' said Kate firmly. "We've both been very much loved and valued by lots of people. Don't forget that. Some people have never had half as much love as we've both known. Try not to blow it up out of all proportion. Don't dramatise. And Mum does love you—I promise.''

Acer, bounding back, covered Ophelia-like in duckweed, heralded the return of Robin and Nick, which effectively put a stop to the conversation. Kate was relieved. She thought the ice on which she and Harriet had ventured was very thin indeed, and the water below dangerously deep.

"Sorry, Kate—we sort of came across this pond,'' said Robin as Acer shook all over Kate and Harriet, generously trying to share her trappings of green slime by twining her-self round their legs.

Robin and Nick had been asked out to dinner with some friends that evening. Before they went Nick had said to his mother: "It's all very exciting, Mum—specially the Midas bit, and I do think you're right to try and move away from here, but I also think you want to be a bit careful of rushing into temporary rent-free arrangements with someone you don't know much about, though I can see it's an ideal house for you. You will get proper advice about your rights and things, won't you? Have a word with Graham Cooper at Cooper and Wilkinson perhaps?''

"I will be caution personified, darling,'' said Kate, who had no intention of being any such thing.

Nick thought to himself that he might do a bit of sleuth-ing about Jack Morley on the quiet. (He would have been interested to know that Gerald Brownlow had exactly the same idea, though with a less worthy motive.)

Kate waved Nick and Robin off, promising not to wait up for them. She couldn't be bothered to cook herself supper so she ate a bowl of muesli and then settled down to some sewing, fingers flying, ideas yeasting away in her head, and a CD of *Così Fan Tutte* filling the room with just the right background music to inspire clothes of elegant frivolity. She had meant to have an early night but lost all sense of time, and it was after eleven when she packed her work away. She had just got into bed when the telephone rang. It was Jack. She was extremely thankful she was alone, and inordinately pleased to hear him.

"What time is it with you?" she asked, after they had been chatting away for some time.

"Oh, nearly seven but it must be getting late for you—midnight. I ought to let you go."

"Oh Jack, don't ring off yet—unless you're terribly busy, that is. Also this call must be far too expensive."

"Couldn't be when you're on the line," said Jack. "Telephone bills are the least of my worries. I'm not nearly ready to say goodnight yet. Are you?"

"No," said Kate, and thought how wonderful it was to talk to someone with whom it was so easy to communicate that she felt as if they shared their thoughts before they had even put them into words—and then proceeded to put them into words for another half-hour.

When they finally said goodnight, she lay back on the pillows without attempting to turn her light out or go to sleep for some time—and her thoughts were miles away from Longthorpe.

ᕯ TWENTY ᕯ

Kate was not the only member of the Rendlesham family to be taking on a local workforce. Joanna had organised a team of helpers to launch her new party catering venture by doing the cooking for Lady Rosamund's psychic lunch party.

"Not too big to start with, not too small, but *medium*," as Harriet and Polly pointed out, killing themselves with giggles at their witticism.

"Why not call yourself 'Out of This World Catering'?" Harriet suggested. She and Polly were furious that they couldn't attend, and thought it very unsporting of Polly's grandmother not to have fixed the event during the holidays. Polly had come over to Longthorpe for Sunday lunch and the two girls egged each other on, suggesting menus for this interesting occult occasion.

"You ought to give them devilled kidneys and angels on horseback, Mum, then you wouldn't risk offending either the powers of darkness or the powers of light," said Harriet.

"How about monkfish followed by brimstone and treacle pudding?" asked Polly. "Granny Roz once got involved with a sinister sect and we had this fake monk living with us at Duntan for weeks. Dad went bananas—he's terrified she's getting involved with the same sort of thing again. What are you giving them to drink—spirits?"

They got sillier and sillier.

Joanna felt the catering business would greatly enhance her cookery writing, and her magazine editor agreed. She was busy experimenting with lavender as a culinary flavouring, and was not amused when she heard Harriet telling Polly that she'd collected all the old lavender bags from

Kate's linen cupboard and dropped them into the *crème brûlée*.

"God, your mother really is sad—she can't take a joke at all, can she?" Polly rolled her eyes sympathetically.

"That's because she's stressing. You don't understand—she really can't help it." Harriet was defensive and sounded sharp. It was one thing to slag off Joanna herself, but she found she didn't like Polly doing it.

"OK, sorry—just chill." Polly, an uncomplicated character, sometimes found her friend's lightning mood swings baffling. "Perhaps we'd better watch our step a bit anyway—we mustn't risk Melissa's party."

Both girls had been left in no doubt that their attendance at Melissa's party would hang in the balance up to the last moment. It was crucial to their plans that they should go to it—absolutely crucial. Sonia had privately impressed on Polly that if it hadn't been for anxieties about Harriet's health, they would not have got off nearly so lightly over the drinking and smoking. Polly couldn't see why they should all be so fussed about Harriet, who seemed perfectly all right to her, but she had reluctantly promised Sonia not to discuss it.

The two girls went riding after lunch, Polly on Harriet's pony, Star, and Harriet on Joanna's eighteen-hand hunter, Flame, whose temperament was remarkably similar to that of his owner. Then they went up to have tea with Cecily, tea being her speciality as a meal. She thought Harriet needed fattening up.

"Oh, Granny-Cis—proper thin bread-and-butter. How scrum." After tea they settled down to play Scrabble and fill Cecily in with all the Essendale Hall gossip, though they avoided any mention of vodka.

"And how is that twittering Miss Noakes who teaches you mathematics? I sometimes see her in Winterbridge. Can't even make up her mind what cereal to buy."

"Wonderful—she gets so livid she's started foaming at the mouth. Sister says if we get her too worked up she'll have to leave, so we're desperately trying to stress her into an epi.''

"Silly creature. I wouldn't let any of you stress me into anything,'' said Cecily scornfully. "And are you still sleeping in the same nice bedroom as last term?''

"No,'' said Harriet, "but we're still together, which is great, and we're in an incredibly cool dormitory.''

"Really? How disgraceful. They should turn the heating on again, even if it is summer. I shall knit you one of my bed-jackets.'' Cecily had a poor opinion of the ability of anyone other than herself to look after her family. Her bed-jackets were famous. She made them on huge pointed wooden needles, always to the same rather curious design in which two ribbed cuffs were joined together by a vast woollen hammock.

"Oh Granny-Cis, I do love you,'' said Harriet. "Cool doesn't mean what it used to in the old days.''

On Wednesday morning Joanna left early for the Dial House with her team of helpers. Those attending had been bidden to arrive for coffee at eleven and had been sent a proposed timetable. During the morning there was to be an opening talk, followed by some sort of demonstration. After lunch there might be workshops and, time permitting, individual readings for those who wished. Connie Tratton, the internationally acclaimed trance-channeller, would also give readings the following day by appointment only.

Kate, together with Robin, who had stayed on after the weekend unable to resist the lure of the world-famous psychic, drove Cecily over to Rosamund's house. There was the usual ritual suggestion that Cecily should drive them— an idea which they all three knew was a non-starter, but which Cecily liked to pretend she had been expecting to do: "Oh well, if you'd rather do the driving today, then we'll go in Kate's car this time.''

Cecily had recently received a summons for reckless driving in Winterbridge. "Perfectly ridiculous,'' she had told the embarrassed local policeman who had come to question her about the alleged offence, "you can't get up enough speed in Winterbridge to *be* reckless. I never heard such rubbish."

Cecily was said to have backed out of the square in the centre of town, causing two pedestrians to leap for their lives, and taking with her most of the wing of the car parked on the far side of her. She had been blissfully unaware of both these little happenings and had driven off without stopping.

"What absolute nonsense, officer. I would have noticed."

"I am afraid I shall have to ask to look at your car all the same, madam."

Unfortunately the scratches and dents were said to match those on the other car. Cecily was scornful: "Well, but my whole car is covered in scratches. You only have to look on the other side of it to see that." This was certainly true. Cecily grazed some portion of her car every time she drove in or out of the garage, and had recently had a little contretemps in a narrow lane with another old lady—whom she described condescendingly as "a poor old trout."

"We just met in the middle of the road. Luckily we both agreed we were neither of us at fault in any way," she told Kate. "We decided to pay for our own repairs, and not bother anyone else."

"Very wise," Kate had said, breathing sighs of relief that it had not been worse. Two dented bumpers seemed a small price to pay. The Winterbridge occasion, however, had not been so easily dealt with.

"You shouldn't let these petty bureaucrats worry you so much, Kate," Cecily said pityingly when Kate tried to offer sympathy. "I shall deal with them very firmly."

Kate was not looking forward to the court case, but Cecily was sublimely confident.

*   *   *

When they arrived at the Dial House, the first person Kate saw was Netta Fanshaw, and her heart sank.

"Sweetie!" Kate noted her reinstatement to the darling rather than the dear category. "What's all this I've been hearing about you?"

"I don't know," said Kate. "It depends what you've been hearing." Netta hated not to be first with the news, and her dashing VW convertible was a well-known sight as it buzzed round Yorkshire, from house to house, gathering information like pollen.

"That you're thinking of living in that ramshackle little house on the Ravelstoke estate that belongs to your American friend."

"What a lot of busy bees have been around."

"Then it's true?" Netta stretched her eyes, rather a difficult proceeding, given the iron-railing spikes of her eyelashes. "I couldn't believe it, at first, but as I said to Gerald Brownlow, perhaps living at Longthorpe is just too painful for her without darling Oliver?"

Ho ho, thought Kate, you're trying to find out all sorts of other things too, aren't you, Mrs. Nosy Netta Fanshaw.

She decided that feeding Netta some carefully chosen truth might be good policy.

"Jo's going to have Longthorpe—which I'm sure would have pleased Oliver—and it's far too big for me alone. The kitchen will be just right for her. You do so much entertaining, Netta—I do hope you'll support her catering venture. I'm going to live in the Observatory because I'm also going into partnership with Jane Pulborough, and we're converting the stables there for our workshops." Kate hoped she sounded casual but matter-of-fact.

"And is your rich new friend going to live in the Hall at Ravelstoke?"

"I believe my rich old friend is forming a charitable trust to turn the Hall into a holiday home for invalids. In fact," said Kate, much enjoying herself, "I had a business lunch with him in London last week to discuss the alterations to the Observatory and he mentioned that he wanted to persuade some influential local people to be on its governing body. I believe your name came up. I said you'd be ideal,'' and she smiled sweetly at Netta.

"I don't think you told me how you met Franklin Morley in the first place?"

"I don't believe I did. Now I think I ought to go and say hello to Roz."

It occurred to Kate, that without realising it, she had become a great deal more self-confident in the last year: partly due to enforced independence no doubt, but perhaps also something to do with no longer minding so intensely what other people's opinions were.

Rosamund, a vision in a simple black linen shift which had cost a fortune, a purple chiffon scarf knotted cleverly about her throat, was receiving her guests in the hall, while Joanna's minions scurried about handing round home-made biscuits and a choice of coffee or camomile tea. Joanna had been very put out that Gloria Barlow had declined to help on the grounds that she now had a full-time job with Kate.

Rosamund proffered a scented cheek to Kate and Cecily.

"Good heavens, Roz, you look as if you were going to a memorial service in Westminster Abbey!" said Cecily, confident that her own ancient tweed skirt was far more suitable attire for a grey summer day in the country. An oblong diamond brooch, of tea-tray design, was pinned slightly askew to the Peter Pan collar of what she always called her blouse. Kate had with difficulty persuaded her that the zip-up woolly boots that she never wore in the winter ("might give me chilblains") were not really ideal for this occasion, no matter how unseasonably chilly the weather had become.

"I've talked to Kate about your shroud," Cecily went on, her ringing voice silencing the general hum of social conversation. "But I've told her she must make you pay through the nose for it."

"And will you do it, Kate?" Rosamund was not at all put out by the riveted attention of everyone around them, attention being as essential to her existence as oxygen to lesser mortals.

"It rather depends," said Kate. "I'm pretty hectic at the moment trying to build up a stock of more mundane garments. Rather an awkward question—but how soon will you be wanting it finished?"

Lady Rosamund glimmered at her. "Who can tell? I have no immediate plans. Put me on your waiting list then, darling, but come and discuss the design sometime."

Eventually everyone was shepherded into the drawing room, the centre of which had been cleared, and sofas and chairs were arranged in a circle round the edge of the room to seat about thirty people. Cecily stumped off to sit next to Babs Mallory, who shrank back in her seat as her old friend advanced towards her, looking as alarmed as if a python had come to settle beside her.

Lady Rosamund then made a brief introductory speech about the amazing powers of Connie Tratton: "I first met Connie in New York, but she originally came from New Zealand: Maori blood courses through her veins," she announced, giving the impression that Connie's circulatory system was driven by a super-charged occult pumping station. Her audience nodded sagely, though not many of them actually knew many Maoris. "We are lucky to have Connie with us," continued Rosamund, "because nowadays, of course, she travels round the whole world."

"Bet she goes on a broomstick," muttered Robin to Kate.

"Connie has brought her partner Sylvester with her," their hostess went on. "He's an expert on precious stones and will also tell us all what colours we should wear. I believe he's brought some gems with him, so we may be able to purchase those Sylvester feels will most enhance our lives." She made it sound as if Sylvester would be doing them an enormous favor to flog the odd jewel or two—no doubt at vast expense. "Now you don't want to hear any more from me,"—Rosamund didn't look as if she believed this for a moment—"so I will now ask you to welcome Connie and Sylvester."

There was a tentative sound of clapping, like a light shower of rain: some of the gathering felt doubts akin to the dilemma of attending a concert in church, when the question of whether to applaud or not to applaud can cause such difficulties.

Neither Kate nor Robin had been sure what to expect: Robin imagined a Minnehaha with a face like a walnut, and Kate had guessed at someone aggressively ordinary, like a particularly frumpy stall-holder at a local bring-and-buy.

Nothing had prepared them for the Madame Tsa-tsa like figure who came lumbering into the room. Over her turquoise tracksuit Connie Tratton wore a silver tunic covered with leather thongs from which dangled an awesome array of coloured stones. Had she not been of such gigantic proportions, Kate thought she might not have held up under their weight, but Connie had the physique of a sumo wrestler. A large plastic orchid was pinned in her multi-coloured hair. Sylvester, balding and pigtailed, also weighed down with rocks, leant against the wall and closed his eyes.

Robin gave a muffled snort and Kate didn't dare to catch her eye.

Connie announced that she was going to start by showing them how to sweep auras, inviting them to ask questions while she got to work. She placed an upright chair in the middle of the room and asked for a volunteer to sit on it. Her eye lit on the luckless Babs Mallory. "Go on, Babs—might do your brain good: improve your bidding," Cecily ruthlessly pushed her forward. Babs perched uneasily on the edge of the chair as Connie thudded round her, beating the air and wildly sweeping away the aural waste, or so she informed her fascinated audience.

"My, my! Your energies must have been low. You certainly needed that!" she said, with one final cleansing whoosh, and Babs crept back to her seat, looking as shame-faced as the lady with the dingy whites in a detergent advertisement. Kate thought she was going to die from suppressed laughter. Robin stuffed her handkerchief into her mouth.

Connie then announced that you didn't actually need a physical presence at all: you could just conjure up the astral body of anyone you wanted to help, pop them in a chair, and start sweeping. She said she was working on Nelson Mandela—she often did. "His psychic kidneys must have got so terribly blocked by all those years in prison." She jumped around the now apparently empty chair whacking poor Mr. Mandela's aura like an old carpet. Kate thought his psychic kidneys must have been badly bruised by the time Connie had finished with him.

"Any questions?"

Sonia Duntan, her voice quivering with giggle, said she didn't much like the idea that anyone could just bung her astral body in a chair and muck about with her aura without a by-your-leave, but Connie was well able to deal with that.

"It couldn't happen unless you consented spiritually," she said reprovingly. No one felt up to asking how one was to know. Kate thought it might be deeply satisfying to knock hell out of Netta's aura in the privacy of one's own home, whether she consented or not, but couldn't help wondering if she was now unwittingly sitting on Nelson Mandela's psychic knee.

"Now we're going to concentrate on a particularly effective form of absent healing." Connie made it sound thrilling. "An important tool in your psychic armoury is your own little vacuum cleaner," she said impressively. She often went round New York with hers, slurping up the negative grey vibes.

"You want to switch on your cleaners?" she asked. There was a cautious murmur of assent. "Right then: hook yourself up to God through the top of your head." Lady Rosamund was the only one to wear the look of someone who would have no trouble with this simple instruction. "Put down roots in the soil to earth yourselves, surround yourself with light as protective clothing and just say: 'Hook up. Ground. Protect.' Then you're all charged up, and away you go. Easy. All-righty, everyone?"

Old Mrs. Northwood, who had been busily tucking into a plate of Joanna's biscuits which she'd managed to smuggle in to the drawing room, objected that she didn't feel as if she had a little psychic vacuum. "Useful for the crumbs if she did," moaned Robin. "Look at the floor round her chair."

Nothing seemed to daunt Connie: "We can't all have the same psychic gadgets. We'll try another visualisation: imagine your friends as refrigerators. Open their doors, defrost them and give them a good clean out. Take out their tubes, get right in there, and *scrub, scrub, scrub*." Connie made it sound a real rubber-gloves job. Kate glanced across to see how her mother-in-law was taking these novel ideas, but Cecily, back ramrod straight, was asleep.

Babs Mallory, emboldened no doubt by her now spankingly clean aura, anxiously asked: "But what about *the Church?*"

Connie said that was fine. Great. She supported Jesus too. She made it sound like a football club.

Sylvester then gave them a talk on energy levels and the help that could be obtained from crystals. Judging by his yawns and monotonously droning voice it looked as if he'd forgotten to charge himself up; perhaps he'd lost the hook on top of his head along with his hair. It was important, he said, always to wear or carry the right gem for you—though the array of multi-coloured stones round his neck seemed to indicate that he hedged his own bets. When he was driving, he said, he always carried an amethyst in his pocket in case he got stuck in a traffic jam. Kate wondered if the AA knew about this tip.

After such an instructive morning everyone was more than ready for lunch, especially Mrs. Northwood.

Joanna's food was perfection. She had produced cold *Boeuf à la mode*, the jelly set to exactly the right consistency of wobbly delicacy and the meat so tender it melted in the mouth, salmon mousse, a delicious vegetarian lasagna and plenty of colourful salads, all of which were easy to eat with a fork, so nobody was left trying to fight with a recalcitrant lettuce leaf which dripped French dressing down their front.

Beryl Northwood, not one to hang back when important things were at risk, made straight for the pudding table: better go back for the beef later and make sure of two helpings of chocolate roulade.

Kate went through to the kitchen to congratulate Joanna, and was surprised to find her standing in the kitchen, a glass of wine in her hand, doing nothing. She would have expected her daughter to be in the front line of the action, relishing every moment of the bustle and challenge of the occasion, and basking in all the compliments that were coming her way.

"Brilliant food, darling. I am proud of you," Kate said, and then: "Jo? Are you all right?" She thought Joanna looked as taut as an overstretched guy rope.

"My head's splitting—got any paracetamol?"

Kate fished in her bag, and produced some. "Would you like me to run you home?" she asked. "Surely you've done your bit now. Couldn't you let everyone else clear up?"

But Joanna wouldn't hear of it. "Don't fuss, Mum. I'll be fine." When Kate reluctantly left her, Joanna, who never took pills, swallowed the paracetamol, recklessly swilling them down with gulps of wine. She couldn't tell her mother how frightened she felt. She who had always been such a brilliant organiser, who prided herself on her orderliness and energy, who had always believed in making lists of things which needed to be done, and then enjoyed the almost orgasmic pleasure of crossing them off as she whistled through her self-imposed agendas, felt on the brink of a threatening void of complete inaction. Lately the list-

making had been getting more and more compulsive, but
the crossing-off sessions were less satisfactory: she was
finding it increasingly difficult to achieve her own goals.
Joanna fought a terrifying urge to curl up in a foetal position in some dark corner and hide from everyone.

She poured herself another glass of wine, and hoped
none of her helpers would notice that her hands were shaking.

During lunch Sylvester did a brisk trade selling little suede
pouches of mixed gems, and he and Connie booked appointments for personal consultations the following day.
Kate couldn't help an unworthy satisfaction when she heard
him telling Netta she was ill advised to choose the particular shade of coral pink she was wearing. Actually Kate
thought Netta looked wonderful, as usual, but Sylvester
said pink was aurally wrong for her.

The afternoon was to be spent dividing into small groups
to practise psychic diagnosis, but a good many people suddenly remembered pressing engagements and made their
apologies. Kate genuinely felt she must go and see Gloria
and get on with some sewing herself, and Cecily said she'd
had enough. Robin, on the other hand, said wild horses
wouldn't drag her away and she would get a lift back later
with Joanna.

"Joanna seems very tense. Anything special the matter?"
asked Cecily on the way home.

Kate sighed: "Things are not good between her and
Mike."

"Doesn't surprise me. Of course it didn't matter that
Mike wasn't like Oliver while Oliver himself was still
there, but I imagine it matters very much now," said Cecily
shrewdly. "But Jo's never going to find another Oliver—
he was unique."

Looking straight ahead of her, she said, "I know he was
a terrible husband to you, Kate, and I'm sorry. I've never

brought myself to say that to you in all these years, but I've often felt I should. When you reach my age you get an urge to leave your life . . ." uncharacteristically Cecily hesitated for the right word: ". . . tidy," she came out with at last. "Oliver was always half devil, half angel. You knew the devil, but for those like Jo and me who only knew the angel, he was irresistible."

"I know," said Kate, much moved. "I've always known—but thank you all the same." She guessed what this speech must have cost the old lady, and though Cecily still seemed astonishingly well and energetic for her years, Kate felt it rang alarm bells for the future.

Cecily gave a sudden snort of laughter. "Must be that silly woman Roz had picked up, with her psychic hoovers! Perhaps I'm doing my spiritual spring-cleaning."

"I thought you were asleep most of the time."

"I may just have nodded off, now and then, but I heard a lot of fiddlesticks whenever I woke up. What about Harriet? I didn't think she looked well on Sunday."

Cecily had always adored her eldest great-grandchild, and there was a special bond between them.

"Crisis time there too, I'm afraid."

"Umm. A time bomb that's been waiting to explode."

"Let's pray the fallout isn't too devastating when it does explode," said Kate soberly.

There was no reply. Cecily had suddenly fallen asleep while she was talking, in the way that only the very young and the very old can achieve. Kate felt choked with love and anxiety. Despite the ups and downs of their relationship she knew she would miss Cecily unbearably when she finally departed.

Robin had come back full of giggles. "You'll never guess what I've got sitting on my shoulders!"

"What?"

"Well," Robin could hardly speak for laughing. "It's my guides. I have an ancient Egyptian called Ramat hovering over my right shoulder and a fairy called Molly on my left shoulder. They're my masculine and feminine aspects, and I can tune into them for advice at any time. Isn't that cute?''

''Bit of a relief the fairy's feminine, I should think,'' said Kate. ''Perhaps you'd better not tell Nick about Ramat.''

Robin still felt sick most evenings, and she went up to bed early, tired out from so much smothered giggling. Kate tucked her up and then sat on the other spare-room bed and had a lovely chat about the baby, and the ever enthralling topic of prospective names. Robin said she and Nick couldn't agree.

''Well, don't ask me to adjudicate between you.'' Kate got up and kissed her. ''Sleep well then, darling. Hope the guides have a good night too. Let's hope Ramat doesn't snore.''

She let Acer out and locked up, then pottered about half-heartedly tidying the kitchen, undecided whether to finish the back of Jane Pulborough's Midas jacket, with its blazing sun, before going to bed herself. She opted for the jacket, and, as always, got absorbed and went on stitching for longer than she had intended, only stopping when she realised that she was in danger of making mistakes. She was just about to go upstairs when Jack telephoned.

Kate much enjoyed regaling him with an account of Rosamund's lunch. It struck her that even after so short a time, she would be devastated if he was not there to share things with. She was conscious that she had started saving up all the trivial little titbits of her days to tell him, knowing he would be amused by whatever made her laugh—it was wonderful.

Jack told her about all the progress that was being made over setting up the trust for the Ravelstoke Hall Centre. He sounded really pleased with the way things were working out. He also told her that something unavoidable had cropped up which would necessitate him staying on in New York longer than he'd expected.

"I'm so sorry, Kate. I was hoping to be back by the end of the month. I want to be with you again so much—don't give up on me. This is something I really can't help."

After they had rung off, Jack Morley, sitting alone on the other side of the Atlantic, prayed that nothing would come between him and this woman who had become so dear to his heart, because if it did, he knew his life would fall apart.

❧ TWENTY-ONE ❧

Though Kate was disappointed that Jack had postponed his return, she was so busy with plans and work that the days flew by. She thought it would be fun to be installed in the Observatory by the time he returned to England. This had the added advantage of setting herself a target date for leaving Longthorpe. It would have been all too easy to allow time to drift gently on with no particular deadline, and having made the big decision, Kate felt the sooner the change in her life was achieved, the better it would be for all concerned. She never knew when Jack was going to ring her up, but she was conscious of acute disappointment on the days when there was no call.

Work was progressing at a fantastic speed. She supposed this must have much to do with the financial resources behind Jack, but it was also because the work was all being done by the same team, who were concentrating on this particular project. Frank was a brilliant organiser and ally. The infuriating delays usually experienced in connection with the building trade, when plumbers are held up because the electricians have disappeared, or plasterers can't start until the carpenters have finished—who, in their turn, go off on another job themselves—did not arise.

Kate had promised to take Jack's Aunt Hannah to the Observatory to look at the work in progress, and went to pick her up one afternoon. On the way they stopped to go into the ancient church at Ravelstoke and Hannah Hartley proudly showed her the hassocks she had stitched. It was so peaceful, Kate would have liked to linger there and try to lay some old hurts and resentments, together with some new hopes and resolutions, before her God, but felt the old lady might think her pretentious if she went to kneel in one of the pews. She gave a quick inner wave to God and hoped, if he was surfing for messages, he'd take these ones as read.

As they walked out to Kate's car, Hannah Hartley said: "I often goes and sits in the church. Don't know if the Good Lord sees me, but one can but hope," and Kate felt ashamed of her own inhibitions.

Hannah Hartley was not impressed by the Observatory. She said with a disparaging sniff that Jack seemed to be getting a lot of fancy ideas these days—Kate couldn't help wondering if she was included in this category. However when she took Jack's aunt into the workshop in the stables and showed her some of the designs for Midas that were already stored in the new cupboards, it was another matter, and Hannah allowed herself a little attack of hyperbole. "Aye. Them'll do," she said.

Frank, who happened to be in there, gave Kate a broad wink.

Ellie Hadleigh came up and spent a night at Longthorpe. Kate loved having her, and unlike old Mrs. Hartley, she was enchanted with the Observatory. Though she was full of ideas, she never pushed her own individual taste. Since Jack had given Kate a completely free hand in the matter of choice, there was nothing to hold up decisions. Kate wanted to preserve the feeling of light and simplicity in the charming little house, and Ellie agreed. They decided to have the same carpet throughout the house, except in the tower bedroom, and to go for a soft apricot colour, chosen from the National Trust range, for the walls in the passages and hall. ''And let's keep all the paintwork white,'' said Ellie. ''I know the two wings of the house are separate, but it would be dreadfully easy to make it all itsy-bitsy. Let's go for unity.''

Luckily there was no immediate hurry to take decisions about curtains as all the rooms had shutters on the windows.

Though Ellie was a good bit older than Joanna, Kate was pleased that she and Jo appeared to get on well together and hoped they might stay in touch. Kate had always felt Joanna lacked women friends. Men had always found her attractive, but contemporaries of her own sex tended to regard her as intimidating, and she didn't seem to make easy, gossipy relationships with the mothers of her children's friends. Even at university she had not become close to other young women or formed the kind of friendships that can be so sustaining later on, through all life's ups and downs. Perhaps she had never needed them before, but Kate suspected that Joanna was beginning to pay a penalty for remaining so aloof and self-absorbed, and thought her daughter was desperately in need of a confidante. Joanna liked Sonia Duntan, and Sonia was easy and friendly with everyone, but Kate wasn't sure how much Sonia approved of Joanna. Harriet, with her quick sense of humour, was really much more Sonia's cup of tea as a person than her mother was.

Discussion about anything to do with Duntan being a taboo subject with the Hadleighs, naturally Kate did not raise this topic with Ellie.

''I adore your mother's new house, but you'll have great fun doing a few things to Longthorpe yourself, won't you?'' Ellie said to Joanna. ''Of course it's gorgeous as it is, but I expect you're longing to put your own stamp on the house, tweak it a bit, aren't you?''

Joanna looked horrified. ''Oh, I wouldn't want to change a thing,'' she said. ''My father chose everything in this house, and he and I had identical taste.''

Ellie raised a quizzical eyebrow. "Mustn't stay trapped in the past though," she said lightly. "Got to move on, don't you think?"

Essendale Hall broke up for the summer holidays in the second week of July. Miss Ellis said Harriet and Polly had tried so hard for the last weeks of term that, as long as they could keep it up next term, they might begin to creep back into her good graces. In view of this Sonia and Archie, thinking that rewards, if at all possible, were a better policy than punishments, decided that Polly should be allowed to attend the coveted party in London. Joanna agreed, and the girls gave firm promises about avoiding drink and drugs and generally behaving in the way their parents would wish.

"God! They are out of the ark! Why can't they trust us?" said Polly, tossing back the lock of hair that so fetchingly flopped across her face, but it was a purely routine flounce, because she was deeply relieved to be allowed to go at all.

Sonia—much to Polly's mortification—had spoken to Melissa's parents, who had assured her that they would most definitely be there all the time. "My husband says it's like being in Customs—all our friends tell us you have to frisk the young on arrival otherwise they smuggle in the drink," said Melissa's mother.

Harriet suggested that perhaps she and Polly could stay with Mike at Oxton Road, an idea which seemed to find favour with everyone. Mike was delighted. Ever since his conversation with Kate he had been feeling bad about Harriet, and was glad of the chance to do something for her. He said he would drive the girls to the party and pick them up afterwards. The following morning he would have to go to the office, but everyone agreed that they were quite old enough to lock up the house and then get themselves back to Yorkshire.

On the appointed day, Joanna gave Harriet a set of keys and a great many instructions, and Kate drove her and Polly to York to catch an early train so that they could go shopping in Oxford Street before making their way to Fulham.

They had a brilliant morning trying on clothes and window shopping, and then went to Cascade, where *everyone* else at school had been, except them, and Polly bought a terrible rubber hat like a condom, and Harriet bought a penis pencil to send anonymously to the dreaded Miss Noakes. If that didn't stress her into an epi, nothing would. They both agreed that she'd probably never seen a man's willy, poor thing, and they laughed so much they thought they might be sick. Luckily a Big Mac and some chips soon put that right.

Like her brother, Rupert, Harriet was enraptured to see Mike again. She had also been thrilled to be back in Oxton Road, though unlike Rupert this was partly for an ulterior motive that was unconnected with any real longing for her old home.

She and Polly had taken hours washing their hair and getting dressed before Melissa's party, squeezing themselves into stretch mini skirts that were so brief they were almost invisible. It had to be admitted that this particular fashion was more aesthetically pleasing on Harriet's long, lean legginess than on Polly's shorter, stouter stockiness— on the other hand, Polly's boobs were really quite something, and Harriet's were almost nothing, so they each happily envied the other.

They had a wonderful time at the party, and voted it brilliant—really cool, they told each other. Alexander Rivers had asked for Harriet's telephone number, and his friend Sebastian had asked Polly if her father had a shoot— notching up the first good mark for Archie that his daughter had given him for some weeks. Sadly Sebastian had been terribly sick before the evening was over, which was a bit of a turn-off, though on the whole Polly felt she would be prepared to let bygones by bygones. Before he was afflicted, he had not only looked utterly gorgeous but had given Polly that much coveted badge of bad fifteen-year-old behaviour—a hickey that really showed. Polly told Harriet she thought she would have to cover her neck with a scarf when she went home because her mother could be so unbelievably naive and stupid about that sort of thing. Pathetic, really, said Polly.

After they had gone to bed and enjoyed a highly enjoyably post-mortem on the party, Harriet set her alarm clock for ten o'clock the next morning. She had things to do before returning home, and if she overslept she might not get another chance. Polly still seemed dead to the world when it went off, and though she was in on the plan—indeed it had mostly been her idea—Harriet felt she wanted a little time alone. She padded down to the kitchen to make herself a mug of instant coffee and sat on one of the stools at the breakfast bar. Mike had left everything out for them, and a note to remind them about locking up and also to say how lovely it had been to have them both, was propped against the milk jug. It all seemed very normal. Harriet helped herself to cereal and put a couple of bagels in the oven.

I must get on with it, she thought, but felt deeply reluctant to do so. Perhaps it was as well that the burglar alarm of a car in the street outside the house went off at this moment, and Polly, who had half stirred when Harriet's clock bleeped, was woken up properly. She came down rubbing her eyes and looked blearily at Harriet.

"What time is it?"

"Tennish." Harriet got the bagels out and gave one to Polly.

"Yum, thanks. OK, then—breakfast and then start the search."

"Oh Pol—I'm not sure I can. It feels so shabby."

"Come on! Desperate situations require desperate measures. It's your only hope. Where shall we start?"

"In the drawing room, I suppose. That's where Mum's desk is."

"Right. Let's get cracking."

Everything in Joanna's desk was immaculately tidy, neatly labelled and deadly dull. There were bank statements, files on household things and files for each of the children containing birth certificates, details of inoculations and, in Harriet's and Rupert's case, some early school reports. There were folders labelled with titillating titles like CAR, HOUSEHOLD, and TAX. Harriet and Polly ploughed through Joanna's first cookery articles and endless recipes. Everything was out of date, because Joanna now had all the information she could possibly require on her computer in the cottage at Longthorpe—but then the information they were looking for was about an event that had happened sixteen years before.

They worked their way from drawer to drawer, Harriet getting frantic at the light-hearted and careless way in which Polly tended to ram everything back in envelopes and folders. "Do be careful. Mum's such a perfectionist she'd spot anything out of order in a twink."

There was no file about unknown fathers.

The last long drawer at the bottom of the desk contained nothing but photograph albums. "Hopeless. I've seen all those often," said Harriet, hovering between despair and relief.

"Let's look all the same. 'Attention to detail, girls, that's what passes exams.'" Polly imitated the dreaded Miss Noakes' twittering falsetto. "Oh look—how sweet. Here's you being a bridesmaid to your mum. Goodness, she was stunning, wasn't she? You look in a frightful bolsh."

"I was. Mummy didn't really want me in the photograph—she pretended it was because my hair was such a mess. She's always on about my hair. It was torture when they tugged that grotty wreath off after the wedding because it got snarled up in my curls. Oh Polly, this is just a waste of time.''

Nevertheless the albums exerted all the fascination that old photographs usually do.

''Funny how many pictures there are of your mother with your grandfather—far more than of anyone else,'' said Polly, then: ''Hattie, what is it?'' Harriet was staring at a page of the particular album through which she was half-heartedly skimming. The album, blue leather, like all the others, had ''Oxford'' printed on it. The page that Harriet was looking at was blank, though something had obviously been removed at some time, because under four places where photographs had once been stuck, the indentation made by Joanna's neat writing still remained, and though an attempt had been made to rub it out, it was still possible to make the letters out. ''J. K. R. with M. G. H.'' it read.

''Look some more,'' said Polly urgently.

They flicked through the pages. There were two more pages from which single photographs had been taken out. Each time the initials underneath were the same: M. G. H.

''I bet it was him! And she's gone and destroyed them all.'' Harriet's voice was choked with frustration.

''Hang on! How do you know she destroyed them? Bet she didn't. Think, Harriet. Where would your mother hide something?''

''I've no idea.'' Harriet looked hopeless.

Polly sat back on her heels. Suddenly she said: ''Mum's got a secret drawer in her desk at Duntan. You feel around inside one of the little pigeonholes in the top, and at the back there's a tiny wooden catch. When you release it a whole section with pillars on each side pulls out and there are two secret drawers in the back. She keeps treasures in it—locks of our hair and a little box with baby teeth and funny little things. She's often shown us. I wonder if this desk has a secret place—old ones usually do. Must be worth a try.''

Harriet looked at her in admiration. They felt carefully in all the nooks and crannies of Joanna's desk. It seemed ages, but was really only minutes before they found a secret drawer in Joanna's desk too.

With trembling fingers Harriet felt inside. She drew out an old brown envelope. In it were some photographs.

"I can't look."

"Don't be wet—if you won't I will."

Harriet took one of them out. "Oh my God," she said. "It has to be him! Oh Polly, look!"

The photograph showed a youngish man—though too old to be an average undergraduate—dressed in casual clothes, with a blazer slung over his shoulder; he was leaning against the arched door of what might have been a church or a college building, and unless it was an exceptionally small door, he must have been tall. He had an arresting face, not exactly handsome, but with an alert, amused expression—but what really caught the eye was his hair: a wild, unruly mop of spectacular curls.

The two girls looked at each other in awe. Then Harriet rushed out of the room. After a minute Polly went after her, and located her by the awful retching sound coming from the downstairs loo. Harriet was being violently sick. Polly thought it was extraordinary the way some people reacted like that. It wasn't as if Harriet had had anything to drink, unlike the beautiful Sebastian at the party the night before— he'd certainly had a skinful—or indeed Harriet herself after the session under the rhododendron bush at school. Most odd. Polly would have expected her friend to be thrilled, but when Harriet finally emerged out of the cloakroom she looked so white and shaky that even Polly, like her father capable of great kindness and loyalty but not by nature the most finely tuned or intuitive of people, could see that her friend was shattered.

"D'you want a mug of tea?" Polly asked.

Harriet nodded. She felt clammy and dizzy and thought she might faint, as she had done in church once when she first got the curse. She lay down on the sofa, and her world spun round her head.

Polly came back and thrust a tepid mug into her hands. "You must brace up, Hat. If you're like this when we go home, they'll think we drank too much at Melissa's—and that would be so unfair."

"Sorry. I'll be OK in a minute."

"What are you going to do?"

"Dunno."

"Well, I think you should shove the photos under your ma's nose and demand an explanation. That's what I'd do."

"Yes, but your mother's not like mine. Mum would kill me if she knew about going through her desk—and anyway I feel bad about that. Besides," said Harriet, with total conviction, "she'd be even worse now. She'd die rather than tell me who he is after this—or who he was," she added. "He may be dead."

"Or married," said practical Polly. "I think he looks quite old even then. I bet he was married with ten children. That would explain everything."

In all her imaginings, this most obvious explanation had not occurred to Harriet. A foreigner, of any colour, but especially one of royal blood, was probable; a criminal—possible; a tragic hero dying young of some transmittable disease like Aids—scary but likely; a rapist—on the cards, though personally she thought it would be a brave man who would try to rape her mother—but a boring old family man had not entered her fantasies. She looked at the photograph again. "But he does look nice," she said wistfully, and tears welled up in her eyes.

"Well come on, get a grip," said Polly bracingly. "Are you going to tell your grandmother?"

"I'd like to. I can say anything to her, but Gran's quite . . ." Harriet groped for the right word, ". . . honour-

able. I don't think she'd agree to do anything behind
Mum's back.''

Polly looked sympathetic—must be awful to have so
many hang-ups. Harriet sat up and stuck out her chin: ''I
have to find him for myself—if he's alive. The time for
Mum to find out about all this is after I've traced my father.
Didn't you say your aunt might help?''

''Martha? Yeah, she'd love to. This is right up her
street,'' said Polly confidently. ''She's up at Oxford as I
told you. All she'd got to do is to wave the photograph at
some old fogeys who were there then and someone's sure
to remember him. Don't forget we know his initials; that'll
help. Dad always remember people's initials. Someone
goes 'John Snooks' and Dad'll go 'Ah yes, J. A. K. S.' or
something like that—it's weird. Finding your father'll be a
doddle now.''

Polly was relieved to see that Harriet was beginning to
look more normal. The telephone rang. ''Want me to answer it?'' asked Polly. Harriet nodded, terrified it might be
Joanna having somehow got a telepathic view of her rifled
desk. She was relieved to hear Polly gassing away—chat,
chat, chat, giggle, giggle.

''That was Mum—had to fill her in about the party,''
said Polly. Harriet felt the usual twinge of envy. Polly
might talk about her parents as a couple of old dinosaurs,
but by Harriet's standards she usually seemed on remarkably good terms with them. ''Great news,'' Polly went on.
''Mum was ringing to say you're to come back to us for a
few nights. She's fixed it with your mother, and Dad'll
meet us off the train that gets in about nine, so we've got
lots of time to do things this afternoon. Let's ring Melissa
and meet her for lunch.''

A delightfully therapeutic plan was then concocted, one
that was guaranteed to take the mind off any emotional
drama; it involved meeting Melissa and several other
friends in Peter Jones, and then all going down the King's
Road together to have hoops put in their navels and several

new holes pierced in their ears. The results were really cool—absolutely amazing—but not, they all agreed, as cool or amazing as Harriet's new hairstyle.

Harriet had her head shaved.

❧ TWENTY-TWO ❧

When Archie met the girls off the London train, he did not immediately recognise Polly's companion and thought Polly had an unknown boy with her. It was not until he had kissed his daughter hello and asked: "Where's Harriet got to?" that he realised that Polly's strange-looking friend actually *was* Harriet.

Archie gazed at her in shocked silence. For a good deal of the journey Harriet and Polly had discussed how they were going to play this first moment of greeting, and had decided to play it very cool, and take their cue from whatever reaction they received, prepared either to joke and laugh, or be very nonchalant depending on whether they were greeted with astonishment alone, or surprise coupled with anger—which seemed more likely—but Archie's total lack of recognition was more than Harriet had bargained for. She felt near to tears, and had a sudden desperate longing to cover her head with anything available and then run away as fast as she could and hide.

"Good God," said Archie, finding his voice at last. "Whatever's happened to you, Harriet?"

"Nothing's happened to her," said Polly, hoping she sounded casual, but succeeding in sounding belligerent. "She's simply had her hair cut, that's all."

"*Cut*? That must be the understatement of the year. I thought you must have been in a road accident. Does your mother know?"

"Not yet."

"Rather you than me when she does," said Archie, gazing at her with awed fascination. Appalled though he was at her transformation, Archie couldn't help noticing for the first time what an interesting face Harriet had. He supposed he had never really looked beyond the hair before. In fact it was a longing to be seen for herself alone—at any rate by her mother—that had driven Harriet to take such drastic action.

Joanna's ambivalent attitude to her wild mop had been a bone of contention for as long as Harriet could remember. Kate, who found it incomprehensible that Joanna could be so irritated by the unruliness of her daughter's hair while at the same time adamantly refusing to allow it to be cropped short, had once taken Harriet to her London hairdresser, and been enchanted by the effect his clever scissors had produced, giving the little girl's head the look of a particularly beguiling baby bacchante in some Renaissance painting. Jo had been more than furious: she had been extremely upset. It seemed as if Harriet's hair exerted a compulsive fascination over her mother. Whether love or hate had been Joanna's predominant emotion Harriet had no idea, but for the first time she felt she had a clue to this anomaly.

It would not have occurred to Harriet to have her scalp shaved had not the King's Road hairdresser, who also specialised in punching holes in some surprising parts of people's anatomy, suggested it. Harriet had immediately been hit by the idea—like a blinding flash worthy of the Damascus Road, as she told Polly afterwards—that if Joanna could only see her without being forced to look at a replica of her missing father's hair, then perhaps the relationship between mother and daughter might start to improve.

"I thought Mum might start to notice the person I am inside, instead of automatically being driven crazy by the sight of me. We might be able to communicate without screaming at each other," she said, twisting her long fingers together while she gazed unseeingly out of the train win-

dow as the flat Midlands flew past. "We may even be able
to explain how we *feel* now. She might even tell me
things."

Polly had looked dubious, but for once hadn't liked to
argue. That Joanna was going to notice the outside of Harriet, was absolutely certain; it was the rest of the scenario
that gave Polly doubts. She was beginning to feel thoroughly out of her depth with Harriet's complicated emotions, and was afraid that if she said the wrong thing, it
might prove too much for her friend's unreliable stomach.
It would be too rank if Hattie was sick on the train all the
way back to Yorkshire. Though she would have died rather
than admit it, Polly could hardly wait to share the responsibility for the newly shorn Harriet with her own parents.
They might be boring in the extreme at times, but Sonia
and Archie had their uses. It was a pity Polly had sworn a
solemn oath not to tell them about the photograph because
she couldn't help feeling that her mother, rather than Martha Campion, might be more use now that the situation was
getting so heavy. Polly rather wished she hadn't thought of
enlisting Martha's help.

When they got home, Archie drove round to the back
of the wing of the house in which the family lived, now
that the house was open to the public all summer.

"Hop out, you two," he said. "I just want to go and
check on the horses."

Polly hopped, seizing the duffle bag in which her party
clothes were now screwed into a ball, and charged into the
house, yelling, "Hi, everyone—we're ba-ack!" but Harriet
remained rooted to her seat.

"Come on, Harriet—out you get."

"I can't," she whispered. "I can't face anyone. They'll
all laugh."

"I'm afraid you're going to have to face everyone
sooner or later." Against his instincts for order and disci-
pline, something about Harriet wrenched Archie's heart.
"I'll tell you something," he said. "I don't approve of

what you've done, I think it was bloody silly, and pretty unkind to your mother—but it must have taken guts and I always admire that. What's more, you don't look half bad. Now you've got to hold your head up and be brave. Do you want me to come in with you?''

''W-would you?''

''Well, I would—but I think you'd respect yourself more if you could do it on your own.''

''All right,'' said Harriet in a very shaky voice, and climbed out of the car as though she had indeed been in a road accident and was suffering from multiple bruises.

''Good girl, well done,'' said Archie approvingly. He adored his own three daughters, and he had a lump in his throat as he watched Harriet's slender figure, with its strangely altered silhouette, walk towards the house, slowly, but with shaven head held high. With or without hair, Archie thought, Harriet Rendlesham would break hearts one day.

In fact it had been easier than Harriet feared. Garrulous Polly had already poured out a dramatic warning by the time Harriet walked into the kitchen, which was the hub of family life at Duntan. Sonia held out her arms, and Harriet flew into them and clung to her. Sonia had just had time to tell Tom, Birdie and Cassie, her three younger children, that any mockery would invoke her most terrible wrath, though naturally they all three gazed at Harriet in wonder.

''God, that's cool,'' said Tom admiringly. ''Might try it myself,'' and he threw his mother a provocative look which she wisely ignored.

''I think you look really beautiful, Harriet,'' lied tender-hearted Birdie, her eyes brimming with tears—she could never bear to see anyone looking unhappy. Polly gave her sister a withering look. The soppiness of Birdie drove her mad.

''I expect people will just think you've had nits,'' said Cassie judicially. ''They'd be awfully hard to get rid of in hair like yours. A girl at school had them and she was simply crawling with lice. We all caught them. Why did you have it done?''

It was typical of Cassie to ask the question everyone else was longing to ask. Like her grandmother Rosamund, Cassie had been born without inhibitions.

Harriet and Polly exchanged veiled glances, and Harriet gave their prearranged reply: ''For a dare.'' Cassie's eyes sparkled: that was something she understood immediately.

But the look that had shot between the two older girls did not go unnoticed by Sonia.

Altogether Harriet felt cheered by the happy-go-lucky atmosphere that prevailed at Duntan, and everything started to seem more like a joke, though she jumped every time the telephone rang. There was much speculation about what Joanna's reaction would be.

Everyone agreed that Joanna must be warned before seeing Harriet. It was a question of who was going to tell her. Harriet shot Archie a nervous look, wondering if his military principles might require this of her too, but in the end it was decided that Sonia should ring up and break the news to both Kate and Joanna. After that Harriet must take whatever was coming.

''Oh Sonia, I'll be grateful to you till I die,'' said Harriet dramatically. ''I'll do anything for you.''

''Just not doing this again will be quite enough, thank you,'' said Sonia dryly.

Later that night, when she and Archie were discussing it in bed, she said: ''There's more to this business of Harriet's hair than meets the eye. Polly's bulgingly pregnant with information she obviously feels she can't tell me. I smell trouble.''

''Trouble between Mike and Jo, too,'' said Archie. ''Did you notice how Jo set her cap at Hugo Coltman at the Van Alleyns' dinner party the other night?''

"I thought it was the other way round—but anyway, potential dynamite. I've never thought of it before, but you know, Hugo looks a bit like Oliver Rendlesham. Oh darling—we had a lucky escape, didn't we?" Sonia put her hand out to Archie, her fingers asking questions up and down his arm.

"Umm—certainly did," and Archie turned his attention enthusiastically to stoking the fires of his own once neglected marriage.

Sonia had told Kate first. "Oh Sonia, how truly dreadful. Thank God Hattie's with you. Jo will kill her."

"That's what I'm afraid of too. Harriet's awfully unhappy, Kate."

"I know, I know. The trouble is, anything I say in her defence always makes Jo worse. How *stupid* of Harriet—how could she be so silly?" Sonia thought Kate sounded really rattled. "But I don't see why you should have to do our dirty work, Sonia. Would you like me to ring Jo, drive over and collect Hattie and take her home?"

"No, no. Polly would be heartbroken. They've planned all sorts of lovely pony things to do together, and we all adore having Hattie. I think the longer she and her mum are apart the better. I'll ring Jo—just wondered if there was any particular line you thought I ought to take?"

Kate groaned. "If I knew the answer to that, family life would be much easier for us all. It's all to do with Hattie wanting to know who her father is—as well as teenage hormones, I suppose. Perhaps I ought to give up the Midas idea and concentrate on being a better granny."

"No," said Sonia firmly. "No, Kate, absolutely not. You've always been a wonderful grandmother, especially to Harriet—and it wouldn't help anyway. Joanna and Harriet have to sort this out together. Promise me you won't go and immolate yourself on the pyre of their mutual pigheadedness? Sorry, Kate—perhaps I shouldn't have said that. I love Harriet and actually I'm fond of Jo too, though

I sometimes long to shake her. I mightn't ever have got to know her so well if the girls weren't such pals—but you form bonds with your children's friends.''

"Well, I won't do anything drastic at the moment," said Kate doubtfully. "You really are kind, Sonia, and thank you for saying that about Jo. You and Archie have been so kind to her this last year—please don't abandon her. Oddly enough I think she needs friends even more than Harriet. She hasn't got that many."

"Don't worry. I won't. I won't let on that I've told you already, but wish me luck—I'm going to ring her now."

All the same Sonia thought of several vital things she ought to do, like giving the dogs a run, and making a shopping list for the next trip to the supermarket, before she could bring herself to dial Joanna's number. It was engaged. Sonia couldn't know that it was Hugo Coltman, whose wife happened to be away taking their two small children to Filey for a week of bracing north-easterly ozone, who was on the line inviting Joanna out to dinner. Hugo, a barrister who had political ambitions, was nursing a constituency in North Yorkshire.

Hugo's call was just what Joanna felt she needed. He had cleverly issued the invitation on the pretext of consulting Joanna about a party for his wife's thirty-fifth birthday, an event not due for several months, and not one which it had previously occurred to him required celebrating in particularly lavish style. The party must be a surprise, he now said smoothly, so naturally this new idea would have to be kept secret from Penny. Naturally, agreed Joanna; of course she wouldn't breathe a word to Penny and it would certainly be easier to plan the occasion if they met. She and Hugo were pleasurably aware that they understood each other very well. Mike needs a sharp lesson to bring him to his senses, thought Joanna, serve him jolly well right. Hugo, who was well used to serving his limply adoring wife jolly well wrong, but was far too ambitious to want a serious marital upheaval (Penny's father had powerful connections), thought a satisfactory little interlude might be enjoyed by Joanna and himself without too many complications.

When Sonia eventually got through to Joanna's number, the answering machine was on. She didn't know whether to be sorry or relieved, but eventually left a message explaining the situation as best she could. She emphasised that all the girls had been very silly, had egged each other on and fallen under the spell of a persuasive salesman. Polly herself had several new holes in her ears and Sonia gathered that Melissa had a stud in her nose about which her mother was far from pleased, so it wasn't only Harriet who had got carried away. "Just wanted to forestall you having a shock when you pick Hattie up after the weekend. I think she's already devastated at what she's done, and naturally she's very worried about your reaction, but I've said I'm sure you'll be very understanding," said Sonia, with more hope than conviction. "Do ring me when you get in."

It was unfortunate that when Joanna got the message, she had just got back from an abortive attempt to persuade Kate to take on full Granny duty for a fortnight in August, so that Joanna could accept an invitation to be the guest cook at a series of gastronomic demonstrations organised by a famous country house hotel in Scotland. She had thought she might have to lean on her mother a bit, but had been unprepared for an absolute refusal.

"How can I, darling? I'm hoping to start moving next week, and I'm snowed under trying to get all the Midas things Jane and I have planned ready for a launch of the new line at the beginning of October. I'm really sorry."

"But that means I'll have to say no. Jenny's booked her holiday then, and it's an important opportunity for me."

"Midas is an important opportunity for me too," said Kate quietly, strengthened by her new-found sense of commitment, but racked by guilt all the same, as she saw the hurt and disappointment in Joanna's face.

Joanna went up to visit her grandmother, expecting sympathy and a fortifying discussion about the unhelpfulness of Kate, against whom they had often ganged up together in the past.

An appalling noise was issuing from Cecily's flat, as though several starving dinosaurs were pulverising bones. The whole house shook.

Joanna knew immediately what the cause must be: Cecily, notoriously resistant to most modern gadgets, had taken an unaccountable fancy to the waste-disposal machine. She had not, unfortunately, taken a simultaneous interest in the manufacturer's instructions, and regularly supplied the unit with a diet of Georgian silver. After these alarmingly noisy episodes, she would then ring the plumber to come and salvage the mangled remains of her spoons and forks. She had amassed an interesting collection that might one day puzzle an expert. Unfortunately they had also made the machine less effective in carrying out its normal duties—usually necessitating yet another visit from the plumber to unblock the drain. Cecily kept the twisted souvenirs in a drawer in the sideboard, and insisted on Mrs. Stokes cleaning them when she came in to do the rest of the silver.

"Oh Granny-Cis! Not more spoons gone!" Jo had to raise her voice above the frightful churning noise.

"Hello, darling. Yes, this naughty gobbler will devour my nice King's pattern teaspoons," said Cecily fondly, in the voice a proud mother might use about a beguiling but wilful child. She switched off the offending machine. "Such a pity—I've only got four left now. Nice to see you."

To her surprise, however, Joanna had not found Cecily sympathetic. "You're really getting boring, Jo," the old lady said sharply. "Time you got over your father's death and came into the real world. Time you stood on your own feet and stopped depending on your mother. I think Kate's being splendid.'' Altogether it had been a disconcerting visit. Boring! Cecily had unerringly picked an adjective guaranteed to rile Joanna, and the idea that she, clever, independent go-ahead Joanna, should be considered dependent on her mother was very unwelcome. She reminded herself that her grandmother could be a naughty old troublemaker, capable of setting the family against each other, but the words stung all the same.

It was not, therefore, in a conciliatory frame of mind that she went back to the cottage to finish her weekly cookery article—''How to Liven up Leftovers and give them a Zing.'' On the rough draft which lay on the sofa, Harriet had scribbled ''Add arsenic?''

Joanna listened to Sonia's message in disbelief. Then she got into her car and headed straight for Duntan.

❧ TWENTY-THREE ❧

When Joanna swept, unannounced, into the kitchen at Duntan, Sonia was about to go and shut herself in her studio to paint, and Archie was just about to take the children for a long ride. They had packed up saddle-bags with sandwiches and were going over the moor. They had all been praying for a fine day, and it looked perfect.

At the sight of her mother, Harriet froze. Her knees felt like castanets and she thought her wildly thumping heart might break her ribcage, but unfortunately her set expression gave her a look of defiant mutiny. Joanna went white with shock at the sight of her and for a moment mother and daughter stared at each other, while everyone else held their breath. Then Joanna dealt her daughter a swinging slap across the cheek.

''For God's sake, Joanna!'' Archie was rigid with disapproval: ''There's no call for that.''

A red mark stood out on Harriet's face. She bit her bottom lip so hard to stop her lips trembling and a cry coming out that she drew blood, and her eyes were full of tears. But now the look of mutiny was real. Joanna collapsed on to a chair at the kitchen table, and buried her head in her arms. Tom felt extremely embarrassed, Cassie looked thrilled, Birdie burst into tears and Polly, her resemblance to her father very marked, went and stood defensively close to Harriet, as though to ward off any further blows.

"Take them all out, darling," said Sonia urgently to Archie. "Go and have your ride and don't hurry back. Have a lovely time."

After they had gone, the children having made a sudden stampede for the door like a herd of frightened buffaloes, there was complete silence in the Duntan kitchen. Then: "Oh Jo," said Sonia, "whatever did you have to do that for?" She went and put her hands on Joanna's shoulders, and suddenly the floodgates of Joanna's pent-up tension burst, and she sobbed, great heaving bouts of unaccustomed crying shaking her thin frame. Sonia went to put the kettle on.

"Come on, Jo—tea or coff?"

"I couldn't have something stronger, could I? A swig of brandy might help—purely medicinal."

"Jo!" Sonia looked horrified. "It's only eleven o'clock. Have you taken to the bottle?"

"Nothing I can't handle. Life's a bit on top of me at the moment and a nip might steady me." Sonia went into the dining room next door, and came back with a tiny liqueur glass of brandy, and then made a pot of coffee. Joanna tipped the brandy straight down her throat.

"What am I going to do about Harriet?"

"How about starting with an apology?" suggested Sonia.

"You mean *me* apologise to *her*?"

"That's exactly what I mean."

Joanna looked thunderstruck: "After what she's done? She deserves to be punished. Don't tell me you wouldn't mind if Polly had all her hair shaved off."

"Yes of course I'd mind. I'd be very upset." Sonia struggled to be fair. "But I hope I'd wonder why she'd done it. And I absolutely don't think you should have hit Hattie, Jo. She's nearly sixteen—it was her hair, and she's going to suffer. She was wretched last night. This is a cry for help."

Joanna said hopelessly: "I've never been able to cope with her. She's always been impossible with me. If I say I'm sorry she'll feel she's won."

"Won what? And would that matter? She might feel you were trying to make an effort to understand her. How can you expect her to say she's sorry to you if you never say it to her?"

"Do you apologise to your children?"

Sonia laughed. "Frequently, I'm afraid. I get so ratty when they come and interrupt my painting."

"Oh Sonia," whispered Joanna, "tell me what to do. I'm so unhappy. I think our marriage is on the rocks too."

"Save it."

"Can I ask you something?"

Sonia pulled a face, guessing what was coming. "I suppose so," she said reluctantly.

"You've never told me about it, but I know you and Archie nearly came unstuck. Have you any regrets about staying together?"

Sonia took a long time to answer. "No," she said at last. "I still have anguish for the loss of something wonderful that lasted a very short time, but regrets at how we dealt with it—no, none." She added painfully: "But it's taken me time to be able to say that truthfully."

"And Archie?"

"Archie was the one who strayed off the track first, but it was my fault that he did. I undervalued him for years. He never got emotionally involved with anyone else, though—it was just a fling for him. But not for me. Don't make my mistake and undervalue Mike, Jo—not if you value your children.''

''I don't know if I do—I'm a useless mother and I'm not as nice as you, Sonia.'' She rested her head on her hands again, and Sonia could hardly hear her next words. ''I've only done one really loving thing in all my life— something that cost me the sort of anguish I think you're talking about.''

''Would it help to tell me?''

Joanna lifted her head, and Sonia saw real pain in her face.

''Deciding never to see Harriet's father again, and then not telling him I was pregnant. You don't know what that cost me—but I did it out of love, and keeping it secret has been very lonely. I vowed that if he didn't know about Harriet, then not even Harriet herself should know about him,'' said Joanna, ''because you see it would have ruined everything that mattered to him most, and it was all entirely—one hundred per cent—my fault.''

Sonia felt wildly curious. Though genuinely sorry for Joanna, she couldn't help thinking impatiently that it was typical of her to be so draconian in her views.

''Come off it, Jo. It takes two to make a baby.''

But Joanna didn't want her responsibility diluted. She had worn a hair shirt for so long, she couldn't imagine what it would be like to take it off.

''I can't tell you the circumstances, but what I did was inexcusable,'' she said obstinately. ''I deliberately seduced Harriet's father—he had no intention of sleeping with me, and I was well aware that he was absolutely out of bounds. All the time I was pregnant I thought the baby might be a consolation, but the birth was awful—I'd had no idea it could be like that—and then from the first moment she was born, I found her a nightmare. Ever since I've always thought of Harriet as my punishment.''

"Well, poor little girl! No wonder she's in a mess."
Sonia knew she sounded sharp. "What are you going to do
about her?"

"I don't know. She gets more like her father to look at
by the day—except now. Without her hair I can't bear to
look at her; at least that was a reminder of him. Hattie's
father had hair just like her—but of course she can't know
that," said Joanna. Sonia suddenly remembered the veiled
look she had intercepted between Polly and Harriet the
night before, and a large question mark ballooned inside
her head, but she didn't pursue the subject.

"Why don't you leave her here for the weekend as
planned, and then let her stay with Kate for a bit? Then
it'll be August and she's coming here to work anyway.
Give you both a bit of space from each other," she suggested. "Couldn't you talk to Hattie as you've just talked
to me? Explain your feelings? You don't have to give her
his name, but she might feel less resentful. Think about it.
Anyway, try to get things sorted with Mike and then start
again. Would you like me to ring Kate for you?"

"My mother wasn't very cooperative with me this morning, but she'd do anything for Hattie. Yes please, Sonia.
You seem better at dealing with my family than I am. I'm
still having to get used to the fact that my mother has
changed—or else I've never really known what she was
like, and that's quite hard to take on board. I suppose I've
undervalued her too," said Joanna, facing Cecily's earlier
criticism, joining it to Sonia's, and drawing an unwelcome
conclusion about herself.

"Of course I'll ring Kate for you. You look absolutely
all in. You go back home—but do go easy on the booze."
Sonia shoved a piece of paper and a pen across the table
at Joanna. "I expect you'd like to leave a note for Hattie
first?" she said.

The two women exchanged a long look. Then Joanna
suddenly smiled. "OK, Sonia. You win. I know when I'm
outmanoeuvred."

As she watched Joanna writing, Sonia thought that when Joanna smiled like that, she was really beautiful. It was a pity she didn't do it more often.

Joanna folded the note, wrote "Hattie" on it in her neat hand, and got up. She gave Sonia an unexpected hug.

"Thank you," she said. "I'll do some real thinking about things, but I don't feel very hopeful. Please say goodbye to Archie, and tell him I'm sorry I was such a pain." She gave a rueful little laugh. "Does apologising get easier with practice?" she asked.

As Sonia watched Joanna drive away, she thought that though she had enjoyed Joanna's company before and often found her stimulating, this was the first time she had really warmed to her. She might get to like her better in the future. She also felt absolutely drained, and knew it was not only due to the dramas of the Rendlesham family. Raking over the embers of her own past fire was something she tried to avoid. She went up to her studio, but spent more time gazing out of the window than applying paint to the canvas she was working on.

Joanna had written: "Darling Hattie, I wish you hadn't shaved your head. Contrary to what you think I've always loved your hair—please grow it again. I'm sorry I hit you. Love, Mum."

When Harriet had read the letter, she folded it carefully and tucked it safely in her pocket to be reread later. It was the shortest letter she'd ever had from her mother—and quite the best.

Sonia, who had already talked to Kate by the time the riders returned, told Harriet what had been decided. She said Kate wanted Harriet to help her over the next two weeks with her move to the Observatory. Then Harriet would come back to Duntan to work in the café with Polly. "After that," said Sonia, "your mum tells me you're all going to Corfu for two weeks before you go back to school. That should be lovely. Now will you all please go and clean the tack—and then yourselves—before tea." It was clear that Sonia now considered the subject was closed, and a sober but more settled Harriet followed Polly out to the tack-room. Archie had taken them all for miles. They'd had a brilliant long ride and were healthily tired.

Kate had been dreading seeing Harriet, instinctively wanting to champion her, unwilling to show disloyalty to Joanna and terribly afraid of making a wrong response, but when she saw Harriet's expression of agonised anxiety, she just folded her in a huge embrace, and rocked her gently to and fro, saying, "There, there, darling; it's all right; don't cry; there, there," as she had so often in the past, after many different stormy episodes.

Then she took her by the shoulders, held Harriet away from her, and started to laugh: "Oh Hattie," she said. "You're not your mother's daughter for nothing—such an extreme thing to do. Whatever made you do it?"

Harriet longed desperately to tell Kate about her discovery, but all she said was: "Oh Gran, I wish I hadn't done it now. I don't want to meet anyone."

Unknowingly, Kate echoed Archie's words. "As a matter of fact you don't look half bad—much better than I expected—but I shall be pleased when the curls grow back in all the same. Mum must let you keep them short now. Cheer up, my darling, in a few months' time this will all seem funny. One day you'll be telling your children about it, and it will be their favourite story about your naughtiness."

Harriet was very useful to Kate during the next weeks. Kate kept her busy and insisted on paying pocket money as a reward for her help, though Harriet would willingly have worked for her grandmother for love. The divine Alexander Rivers had telephoned, which was just what Harriet's morale needed, though she couldn't help being secretly relieved to hear that he was off to Spain with his family for the rest of the holidays, and she wouldn't have to put his reaction to her altered appearance to the test. As it was she was able to make a marvelously funny confection out of the story, and Alexander was much impressed. He thought Harriet was really cool.

Together Kate and Harriet made lists, sorted out cupboards, took endless measurements and put coloured stickers on everything Kate intended to take from Longthorpe. She was appalled by the clutter that had accumulated over the years, and was determined not to take anything with her that wasn't either essential, or so much part of the fabric of her being that she felt she might bleed without it. This has to be my fresh start, she told herself—but there were some hard decisions.

She had a feeling of unreality as her last days at Longthorpe raced by, but Jack's telephone calls were always a highlight. She was longing for his return, but felt relieved, after its whirlwind start, that their friendship was having the chance to unfold more gradually. He told her he wanted to give a grand party at Ravelstoke Hall in the autumn, before all the major alterations turned it into a nursing home. He asked Kate to make a list of all the people she thought should receive invitations. Kate suggested that Joanna might do the catering.

Jack was not the only man to telephone Longthorpe House. Gerald Brownlow had also got into the habit of making regular calls to Kate. She came to dread them. Unlike her conversations with Jack, which neither of them ever wanted to finish, she and Gerald ran out of things to say to each other very quickly. Kate did not want to talk to Gerald, and Gerald had no talent for chat. Unfortunately this did not mean that he was prepared to ring off. After lengthy pauses and several attempts on her part to say goodbye, Kate was usually driven to saying, "Nice to talk to you, Gerald, but I'm afraid I have to dash," whereupon Gerald would say, "Just one thing I wanted to talk to you about . . ." But then could never think what it was. Kate felt she was always telling him she must dash. It became a challenge to see how often she could vary the formula. Jack was highly amused when she told him about this private game of hers, but all the same he felt a fierce little stab of jealousy. Gerald Brownlow might be a dull dog—but he was on the spot.

Most days Kate and Harriet went over to Ravelstoke. Gloria's friend, Jessie Worsencroft, was already working in the stables and was a brilliant success. Her tailoring was immaculate, and left Gloria and Kate free to concentrate on embroidery. Though Harriet felt very self-conscious to start with, it was amazing how quickly the family got used to her altered appearance. Rupert, predictably, had been very bothered to start with, but Tilly was thrilled because she said Harriet now looked like the rubber-headed Cleareye Clikes—not a compliment in everyone's eyes. The hairdresser in Winterbridge told Kate that it would be at least eight weeks before anything approaching a short covering of hair grew back. Harriet's hair was so fair that the first growth was almost invisible.

Harriet and Jo treated each other with caution, and though there was still considerable tension between them, the hostility had toned down and they were both obviously making an effort. Harriet exercised the horses with either Jenny or Joanna, but slept and ate with Kate.

She and Polly were constantly on the telephone or writing endless notes to each other on the fax machine that was now installed in the stables at the Observatory. The calls or messages frequently ended with the words, "See you in an hour then." Kate quite saw how this must drive Joanna crazy, but it is easier as a grandparent to be amused rather than irritated by the lifestyle of the young, and she loved Harriet's company so much that it seemed a small price to pay. There was much coming and going between Duntan and Longthorpe. It was music to Kate's ears to hear the girls' shrieks of laughter when Polly came to spend a night at Longthorpe. She thought Harriet was beginning to look a little less hunted.

Polly was a mine of information about Lady Rosamund's involvement with the paranormal. Apparently Rosamund was learning astral projection.

"Mum says Granny Roz has taken to popping in and out of the spirit world like a trip to Sainsbury's," Polly informed Kate. "She says Connie and Sylvester have got themselves a cushy pad, and know they're on to a good thing: They've settled in at the Dial House and are using it as their base to give Granny-Roz's friends readings about their past lives. Imagine! Granny-Roz has had three hundred and fifty incarnations," Polly doubled up with laughter, "sometimes as a woman but often as a *man*! So Mum goes, 'Bet you were always in the upper income bracket though,' and Granny-Roz goes: 'Naturally.' She had some grizzly deaths though, toppling off battlements and being knifed by lovers. Wild! Dad hates it all, but Mum thinks it's hilarious and says Granny-Roz will get rid of them both the minute she's fed up. She's quite ruthless, you know."

Polly told Harriet that Martha was coming to stay at the Dial House in August, and they planned to give her the picture then. Harriet had put all but one of the photographs back in Joanna's desk, but the one they had kept was now in Polly's care, hidden at Duntan. Harriet didn't dare keep it at home in case her mother found it.

Joanna had rung Mike and been surprised to find what a relief it had been to talk to him about Harriet. It was the first time they'd had a call that wasn't acrimonious for ages. Mike had been sympathetic to both sides. Joanna volunteered to send Jenny down with Rupert and Tilly to spend a fortnight with Mike, and he promised he would come up to Yorkshire later for a weekend to talk things over. They both agreed that they should stick to their plan for a family holiday in Greece at the end of August. It occurred to Joanna, in her unaccustomed mood of introspection, that Mike had always had the balance she herself lacked. It was more food for thought—but it didn't stop her lunching with Hugo Coltman.

She did not know that Kate, so fired up with life that she was waking early at the moment, had been surprised to see a car disappearing from outside Joanna's front door at six o'clock on a beautiful July morning the day after Jenny and the children had gone up to London. Kate had been letting Acer out. Three days later she saw the car again. This time she saw who the driver was.

◄ TWENTY-FOUR ►

Kate had booked the removal firm for August the first.

"It's as well you didn't pick the fourth," announced Mrs. Stokes, leaning on her mop and blocking Kate and Harriet's path, "else I shouldn't have been able to help you flit." Kate obligingly asked why.

"The fourth of August," said Mrs. Stokes impressively, "is my birthday—me and the Queen Moom, both." Kate resisted an urge to say that she hadn't actually had it in mind to ask for the Queen Mother's help with her move, or Mrs. Stokes' help either. Help from Mrs. Stokes was a very mixed blessing.

"Yes, it's funny what a link we have with the Royals in our family. I'm not the only one." Mrs. Stokes half closed her eyes as she contemplated this pleasurable claim to fame. Harriet gave a muffled snort.

"My Herbert's birthday's on July the fourth, which is only three days off the Princess of Wales," she went on. "Our Sandra's five days off Princess Alice, Doochess of Gloucester, *and*," Mrs. Stokes was clearly reaching a thrilling climax: "our Kevin's birthday is on April the twentieth—only one day off Her Majesty's own!"

"And the same date as Hitler," said Kate.

Mrs. Stokes ignored this unworthy interruption. "Quite a lot of coincidences," she said smugly—adding inexorably: "So luckily, on the first, I'll be free to help with your flit."

Like Netta Fanshaw, not that they resembled each other in any other way, Mrs. Stokes hated to be out of things and could have been invaluable to the Ministry of Information.

Cecily, who had always kept up the fiction that she had never been dependent on anyone in her life, least of all her daughter-in-law, was undergoing private agonies at the thought of the impending upheaval. Naturally this could not be admitted and had to be disguised by extreme contrariness. She puffed up and down the stairs at Longthorpe, wearing herself and everyone else out, and claiming, quite erroneously, that pieces of furniture which Kate intended to take to the Observatory were in fact hers, and she might need them. Though normally the problem was to try to keep Cecily off the road, now she demanded to be driven out to lunch, or into Blaydale, because she said her car wouldn't start; or, worse still, she appeared in the kitchen announcing that she was foregoing her bridge morning in order to "help."

"I might even move with you. You may need my assistance more than Joanna does." They both knew she would have hated to leave Longthorpe, and that had it been suggested, she would certainly have refused to go, but it was a charade that had to be played out. Kate understood, ached for the old lady—and was driven crazy.

"Do me a favor, darling," Kate said to Joanna, who had come over one morning to find her mother slumped at the kitchen table after a particularly bruising encounter with Cecily: "Go and tell Granny-Cis that you wouldn't contemplate moving in here if it weren't for the fact that you know she'll always be there to keep an eye on the children for you." Joanna, aware that there was much in her own personality that came from her grandmother, was suddenly overcome with sympathy for Kate and went straight upstairs to Cecily's flat and did a wonderful job in presenting herself in an uncharacteristically needy role.

August the first dawned fine and clear. Kate slept very little on her last night at Longthorpe. Her brain relentlessly reviewed a succession of films of the vanished years of her life. It was as though she had switched on a video and then been unable to turn it off. Some of the scenes were sunlit, with Joanna and Nick as children running wild in the garden, making tree-houses, riding their ponies, and playing sardines all over the house with their friends—but the dark presence of Oliver kept intruding. Kate also viewed herself as a young wife and mother, deeply lacking in self-confidence, wildly in love with her glamorous husband but constantly on the edge of terror. She saw him taunting Nick, while flaunting his adulation of Joanna and constantly undermining her own maternal role. She saw herself torn between a dread that Oliver might leave her and, eventually, a longing for him to do so. Then she saw the brave, uncomplaining and defiant figure of his final years when the flesh seemed to melt from his bones and his restless, destructive spirit inhabited a translucent shell.

During his last weeks, Kate had allowed herself to indulge in a fantasy that she and Oliver might have a touching reconciliation before the end, despite the fact that though his body had altered, his personality had not, and anyway breath had become too valuable a commodity by then to be wasted on unnecessary words. She would have liked to part on a note of love, and gave him several openings to which he did not respond.

"Well, you'll be free of me soon, Kate," he had whispered one day, in the barely audible voice that wheezed out as though he were trying to fan a damp fire with leaky bellows. His old mocking look flickered across his emaciated face, daring her to give him the bland, palliative answer she would once have done. "How will you like that?"

And she had answered painfully and truthfully: "I don't know, Oliver. I really don't know. But I shall remember your courage as well as all the other things. You will leave me a stronger person than when you found me and I can be grateful for that. I shall cope—and I shan't ever forget you."

And he had said, as though it brought him satisfaction, if not comfort: "No, you won't forget me."

Kate had left Oliver's study unaltered. She wanted nothing from it for herself. They had decided that after Kate had settled in the Observatory, Nick and Joanna would go through the house taking it in turns to pick what they wanted. She thought Joanna would probably use the study as her own office, and run her business from it—depending on how much life with Mike she wanted to salvage from the wreck of her marriage—but Kate hoped Joanna would resist the temptation to turn it into a sort of shrine to the memory of her father. At the moment Oliver's big mahogany kneehole desk with the silver inkstand and pen tray, and dark green leather blotter, were to outward appearances exactly as he had left them.

Kate had removed only one item from that desk. She would never forget the horror of finding it. Now it was safely lodged with her solicitor—who also happened to be her son-in-law, Michael Maitland. The week after Oliver's death, Mike had asked Kate to look through Oliver's filing cabinet for an inventory, and having failed to locate it, she had opened the middle drawer of the desk, not really expecting to find what she was looking for. She had opened the large brown packet without any feeling of apprehension—and an abyss had opened in front of her.

She had known about Oliver's flagrant unfaithfulness for years—he had delighted that she should know—but here was evidence of something much darker. She had been stunned and sickened by what she found. She had sat in the study shaking with shock and disgust, remembering a conversation they had once had which she had not taken seriously.

"What would you do if I was ever publicly disgraced?" he'd asked, glittering at her mockingly. He was rather drunk at the time and she had thought he was just tormenting her. Oliver revelled in the admiration he inspired in certain quarters, relished the power of money and success. She had not believed he would be capable of jeopardising his whole lifestyle. Now she supposed that taking risks must have been a kind of addiction. Mike had been wonderful to her. He thought she ought to tell Nick, but she had been desperate for neither of her children to have to face something so unpleasant about their father, especially so soon after his death, so they had agreed to say nothing. Kate would never be sure whether Oliver had deliberately left the package for her to find—as if he had wanted to inflict one final humiliation on her from beyond the grave. If so he had succeeded.

Two removal vans arrived at eight o'clock. It would have been impossible for one large pantechnicon to get through the gates and under the archway that led to the Observatory. Kate, Joanna and Harriet were ready waiting in the kitchen. After so much planning and sorting there seemed curiously little for them to do except hand over to the professionals. Mrs. Stokes arrived early. She leant on her mop midway between front door and stairs and tried to engage anyone who crossed her path in conversation. The golden voice of Pavarotti singing "*Nessun dorma*" wafted from the radio of one of the vans.

"That song always puts me in mind of my Herbert," said Mrs. Stokes. "Herbert is gifted with a fine tenor voice too."

"Did he ever think of making singing a career then?" asked Harriet, fighting giggles and not daring to catch Kate's eye. The idea of scrawny little Mr. Stokes having anything in common with the gigantic opera star in the parachute kaftan, made imagination boggle. Mrs. Stokes gave her a baleful look.

"Well, no," she said confidentially, "because you see, oonfortunately, my Herbert was gifted with the fine voice, but not with the musical ear. He sings in the pub sometimes, on special occasions, but . . ." Mrs. Stokes paused impressively, ". . . he's always had trouble with picking out a tune. It's been a disadvantage."

Luckily at this moment Cecily appeared, and Mrs. Stokes, recognising a stronger force, retreated unwillingly down the kitchen passage, dragging her mop behind her. It left a wavery damp line on the stone flags like a snail's trail.

Kate and Harriet, leaving Joanna to supervise the loading of the vans at Longthorpe, set off in the car for Ravelstoke with Acer, so as to be there when the first one arrived.

"Are you sad, Gran?" asked Harriet.

"Yes and no, darling. In some ways I am, of course, but excited and a bit scared too."

"Everything's changing, isn't it?" said Harriet sadly. "I remember when I was little thinking it was such fun to blow the seconds out of dandelion clocks. Now I don't want to."

Kate put out her left hand and closed her fingers round Harriet's, and they drove in silence until a steep hill, requiring a change of gear, forced Kate to take her hand back and concentrate on the road. When they drove through the gates of the Observatory she didn't like to tell Harriet what a lightness of heart she felt, as though a constriction had been removed. Like being given oxygen at a high altitude. I shall breathe more freely now, she thought.

Gloria and Jessie were both there to greet them. Gloria had got her sister-in-law to sit with Jim so that she could help unpack china and glass. She was armed with a huge bunch of yellow roses from her garden.

"Oh Gloria—how lovely. What a welcome!" Kate was much touched. Gloria beamed.

"Nothing quite like yellow for a special occasion I always say—so pleasant and cheering." As though to match the roses, Gloria's hair had changed back from burnt sienna to pale gold. It was like being greeted by a sunbeam.

The rest of the day had a carnival feel to it. Frank and Walter, both of whom had been sworn to secrecy about Kate's move in case Jack got wind of it, had turned up to help, and in no time pictures were up on walls, and furniture placed in its new setting. The little house seemed to open like a flower in the sun to all the loving attention it had received. Joanna had excelled herself and came over after the last van-load had arrived bringing not only a delicious picnic lunch for everybody to share, but a supply of wonderful dishes ready to put into Kate's deep freeze. She had also brought champagne.

"Save you having to cook for a while and you deserve a bit of spoiling," Joanna said unexpectedly and kissed her mother. Then she expertly opened the champagne: "Let's drink to Midas and Mum's new life," she said to everyone. Kate was so moved she felt near to tears as they all sat on the terrace where she had first had lunch with Jack only two months before; she wished he was there now. Everybody raised their glasses to her.

"To Kate and Midas," they chorused. At this moment, the grinding noise of an unbelievably bad gear change plus a violent tooting drowned their good wishes, and Cecily arrived in her battered little car, swerving jerkily through the arch and narrowly missing one of the stone pillars. The brakes screamed their usual protest as she drew up in the courtyard, only inches short of the house. One of the removal men, who had nipped back to his van to collect his packet of fags, witnessed this exciting approach. "By shots! That was a close-run thing," he said admiringly as Cecily heaved herself triumphantly out of the driving seat.

"You didn't think I was going to be left out of all the fun, did you?" she asked as she joined the rest of them at the back of the house. Frank, inhibitions having popped off with the champagne corks, gave them a taste of the impersonations at which Jack had told Kate he was so brilliant, and had them all in hysterics.

It seemed that the move had turned into a party.

By six o'clock the house looked shipshape, and the kind helpers left, to many expressions of gratitude from Kate, and with many good luck wishes from all of them to her.

Four generations of Rendlesham women were left together. Kate could hardly believe they had spent a whole day in such accord. Cecily, Joanna and Harriet had all offered to stay and keep Kate company on her first night in the new house, but she had insisted that she needed to start her new independence on her own. Cecily left first, suddenly more tired than she liked to admit, not looking forward to Longthorpe without Kate. It was not that she felt nervous. The unexpected creak on the stairs or the little moan that might—but might not—be caused by the wind, held no terrors for Cecily, who felt equally capable of seeing off ghosts or burglars, but she knew that the absence of the daughter-in-law she had once despised would leave a hollow which would echo round her heart.

Joanna and Harriet stayed to have supper with Kate, and then Joanna said they must go. She was driving Harriet to Duntan as she and Polly were due to start their holiday job next day, and they mustn't be too late.

"Did you hate leaving Gran alone?" Harriet asked Joanna suddenly, after a silence, as they left the village of Ravelstoke and headed towards the main road.

"Yes, Hattie, I did. But I felt it was what she wanted. Do you think I was right?"

"Umm—I think you were. Glad you minded too, though." Both Harriet and Joanna felt that they had edged a little closer together through this brief exchange.

* * *

It was after nine when Kate waved them off, and she and Acer were finally alone. She walked round the house from room to room with a sense of wonder. I have made all this happen, she thought. I took a decision for myself and all this has flowed on from there.

Because of the spiral staircase, which led up from the tower bedroom to the observatory proper, Kate's big bed had had to be placed in the centre of the room. Walter had built a dais to raise it up a little, so that Kate would be able to see the view while she lay in bed. This gave it a theatrical look and as she lay there now, propped up on pillows, she felt as though she were in the middle of an opera set. She quite expected the door to fly open and someone to leap in and sing an aria—though preferably not Mr. Stokes. There were windows on three sides of the room and Kate had left them all open, very much hoping a bat would not fly in, but unable to resist the warm summer air—warm evenings being a special luxury in Yorkshire. I am like a bird in a tree; a partridge in a pear tree perhaps, she thought, remembering how she had once compared herself to a hen partridge to Jack. The moon was nearly full, and she could see the branches of the great beech tree, black against the sky. It cast fantastic shadows across the bedroom floor. It was very still—again untypical for Yorkshire. An owl hooted, and was answered by another, like an antiphony sung at compline. Kate drifted into sleep.

She woke with a suddenness that immediately made her certain that something had roused her, though she was not sure what. She had no idea what time it was and looked at her clock—it was nearly two o'clock. Then she heard Acer bark from the kitchen below. She listened intently but could hear nothing else. Acer never barked for no reason, but perhaps it was just her new surroundings, or she'd heard a fox or a badger. Then Acer barked again, and Kate thought she heard the sound of car wheels crunching on the gravel at the front of the house. Don't be ridiculous, she told herself, it must be on the road above the house. Her heart started to thump, and she very much regretted that she had not set the burglar alarm before coming up to bed. Earlier in the day, Frank had given her a bunch of keys, clearly labelled, one for each room—but she hadn't got round to putting them in the appropriate doors. They were all sitting on the kitchen table, and she realised with a sinking heart that she had left her mobile panic button in the kitchen too. She got out of bed, and without turning on the light padded in her bare feet to the door, opened it cautiously, and stood in the dark at the top of the stairs, her hair rising at the back of her neck and her hands going clammy—because what she now heard, without any doubt, was the sound of the front door being very quietly opened. Quick as a flash Kate was back in her room, up the spiral staircase, and through the trap door into the observatory. She lowered the door, and then sat on it, panting. She wished it had a bolt on, but surely no one would be able to push it open from below with her weight on top? Acer had gone quiet. Kate thought of awful stories of dogs being given poisoned meat by burglars.

The moonlight flooded in through the four quarters of the dome. Kate listened. She heard footsteps: somebody was definitely coming upstairs.

Then she heard a voice—a man's voice. "Kate?" it called. "Kate? Where the hell are you?"

Kate's heart, which had been pounding in fear, now started to pound for a completely different reason.

"Who . . . who is it?" she called, knowing perfectly well, but still sitting frozen on the trap door like a child playing statues when the music has stopped. She felt the door heave beneath her. There was a bellow of laughter. "Kate—darling Kate, I know you must be up there. I'm not Hercules—for God's sake get off the lid and let me up."

She moved then, and when the flap opened, and first Jack's head, and then his shoulders appeared through the hole she was standing in her white nightdress in a patch of moonlight.

"Hello, Puss-in-Boots," said Jack, and stayed on the steps gazing at her as if he couldn't get enough of the sight. She wasn't beautiful, Jack thought, this woman he had grown to love so much, she wasn't even young, but for him she was something far, far better. He felt as if he'd come home at last after a long and arduous journey—and he was certainly not thinking of the luxurious first-class flight from New York which had delivered him to Heathrow some hours earlier.

"Jack Morley—you . . . you monster!" said Kate. "You've just scared me half out of my wits."

He laughed at her. "How could I possibly know you'd moved already? You never even dropped a hint. I wanted to surprise you and turn up unexpectedly tomorrow."

"Well, you've nearly killed me with shock tonight instead," she said tartly. "I might easily have died of fright."

"Oh Kate, I'm so glad you didn't," he said. And then he was through the trap door and she was in his arms, and they both knew what would follow.

So it was that first time Jack made love to Kate was on Raving Ravelstoke's dilapidated old Wield observation couch, but the stars they gazed at that night were not seen through a telescope. They were in each other's eyes.

❧ TWENTY-FIVE ❧

Kate woke the next morning when Jack appeared with a cup of tea for her, Acer bounding enthusiastically in his wake. Kate held her face up for a kiss. Jack put the tray down and then got back into bed with her. The kiss was totally satisfactory.

"I've let your hound out," he said. "One exciting but fruitless chase after a squirrel, and a good many impertinent messages left by rabbits picked up round the garden, which she says she'll deal with later. That all right? She seems to have accepted me as part of your new life—hope that goes for other people, but I thought Acer was an important first test."

"Quite right," said Kate. "If she'd disapproved you'd have been out on your ear, landlord or not."

After they had come down from the observatory, opting to spend what was left of the night in the deep peace of the comfortable bed after the hurly-burly of the horsehair astronomical couch, they had talked for ages.

"I'm so glad you're here, Jack. How wonderful to spend the first night together in this house," she had whispered drowsily into his chest before she finally fell asleep in his arms.

"Jack—your car! It's not there," said Kate, looking out of the kitchen window that gave on to the courtyard at the front, as they had breakfast. He looked surprised: "Oh, I didn't drive myself last night. Leslie drove me straight up from Heathrow and dropped me here."

"Where is he now?"

"I don't know. He always makes his own arrangements. He may have driven straight back south. He lives in Cricklewood and probably wanted to get back to his family. I shan't be needing him this weekend. I left the Range Rover at Ravelstoke before I went away. I want to go and look at things there anyway so I thought we might walk over to collect it?"

"Oh you did, did you, Mr. Powerful?" Kate rolled her eyes upwards. "What would you do now if you suddenly got the urge to have Leslie back and wanted him to drive you about today?"

"I should call him on his mobile—which of course is permanently switched on in case I want him." Jack came and put a finger on her nose and laughed down at her. "You don't have to be sorry for Leslie, Mrs. Puritan. He has an extremely well-paid job which he genuinely loves. He drives a bloody great car which he's mad about, and," said Jack, still laughing at her, "believe it or not, he actually likes me too. When I'm in the States, or anywhere abroad, he can take other driving jobs as a bonus."

"Provided you don't suddenly turn up without warning—and then he'd have to ditch the other people?"

"Exactly. Look, Kate," Jack was suddenly serious, reading something in her eyes which still worried him, as it had in London the last time he'd seen her. "I really do need to be able to work on my papers in a car, not to waste time looking for parking places or risk being late for important appointments—but yes, if I'm honest there is a bit of me that revels in all that luxury side of life too. I love going to the best restaurants, being able to get and afford tickets for the opera, and travelling in style. I'm proud of what I've achieved. I've had to take huge risks—never, I hope, dishonourable ones—and I could live without any of these trappings again if I had to. I started without them, and I hope I haven't forgotten what it was like. Because you've had a bad experience of what you call 'power,' you mistrust all these things. I can see why—but the so-called good things of life aren't wrong in themselves, though what people do with them can be. They're not the *really* good things, of course—those can't be bought—but they sure as hell make life more comfortable. If you can't accept this part of my life you won't be happy with me. And I do so badly want us to be together."

Kate scanned his face.

"Just don't ever play power games with me," she said.

"Kate, there are things I must say to you," said Jack, bracing himself to take the risk that mattered to him more than any he had ever taken in his life. "There is something I need to tell you and something I want to ask you."

At that moment the telephone rang. "Don't answer it," said Jack urgently, but Kate had already stretched out her hand for the receiver from force of habit.

"Oh hello, Gerald," Jack heard her say, in a less than enthusiastic tone. She made a thumbs-down sign at Jack and pulled a frightful face. "Yes. No. Well, I'm sorry you feel like that." Kate walked through the hall and out on to the terrace with the cordless telephone. Jack put the breakfast things in the new dishwasher. He felt like smashing up the china, and Gerald Brownlow with it.

Gerald, turning up at Longthorpe to ask Kate out to lunch, had first of all found no one, and then seen Cecily. He had been appalled to hear that Kate had actually moved already. He gave vent to his hurt feelings that she had not only not consulted him, but hadn't even bothered to tell him, and he followed this up with a string of cautionary advice for the future—a future in which he still intended to play a major part. Kate answered him mechanically, her mind on the conversation he'd interrupted.

Jack is going to ask me to marry him, she thought in a panic. I must stop him asking me, because I don't feel ready to say yes, but I certainly don't want to have to say no either. She was sure that she loved him, indeed was mad about him in every way, including one which would, she thought wryly, have utterly astonished Harriet—but after years with Oliver, the thought of marriage was deeply threatening to her. It might spoil everything. I am not ready for this yet, said Kate to herself, while Gerald Brownlow droned on down her right ear. She was absolutely terrified that if she turned down a proposal from Jack now she might lose him, and that would be the worst scenario of all.

Jack was standing looking out of the window when she eventually walked back into the kitchen. She came and stood behind him, put her arms round him and leant her cheek against his back.

"Please don't tell me or ask me anything yet, Jack," she said. "It's so wonderful being together. Can't we just enjoy each other and be carefree and irresponsible? I've never been able to be like that. Can't we just dance barefoot in the grass? I'll put up with your power fetish if you'll put up with my chronic anxieties. Isn't it enough to be happy *now*?''

So because the right moment seemed to have disappeared, because he couldn't resist her appeal, and although he knew the stakes got higher with each postponement, Jack put off telling Kate what was on his mind—yet again.

He turned round and held her close. Then he gave a great shout of laughter. ''You daft creature!'' he said, the trace of Yorkshire that still underlay his not-quite-American-either accent, deliberately more pronounced than usual. ''Dance barefoot in the grass indeed! At my age and size? I'd look a right Charlie—but all right then, Mrs. Puritan-Puss-in-Boots-Rendlesham, if you want to dance—we'll dance.'' And bellowing the Blue Danube at the top of his voice, he swept her into a Viennese waltz and whirled her through the hall and the drawing room, and round and back again at a breathtaking speed.

Mr. Stokes would have been most impressed; unlike him, it seemed, Jack Morley had not only been gifted with the musical ear as well as the fine voice, but with an excellent sense of rhythm and an amazing lightness on his feet for such a big man.

Joanna and Harriet would have been most surprised.

Gerald Brownlow would have been flabbergasted.

Jack wanted to inspect every bit of the house, and approved of all Kate's decorating. When she took him into the stables, he was extremely complimentary about the garments already finished for Midas, and was genuinely surprised at how much work the three women had already managed to do.

''You must have worked like beavers—and you with the move too. I don't know how you've achieved so much. You're going to have a real success on your hands,'' he said seriously—and then grinned. "Soon be getting a chauffeur of your own!" he teased.

They walked across the fields to the Hall with Acer. A transformation had taken place there too. Jack was very pleased with the office that had been set up in the billiard room, and the whole house had been cleaned. Instead of a smell of must and mould, there was the scent of beeswax polish; the furniture gleamed, the diamond panes of glass in the casement windows sparkled and the dust and cobwebs had gone.

But the house still gave Kate the shivers.

They discussed the party Jack wanted to give in October. He agreed at once that Joanna should have the chance to do the catering if she wanted it. He didn't tell Kate that he had got the invaluable Sylvia to do a little research about this, and she had come up with the information that Joanna's food would be excellent, absolutely up to the high standard he always required, but that they would probably need to import extra staff to help out with the service; Joanna had not yet got a big enough team together to cope reliably with such large numbers. Kate had made a note of all the people she thought should be invited. She had kept the lists from the year that Oliver had been High Sheriff, and added the names of some younger people too. Jack said he would hand it all to Sylvia.

"The good life?" asked Kate slyly.

On the following morning, which was Sunday, they woke early, made love, and went back to sleep again. Then, because it was another lovely day, they took their breakfast out on the terrace. Kate, still in her dressing gown, was sitting there in a blissful trance, her eyes closed and her face turned up to the sun, when Joanna walked round the side of the house.

"Hi, Mum! Just thought I'd check you were all right. The children are still away in London and I'm going to a drinks party at Roz Campion's and then on to Sunday lunch at Duntan. Thought I'd take a cup of coffee off you on the way. Goodness! You look blissful. I have to admit it really is lovely here.''

''Oh darling, how absolutely wonderful of you to come.'' Kate was very taken aback to see her daughter, and though much touched at the unaccustomed solicitude behind the gesture wondered what on earth she was going to do about Jack. It had been so gorgeous the day before that they had decided to walk back from the Hall instead of picking up the car, so luckily Jack's Range Rover with its personalised number plate was not outside the house.

''Sit down, darling, and I'll go and make us a fresh brew of coffee,'' said Kate, playing for time, and wondering if she should nip upstairs and ask Jack to disappear. Furtively she pulled her dressing gown further round her, and winched in the sash, hoping Joanna wouldn't notice that she had no nightdress underneath. At that moment there came the unmistakable sound of a man's voice from up in the tower. Jack, in the bath, was giving a fine rendering of *''La donna è mobile.''*

Joanna's mouth opened in surprise but no sound came out. She looked at her mother very hard. Kate looked right back.

La donn'è mobile
Qual piuma vento,
M'uta d'accento
E di pensero.

Jack was in truly splendid voice.

''So this is why you wanted to come here! I did wonder at first but I couldn't believe it of you,'' hissed Joanna, white with unreasonable fury, all the difficult emotions she had been going through lately finding a wonderful scapegoat, her easily ignited flash-point already sparked.

"No," said Kate. "Actually that isn't why I wanted to come here—but I have to say it's a quite terrific bonus."

"Mum, how could you! When I think of Dad . . ." Joanna choked on her words.

"Your father had been dead for over a year. I am a free woman, Jo," said Kate gently. "Jack and I are both free."

"Loose might be a better word. A vulgar, jumped-up, go-getter after someone like Dad!" Joanna was almost spitting.

Suddenly Kate felt very angry. "Jack Morley is a self-made man—all credit to him. He also happens to be a very rich one with some altruistic ideals for helping other people. I think he's the most wonderful person I've met in years— and don't you dare take the high moral ground with me, Joanna, you're not in a strong position."

"Leave Harriet out of this!"

"This had nothing whatever to do with Harriet. I never cheated on your father while he was alive, though goodness knows I had provocation! Can you say the same? How was Hugo Coltman last night, Jo?" Kate fired off a bow at a venture, and hit the bull's eye with a deadly arrow.

A dark flush, spreading up from her neck, crept slowly over Joanna's face. All the military went out of her. She looked like something left out of the deepfreeze by mistake, which had unexpectedly gone soggy.

"How did you know?"

"Sometimes I let Acer out quite early."

"You never said a word."

"It wasn't my business, Jo. Any more than this is yours. Oh darling, you do take life so hard! Why make it so rocky for yourself and everyone else? Life's tough enough anyway without making it worse."

"Will . . . will you tell Mike?"

"Of course not. That's for you to work out." Kate took a snap decision. "But you, on the other hand, can tell anyone you like about us," she said airily. "It might even be helpful; we'd never be able to keep it a secret for long even if we wanted to. If anyone gets nosy, say, 'Yes, my mother's having a fantastic affair with Jack Morley—and loving every minute of it.' And you can specially tell snaky, two-faced Netta and worthy, disapproving old Gerald,'' added Kate, recklessly throwing discretion to the prevailing Yorkshire winds, and relishing the sensation.

Jack, who had been coming down the stairs still happily humming, though he had turned the volume down and switched to Mozart, had heard their angry voices through the open windows. He had paused, wondering what Kate might want him to do under the circumstances. But when he heard this last speech, which both filled his heart with delight and greatly amused him, he decided disclosure would be in order. He sauntered out through the French window in the drawing room and held out his hand.

''Ah, Joanna. We met briefly at the Fanshaws. How very good to see you again. I'm sure you've come over to check that nothing untoward has happened to your mother since her move. Quite right too.''

Joanna, not normally given to uncertainties about social responses, felt she had been completely wrong-footed, and was so disconcerted by the understanding and amused gleam in Jack's eye, that she found herself politely shaking hands with her mother's lover as though they had just met for the second time at a formal party.

''How . . . how lovely to see you too,'' she said inanely, wondering what to do next.

Kate started to laugh. ''Darling Jo, I'm truly thrilled you've come. *Please* don't go now. Sit down and I'll get that coffee for all of us.''

''Better still,'' said Jack, enjoying himself no end, ''*I'll* get the coffee—or why not champagne? I brought some with me, and it always tastes best drunk out of doors before lunch. We can make it into buck's fizz if you'd rather. Why don't you go up and put some clothes on, Kate? I know you've already sounded Joanna out, but I want to ask her formally myself to take on the catering for my proposed party. You see, I'm trying to buy my way into the York-shire County set with tremendously nouveau-riche display of vulgar opulence," he said blandly to Joanna, "and I thought you might be my passport to their acceptance of me?" He raised a quizzical eyebrow at her.

For the second time that morning, Joanna turned scarlet.

Kate left them to it and fled upstairs.

When she came down, feeling ridiculously relieved to be properly dressed in front of her daughter, Jack and Joanna were doing what they both excelled at—making lists and discussing plans. Jack looked completely relaxed but Joanna looked as if she'd had a poker stuck down her back.

Jack got to his feet as Kate appeared.

"She's very efficient, this daughter of yours," he said. "And full of original ideas too. She's got herself the job if she wants to do it. What about it, Joanna?"

"Yes, I'll take it on for you," said Jo coolly, equilibrium recovered, adding with a glimmer of her own: "Perhaps it will be good publicity for us both." Jack gave her an appreciative look. There might be more of Kate in her than he had thought.

"Refreshment time now," he said. So champagne was opened again on the terrace at the Observatory, and another toast drunk to future happiness and new ventures. Kate passionately hoped the happiness would include Mike and Harriet as well as the three of them present.

ᕯ TWENTY-SIX ᕔ

The next two months were a golden time for Kate.

Together she and Jack had fun rearranging the rooms in the house. Oliver had never consulted her about anything to do with furnishing Longthorpe, so it was a new kind of pleasure for her. She and Jack by no means always agreed and had some enjoyable arguments. He brought over a few small choice pieces of furniture from the Hall, though to Kate's relief most of what was in the big house was of the wrong period and too large to suit the little Regency folly. Jack had a good eye, however, and found some beautiful Jacobean glass which she liked, and some lovely Bow porcelain. In one of the gloomy bedrooms, Kate found a pair of Derby milkmaids, bearing little wooden yokes on their shoulders from which tiny milk cans were suspended, which looked far more at home in the Observatory than in the grander establishment. She also fell for a small Dutch flower painting by Rootius which looked wonderful in the drawing room. Jack got Frank to help him move the portrait of Raving Ravelstroke, and they hung him in the dining room. "Must have the old Raver in his own house," said Jack.

They went to a brilliant production of Verdi's *Falstaff* by Opera North in Leeds, and discovered a mutual passion for poking round antique shops. Jack took Kate all round the estate and showed her his plans for renovating the farms. Acer had never had so many wonderful walks.

Jack had to be away quite often, sometimes only as far as London, sometimes in the States, but Kate, who had for years been used to Oliver's absences on business trips, accepted this necessity. Though she now missed Jack terribly when he wasn't with her, their reunions were so wonderful that she felt it was worth it. She was also extremely busy herself.

She had wondered how Gloria and Jessie, not to mention Frank and the Ravelstoke Estate workers, would take her involvement with Jack. It wasn't the affair that would have worried them, but the open living together that she thought might offend. She needn't have worried. Gloria was entranced.

"I've always thought Jack was such a pleasant man," she glowed to Kate. "It's like a fairy tale!"

Kate told Jack she was afraid Gloria might feel impelled to do an embroidery portrait of them in the guise of an elderly Cinderella and Prince Charming, dressed in shades of primrose, sipping cowslip wine. "Or knowing her penchant to anthropomorphise everything, I'd probably be a field mouse in a party frock and you'd be the frog prince."

"Thanks," said Jack.

Frank was too much of a gentleman to let Kate see he was even aware of any altered situation, though what he said about her privately to Jack when they were having a drink together in the Ravelstoke Arms one evening would have made Kate blush, and Frank's wife slam a few doors and deliberately burn his tea.

Naturally neither Jack nor Kate said anything to Hannah Hartley about their relationship, though when they paid her a visit, she allowed herself one sagacious sniff which spoke volumes.

"What a lovely evening, Mrs. Hartley," Kate greeted her.

"No need to get in a lather about it," was Jack's Aunt Hannah's enthusiastic response—but she produced the dreaded parsnip wine all the same. Kate had to resort to taking Anadin afterwards.

As for the Yorkshire social set, most of them immediately liked Jack in his own right and were too fond of Kate to be anything but pleased for her obvious happiness. How she chose to live was her own affair. A few others were too absorbed in their own private games of general post to be interested, and as with any new bit of gossip, it provided an interesting topic of conversation for a short time but was quickly yesterday's news.

On the other hand, Netta Fanshaw and Gerald Brownlow both found the situation very difficult. Gerald was deeply hurt and very jealous. He labelled Jack a bounder, and in his imagination indulged in fantasies of horse-whipping him. Unfortunately, not only had this satisfying occupation gone out of fashion, but Jack was bigger than Gerald and looked alarmingly fit.

It would only have been fair to admit that Gerald felt genuinely concerned for Kate too, and was anxious that she should not get hurt. He had no idea of the wounds she had already sustained over the years from Oliver, whom he had greatly admired, and would have considered quite beyond suspicion as a terrorist on the domestic front. Gerald's horizon was limited to what he could see through his ex-army field-glasses and he had a deep mistrust of the territory that might lie to either side of his direct line of vision. After all, what did one know about this pseudo American fellow—apart from his money and his humble origins (not two things that went too well together in Gerald's opinion)? Back to reconnaissance.

Netta's problems were different As Kate had predicted, she couldn't resist the invitation to sit on the governing body of the Ravelstoke Hall Centre, especially when she discovered that Archie Duntan, Lady Van Alleyn and the Bishop were also to be on it. Like Gerald, she was a snob, but her angle of vision was spread wider than his. What Netta really admired, unlike Kate, was prestige and influence. She would have liked to take up Jack herself (had she not been the first to discover him?), stamp him with her personal seal of approval, and then organise his social life. That Jack's acceptance of any social invitation now depended on Kate being invited too, was a pill that stuck in Netta's gullet. She got round this by saying that Oliver's old friends must all stand by to help pick up the pieces when Jack Morley got tired of poor little Kate Rendlesham—as he almost certainly would.

She lent Gerald a very sympathetic ear, and applied aromatherapy to his ego.

Kate told Jack that after meeting Joanna everyone else would be a doddle, and she was right. Cecily, who might understandably have been the most difficult, took one of her unpredictable fancies to Jack. He not only made her laugh, but he also stood up to her. Nick and Robin had liked him immediately. Robin's father in the States, pumped by Nick, had made enquiries about Franklin J. Morley.

"Supposed to be a good guy—don't know anything about him personally," he had told Nick.

"I guess you can stop fussing about your mother now, darling," said Robin. "Anyone can see she's blissful and I think Jack's just great. You concentrate on getting your mind round being a father."

Kate took Jack over for supper to Duntan one evening. All the family were at home, including Lady Rosamund and Martha, who came over from the Dial House for supper. Harriet, still self-conscious about her lack of hair, and therefore prickly about meeting anyone, regarded Jack with considerable caution, although she was bursting with curiosity. She was not very forthcoming with him, and Kate felt anxious. Jack did not make the mistake of trying to win Harriet over.

The other children all fell instantly under his spell and vied shamelessly for his attention. As he was obviously brilliant with the young, it made Kate wonder why he was so reticent about his own daughter. She felt she could talk to Jack about any subject under the sun, except this one. Lady Rosamund flirted outrageously with him, to their mutual enjoyment and amusement—and that of everyone else, including Kate.

Connie and Sylvester had recently held a seance with Rosamund, and her dead husbands and several ex-lovers had "come through" she told the riveted company. They would, apparently, all be waiting for her when she "crossed over."

"Better stay alive as long as possible then," said Archie.

His mother flashed him a pitying smile. "You've always had such a one-track mind, Archie darling. I've never had a problem with juggling several projects simultaneously."

"You mean keeping several balls in the air at once?" asked Tom innocently. Archie tried to glare at him, but it was too late. Everyone, including his grandmother, laughed. Tom looked horribly pleased with himself.

"Talking of death," said Rosamund, "how is my shroud doing on your list of commissions, Kate?"

"Still on the back burner I'm afraid, Roz," said Kate, and then, amid more laughter, realised she might have put this better.

During dinner, Harriet and Polly regaled everyone with their experiences as waitresses in the café.

"Hoggish Mrs. Northwood brought some other old bean round the gardens the other day and ordered *three* helpings of raspberries and cream just for herself. I promise you she was drooling," said Polly.

"You could see it running down her chin, like Acer when she sees Granny opening the dog food," said Harriet.

They were both thoroughly enjoying their stint as waitresses in the café, though it was far harder work than they had expected, as Sonia had known it would be. Still, the money was rolling in; they had bought Archie his bottle of vodka and some spotted cotton handkerchiefs as a "sorry" present for having pinched the original one; Polly's 501s were well within her sights and Harriet was secretly saving up for a travel fund which she thought she might need when—if—her father was found.

A few days before, Harriet had given Martha the precious photograph, and Martha had promised to do what she could.

"Shouldn't be difficult," she said. "Some of the college porters are geriatric. Someone's sure to remember. Once we find his name and the right college a letter would get forwarded even after all this time, I'm sure." Martha, who was at Trinity herself, had a house up the Iffley Road which she shared with her current boyfriend. "May take time and you'll have to wait till I next get up," she warned, "but I might be there before terms starts to do a bit of work.

Which college was your mother at, Harriet?"

"Brasenose, I think."

"I'll try that first, then."

As they were leaving the dining room Martha whispered to Harriet: "Don't worry—I won't forget your secret mission."

They had all played Pictionary after dinner. It was a happy evening.

Harriet had walked out to the car—Jack's car—after Kate and Jack had said their farewells and thanks to the Duntans. Harriet twined herself round Kate: "Gran, can I come over for supper one night before we all go to Corfu? Just me on my own, not Polly? We finish at the caff at six."

"Of course, my darling. I'll come and collect you."

She had kept her promise, and Jack had tactfully taken himself down to London on business. Harriet had been both relieved and disappointed.

She and Polly had enjoyed endless discussions and much speculation about Kate and Jack's relationship. Polly, used to her own particularly glitzy and notorious grandmother, imagined them in a far more active role than Harriet either could or wanted to. The only thing they agreed on was that it was weird that ancient people should need any relationship at all.

"I think they've got the hots for each other though," said Polly knowledgeably, but Harriet had ambivalent feelings about this idea. She had secretly liked Jack, but that didn't stop her resenting him and wanting her grandmother to herself.

Jane Pulborough came to stay at the Observatory, and was enchanted by it. Gloria and Jessie were thrilled by her obviously genuine admiration for their work.

Gloria's Jim was getting worse. Eating and speaking were becoming a major problem for him. Gloria mostly took work home and was finding it increasingly difficult to come and sew at the stables even for the odd morning. She badly missed the chat and laughter with Kate and Jessie, but she was amazingly cheerful. Jack had long conversations with her about the difficulties of being a carer—about the necessity for the occasional break, versus the anguish of leaving a beloved invalid at all; about what sort of facilities would be really helpful.

One day, when Gloria arrived to collect a pile of new designs, she said to Kate: "Do you know what your Jack's just asked me to do?"

"No. What?"

"He's only asked me to go on that there governing body of his up at the Hall—that's all."

"Gloria, how brilliant of him! Why didn't I think of it myself? You're the very person."

"I said no, of course."

"You said no?" shrieked Kate. "Gloria, you must do it. Is it because of leaving Jim for the meetings?"

"Not entirely. Jack said he'd always get a nurse in to cover if I wanted—it's the sort of thing he says he wants to be able to do. No—it's just not my scene—all those people like that niffy-naffy Mrs. Fanshaw and the Bishop on the committee. I don't object to Sir Archibald, mind," said Gloria graciously. "He's got all his buttons done up, and he's always so pleasant to everybody . . ."

"But you'd be a star. Look how well you and I ran those classes together. Look what a good president of the WI you were. OK, Mrs. Fanshaw's a pain—I can't stand her myself and she loathes me—but she's really good at committees. I actually suggested her to Jack, though it sure as hell went against the grain to do so. She'll be ace at the fundraising stuff—but you'll know what's really needed for the centre. You have to think again, Gloria." In the end, Gloria agreed.

"How clever of you, Jack," said Kate admiringly. "I begin to see why you've done so well."

Jack roared with laughter. "Oh we are progressing. Approval from you! Don't get too carried away—I might get above myself."

* * *

Jane had shown Kate's work to the fashion editor at *Vogue*, who had been enchanted by the embroidered jackets and waistcoats for both men and women, and agreed to run an article on Midas in the Christmas number. There had been an interview with Jane and Kate in the shopping feature of a major Sunday newspaper. Kate's designs were described as "borrowing the best from the past and lending something exciting to the future." She was stunned. Sonia was going to hold a big charity fair at Duntan again, in November—after the house had closed to the public but well before Christmas started to submerge people in ever more complicated preparations. It was all getting very exciting.

"Oh Jack, this magic house, this amazing job—but best of all you," Kate said to him one evening, leaning back against his knees. "I can't believe my luck." They had just had their favorite kind of supper, alone together. She was sitting on the floor, stitching away, surrounded by her usual rainbow of coloured silks, which often spilled out of the workshop into the house. Under her clever fingers blue auriculas with yellow centres (Gloria would approve) were rapidly growing up the side of what, when Jessie had finished with it, would be a long evening coat of fine black broadcloth. Jack was on the sofa working at some papers and the air was filled with Chopin's Piano Concerto No. 1 in E. Jack stroked her cheek.

"Nor me," he said. "I want to tell you, Kate, that I have never been so happy in my life."

The Maitlands, plus Harriet, had their holiday in Corfu. They had taken a villa with another couple, Piers and Abigail Jackson, whose three children were the same age group as Rupert and Tilly. Mike and Piers had been at school together and were old friends, but Joanna and Abigail had little in common.

The villa, whitewashed and simple, was delightful. Set in an olive grove above a secluded bay which could only be approached on foot or by boat, it was as private as it was possible to be. A wide terrace, half covered over in places to provide shade, ran all round the house; the garden walls, made of local stone, perfectly showed off the pink and scarlet geraniums which cascaded over them; delicate plumbago, its colour melting into the sky, waved gracefully from huge terracotta pots and beckoned invitations to butterflies.

Piers, who fancied himself as an authority on lepidoptera and was a great one for trying to improve each shining hour, though not with notable success, tried to teach the children to identify all the many different varieties that fluttered and drifted round the garden, from Southern Swallowtails to Yellow Brimstones and White Admirals.

"What are those really teeny little orange ones, with bright blue edges round their wings and black dots underneath?" asked Harriet, opening her wonderful eyes wide at Piers and looking intensely interested. Piers looked disconcerted.

"Are you sure you've got the description right?"

"Absolutely certain." Harriet was all innocence, and Mike's lips twitched.

The children spent most of the day with arm-bands on, flopping in and out of the incredibly clear sea, and splashing about on blow-up dinosaurs and dolphins. Tilly was quite fearless from the start, but Rupert was initially terrified about absolutely everything from wasps in the honey at breakfast, to trips in boats for picnics—not to mention lizards on the wall of his bedroom and the fear of what strange monsters might lurk in the deep. Harriet had sent him into screaming hysterics the first day by swimming underwater, clutching him round the ankle and pretending to be an octopus. Joanna, predictably, was furious with them both, but Mike had been unexpectedly sharp with Harriet, something she wasn't used to from him.

"Take on someone your own equal if you must, Harriet. Bullying's despicable," he had said. Though she shrugged a scornful shoulder, and wagged a bikinied bottom as she flounced off, she had secretly minded a loss of Mike's good opinion, and felt ashamed of frightening her little brother.

However, as the days went by, Rupert blossomed under his father's endless patience and encouragement, and actually learned to swim unaided. Joanna was forced to admit to herself that Rupert was a changed child when Mike was there—even Tilly was marginally better behaved. Harriet fought a running battle with her mother about how many evenings she was allowed to attend Fresh, the nearest, misnamed disco dive, and how late she would be allowed to stay if she went there. Unless a lift was forthcoming from other parents, this involved Joanna or Mike in a very unwelcome taxi service. The trouble was that there was no one else in the villa of Harriet's age, whereas at the disco she met other congenially moody teenagers, all of whose mothers, Harriet assured Joanna, were far more enlightened and less stuffy than she was. Harriet's still sparse supply of hair seemed to be no impediment to acquiring admirers. Gangly youths were always turning up on mopeds asking for her, and when permission was refused—as it always was—for Harriet to go off pillion behind them on the terrifying Corfiote roads they had a tiresome tendency to hang around the villa looking hungry. Having successfully lured them into her parlour, Harriet then largely ignored them and ran a new and fascinating video through her head while she pretended to be buried in her book. She had temporarily replaced the image of the alluring Alexander Rivers with that of Socrates, the waiter at the local Taverna.

Mike and Piers Jackson disappeared to play golf several times, and Joanna found being left with the mumsy company of Abigail and the children almost more than she could bear. Abigail, who was petrified of Joanna's sharp tongue and even sharper brain, and whose scintillating flow of conversation was limited to the possible risks of allowing the children to progress from total sun-block to factor twenty, drove Joanna to the bottle of ouzo in the fridge much earlier than was desirable. As Abigail didn't at all mind keeping an eye on all five children, Joanna would leave her—to their mutual relief—with the nursery party, and swim miles out to sea, where she would turn over on her back and float about thinking of Hugo Coltman. When the husbands returned from a thoroughly enjoyable morning spent ambling round the golf course near Corfu town, Joanna could hardly believe the fuss Abigail made of Piers, worrying if his nose was peeling, and rushing to greet him with a chilled glass of wine.

"God she does get up my nose," she complained to Mike. "Anyone would think Piers was Ranulph Fiennes back from the Arctic. It makes me sick. And if Piers tells me one more time about the trouble he's having with his swing, I might just take a swing at him myself."

On the whole, the fortnight was a qualified success. The Maitlands came back without a definite resolution to their problems, but Mike had agreed to extend his deadline for sorting things out till Christmas. He was more certain than ever that he did not want to miss out on his children's lives, and found he had forgotten over the last resentful year what interesting company Joanna could be, if she chose, or how much she sometimes amused him—though not always on purpose. He decided that if Jo was prepared to compromise, then he would do his best to meet her halfway—but she had to want the marriage to work. He was not going to be pushed around by his wife any more.

For her part, Joanna might dream about Hugo, but he had never left her in any doubt that the slightest suspicion of their affair becoming public would send him scooting back to the matrimonial bed in record time, denials scorching from his lips. It was not a satisfactory relationship, and Joanna despised herself for not having ended it yet. Hugo Coltman was undoubtedly second-rate goods—and that could not be said of Mike. She wished she could roll them into one and have Mike's kindness and integrity spiced up with Hugo's sleazy sexiness.

As far as any attempt by the Maitlands to re-establish a sex life for themselves was concerned, conditions had not been favourable: the house was all on one level, and because it was so hot everyone slept with their French windows wide open—all of which opened on to the terrace. Mike decided not to court disaster by trying. Joanna, having decided to spurn any sexual overtures Mike might make, was needled when he didn't make any.

She felt furiously jealous of her mother, who seemed to have landed all the things Joanna most coveted, and was very resentful of Jack Morley—though she had to admit that he was an attractive man. She hoped he was not going to be a permanent fixture in her mother's life. She gnawed on her own perception of Kate's disloyalty to her father's memory. Deep down she knew it was monstrously unfair, but it was as irresistible as checking a sore tooth for pain. The tooth got more painful with each testing bite.

After the usual shambolic chaos at Corfu Airport and a long, hot wait for delayed flights, Mike returned to Oxton Road, and Joanna and the children returned to Yorkshire and their move into Longthorpe. Joanna tried to convince herself that once she was installed there, Mike would be unable to resist its charms. She couldn't wait to get the kitchen organised for party catering. It was still the only room she wanted to change.

Nick and Robin were coming up the following week to negotiate who was going to have which bits of furniture. Kate had stipulated that neither Mike nor Robin should enter into this, and that Joanna and Nick should go from room to room, picking alternately without regard to financial value.

"Oh, but Mum, there are one or two things that I know Dad always specially wanted me to have," said Joanna.

"Oh, but Jo, they all belong to me now, and these are my conditions," said the new, more assertive Kate. She added consolingly: "You might well find that Nick doesn't

actually want the same things as you anyway, darling.'' She
had been right. She had also suggested that Joanna should
let Nick and Robin have the cottage as a weekend retreat.
Unlike Mike, Nick loved the country, and once the children
started arriving Kate guessed he and Robin would want to
leave London.

"You let them have it rent-free for one year. I will let
you have Longthorpe rent-free, and in a year's time when
Jack and I review the situation at the Observatory we'll see
where we all are.'' Cecily, of course, was to stay put.

Soon after the Maitlands returned from Corfu, school
started and Harriet went back to Essendale Hall. Polly had
not received any news from Martha yet.

⦗ TWENTY-SEVEN ⦘

There had been far more than the usual two-thirds rate of
acceptances for Jack's party at Ravelstoke Hall. Curiosity
played its part of course, not only about Jack himself, but
because the late Lord Ravelstoke had been such a recluse
that very few people had ever been in the house at all. Kate
had taken no hand in planning the party. "I'm not going
to turn into one of your minions,'' she had teased Jack.
"You've got quite enough of them running round you already. Besides, that house gives me the heebie-jeebies. The
sooner it turns into something useful the better.''

Kate had now met the famous Sylvia, who ran Jack's
business life. She had expected to hate her, but actually
liked her very much, despite the fact that she looked so like
a cartoon of the personal assistant to a powerful boss, that
Kate asked Jack if he'd bought her ready packaged. She
was clearly devoted to Jack, but not in a way that Kate,
who had absolutely no desire to organise Jack's schedule
or arrange his meetings herself, found threatening—and as
Jack had said, Sylvia had a sense of humour.

Jack was determined to make the party, with which he hoped to publicise his prospective holiday home for the disabled, a very lavish affair indeed. The invitations which went out in the name of Mr. Franklin J. Morley, promised Dinner, Entertainment, and Fireworks at Ravelstoke Hall. Jack had been lucky enough to get Kit and The Widow to come and amuse his guests. That in itself guaranteed success.

Joanna had wondered whether to dream up a clever name for her party planning, but as she always used her maiden name professionally, she settled simply for Joanna Rendlesham Catering. She knew she should feel grateful to Jack for giving her such a splendid launching pad for her new venture—she just wished the chance had come from someone else. Between them, Joanna and the efficient Sylvia had organised everything for the party to the last detail. They got on extremely well together, and both enjoyed it.

The party was to take place on the second Saturday in October. Kate walked over to the Hall with Jack in the morning. She had been to many grand occasions with Oliver over the years, but she had never in all her life seen such flowers as the florist engaged by Sylvia had produced. The main hall was a riot of autumn colours, but every room had a different colour scheme. There were swags of flowers all the way up the great staircase and huge pedestals were placed in strategic corners. Some of them, Kate knew, skilfully hid damp patches. Much of the furniture had been moved and only the very best pieces were left. Floodlighting had been set up, and there were lights all the way up the drive, making the sinister yew trees look unexpectedly festive; the fountain in the courtyard was sending up a spectacular jet into the air and the old cascade in the gardens had been made to work. Clever lighting turned the water of both of them into shimmering rainbows at the flick of a switch. "Heavens!" said Kate. "You have been busy!" A shuttle service of minibuses was standing by to transport guests from the car park. Most importantly, announced Sylvia, there were dozens of loos in a very elegant marquee joined to the back of the house that looked fit for a party in its own right. "No loo or coat queues. Vital!" said Sylvia.

Jack, who could read Kate's face like a book now, was highly amused at her expression. "You're afraid it's too much," he said, mocking her gently. "But I can tell you people will expect a splurge and that's what they're going to get. They'll simply love it—and then they'll love it even more afterwards when they can say how thoroughly over the top it all was. Gerald Brownlow will be able to say, 'What did you expect from someone from his background?' Think what pleasure that will give," he said ironically.

"Oh Jack, I do love you—I'd kill him if I heard him," said Kate.

At least four people were definitely going to wear Midas outfits: Kate herself, who had decided to wear the blue silk jacket with the shell motif that she had worn to Netta's party; Jane Pulborough, who was coming up specially and was going to stay at Duntan; and Sonia—for whom Kate had made a fantastic scarlet waistcoat embroidered with a riot of flowers which she wore with a white silk shirt and an extremely short matching scarlet silk skirt to show off her elegant legs. Even Archie had whistled when he saw it. The fourth person was Nick, for whom Kate had designed a dark green Pandit Nehru type coat in heavy slubbed silk, with gold embroidery down the front and round the stand-up collar. The tailoring of this was beyond Jessie, but Jane had got a shop in Jermyn Street to make it up after Kate had done the embroidery. They were enthusiastic about doing more. Nick had been a bit doubtful to start with. The invitation had read "Black tie optional" and he said he would have much preferred to wear his ordinary, safe dinner jacket. Kate said firmly that nowadays the interpretation of this was so wide that you never knew what anyone might wear.

"Only for the sake of your career, Mum, would I dream of going in for modelling," said Nick gloomily, but Robin said she had caught him trying the jacket on and preening at himself in her long looking-glass. She thought it uproariously funny.

"Let's hope you don't just turn up in your old shorts and sneakers," he'd retorted. Robin was not a snappy dresser.

After the party was over, Jack was going to take Kate away for ten days—their first holiday together. He wouldn't tell her where they were going except that it was to be Italy.

Kate hadn't had a proper holiday for over two years, and the idea of going with Jack was so wonderful she could hardly think of anything else. She was counting the days.

One day when he had returned after one of his trips to New York, he had said to her, very seriously: "Darling Kate, we have to discuss certain things about your life— and mine. We can't go on 'dancing barefoot' for ever. You wouldn't let me tell you what was on my mind last time I tried. When am I to be allowed to try again?" And Kate had answered: "Save it for Italy."

She was convinced that Jack was going to propose to her on their holiday, and whereas two months earlier she had felt completely satisfied with their relationship just as it was, only terrified of spoiling it and dubious as to whether she would ever want to make the commitment of marriage again, now she knew that if Jack asked her to marry him, her answer would be an unequivocal yes. She would even be prepared to give up Midas for him, though she didn't think for one moment that he would want her to do so. What more romantic place for a proposal than Italy? thought Kate happily.

Jack had wanted a sensational evening, and he got it. The great party at Ravelstoke Hall was a Yorkshire talking point for years afterwards. Not one detail of the immaculate organisation went awry. Joanna's food was superlative—even Mrs. Northwood had enough—the service was faultless, there was the right amount of space for those who liked to be in the thick of a throng, but always chairs in a more peaceful side room for those who did not. Everyone was dressed in their best—Gloria resembled a mobile primrose, Lady Rosamund looked like a bird of paradise. Frank, in the suit he kept for weddings and funerals, was almost unrecognisable without his old cap stuck back-to-front on his head; his hair was brushed sideways over his bald patch and his face was so smooth, red and shiny from shaving and scrubbing that he looked like a ventriloquist's dummy.

Joanna, having done all the hard work beforehand, changed into an evening dress and joined the party. She basked in all the compliments that rightly came her way about the food, and revelled in the ones that wrongly came her way from Hugo Coltman. Penny Coltman was notably unfriendly, but Joanna was too high on admiration and Jack's champagne to care.

After dinner everyone trooped up to the Long Gallery, where rows of gilt chairs had been laid out for the entertainment. Kit and The Widow excelled themselves.

"I'll die if they go on like this," gasped Sonia who was sitting next to Kate. "I feel ill from laughing so much." Jack sat between the Lord Lieutenant's wife and beige-clad Lady Van Alleyn, who always dressed as if she was afraid of being spotted in the desert. Several members of the newly appointed governing body, including Netta and Miles Fanshaw, separated Kate and Jack. Robin was on Kate's other side and Cecily was between Robin and Nick.

After several encores, and wild applause, Kit and The Widow finally took a last bow and Jack got to his feet and walked on to the platform that Josh had made for the occasion. He thanked everyone for coming and said what a privilege it was for him to be their host. "Some of you may know that as a small boy I came often to this house—by the back door." Laughter. "I'm glad this great house has had the chance to wear its formal party dress tonight," he went on, "but from now on it's going to be put to a very different use—one I hope you will all approve of and be proud of as I am proud to be its owner tonight. But," Jack paused, "as from tomorrow it will really belong to all of you. Next week the alterations start, and because I know there has been much speculation, I thought I would take this chance to tell you about the plans." He spoke briefly and movingly of his ideals for the centre and appealed for support for the project, but he did not overstate his case. He possessed that mysterious power to command immediate attention without appearing to try, and he had his audience eating out of his hand. Kate was filled with pride and happiness.

"That's enough from me," Jack finished, smiling. "Now for fireworks. If anyone would like to go out into the courtyard they will have time to collect a coat—but for those who would rather stay indoors, I think you will all see perfectly from here." He was about to step down amid a burst of spontaneous clapping, when Netta Fanshaw came and stepped up beside him. She held up her hand.

"Oh Lord, wouldn't you just know it!" muttered Sonia to Kate. "She can't resist the limelight, can she?"

Netta gave everyone her sweetest smile. Robin rolled her eyes and whispered to Cecily: "Wouldn't she make a great coughdrop—all honey and glycerine."

"I sometimes get accused of being bossy," said Netta, leaving a little pause for murmurs of dissent which were not forthcoming. She went on undaunted: "As a member of the new committee I felt I had to take it upon myself to thank Jack on behalf of all of us here for this wonderful evening." This time, there was polite assent. "Jack has told you about the exciting future for this house, which is obviously so dear to his heart—but Jack himself is so modest that there is one thing I'm sure he hasn't told you." Netta looked so arch she might have been a gothic window. "He knows what he's talking about at first hand." She paused dramatically. "Jack Morley is himself the devoted husband of a paraplegic wife."

Jack's face was completely impassive. Kate thought she was going to faint. She knew she must escape and get out of this terrible house which had always seemed to threaten her. Urgent fingers closed round her arm. "Don't go, Kate," hissed Sonia. "Stay right where you are and keep smiling even if it kills you. Don't let bloody Netta win."

Afterwards Kate had no memory at all of the fantastic fireworks, which everyone said were the best they'd ever seen. She felt the next hour was the equivalent of a full training at RADA plus several tours with leading repertory companies. She laughed and chatted with everyone there— everyone except Jack that is—then oohed and aahed at the explosions in the sky with all the other guests, all the while flying on automatic pilot. Joanna left the Coltmans abruptly and came to join the rest of the family. Together with Archie and Sonia, they made a sort of bodyguard round Kate and moved with her wherever she went.

A lot of people came up and were specially warm to her; several people gave her curious looks; a few avoided her with the look of panic that is sometimes reserved for the newly bereaved—but Kate got the feeling that the implication of Netta's announcement was not lost on many of her acquaintances.

Gerald Brownlow came striding over, looking ponderous. He took Kate's elbow, a habit he had with women, as though he thought they all needed help with walking. It usually drove Kate mad. Tonight she didn't even notice.

"Kate, I have to know—were you aware Jack had a wife?" he asked, then just to be on the safe side and clarify the question, added, "Did you realise he was married?"

"Of course," lied Kate, smiling brilliantly. "I get an extra kick out of adultery." She quickly turned away to sparkle at someone else, leaving Gerald disconcerted—but quietly hopeful for the future. It had been Gerald's idea to ask the Fanshaws to make some searching inquiries about Jack. Miles had been attending a business conference in New York, and he and Netta had just got back. Gerald had not known Netta was going to make her announcement—and would certainly have dissuaded her if he had—but he had always known sound reconnaissance would pay off.

Kate had arrived at Ravelstoke with Jack, but as soon as people started to go, she asked Nick and Robin to drive her back to the Observatory. Joanna said she would take Cecily home with her. Cecily looked helplessly at Kate. She suddenly looked very old and very tired. When Joanna offered her an arm, she took it.

"It may not be true, Kate," said Robin in the car, anguished by the look on her mother-in-law's face. "It could be only Netta making trouble?"

"Of course it's true. Jack would have denied it otherwise."

"Shall we stay with you, Mum?" asked Nick. "Please let us."

"No thank you, darling. I need to see Jack alone."

Nick and Robin drove unhappily back to Longthorpe, where they were staying with Joanna. "I can't believe Jack deliberately deceived her," said Robin. "He seems such a lovely guy. Really special. I still think he is—there must be more to it than we know."

"Bloody awful way for Mum to find out though. Did you see the look Netta gave her after she'd burst her little bombshell? I'll never speak to the woman again—ever."

When Jack came back to the Observatory, Kate was waiting in the drawing room. He stood in the doorway.

"Oh Kate. I don't know what to say to you. I am just so sorry. It's all my fault—what a bloody fool I've been."

"No," said Kate. "It's me that's been the fool. You wouldn't believe I could be so stupid as to do the same thing twice, would you?"

"Do what?" asked Jack, with a terrible sinking of the heart.

"Fall in love with a powerful shit for the second time in my life."

Jack looked as though he'd been knifed.

"You told me your wife had been killed," said Kate. "You *lied* to me."

"No," he answered. "I didn't actually lie—not with words. But I might as well have done. I told you a car crash had dealt with my marriage, and that was true. You assumed that Sheila was killed, and I, unforgivably, let you think that."

"Sheila? Oh, we have a name now, do we? How cosy!"

"Kate," he said desperately, "darling Kate, don't be like that. It really isn't quite as you think."

"Don't you call me darling," she flashed.

"Will you let me explain?"

"You've had months and weeks to explain. You've had nights," said Kate pointedly, "when you could have explained. But you didn't. It's too late now."

"I've tried to tell you several times—missed my chance and then funked it. I fully admit it. Once that stuffed-shirt Brownlow rang up at the crucial moment. Once when I tried, you stopped me. I blame myself entirely. I should have insisted then, but I was so afraid of losing you I let it go again. Last time you told me to save what I was going to tell you for Italy . . ."

"And I," said Kate in a deadly voice, "thought you were going to ask me to marry you in Italy. Well, we won't be going now." She gave a little laugh. Jack, who had so loved the sound of Kate's laughter, had loved her particular laugh as much as anything about her, didn't recognise this one. "And I'd decided to say yes," she said, "fool that I am. I've had a lucky escape."

"Please let me tell you what really happened to Sheila."

Kate put her hands over her ears. "*No! No! No!*" she shouted. "You've had your chance and you've blown it.

You could have told me, but instead you told fucking Netta Fanshaw.''

Jack suddenly felt furiously angry. ''Stop it, Kate!'' he said. ''You've every right to be angry but now you're being ridiculous. You know perfectly well I wouldn't tell Netta anything.''

He came and took her by the shoulders, but she shook him off.

''Well, I can guess it all for myself now, thank you: your invalid wife wasn't enough for you any more—perhaps she can't give you all you want—so you pop safely across the Atlantic and have your nice little bit on the side—*me*—set me up in a dear little house, then salve your conscience by endowing a home for the handicapped which you can well afford to do. Am I right?''

Jack stared at her in silence. ''You can put it like that if you like,'' he said slowly—disastrously. ''Yes, if that's how you choose to see it, I suppose you're absolutely right.'' He turned on his heel and walked out of the room.

Kate dragged herself slowly upstairs. Somehow she got undressed, throwing the shell-embroidered jacket that she never wanted to wear again across the room, and climbing into her high bed from which she could see the stars. The sky looked very clear and cold to Kate. She lay like a stone.

How funny, she thought. I'm not feeling anything. It doesn't hurt. How *strange*.

She could hear Jack moving about in the bedroom downstairs in which he still kept his things, though this was the first night they'd spent in the house together that he hadn't shared her bed. She had no idea how much later it was when she heard his steps coming upstairs.

He tapped softly on the door. She turned the light on. She didn't want Jack to think she was asleep.

''Kate? Kate, will you let me talk to you?''

Silence. Kate watched the door handle turn.

But there was a key in the lock now. Kate didn't need to go up into the observatory this time—she had locked the door.

She held her breath, punishing him, making him sweat for it. But Jack didn't plead or try the door a second time, as she had felt certain he would. She heard his steps going down again.

It was as though she had no vocal cords. She longed to cry out to him, but remained mute.

After a moment a door slammed and she heard the sound of a car being started—and driven away.

Then Kate turned into her pillow and cried as she had not cried for years—as she had thought she would never in her life cry again.

In the morning she looked into the downstairs bedroom. All Jack's things had gone. There was nothing of his left in the house at all.

ↄ TWENTY-EIGHT ⊱

There had been a sacred building at Betws-y-Fridd—or, to give it its English translation, "the church of the high pasture" since time immemorial. The present church dated back to Saxon times, a small stone building, whitewashed inside, with no stained glass or elaborate memorials. The carved figure on the worn stone above the main door, which for years had been presumed to be Christ on the cross, was now thought by scholars to date back much earlier—possibly even to pagan times. It was so eroded by the elements that it was impossible to make out what it had originally depicted. The church at Betws-y-Fridd was known locally as "The Drovers' Church." Tourists loved the square wooden enclosure in the nave where, in previous centuries, working dogs could be put during the service. Now there

were usually sheep reclining against the old headstones
which stuck out at drunken angles like broken teeth; occasionally half-wild Welsh mountain ponies that had been
turned loose on the hill wandered through the churchyard
or cropped the grass. You had to be careful where you
walked—though most of people who flogged up the steep
track wore proper walking boots, sported orange kagouls
and didn't worry too much about what they trod in. Some
came for the challenge of the walk, some came for the
view, and a few of them found a silence which they were
able to keep inwardly and take out later to sustain them in
their busy urban lives.

There were still occasional services in the church—in
both Welsh and English—but only of course in the summer, there being no artificial light or heating. The building
belonged to the Church of Wales but the services were
usually ecumenical, catering mostly for youth hostel
groups, or serious walkers, rather than for modern farmers.
Father Paul, from the Benedictine foundation below Betws-
y-Fridd, loved to go there and was always pleased if he was
invited to take a service in either language. There had once
been a wood round the church but not much remained.
Some hazel bushes, a few mountain ash trees, bent by the
wind, and some old fallen trunks encrusted with lichen and
almost embedded in the ground, were a reminder of it—
but that was all.

Father Paul, the housemaster of St. Anthony's at Nant
Dafydd College, the Roman Catholic boys' public school,
was an acknowledged expert on Gerard Manley Hopkins.
Many teachers of English literature used his books in both
universities and schools. Father Paul considered himself incredibly lucky to live and work in Snowdonia. The river
Dafydd ran through the bottom of the famously beautiful
college grounds, which were always opened to the public
in rhododendron and magnolia time. People came from
miles to see them, but though Father Paul appreciated their
beauty, like the poet he studied and wrote about, he would

have been bereft without the wildness of the weeds in the wilderness—though there were days when he felt he could have done with a little less of the wet. He specially loved the unkempt hillside round the little church at Betws-y-Fridd. Except for the occasional croaking of a raven, or the cry of a plover, it was so quiet up there you could almost hear the harebells ringing in the grass.

The Abbey was modern compared to the drovers' church—only a hundred years old, though the school chapel was a good example of the architecture of its period.

On this October morning, Father Paul had just handed out the mail to the boys in his house and after the juniors had scurried off, he sat chatting in the refectory to a few sixth formers who, like him, were having a second cup of coffee. The school had gone over to a cafeteria form of catering several years before; some of the older monks deplored this, but the boys greatly preferred it. They still sat with their fellow house-mates, however, and always brought their trays of chosen food back to the appropriate section of the dining room.

"You really ought to tell your girlfriend to give up those frightful purple envelopes, Carter," said Father Paul, "and what does SWALS stand for? In my day we put SWALK."

"Oh, you're very behind the times, Father. We seal letters with a loving snog now."

"How much less romantic." Father Paul was going through his own letters—some from old boys, some administrative and a good many connected with his writing. His last book, written about an inner and an outer pilgrimage, triggered by walking in the foothills of the Himalayas during a sabbatical term he had been granted, had become a surprise best seller. It had engendered a lot of correspondence. Father Paul, who was an inspired and inspiring teacher, was secretly afraid his superiors might feel he should give up his house at the college to live in the monastery and concentrate full time on his writing. He very much disliked the idea.

Still half chatting to the boys, he skimmed through his letters, putting those he knew to be dull or non-urgent to the bottom of the pile. One, with a Yorkshire postmark, attracted his attention because it had been forwarded on from Oxford and was addressed to Mark Hughes, which had been his name before he entered the order sixteen years ago. Someone had scribbled "Try Nant Dafydd Abbey" on it. The writing meant nothing to him, though he thought it was in a youthful hand. Strange, really, because his books came out under his Benedictine name. Curiosity aroused, Father Paul opened it. But after reading the first paragraph, he quickly put it back in the envelope, so shocked he felt ill. This was a letter to be read in private. With an outward show of calm, he shooed the remaining boys off to their various ploys, thanking God that he had a free period and wouldn't be teaching for the next hour.

Then he walked over to St. Anthony's and on reaching his study sat down in his chair. He was trembling. It took all his strength of mind to force himself to take the letter out of its envelope again. He looked first at the signature: Harriet Rendlesham. With a terrible lurch of the heart, Father Paul knew that what had shocked him so much when he had read the first few lines of the letter in the refectory, must be true.

"Dear Mr. Hughes," he read, again:

This letter may come as an awful shock, but I think you could be my father. I do hope you don't mind me writing. If you have a wife and family I don't want to cause trouble, but all my life I've longed for a father—or at least to know who mine is. My mother, Joanna Rendlesham, would never tell me or anyone else who you were. Not even my grandmother knows, and I lived with her till I was six, and still do sometimes. All the time I was little I imagined you trying to find me—but you didn't. Then a few weeks ago my mother told me that you don't even know I exist so I feel I must look for you myself. I've done a very dishonest thing—I've been through Mum's desk and found this photograph hidden in it with just initials on. I have violent hair like yours. I enclose my photograph so you can see. I don't look quite like that now because the day I found your picture I had my head shaved. I wish I hadn't now, but it's growing again at last. A friend of mine has an aunt at Oxford where Mum was before I was born. I gave her the photo and she said she would try and find out who you were. An old porter at Christchurch recognised it and thinks you are Mark Hughes who was a don there. He said a letter would still get forwarded to wherever you live now.

My mother is married and has two more children. This is not her address but it would reach me. Please will you write to me if you get this letter? I long to meet you—if you wouldn't mind? I have dreamt of you so often.

> With love,
> Yours sincerely
> Harriet Rendlesham

P.S. Please, please don't tell my mother until we've been in touch—though I realise she'll have to know sometime.

Father Paul sat, reading and rereading the letter, in a state of shock. He looked at the photograph of himself as he had been sixteen years before, and then at the one of a very blonde girl with wild curls and a vivid, vulnerable face. He had no doubt at all that he was looking at his own child. "I have dreamt of you so often" she had written. Yeats' lines came into his head:

But I, being poor, have only my dreams;
I have spread my dreams under your feet;
Tread softly because you tread on my dreams.

What shall I do? thought Father Paul. Whatever shall I do?

Then he did what he always did in times of trouble or joy—went over to the monastery chapel. His thoughts and emotions were in turmoil, but he tried to centre himself. He prayed for guidance and for help: for himself, for his vocation, for this daughter of whose existence he had been completely unaware, and for whatever the future might hold. He was torn between horror and delight. Long ago he had renounced the possibility of having a family of his own. Because he had always loved children this had been, for him, one of the things it had been hardest to give up.

He came out of the chapel feeling calmer, and went straight into school to battle with teaching *Measure for Measure* to a class of rugger fanatics. Trying to wrench their minds away from the forthcoming match against their great rivals, St. Peter's at Morfa Castell, was an uphill task.

It wasn't until much later that Father Paul got a chance to talk to his friend Father Dominic. They settled in front of the fire, and Father Paul thrust the letter at him.

Father Dominic, not one to be profligate with words or gallop at uninspected fences, read the letter twice, and looked carefully at the photographs before speaking.

"True?" he asked.

"It has to be."

"You had an affair with the mother?"

"An affair—no. I slept with her for one night the week before I entered the order."

"Were you in love with her?"

"No."

"But you were attracted to her?"

"Yes. Oh yes—she was a very beautiful girl. My star pupil."

Father Paul looked haggard. In his state of heightened sensitivity, his truthful answers to such bald questions sounded terrible to his own ears.

"Would you like to tell me?" asked Father Dominic.

So Father Paul told him, and went back in time to Oxford, to Mark Geraint Hughes, aged thirty-five, Welsh-speaking son of a country doctor from North Wales, who was a don at Christ Church, and to the dazzlingly good-looking young student from Brasenose who had come to him to study English literature. An exceptional student, a brilliant girl, with a thirst for knowledge and a sharp incisive mind: a wilful, spoilt girl who lacked a sense of balance but knew exactly what she wanted and believed she could always have it— and she had wanted Mark Hughes from the moment she met him.

As her tutor, Mark automatically considered her quite out of bounds as far as any relationship with himself was concerned—though these things happened occasionally, of course—but by the time Joanna Rendlesham came up to Oxford Mark had already decided, after long heart-searching, to become a Benedictine. He was aware of Joanna's feelings for him, but he was well used to handling student crushes and had not been unduly worried to start with. A lot of his female students fancied themselves in love with him for a short while.

Joanna had gone to considerable lengths to disguise her feelings from her fellow students, but had not gone a centimetre with her tutor himself. Indeed. her directness had taken his breath away. He had tried to tease her out of it, laughed at her gently, and then resorted to some astringent straight talking. Nothing had the slightest effect. When he continued to refuse all her overtures, she had proposed marriage to him. When, in desperation, he had explained to her that he was about to become a monk she had been appalled—and disbelieving. It did not enter the mind of Joanna Rendlesham, as she had been then, that he would hold out against her for long. No one else had.

Mark Hughes' parents were both dead—indeed, it had been partly consideration for the feelings of his chapel-going father that had delayed his entry to Nant Dafydd for so long—so he had no particular ties. Before he went into the monastery he had taken himself to Tuscany for a walking holiday. He had stayed at Fiesole, and listening to the sound of the bells that filled the air each evening and to oratorios sung by nightingales in the woods, he had felt a deep sense of the rightness of the commitment he was about to make—though he had also indulged himself in occasional half-pleasurable melancholy, as he looked out over the curved red roof-tiles, and breathed in the voluptuous scent of wisteria. These are my last days of freedom, he had thought. What will it be like to lose that?

Then Joanna had turned up.

"I told her it was impossible," said Father Paul now. "I tried to send her away, but she had found out where I was, and come all that way. I agreed to take her for a last farewell dinner together. It was very stupid of me, but I felt so sorry for her . . ."

"And she was so beautiful," prompted Father Dominic, inexorably.

"Yes," said Father Paul, sadly. "So beautiful, so clever, so vital—and so determined. We had a wonderful evening. We went to Florence to a trattoria which I knew about, but which was still undiscovered by tourists, and we had marvellous pasta and a lot of chianti. Then we kissed properly for the first time and said goodbye—or at least," he corrected himself painfully, "I let myself think it was a last goodbye. Joanna had booked in at the pensione where I was staying. Of course I should have moved out," he said heavily. "I knew it really. Later that night she arrived in my bed."

Father Dominic thought his friend looked utterly drained.

"And this time you didn't try to send her away?"

"No."

"Was she a virgin?"

"No."

They'd had a desperate time in the morning. Joanna had been unable to believe that after such a night, Mark could still be determined to follow his vocation. "You accepted all I've just given you and then think you can reduce me in your mind to a little sin of the flesh," she had hissed at him. "Final fling, no broken vows, off to confession and everything in your Garden of Eden is lovely again. 'The woman she tempted me,' you'll say. You're despicable!"

Mark Hughes, mortally ashamed, thinking the sin of the flesh had been greater than he felt he could bear, knowing it was his rejection of her, not his acceptance, that had shattered her pride and lacerated her feelings, thought he was despicable too. He had never forgotten those words.

They had parted in terrible distress. Afterwards he had written to Joanna and tried to tell her how deeply sorry and ashamed of himself he felt, but at the same time how greatly honoured to have been given her love. He had tried to restore her self-respect without holding out false hopes; to blame himself, and at the same time say that what they'd had together had been beautiful. Mark Hughes, the distinguished writer, had not made a very good job of this letter. Joanna wrote a scorching answer saying she never wanted to see or hear from him again—and he had compiled with her wishes.

He could not know that the worst of her anger was largely directed at herself, or of the sacrifice she had subsequently made for him.

"And now there's Harriet Rendlesham," said Father Dominic. "What do you want to do about her?"

"Certainly not reject her."

At least that was something Father Paul felt positive about. "I have a feeling from her letter she's felt rejected by both parents. I can't fail her."

"Whatever it costs?"

"Whatever it costs."

"It won't be your decision, of course. You'll have to
see Father Abbot. Sleep on it," said Father Dominic, aching
for his friend and yet at some level feeling envious of him
too. "I shall pray for you."

Father Paul had spent a sleepless night before he went to
lay the story before his superior.

The Abbot had been very gentle with Father Paul—and
implacable. He agreed that this vulnerable teenager ought
to be able to count on her father's support, and should be
helped in every way possible, but—and it was a big but—
Father Paul could not remain as a housemaster in the school
while openly acknowledging an illegitimate daughter, no
matter that her conception had taken place prior to his entry
to the monastery. Father Paul had been equally sure that he
could not, with one breath, make offers of love and support
to this child who had dreamt of him for so long, while
telling her in the next that his identity as her father must
remain secret and he could not acknowledge her as his
daughter. The Abbot, who was a great admirer of Father
Paul and knew him to be a wonderful schoolmaster, regretted the decision he had to take, but was clear about it
in his own mind. Discretion was called for. The school
must not be touched by scandal, and if the media got hold
of the story there was no knowing what they might make
of it, or how they might distort it. Parents would not like
that.

"You could do pastoral work, and you can certainly
concentrate on your writing. You are luckier than most with
that. Perhaps another walk, another book, a different journey? This new experience, however difficult and unexpected, may give you greater insights that could ultimately
be of value. Stay at St. Anthony's till the end of term, then

come back into the monastery and write. Meet your daughter in the Christmas holidays.''

Father Paul had bowed his head. He had feared this would be the verdict.

◦ TWENTY-NINE ◦

Kate felt as though she were walking through thick fog down a long dark road, weighed down by a sodden overcoat, with mud on heavy, leaking boots. She couldn't even pick out the verge on either side of her road for the swirling, choking mist, let alone see any side roads that might offer alternative routes. The road ahead was completely blotted out, but Kate didn't want to look anyway—it might stretch too far into the distance. Just keep on walking, she told herself; don't look up, don't look down—keep walking. Sometimes she felt that if she stopped she might expire. Sometimes she wanted to expire.

It was a far cry from dancing barefoot in the grass.

She tried to throw herself into her work, stitched away like a revved-up automaton—and got no joy from what had previously been her solace in times of trouble. Her output as far as Midas was concerned was prodigious.

Gloria and Jessie Worsencroft watched miserably and felt helpless. Kate had a feeling that most of Gloria's indignation on her behalf was directed against Netta Fanshaw rather than against Jack. Gloria made several tentative attempts to raise the subject, but Kate made it clear that mention of Jack was taboo. She felt terribly hurt and angry with him. How dared he deceive her—and how dared he not have made one more attempt on the door handle?

After her first passion of shock, humiliation and fury had dulled a little, Kate admitted to herself that she did not really believe that Jack was a second Oliver—she had simply said the most wounding thing she could think of. She wondered where Jack was, what he was doing—above all what he was feeling. Hardly a second went by when he was not in her thoughts. The idea that he might even visit Ravelstoke and be close but unseen, was more than she could bear. Every time the telephone went she jumped. She rushed to the door when the postman came. The sound of a car sent her dashing to the window.

As the days went by and there was no word, she came to accept that Jack could not want a reconciliation as passionately as she did. He was the one at fault, Kate told herself, so it was for him to make the move. Her own words came back to haunt her. Had she really only been "just a little bit on the side"? It began to look like it. She would die rather than be the first to get in touch.

Acer, sensing Kate's distress, watched her every move and wouldn't leave her side. She drove Kate mad by leaning against her when she was trying to sew, whining mournfully, and placing a paw in her lap—usually on top of whatever Kate was making. Kate would send her sharply to her basket, and Acer would slink sadly off, looking deeply reproachful at having her sympathy rejected. Acer was not alone in that. Kate rejected everyone's attempts at sympathy. All her family were deeply worried about her. They had never seen her so withdrawn, so utterly without any spark.

Their attitudes towards Jack varied, though they united in outrage at Netta Fanshaw's meddling act of spite. None of them knew what had actually transpired between Kate and Jack after the party, because Kate refused to talk about it.

Harriet, home for the weekend, couldn't bear to see her grandmother looking so unhappy, but no one seemed prepared to discuss the events of the party or its implications with her. She asked what had happened to Jack and got her head snapped off by her grandmother for the first time in

her life. Joanna thought she should talk to her about what
had happened but felt quite at a loss to know how to discuss
her mother's lover with Harriet. She desperately envied
Sonia Duntan the ease with which she communicated with
her children. No subject seemed to be taboo round the
kitchen table at Duntan. Polly, with her open, gossipy relationship with her own mother, was Harriet's best source
of information.

Harriet was also very absorbed in ploys of her own.

Robin rang Kate up often, as she always had, hoping to
cheer her with the light-hearted chats they'd always enjoyed
together; she tried to beam Kate's attention on to the
baby—something that normally required no effort—but
though Kate listened and answered, Robin could tell her
mind was elsewhere.

Robin, personally, was disposed to give Jack the benefit
of the doubt. Nick angrily asked what doubt? He said he
simply wanted to round up Jack, the Fanshaws and Gerald
Brownlow and shoot them all—and though Robin was well
used to her sister-in-law gunning for people, she thought
this wasn't a typical Nick reaction at all. They all wondered
what would now happen to the arrangement over the Observatory, but no one liked to ask Kate. Kate thought about
it herself, but the idea that perhaps she ought to leave the
house she loved so much—and at the same time sever her
one remaining link with Jack—was more than she could
face at the moment.

Joanna, expecting indignation against Jack Morley from
her grandmother, was surprised to find that she and Cecily
did not see eye to eye.

"How can Kate be so stubborn and silly?" said Cecily,
crossly, who missed her daughter-in-law's bright company
more than she would admit. "She should patch things up.
What can it matter at her age if Jack Morley is married or
not?"

"How can you say that, Granny-Cis? He cast a spell
over Mum, and then behaved monstrously." Joanna felt

passionately protective of Kate—not an emotion she was used to. "Such double-dealing was outrageous," she said, conveniently forgetting about Hugo Coltman.

"Rubbish. Kate's had a lifetime of being the wronged wife herself," said Cecily briskly. "You'd have thought she might relish being the mistress for a change." Joanna goggled at her grandmother.

"I've grown fond of your mother," the old lady went on, picking up her binoculars with shaky hands. "I was disappointed when your father married her—thought she wasn't good enough for him. I was wrong—it was the other way round. Now she's found the right man for herself after all these years—I think she's very stupid to let pride spoil it all. I liked Jack. Anyway, how do we know what truth there was in Netta's version of events? Netta was in love with your father for years, but she was one of the few women he didn't bed. Netta has a grudge."

"You make Dad sound like a compulsive womaniser," said Joanna.

"He was." A kestrel hovered outside the window. Cecily gazed intently through her binoculars. "And probably worse, too," she added, deliberately trying to shock her granddaughter. Then she relented. "He was also a special, irreplaceable person for you and me, Jo. Nothing changes that. Keep him on his pedestal for yourself—just don't expect your mother to worship at the shrine. Where's that damn bird gone? I can't get these wretched glasses focused properly." She kept them rammed up close to her eyes, but Joanna could see a telltale tear creeping slowly down Cecily's cheek, and knew there was nothing wrong with the focus. "It's a bit early, but would you get my sherry for me, Jo? I feel very tired tonight. Don't know what's the matter with me." She added sharply: "I expect it was having your badly behaved children to tea."

Joanna had never heard Cecily own to weariness before, certainly never seen her shed a tear, let alone make such admissions about Oliver. Joanna Maitland felt she'd been force-fed so much food for thought lately that she might die of indigestion.

She rang Mike up and found herself spilling out a tale of woe.

Jack Morley, back in New York, was more miserable than he had believed possible—and he had known much trouble in his life. His anger was almost all directed against himself—against Netta Fanshaw too, of course, but it was himself he blamed most. How could I have been so stupid? How could I have gone on putting off telling Kate something I knew she had to know? he asked himself. He, Jack Morley, renowned for being so astute in his dealings with people in the property world, always so shrewd and ahead of the game, had just made a complete cock-up of his personal life, and ruined his relationship with the one woman he had really loved. The hurt of Kate comparing him to Oliver filled him with pain. Almost as bad were her remarks about his motives in setting up the Ravelstoke Hall Centre. Though the jibe was distorted, Jack felt there could be just enough truth in it to hit him where it hurt most. He flagellated himself with the sting of her words. If Kate, after all they had been to each other, all the intimacy, the precious friendship they had shared, could imagine he had only thought of her as a little sidekick, and was not even prepared to listen to his side of the story, then she couldn't love him as he had dared to hope she did. Jack was a proud man. It had cost him dear to go up the stairs and try to make one final apology. The switching on of Kate's light had not been lost on him. That message, together with the silence that followed and the locked door, had been horribly clear to Jack. It didn't stop him hoping against hope that there might be a letter from Kate offering him a last chance to tell his story—but the invitation would have to come from her.

He could not escape going to England from time to time, but the affairs of Ravelstoke Hall Centre would have to be run from London. There was no way Jack was setting foot in Yorkshire at the moment.

Jack and Kate were not the only ones to be watching for the post. In her letter to Mark Hughes, Harriet had enclosed a stamped envelope addressed to herself c/o The Observatory, Ravelstoke. She and Polly had thought this was frightfully clever. Kate, recognising Harriet's handwriting, imagined she must have written to some boy she didn't want Joanna to know about, or sent off for something that would not meet with parental approval. She'd forwarded it on to the school without a thought. There were other things on her mind.

When Harriet saw the re-addressed envelope, she could hardly bring herself to open it. A Welsh postmark. Her fingers trembled as she tore it open.

The letter was both a delight and a disappointment. Yes, she had almost certainly found her father, though her letter had come as a complete surprise. He was touched and thankful she had written. Yes, he wanted to meet her, and was ready to give her his love and support. He too was struck by the likeness of the hair—he added that they might still be alike even after her drastic action, since he had not got much hair either now, though this was due to anno domini rather than a razor.

This much was all wonderful to Harriet.

But it was a brief letter, restrained, not the long, passionate, detailed screed of Harriet's imaginings. Her father wrote that he thought she should tell Joanna what she had done, and suggested they might meet—with her mother's permission—in the Christmas holidays. He would come and meet her at a suitable rendez-vous.

"I had a brief love affair with your mother before I joined the Benedictines," Father Paul had written carefully, after much thought. He said he was a housemaster at Nant Dafydd College but was giving up schoolmastering at the end of this term to concentrate on his academic writing.

Rather curiously, Harriet thought, he signed himself Paul—
but he'd put a little kiss in front of his name. Really sweet.

"Well—come on, Hattie, spit it out." Polly was bursting with curiosity. Somewhat reluctantly Harriet gave her
the letter, but: "A monk!" breathed Polly, much impressed.

"What do you mean—a monk?"

"That's what Benedictines are, stupid. Now that's something we never thought of. Explains everything—the mystery and things."

Harriet looked horrified.

"Wonder if their affair really was over before he became
a monk," speculated Polly happily. "You read about things
like that in the paper sometimes. You know the sort of
thing—Jealous Jilted Jesuit Stabs Secret Lover. Granny-
Roz will adore this, we must tell her. She's mad about
monks. Unstoppable passion—broken vows—blighted
hopes. Wicked!"

"Stop it! Shut up! You're making it horrid!" shouted
Harriet, and burst into tears.

Polly felt aggrieved. She shrugged her shoulders at the
unpredictability of her friend. "It was you that wanted the
drama . . ." she started defensively, and then, "Oh Hat! I'm
so sorry—please don't cry. I'm sure he's lovely—it's a
really nice letter. What are you going to do now?"

"I don't know," wailed Harriet. "Everything's so difficult. I'd love to tell Granny, but she's so miserable at the
moment I don't like to bother her. I've waited for this moment all my life—I can't possibly wait till *Christmas* now.
As for asking Mum first! He can't remember what she's
like."

"Why don't you just go?"

"You mean turn up unannounced? I don't want to tell
more lies after what I've done already."

"You won't need to." Polly as usual was blithely confident. "It's half term soon. I'll just ask your mother if you
can come to us—we don't need to mention it to my parents
because you won't actually *be* coming. Your mother's

bound to say yes—you know she's always thrilled for you to be away for exeats.''

Harriet winced.

''Worth a try,'' urged Polly. ''Melissa's got a cousin at Nant Dafydd—you know, it's that RC boys' school. She'll know exactly how to get there, and you've got lots of money saved up.''

Suddenly it all seemed amazingly simple.

◦⟨ THIRTY ⟩◦

Polly had been right. Joanna readily agreed that Harriet could go to Duntan for the exeat.

Joanna had decided she must end her affair with Hugo; there were signs that he might do so first, which would be intolerable. Whereas to start with, Joanna had thought it would be good for Mike to know she was looking elsewhere, now she most definitely did not want him to find out by accident. Mike had been up to Yorkshire twice since the holiday in Corfu, and Joanna had spent a few nights in London. With Harriet safely out of the way, Joanna thought this weekend would be as good a time as any for a last fling—and then she'd given Hugo his congé.

All might have gone as the girls had planned, had Joanna not had a severe attack of conscience about Harriet. Kate and Cecily had both looked very disappointed at the news that Harriet was to be at Duntan—yet again. Kate, miserable anyway, and longing to see her, had made no comment on the telephone, but Cecily had taken it upon herself to give Joanna a sharp piece of her mind.

''You'll only have yourself to thank if that child goes wrong, Joanna,'' said Cecily, voicing with typical bluntness what Miss Ellis had tried to infer with more delicacy last time she had seen Joanna. ''She's never at home. Don't you care about her at all or are you so selfish you can't be bothered with her?''

She looked so fierce that Joanna felt her grandmother might whip out the aggressive-looking sword, stuck through a sort of tortoiseshell gate, that held up her heavy white hair, and stab her with it. Cecily had wheezed off upstairs—something that was becoming an increasing effort for her—her back-view expressing volumes of disapproval, her breathing distressing to hear. Going into the transformed Longthorpe kitchen, the redesigning of which had taken up much of her time lately, Joanna soon heard the appalling juddering noise from overhead that meant Cecily's grinder had just gobbled up another spoon. The house shook as though hit by the wrath of God.

Cecily's words stung.

Jenny was giving Rupert and Tilly tea. There were shrieks of laughter coming from the playroom, but Rupert went silent and started to chew his thumb the minute Joanna walked in. His mother looked at him in despair. I am a total disaster as a parent, a useless selfish wife, and very little cop as a daughter, thought Joanna. She had meant to go over to see Kate for the last few days, but somehow hadn't done so. Suddenly her successful career didn't seem quite enough.

''Hello, you two. How was school?''

''All right,'' said Rupert cautiously. It had been football which he dreaded and he'd had a bad day—but he wasn't going to tell his mother.

''Lovely,'' said Tilly, who went to kindergarten in the mornings. ''Matthew Naylor thumped Beth. He laid a big egg on her head and she cried and cried. Mrs. Sweeney sent Matthew to the wall.''

''Oh dear. So did Matthew cry too then?''

''No, he laughed.''

''He sounds a horrid little boy.''

''I think he's *very, very* nice,'' said Tilly, her eyes sparkling at the recollection of this pleasurable drama.

After the children had been put to bed and Joanna had poured herself a sizeable vodka and tonic, she was just about to ring Hugo on his direct number at the office, where she knew he would be working late, when she was struck by a different idea. Why don't I ring Sonia and offer to go over to join Harriet tomorrow, Joanna thought—put Flame and Star in the box and ride with Archie and the girls? Then maybe we could all go to a film together? She had finished writing her weekly column. She dialled the Duntan number.

"Heavenly idea," said Sonia. "We can go and be harrowed by *The English Patient* in the evening. Polly and I are dying to see it, but Archie doesn't want to, so we can have a lovely weepy time without him. I've got to take Birdie to ballet in the morning, but you can bring Hattie over to ride any time. Bring her for lunch if you like. It'll only be larder scrapings but there's lots of bits."

"Bring Hattie over? But she's already with you." An awful thought struck Joanna. "You did pick her up this morning, didn't you?"

"No—were you expecting me to?"

"I thought she was with you for the whole weekend. Polly asked if she could stay, and I never gave it another thought till now. I suddenly felt rather mean that I wasn't going to see her this weekend at all."

"Oh dear." Sonia smelt trouble. "I knew nothing about this. Polly hasn't said a word to me. Hattie's not here."

Joanna felt the bottom drop out of her stomach. Cecily's searing words rang in her ears.

Sonia didn't waste time: "I'll talk to Polly and ring you back." The moment Polly saw the look on her mother's face she knew that at least one of Harriet's cats must have leapt out of its bag.

"What is going on, Polly? Where is Harriet?"

"I can't tell you—but I promise she's OK."

"That's not good enough. *Where is she*?"

"I'd love to tell you, Mum, truly—actually I'm dying to—but I'm vowed to secrecy. But I swear she's somewhere incredibly respectable." Polly looked solemn.

"And do you know if she's arrived safely at this respectable destination?"

"Well—no. But she must have done by now. Honestly, Mum."

"Darling, I understand your loyalty, but this is serious. Joanna must know where she is."

"Joanna doesn't give a stuff where Hattie is. She was thrilled when I asked if she could come here—she always is. And I didn't lie. I just *asked*. Sometimes I hate Joanna." Polly looked mulish—Sonia, recognising the expression, thought she looked exactly like Archie in a certain mood.

She reported an edited version of this conversation back to Joanna.

"Could I come and talk to Polly myself?"

"Yes, of course." But Sonia's heart sank.

Once again, Joanna found herself driving over to Duntan in a state of anxiety about Harriet. Polly stonewalled with a barely veiled hostility which did not disguise the fact that she was becoming thoroughly rattled. Suppose something did happen to Harriet and it would be partly her fault?

"Please, Polly—just give me a clue," pleaded Joanna desperately. Pleading wasn't normally a word in her vocabulary.

"A boy?" Sonia suggested helpfully. "Is it perhaps about a special boy, darling?"

Polly looked accusingly at Joanna: "*You know*," she said. "*You know*. It's to do with the most important thing in Hattie's life—only you won't help her. And it was my idea to ask if she could stay—she specially didn't want to lie to you, because of what . . ." Polly stopped herself. She had been going to say "because of what we'd already done." She changed it to a defiant "because she's so scared of you."

"Polly!" said Sonia sharply, but Polly banged out of the room.

"Oh dear God!" said Joanna slowly. "I suppose it has to be about her father. But whatever has she done?"

Everything had been very easy for Harriet. Earlier that morning, the Friday of half term, she had sneaked a lift to York station with some girls for whom a taxi had been ordered, Melissa having provided the information that the nearest station to Nant Dafydd was Bangor. Harriet stuffed her sponge bag and some spare clothes in her backpack and felt she had embarked on a real adventure.

She had to change trains at Manchester and Chester. After Chester she gazed out of the window at the sea as the train followed the North Wales coast. Names like Llandudno Junction, Penmaenmawr, and Llanfairfechan seemed wonderfully unfamiliar. Two women opposite were nattering away in Welsh. Harriet had never heard it spoken before; she felt as if she was in a foreign country. Then it occurred to her that as her father's name was Hughes, she might be half Welsh herself. It was after three when the train stopped at Bangor. The two women got out there too. Harriet asked them if they knew how she could get to Nant Dafydd Abbey—would there be a bus?

"Nant Dafydd? D'you mean the College?" Harriet said she did.

They looked doubtful. The fatter of the two, rolling her eyes as well as her Rs and drawing the word out as though she were chanting a response in church, said: "It's that Rrow-man place she'll be wanting."

She sniffed disparagingly. Always been Chapel herself, but it took all sorts—no one could say she wasn't broadminded.

"You'd have to get a taxi," said the other one kindly.

"How far is it?"

"About ten miles, it is. Got the money, then, have you?" They looked at her curiously.

Harriet felt grateful for her weeks of working in the café at Duntan. She hadn't thought the Abbey would be so far from the station.

The drive was beautiful; the mountains took Harriet's breath away, which was just as well because the taxi driver never drew breath himself so there would have been no hope of her getting a word in edgeways. He pointed out various peaks with unpronounceable names: Pen Llithrig y Wrach, he told her meant the Slippery Slope of the Witch. She liked that. The roads were steep and twisty.

The driver dropped Harriet at the main entrance, and charged her less than his usual fare. He had daughters himself—he thought this girl looked pale and hungry.

Harriet felt extremely nervous. There seemed to be no one about at all. It dawned on her that it might also be half term for the College as well as Essendale Hall. What if everyone was away and she had come for nothing?

The heavy oak outer door was open. Harriet went in, and then pushed through swing glass doors into a vast hall. She was relieved to see a reception area with armchairs and a woman behind a desk, busy at a computer. Harriet coughed. The woman glanced up, obviously surprised, but gave her a welcoming smile.

"Good afternoon. What can I do for you?"

Harriet didn't quite know who to ask for: "I'm—I'm er, looking for a monk," she said, feeling foolish.

"Well, we have quite a lot of those here," said the woman kindly, looking amused. "Any particular one?"

"He could be called Mark or he could be called Paul."

"We have both a Father Mark and a Father Paul."

"Do monks still have surnames?" asked Harriet. "If so it's Hughes."

"I think it will be Father Paul you want—but I'm not sure where he is. It's the long exeat. Do you have an appointment?"

Harriet was just about to say: "No, but I'm his daughter," when the receptionist said, "Oh, here's someone who may be able to help us,'' and Harriet turned round to see a dark, stocky man in a black cassock. "Father Dominic, this young lady thinks she's looking for Father Paul. Do you know where he is by any chance? Is he away for the weekend?''

Father Dominic took in the situation in a flash. One look told him exactly who this girl must be. He must at all costs forestall her from blurting out her relationship in front of nice Mrs. Griffiths—a treasure, but not always the soul of discretion. With a bit of luck all the boys were away.

He held out his hand to Harriet, and she shook it, shyly. She was very afraid her wonderful surprise might be going to misfire.

"Come along with me," said Father Dominic. "I'm a housemaster here too. We'll go over to my house and we'll make tea—I might even rustle up some toast. Mrs. Griffiths, will you leave a message on Father Paul's answering machine and ask him to come and join us as soon as he gets in? He's not away, but I know he's gone walking. He can't be that long because it's getting dark and anyway he'll be back for Vespers. You're Harriet, aren't you?''

"Yes," said Harriet, greatly relieved.

"Then please tell Father Paul that Harriet Rendlesham is here to see him, Mrs. Griffiths. Come along, Harriet," and Father Dominic strode off so fast that Harriet almost had to run to keep up with him.

It had been a wonderful day for walking. On his way down the mountain, Father Paul had dropped in at the little church at Betws-y-Fridd that he loved so much. The rowan berries had turned scarlet and orange, the late October sky was blue and the wind raced the white clouds across it like sailing ships. Inside all was still. Father Paul knelt in the hideously uncomfortable narrow pews and made an offering of his misery at having to give up schoolmastering; he asked for it to be turned into a prayer. He thought of his as yet unknown daughter, and like St. Francis, hoped he could "not

so much seek to be consoled as to console, to be understood
as to understand, to be loved as to love.'' But it occurred
to him that it would be wonderful if he could be loved by
her too—and felt consolation.

When he got back to St. Anthony's, intending to have
a shower and change and then do some reading, the red
eye of his answering machine was winking urgently. Its
message made his heart lurch.

There was a strong smell of burnt toast coming out of
Father Dominic's house. Father Paul stood for a moment
in the hallway. He could hear voices—and then laughter.
He opened the door of Father Dominic's study. Father Paul
was so tall that he sometimes had to stoop in doorways.
He stood in this one, gazing at a tall thin girl who was
curled up on the floor by the fire. Tight fair curls, short as
a baby's, just covered her head. She was devouring hot
buttered toast with a scraping of honey on it from the almost empty pot that was all that could be found in the
kitchen. A square open tin of biscuits was beside her on
the rug. She and Father Dominic both had mugs of tea.

"Hello, Harriet," said Father Paul.

⸙ THIRTY-ONE ⸙

Sonia had to point Joanna gently towards home: "We'd
love to ask you to stay for supper, but I'm afraid we're all
going over to the Brown-Gorings—we're a bit late as it is.
Also, don't you think perhaps you ought to be at home in
case Harriet rings you?"

"I suppose so. I hadn't thought of that, but I don't think
she's likely to ring. I'd thought lately that we were beginning to get on a bit better," said Joanna sadly, "but I seem
to have alienated her totally."

"You go home," said Sonia firmly, feeling desperately
sorry for her, but knowing she was far more likely to get

something out of Polly if Joanna wasn't there. "I'll have another go at Pol. I don't think she'll spill Hattie's beans to me, but if she really knows where she's gone, she might agree to ring up and see if she's arrived. At least then we'd know if she was safe. I'll telephone if we have anything to say—and please let us know if you have news. Poor Jo— you have got problems. Have you told your darling mum? How is she?"

"Not well," said Joanna. "I've never seen her like this. She won't talk to any of us about it, and she looks awful. Nick and Robin are afraid she may get ill. I dread telling her about this, but I'll have to, of course."

"That bloody Fanshaw woman," said Sonia. "I could kill her. She certainly hasn't done herself much good. All Kate's friends are livid with her. Good luck."

It was after eight by the time Joanna got back to Longthorpe. There was no message.

She rang Kate, but only got the answering machine and didn't like to leave such worrying news without actually speaking to her. Then she rang Mike. At the sound of his voice, Joanna cracked. She burst into tears, words spilled out and she became completely incoherent. Once she started to cry she simply couldn't stop. It was some time before Mike could make head or tail of what she was saying.

"Oh Mike," she sobbed down the telephone. "It's all my fault. I've done everything wrong. Way back, for once, I tried to do something unselfish, but it misfired and now I've lost Harriet and I don't know what to do. I can't handle this. I know it's a lot to ask but could you . . . could you possibly come home?"

It was the first time Joanna had ever appealed to Mike for help.

"Of course," he said at once. "Of course I'll come. Just tell me quietly exactly what's happened." When he'd got a clearer picture he said with comforting briskness: "I'll get in the car and be with you as soon as I can. The worst of the Friday traffic should be dying down. I'm sure we haven't lost Harriet. She's not a little girl any more, she's highly intelligent and Polly knows where she is even if she isn't telling. Good for her, really. We'll find Hattie tomorrow and we'll go together and get her from wherever she's got to. Now listen, Jo—take a pull on yourself. If Hattie rings, and I think she may, for God's sake don't fly off the handle. Just find out where she is, say you're not cross, *no matter what she's done*, and tell her you want to talk to her. It's about time you did—so make that clear. And try not to drink too much. It always makes you worse.''

"Thank you, Mike," said Joanna shakily.

"And Jo?"

"Yes?"

"I love you," said Mike.

It was half past nine when the telephone went. Joanna grabbed it.

"Hello?"

"Mum?"

"Hattie? Oh thank God. Where are you? Are you all right? I've been worried sick."

"Oh Mum—how did you know I wasn't at Duntan? You're going to be terribly angry with me. Has Polly told you then?"

"No. She wouldn't say a word, and I only discovered because I tried to go and see you there. I promise I won't be cross. Just tell me what's happened."

"It's going to be an awful shock for you."

"Try me."

"I'm with my father." On the other end of the line, Harriet held her breath. Father Paul had been adamant that she must ring Joanna, but it had taken all her courage. If she had not wanted, so badly, to gain and keep his good opinion she might have refused. There was a moment's dead silence, then:

"I rather thought you might be," said Joanna. "But how on earth did you find out?"

Falteringly, Harriet told her and waited for the explosion. It didn't come. "I should have talked to you," said Joanna, "I should have told you something when you asked. I see that now. But believe it or not, originally I kept the secret for your father's sake. Perhaps you can see why now. I behaved terribly badly to him, and I'll tell you all about it sometime. He may not believe it, but will you tell him that when I didn't tell him about you, I did it out of love—but I think I was wrong. Tell him I've read all his books. Is he still at Nant Dafydd?"

"Yes. I'm ringing from there now. I'm going to spend the night at a b. and b. nearby. He's made me ring you. Oh Mum, he is so lovely."

"Yes," said Joanna, "and you're very like him."

"Only I've got your temper." There was a wobbly attempt at a laugh.

"Yes," said Joanna. "Our downfall. Mike and I'll be with you tomorrow. We're both coming. I'm so pleased you rang me. Goodnight, Hattie."

"Goodnight, Mum—God bless."

Joanna rang Kate again, and this time left a message. She also rang Duntan and left one for Sonia. "Tell Polly there's no need to worry," she said.

It was late when Mike walked into Longthorpe House. Joanna was crashed out, fast asleep, on the sofa in the drawing room. Her normally immaculate hair was a mess and she had cried all her makeup off. She looked exhausted and vulnerable. Mike looked down at her for a long moment, before he started, with great tenderness and the stirring of a desire which was different and better than anything he had felt for her before, to kiss her gently awake.

Driving down to Wales the next morning, Mike and Joanna each learnt some unexpected things. Joanna told Mike her story.

"I went to Mark Hughes to study English literature. He woke me up to words. He was one of those teachers who opens new windows for you—and then makes you feel you've been brilliant to see the view. He was so clever and stimulating and alive—terrifically attractive too. Everyone he taught adored him. I'd had a couple of experimental affairs with dull contemporaries but they meant nothing. This was the first time I'd met anyone who I felt would measure up to my father—but I couldn't get him to take me seriously as a woman at all. He treated me like all his other students—which is why no one guessed afterwards—and it drove me absolutely crazy. I made up my mind to marry him. I knew he was a Catholic but I couldn't believe it when I discovered he was going to become a monk. I didn't understand at all. I still don't. It seemed such a bloody waste to me. I was convinced that if I could only get him into bed with me he'd give it all up. I told him how I felt, and he would have none of it. He'd made his choice and said I only had a passing fancy for him. He said goodbye at the end of term because he was going on to the monastery at Nant Dafydd in Wales after a final holiday abroad. I was devastated. I found out where he was going and followed him to Italy. I meant to seduce him and I did. He was agonised at what he'd done, but he wouldn't change his mind. Then I was so angry I could have killed him. Later I was terribly ashamed of myself.

"It was a frightful shock to discover I was pregnant. I'd been on the pill, so it hadn't crossed my mind it could happen. At first I wanted an abortion but I knew it would be against all Mark's most dearly held beliefs." Joanna added ironically: "And I'd had proof of just how important those were to him. I couldn't do it."

"Have you stayed in love with him all these years?"

"He's always been inside my mind—perhaps because he was unobtainable." Joanna was nothing if not honest. "But actually in love, after so long? I don't know. Perhaps I'll find out today. Are you willing to risk it?"

"I don't have much choice," said Mike dryly, but he put his hand out and touched hers briefly.

"I've done a lot of rethinking lately. I seem to have been wrong over most things—including Dad. Granny-Cis gave me a shock the other day that really hurt. Seems he wasn't quite the hero I thought."

"But he was one for *you*," Mike echoed Cecily. "And to lots of other people too."

"But not to my mother."

"No. Not to Kate."

"What do you really think about him, Mike?"

"I think you should hang on to your own vision—just don't blow your idea of him up to such impossible heights that no one—not even your father—could ever come near it."

"I've got a feeling you know things you don't want to tell me. Why was there so much less money than everyone expected? I have to know everything. Please, Mike."

Mike hesitated. Then, thinking of Joanna's long secrecy over Harriet, decided it was time for truth. Kate had given him permission to tell Joanna what he knew, but only if he ever felt it was in her best interests. He said now: "Your father was being blackmailed. There were a lot of letters, and some dreadfully compromising and unpleasant photographs and videos. Not good. He had got them all back, but he'd had to pay heavily."

Joanna's face drained of all colour.

"I feel sick. I think I'm going to faint," she said.

Mike pulled on to the hard shoulder, turned off the engine and opened the window: "Put your head between your legs," he said.

She did as he told her, and after a moment or two her eyes started to focus again and the buzzing in her ears lessened though she still felt cold and clammy. Then she straightened up and got out of the car. Mike watched anxiously while she stood there, leaning against the passenger door facing the embankment, while lorries thundered terrifying past on the far side of them, making the whole car shake. Then to his relief she got back inside.

"Oh Mike," she whispered. "That's too horrible. Everything feels tarnished. Does Mum know?"

"Yes—he left them all for her to find. That was cruel. She'd known about his mistresses for years, but this was much nastier. She asked me what to do. We agreed not to tell you at the time. I think Nick guesses something, and he'll need to be told now that you know. Oliver was split, Jo. A brilliant, gifted man with some fatal flaws, but a brave one too. Don't judge him too hard."

"Poor Mum," said Joanna. "Oh poor Mum. No wonder she's taken the Jack thing so hard."

"I'm dreadfully sorry, Jo. It's a shame you had to find out."

"Mike?"

"Yes?"

"Ought—ought I to see what he left?"

"Most emphatically not. There's nothing you can do. D'you feel up to going on yet?"

"Yes," she said. "Yes, please go on now."

They didn't discuss their own future. There was enough to be coped with in the present and negotiations could come later. But each had decided that it was at least worth trying to save their marriage.

All the parties concerned had been very nervous about the meeting at Nant Dafydd. Mike thought his wife looked terrible as they stood on the step outside St. Anthony's house.

"All right?" he asked. Joanna nodded, and Mike pressed the bell. Harriet answered the door. Mother and daughter stared at each other for a long moment, and then clung in an uncharacteristic embrace.

"Please come in, Mum," said Harriet, rather awkwardly, and led the way into the study. Father Paul was standing with his back to the fireplace. Joanna stood in the doorway. Constraint hung in the air.

Then Father Paul held out both his hands to her. "Oh Joanna," he said, "you've given me something so precious. How lovely to see you again." When Joanna went and put her hands in his, Harriet and Mike, who had both been waiting in acute anxiety, were able to breathe again.

Joanna no longer saw the charismatic figure of the dashing don aged thirty-five, who had exerted such a hold over her heart and body, and whose image she had glorified for so many years. Father Paul was fifty and looked more: a little faded, a little worn, a little stooped. Humour and warmth were still there, she thought, but the old exuberance had been replaced by something more cautious, and infinitely less exciting. It was a huge relief to her. Mike, watching her, was relieved too.

In place of the brilliant, passionate girl he remembered, Father Paul saw a beautiful woman—he thought she had the potential to become more beautiful still, but she fanned no sexual desires for him, only the embers of a lasting regret that he could have hurt anyone so much. Both of them felt they might be able to share their daughter's future, and cautiously work towards a new and different relationship.

Joanna also thought Harriet had never looked happier. Father and daughter had obviously achieved in twenty-four hours more of a rapport than she and Harriet had managed in fifteen years. It gave Joanna a very lonely pang.

Together with Father Dominic, they all went out to a pub lunch and, high on that release that a sudden relaxation of tension brings, had a convivial time. Father Paul was still wonderfully stimulating company. After lunch they walked through the College grounds to the path by the river. Joanna and Father Paul fell into step together, and the other two men hung back and let them walk ahead. Harriet would have joined them, but Mike put a restraining hand on her arm.

"What would you have done if I'd told you I was pregnant?" asked Joanna.

"Asked you to marry me and given up my vocation."

"Yes," she said. "That's what I thought."

"You were very brave, Joanna. Thank you for your courage and your sacrifice."

Before they left Harriet hugged her father goodbye, and beamed when Mike suggested that he might like to come and stay at Longthorpe during the Christmas holidays. Subject to the Abbot's approval, the invitation was accepted. Joanna wondered how she would cope. It had been hard enough to watch Harriet's love for Kate at close quarters.

As the Maitlands drove off with his daughter, Father Paul thought there would be a great compensation in his future, no matter how much he missed the College. He stood looking after them until the car went out of sight.

"That daughter of yours will go far and you will have much in common with each other," said Father Dominic. "I think you are a lucky man."

◄ THIRTY-TWO ►

When Rupert discovered his father's presence on Sunday morning he went mad and gambolled round his parents' bedroom like an over-excited puppy, finally ending with a series of head-over-heels somersaults that took him from one end of the room to the other.

"Could this be a subtly coded message for me?" Joanna enquired, raising an eyebrow at her husband.

Kate had been shattered by the message on her answering machine, and had not dared to go out of earshot of the telephone all day. She flew to answer it when Joanna rang as soon as they got back home in the evening. Kate was stunned at the developments in their lives. Mike and Joanna asked her to Sunday lunch at Longthorpe.

They all told Kate the story, several times, from their different points of view, and she thought it would take a long time to digest.

"How brave you've been, darling, all these years," she said privately to Joanna, after Harriet had gone off to exercise her pony. "How lonely it must have felt for you to keep all that locked up inside you—and how wonderful that Harriet has such a special father. I'm so happy for you all."

"You've kept things locked up inside you too, Mum," said Joanna. "Mike has told me. We've both had our lonely secrets. I think you're pretty brave as well."

Kate didn't enquire what the Maitlands' own plans were: it was obvious that Joanna and Mike had found something new together but she guessed it might still be too fragile to be exposed to family discussion.

At Kate's suggestion, Harriet came back to the Observatory for the night to keep her company. Curled up in front of the fire, Harriet poured out her version of the story to her grandmother.

"I feel as if a blank space inside me has been filled," she said. "It's my dream come true, but different and better than I ever thought. It's done something wonderful for me—and for Mum too. I think she and Mike might be all right again. I do hope so. Shall I tell you what my father said?" Harriet looked at Kate with enormous eyes.

"Tell me."

"He said I'd brought everybody healing," whispered Harriet, shyly. "Me!"

"I'm sure you did, my darling," said Kate, and then in order to make them both laugh and to stop herself from crying added: "Another little example of God's mysterious ways, perhaps. He certainly has some odd ones."

"What about you, Gran?" Harriet asked, before they went to bed. "Mum's told me what happened. Will Jack come back?"

"I don't know, darling," said Kate sadly. "It doesn't look like it."

You out there—if you're there—she said to her God, what about a cosy little miracle for me? But all was silence.

In November Midas was the star attraction at the big charity autumn fair at Duntan. Kate knew she should have basked in its glory and tried to pretend to Jane that she was enjoying her share of the praise and attention. Jane was not deceived.

It was the first time Kate had been in the same room as Netta since the terrible Ravelstoke evening. Somehow they managed not to bump in to each other: it was as though both women had an efficient built-in radar system like bats. They swooped dangerously close, but never quite made contact. Netta got short shrift from Sonia when she treacled up to offer congratulations on the organisation of the fair.

"Do tell me. How is poor Kate nowadays?"

"Enjoying celebrity as you see," said Sonia, and added: "So pathetic that some people seem to feel so threatened by her sudden success that they have to be spiteful."

"Wow! Take that, Mrs. Fanshaw!" said Jane as Netta retreated, full of shot, but not brought down. "You enjoyed that, Sonia."

"Umm," Sonia laughed. "And I feel much, much better for it."

"Poor Netta, one doesn't have to stand on tiptoes to see what drawer she comes out of," said Lady Rosamund. "She's the kind of person who does her seat belt up the minute she gets in a car. Such a social giveaway."

Gerald Brownlow plodded bravely on with his unrewarding courtship. He told Kate that his family motto was *Perseverando*.

"Then I wish you'd change it," said Kate wearily. She hated it when he turned up unannounced—as he frequently did—at the Observatory and could hardly bear to let him over the threshold of Jack's house. He had tried to explain to her—in a lot of words of very few syllables—just how unsuitable what he called her "arrangement" with Jack Morley had been, and how well-intentioned his own role in seeking to unmask someone so unreliable, though he admitted, magnanimously, that in his opinion, Netta had completely overstepped the mark.

"How perceptive of you," said Kate.

She felt like an empty husk.

In early December, Gloria's husband, Jim, gave up his long struggle and died.

"I am relieved he's at rest," said Gloria to Kate. "I couldn't have wanted him to go on any longer—but oh Kate, the awful emptiness! I can't look at his chair. And I can't seem to remember the fine man he once was—I just see this sad ghost, not my Jim at all."

"The proper Jim will come back in your mind in time. It's the last few years that will fade eventually," said Kate, hoping she was right. She sat by Gloria's kitchen fire, drank endless mugs of very black tea with her, and listened. It seemed all she could do.

"I know you understand—it's a real comfort. You've been through it too."

Kate didn't know if Gloria was referring to the dead husband Kate didn't miss, or the live lover she mourned so grievously.

The funeral was in Ravelstoke church. Kate and Jessie Worsencroft did the flowers in golden colours. It was a simple service. Jack's Aunt Hannah played the organ with excruciating effect. If all the music had "Largo di molto" printed on it, then she generously exceeded the instructions. A black felt hat, anchored by an uncompromising-looking hatpin, was set so flat and centrally on her head that Kate felt Hannah Hartley must have used a spirit level when she put it on. Kate had forgotten she played for the services, and her heart sank at the sight of her. The congregation sang "All Things Bright and Beautiful"—Gloria's favourite hymn—and "Abide With Me." Tears poured down Kate's face. She felt ashamed to cry so copiously when she knew her tears were not really for Jim. The congregation huddled in the freezing church and stood afterwards at the grave-side in chilling drizzle.

"Ah, there'll be a few more carried off by this," said Mrs. Stokes encouragingly. "You mark my words. My Herbert always says one funeral begets another. His Aunt Joan was took two weeks to the day after her cousin's husband's burial."

Neighbours produced cakes and sandwiches for the tea after the service and Joanna had brought plates of vol-au-vents and baby quiches.

Kate was just about to say her goodbyes when Hannah Hartley came up to her.

"Well, you turned out to be a fair-weather friend, Mrs. Rendlesham," she said. She had been calling her Kate before.

"What do you mean?"

"Not one to stick by their man in trouble, obviously," said Hannah Hartley. "Not that I approved of the way you lived, mind."

"It was Jack who let *me* down," said Kate fiercely. "I didn't know he was married. You did."

"If you call it a marriage. Not every man would stick with a brain-damaged wife who doesn't even know who he is—let alone if it's Christmas or Easter—and he looks after her by himself at times too. He's had fifteen years of that— and divorce is even easier there than here, they tell me. A lot of men would have wanted out. It's not as if Jack was a poor man either—he could have settled a lump of that alley money on her if he'd been so minded, and there'd be plenty of folks as wouldn't blame him."

"He should have told me. He had plenty of chances."

"Ah." Mrs. Hartley sniffed. "And I suppose you asked, didn't you—just to make sure you wasn't taking up with another woman's husband who happened to own a house as had caught your fancy?''

Kate felt her face burning.

''Oh well, maybe he's well out of it. I allus say as folk should stick to their own class. Our Jack came to see me the other week when he was visiting his new Centre or whatever he calls it,'' said the old lady, squeezing the last drop of blood from Kate. ''Not welcome in his own house at that star-gazing place, seemingly—though there's some as is comfortable enough to stay in it. Goodbye, Mrs. Rendlesham.''

Hannah Hartley walked out into the December dusk, snapping open her umbrella in a way that made it plain she hoped it would protect her equally from the damaging effects of rain and from worthless, well-born, fancy women.

Kate went home in a state of acute misery. The knowledge that Jack had been so close and had not even attempted to see her filled her with despair. The picture his aunt had painted of Jack's home-life both horrified her and made her ashamed she hadn't given him a chance to tell her about it. But worst of all, Hannah's words about her living in the house bored a hole in her brain. I can't stay here after that, she thought, in despair. I must have been blind—crazy—all these weeks to imagine I could. I suppose that's what everyone thinks round here. She felt utterly humiliated.

It was true, she thought, it had been the house she had fallen in love with first, but this had been rapidly followed, and far superseded, by love for its owner. Could Jack possibly think that she had started a relationship with him *because* of it? That she had used him? Kate could see it might look like that to the outside world—but to Jack himself? Deep down she could not accept this, but a little self-destructive demon would not let the thought go—after all, what had he said to his aunt to cause such an outburst? Kate felt furiously angry with him all over again. Such had been her longing for Jack that she had been on the point of burying her pride, risking a rebuff, and sending him a tentative olive branch: nothing too direct, but a subtle indication, delicately implied, that a meeting might be possible if he wanted one—the sort of letter that could be read either way by someone with the wit and the wish to read between its lines. But now? Now I shall write a business letter to his office, giving six months' notice, she decided. Something cool and impersonal. At least it would remove the awful possibility that he could think she had moved into his life and his bed with an eye to securing his property for herself. She spent an entire day composing the letter.

She had no idea where she would go. She certainly couldn't go back to Longthorpe now. Perhaps Jane Pulborough might know of something? Kate knew they let a flat in their house, but then what about Gloria? Gloria was going to need Midas even more than she was herself, and anyway Kate didn't like the idea of cutting herself off from the family. She was locked in misery. She now needed workrooms as well as somewhere to live. She decided to go house-hunting in the New Year.

Meanwhile there was Christmas to be got through. Kate dreaded it.

Having sworn not to go near Ravelstoke, Jack Morley had been forced to be present at an interview with a prospective matron for the Centre. It had been agony to be so near Kate and not see her. He had taken a huge gulp at his pride, decided to have one more try at making things up, nerved himself to telephone, got the answering machine and felt quite unable to leave a message.

The applicant for the post had not turned out to have the qualities of compassion, humour and competence for which Jack, and the rest of the governing body (from which Netta Fanshaw had felt it expedient to resign) were looking, so the trip had been unproductive.

Jack had then paid a visit to his aunt, secretly hoping for news of Kate. Leslie had parked the Cadillac well out of sight of the farm. Jack had only once made the mistake of turning up to visit his aunt in his opulent chauffeur-driven car. This time, Aunt Hannah, at her most unresponsive, had given Jack a dour greeting. Over a grudging cup of tea—no sniff of parsnip wine on offer—she had then *spoken her mind* about the terrible wound he had inflicted on that poor Kate Rendlesham. "Made her a laughing stock to all the county, by all accounts. Gloria Barlow says she couldn't hold her head up, poor lady. She had no idea you was a married man at all—very deceived, she was. Told Gloria Barlow she never wanted to see you again."

After this broadside, Jack had not tried to ring Kate again before being driven back to London. He decided he would write to her instead, not pleading or whining—just stating facts. She could make of them what she would. Let her read between the lines, he thought.

But back in New York, before he had got this letter finished to his satisfaction, Kate's cold communication arrived, faxed by Sylvia from the London office. He read it with despair. "Dear Jack," Kate had typed, "For reasons which I am sure will come as no surprise to you, I no longer wish to go on living in your house. Please take this letter as six months' notice. If I find suitable premises sooner, I will of course let you know." The letter was on Midas official paper and simply signed: Kate. He had thought that while she was in the Observatory there was still at least a link between them. She must indeed not want to forgive—only to forget—if she wished to sever that connection as well. I have hurt her beyond repair, thought Jack, terribly hurt himself by what he took to be her unyielding attitude. Suitable premises indeed! He reread the letter several times, searching for a hidden message of comfort. He could not find one. There seemed no room between these lines at all. He tore the letter into little shreds.

The family celebrated Christmas at Longthorpe. Robin's doctor had been doubtful about allowing her to travel only

four weeks before the baby was due, but had been persuaded. Kate, who had organised so many Longthorpe
Christmases in the past, intended to enter into all the preparations with enthusiasm, while at the same time appearing
to take a back seat. It might have been a difficult balance
to achieve, but she was so inwardly wretched at the moment
that she was thankful to let Joanna take over and organise
them all. It was wonderful to see Harriet so happy, and the
Maitlands edging their way carefully towards a new to-
getherness as a family, but through she forced herself to
display a glittering show of good spirits which everyone
secretly found rather wearing, Kate berated herself for being unable to feel happy. She counted her blessings and
only saw a gap.

"I wish Mum wouldn't be so bloody cheerful," said
Joanna to Nick. "It makes me feel so darned inferior. It's
like having St. Sebastian staying for Christmas—putting a
brave face on all the arrows, and imagining no one else can
see they're there providing he doesn't make a fuss."

"She doesn't even drown her sorrows in drink. Perhaps
she could switch to being St. Stephen—at least he got well
and truly stoned," said Nick, who was also finding his
mother's laboured gaiety hard to bear.

Of course there were still occasional outbursts at Longthorpe—nobody had changed their personality, and in any
case the traditional festival of peace and goodwill does not
always make for domestic harmony—but on the whole the
emotional weather forecast looked better than it had for
ages.

Harriet had been much exercised as to what to send her
father for Christmas. "Why not write him a poem?" Kate
suggested, so Harriet had done so. Father Paul had been
enchanted—and impressed.

Cecily was shrinking. Always a big woman physically,
her clothes and her skin now seemed to hang off her. Kate
told herself she was probably more aware of any changes
now than she had been when they were both living under

the same roof, though she still saw her mother-in-law several times a week. Cecily denied that there was anything wrong, but all the family noticed that she no longer sailed into the fray with banners unfurled and her usual relish if an argument blew up. When anyone dropped in to visit her, Cecily was often asleep with her binoculars on her knee. Her court case had come up, and much against her will she had been persuaded by her solicitor to plead guilty—"Perfectly ridiculous." To everyone's surprise she had not had her licence removed and was considered to have got off extremely lightly with penalty points and a hefty fine. She pretended not to mind, but some of her nerve had gone. The family had been trying to stop her driving for years. Now they all longed to see her get her battered little car out of the garage and go jerking off up the drive again.

Despite her misery, Kate found herself full of ideas for designs. She worked endlessly and the stables were overflowing with partly finished garments, needlepoint cushions and bits of embroidery. She spent hours working there, long after Gloria and Jessie had gone home.

It was a relief to Kate when Christmas was over. She wondered if there would be a card from Jack.

She neither received nor sent one.

♦ THIRTY-THREE ♦

Robin gave birth to a daughter, a fortnight early, in the New Year, popping her out like the proverbial pea. Nick was beside himself with pride and delight; Robin complained he took all the credit for himself. "Just because you did your bit nine months ago, attended one father's class and got bossy about my breathing doesn't mean you actually gave birth. Why don't you go sit outside the house with 'All My Own Work' chalked on the pavement and your cap out ready for offerings?" she asked.

"I might just do that," said Nick, gazing dotingly at his two women.

The moment the news came through, Kate went down to help until Robin's mother arrived from the States, thereby missing the visit to Longthorpe of Father Paul. In fact, helpers were almost superfluous, since Robin proved to be totally unfazed by parenthood and knew exactly what her baby wanted from the start. Apart from a bit of cooking, Kate spent most of her time gossiping to Robin and having doting sessions with her about the baby. Joanna, leaving Harriet and her newly found father together for the day— in a state of blissful companionship, she reported slightly tartly to Kate—came down to inspect her new niece and was astounded by mother and child. "You're so calm, Robin," she said enviously. "I was terrified by all my babies." She pulled a face. "If they weren't screaming, I was."

"Oh I just lob Chloe on the tit and she seems to settle," said Robin happily.

Kate stayed with the new family for a week, grateful to have something so happy and hopeful to occupy her. She could hardly bear to leave the three of them, and a weight of grey gloom settled on her as she drove back up north. This ought to be a joyful journey too, she thought sadly. I ought to be returning to the man I love in our magic house, instead of which we've blown something special into fragments.

She knew there had been snow in Yorkshire while she was away, though there had been no sign of it in London. As she reached the Leicester Forest Service Station and pulled in for a cup of coffee it started to deluge with rain. The rest of the drive was a nightmare. The wind got up, and the rain became so violent that the windscreen wipers couldn't cope. It was like driving through billowing curtains of water. Visibility was so bad that several drivers had given up and pulled on to the hard shoulder to wait for things to improve, but Kate ploughed recklessly on.

It was a huge relief when she finally reached the Observatory. She hadn't dared stop again because she wanted to get back before evening, though it was so dark already it was hard to tell whether this was due to the storm or failing daylight. The drive had seemed interminable and she was exhausted. As it was a Saturday, she was very surprised to find several cars—including Joanna's—parked in the courtyard. Someone had shovelled the snow to one side and it lay in trickling brown piles like melting coffee ice-cream. Kate tooted the horn. Out from the workshop in the stables appeared Joanna, followed by Frank and Josh, Gloria and Jessie. It was hard to distinguish who was who. They were all muffled to the eyes in full storm kit—boots, waterproofs, scarves and gloves—and they all had faces as long as Lent. Kate climbed stiffly out of the car into the driving rain. Her feet were soaked immediately.

"Hello, darling. What on earth's going on?"

"Mum. Come inside the house first."

"What do you mean *first*?" asked Kate, standing there, letting herself get drenched.

Joanna tried to block her way to the workshop. "The heating's on, we've lit your fire and the kettle's boiled. Let's make you a cup of tea."

"Why are you all here?" Kate pushed past Joanna and went towards the workshop. Gloria was crying.

Frank said: "There's been a bit of a disaster, Mrs. Rendlesham. Bit of a leak like, what with all the snow, a treacherous sudden thaw and now the storm—a branch has come down on the roof." He looked miserable.

"She'll have to see sometime," said Gloria to Joanna. "Better get it over now."

They stood aside while Kate went through the door into the workrooms. A scene of devastation met her eyes. Part of the ceiling was down, and the floor was flooded, though Frank and his team had managed to do some sort of temporary job on the roof with polythene sheeting. Heroic efforts had clearly been made to sop up the worst of the water: there was a pile of sodden old towels, mops and brooms had been propped up against the wall; and various buckets and bowls were strategically placed to catch drips. Three overflowing dustbins bore witness to the chunks of plaster that had already been swept up. Kate was too shocked to speak. Then she followed Gloria's gaze. In the only dry spot at the far corner of the room stood the dressmaker's dummies wearing the exotic coats and waistcoats for Midas that had either been finished or were nearly completed. They had obviously just been moved there and were huddled close together like refugees. All the garments were completely ruined.

Kate gave a strangled cry. "All our work. *Weeks* of work. Our whole new collection." She looked at Gloria and Jessie. "What shall we do?"

"Start again," they said with one voice.

"What about the silks?"

"All saturated."

Joanna put an arm round her mother. "You've seen the worst, Mum. You've lost your stock of materials—but you'll be insured for that and the damage. I've rung Janey and warned her. You can talk to her tomorrow. It's the work that's the awful bit for the three of you, but at least you know the worst. We've done what we can for now and everyone's been marvellous, but I think they should all go home before pneumonia sets in."

"I'd stay with you, Kate, if I wasn't so wet," said Gloria. "We'll ring you in the morning and come over tomorrow, won't we, Jessie?" Jessie nodded. Kate hugged them both. "I can't bear it—it's just as bad for you," she said sadly.

Frank got a couple of Calor Gas lights out of his van. "The electric's all off in here," he said. "There's nowt you can do tonight, but I'll leave you these in case you want to look at anything. I'll be off too then." He looked awkwardly at his boots. "I'm ever so sorry. Don't take on. It'll be right again."

Kate thanked them all as one in a dream. A very bad dream.

Apparently the falling plaster had caused the burglar alarm to go off and the police had rung both Frank and Joanna, who were key holders.

"Oh Jo," said Kate as they made tea in the kitchen. "Now I've really lost everything. What shall I do?" There was no false glitter this time.

"I asked you much the same question this summer when I felt my life was falling to bits," said Joanna, thinking her mother, whose face had always remained remarkably youthful, suddenly looked her age. "D'you remember what you said to me? You told me to pick up the pieces and make a patchwork quilt out of them. I think I've started to make my own patchwork quilt now, Mum. You'll have to do the same."

"I thought I'd only just made one," whispered Kate. "I don't think I can do it twice."

"Yes, you can. This one will be even better." Joanna got up. "I'm terribly sorry, Mum, but I have to go. I've been here most of the day. I'm afraid I came over in such a hurry I never thought to bring Acer back. Will you be all right?"

"Of course," said Kate dully. "You've been wonderful, darling. I'll be fine."

She longed to scream: "Stay with me, stay with me!" but pride and habit prevented her. Joanna gave her an unfathomable look, and then a real hug. "Don't give up," she said fiercely to her mother, before diving into the cold and wet and making a run to her car.

Kate hated being without Acer. She had never spent a night alone, either here or at Longthorpe, without the dog's comforting presence. She mooned hopelessly round the house and couldn't bring herself to unpack. Despite the fact that they'd all implored her not to, she decided to go and have a detailed look at the damage. She put on her Puffa and boots, lit one of Frank's gas lamps and fought her way against the wind to the stables. After the warmth of the house, Kate felt it was like walking into a morgue and just about as cheering. She opened cupboard doors and found rolls of sodden silk and velvet, canvas that felt like muslin, and soggy folders of ruined transfers and designs. She nerved herself to inspect the sad refugees in their gloomy group at closer quarters—and wished she hadn't.

Water was still trickling down the workshop's walls in places; tears trickled down Kate's cheeks. It's all a hopeless wreck—like me, she thought. But even in the face of such outward dereliction she knew that the hollow inside her heart had done far more damage to her will to survive than any hole in the roof could have inflicted. She felt utterly desolate.

I ought to leave all this, thought Kate; there's nothing I can do now. But she couldn't make the effort to move and just went on standing there, getting chilled to the bone. It was a huge relief to hear the sudden sound of a car door slamming. She had a wild hope that Joanna might have brought Acer over after all.

She'd had to bang the workshop door and then push all her weight against it to click it shut against the force of the wind. Now it was suddenly wrenched open letting in a hurricane of cold air.

Jack Morley stood in the doorway.

They stared at each other, still as statues, their breath freezing in the air, their gaze burning.

"Jack! Whatever are you doing here?"

"Joanna telephoned me this morning."

"*Joanna!* She never said! So you've come about the damage?"

"Oh I've come about the damage all right—but not the damage to the stables. I've come to ask you out to dinner with me. Will you come?"

"Could—could we just stay here? Talk?"

"Darling Kate," said Jack. "So long as you'll let me talk to you, as far as I'm concerned you can do whatever you want. It always has been like that for me, only I've been such a criminally bloody fool I deserve to lose you."

Slowly Kate walked towards him. He took her face in his hands and looked down as if he could never see enough of it. It was a dirty, tear-streaked face. Her soaking wet hair, usually silver-grey, was almost white with plaster from the ceiling.

"Oh Jack," she said, leaning against him, and covering his immaculate navy-blue pin-stripe suit with dust and debris. "I've been having such terrible withdrawal symptoms for you. I wanted to kick the habit of loving you, and I've tried and tried—but I can't."

Later they lay in the bath thawing out their hearts and bodies. Before she got in, Kate had used three lots of shampoo under the shower to get her hair clean.

"I can't get over Joanna ringing you. How did she find you?"

"She rang Sylvia—you know how well they got on together."

"And you happened to be in the London office?"

"No. I was in Paris."

"Jack! Whatever were you doing in Paris?" Kate, who had been lying back against him, sat up. He slid his hands down her arms and pulled her back against him. "Not what you think. Not what you like much either though—playing power games, you would say. I'm going in for wine-making. I was negotiating to buy a very prestigious vineyard."

"And Sylvia rang you in Paris to tell you about the roof?"

"No. Joanna rang me in Paris to ask me how much longer I was prepared to go on breaking your heart."

"*Jo* said that? Never!" Kate was astonished and entranced. "And what did *you* say?"

"I said I was fed up with lugging my own broken heart about. I said it was beginning to get tiresome—interfering with my business acumen." Jack started to soap Kate's throat, strangling her outraged protest and gradually working further down. "Actually I said I'd give anything for a chance just to see you and eat humble pie. She promised to try and see that you were on your own before I arrived. I hopped on a flight from Paris to Leeds—and here I am." He didn't tell her he had chartered a plane.

They decided not to go out for dinner. The rain was still bucketing down and it was too blissful to be together. Propped up on the kitchen table was an envelope which Joanna must have put there just before she left; it was addressed in her strong, tidy writing: "Mum—not to be opened before 7:30." Inside was a note which read: "Humble Pie for two in fridge. Have a good feast. XXJo."

After they'd had supper Kate had rung Joanna.

"Better now, Mum?"

"Much, much better. Blissful. Oh, darling, I don't know how to thank you."

"Don't try. Come to lunch tomorrow. Glad you enjoyed the pie. Night, Mum."

It was not till they were finally in bed, having eaten Joanna's delicious supper and drunk champagne, that they felt strong enough to broach the subject of Jack's marriage.

"Until I met you," he said, "I had no hope or expectation of having a satisfying emotional relationship with a woman—a friend of the heart. Contrary to what you may have reason to think, and wonderful though the physical bit is, that's not the side of you that's most important to me. I love you, Kate. Love every bit of you with every bit of me—body and soul. I know now what I've been missing all these years.

"My first marriage was a disaster as I told you. We had one daughter, Jean—and I've never been *absolutely* certain she was mine. I wasn't a good father to her, always too busy, and when I was at home I so disliked the way Tania, my first wife, brought her up, that I was always trying to put her straight. After the divorce she spent most of her time with Tania and her succession of husbands. We never really got on and now we're hardly ever in touch. We fulfil each other's expectations: she sends me a Christmas card, and I''—Jack raised an ironic eyebrow—''I send her money. Parenthood is the big failure of my life.

"Then I married Sheila—a pretty, fluffy kitten. Tania was tough as old boots. It would have taken a hurricane to rock Tania, but Sheila caught a chill from the slightest breeze. It took me a few years before I came to terms with the fact that I'd married a hopeless neurotic. I longed for a family, and swore I'd make a better job of being a father this time. It was a terrible disappointment when she refused to have children. There was no physical reason why she shouldn't, but she was terrified. I only discovered after we'd been married that she'd already had psychiatric problems before we met. There were several spells in clinics. In and out—more and more opinions, more and more doctors. Her latest therapist was her god but nothing helped. I wasn't very patient—I'm far from blameless in all this. She accused me of not loving her enough and she was right. Soon she both bored and irritated me—though I really did try.

"She was a hopeless driver, and if we were together I always did all the driving. Then one day, after a business lunch given by some clients, I realised I'd had far too much to drink and knew I was well over the limit. I was afraid I'd be breathalysed and I let her drive me home. It wasn't far, but it was unforgivable. We had an appalling car smash. Sod's law, I, who was to blame, was thrown clear and miraculously escaped with minor injuries, but Sheila was in a coma and on a life-support machine for weeks. She's paralysed from the waist down and brain damaged—but she survived. Now she lives in a twilight world of her own.

Very occasionally there seems to be a faint spark of aware-
ness, but for the most part she doesn't recognise anyone.
She has to have everything done for her. She can't even
feed herself. She lives in our house on Long Island—if you
can call it living—looked after by a team of nurses. I cannot
describe my guilt. The accident was fifteen years ago. I was
forty-five. Sheila was forty. Not a pretty story.''

''Oh, Jack. I'm so sorry. So terribly sorry.''

''Well, now you know. Being the person you are you'll
understand that I could never divorce Sheila. She gets fre-
quent infections and it's often touch and go whether she'll
recover. God forgive me for the number of times I've secretly hoped she'd die. She could go at any time, but she
could also hang on for years. You know what the Yorkshire
expression is—it's the creaking gate that swings longest. I
should have told you at once, that first time we had lunch
here. I knew I'd fallen in love with you, but once I started
missing chances it got more and more difficult. I was so
terrified I'd lose you, so afraid that if you knew I was married your puritanical little conscience would make you give
me up.''

''I don't think anyone seeing me now would think I was
a puritan,'' protested Kate.

''I would so love to marry you, Kate. It may never be
possible.''

''Can I ask you something?''

''Of course.''

''I don't give a toss about marriage for myself now,''
she said. ''It seems irrelevant. I do believe passionately in
family life—it's what kept me with Oliver—but surely
there can be occasional dispensation of vows? I used to feel
rather smug about the fact that I'd kept my marriage vows,
but now that I've met you I know quite well that I was
never tempted badly enough to break them. If I'd met you
earlier I'd never have stayed faithful to Oliver. I don't want
you to divorce Sheila; what I'd like to be sure of is that if
she suddenly died, you wouldn't let this guilt become so

obsessive that it might ruin the relationship we have together. You've surely paid your price, Jack, for one error
of judgement that happened to have horrendous conse-
quences.''

"I promise you I won't let that happen," he said. "You
are my undeserved benediction and I nearly lost you. I
couldn't risk that again."

They lay in silence hand in hand.

Then: "Your Aunt Hannah says you sometimes look
after Sheila yourself?" said Kate.

"I do occasionally, and I have to check that the nurses
care for her kindly as well as efficiently. I lead my own
life, but I keep closely in touch. I owe her that—but I
suppose it's just to make me feel better, really. A hair shirt.
It certainly doesn't help her. What you said to me about
setting up the Centre to salve my conscience really hurt. I
hadn't thought of it like that, but there was enough of an
element of truth to be extremely uncomfortable."

"Oh, Jack, how awful. I was just lashing out at you. It's
a great thing you're doing there, and that's what counts.
Motives are too complicated to cope with sometimes."

Jack turned out the lights. "I think we've talked enough
for now," he said, letting go of her hand, and turning towards her. "How puritanical are you feeling now, Mrs.
Rendlesham?"

"Not at all," said Kate.

❧ THIRTY-FOUR ❧

Next morning January, having bitten hard, decided to pretend it had no teeth left. The wind had dropped, the sky
was clear, and what snow was left sparkled from the hedge-
rows. Yesterday Kate had felt she hated Yorkshire, but
standing outside the tower bedroom, Jack's arm round her

shoulder, she couldn't wish to be anywhere else. I want this moment to go on for ever, she thought.

"Come to Paris with me?" said Jack.

"Mmmm. Lovely. When?" Kate rubbed her cheek against his hand.

"Say in a couple of hours?"

"You mean *now*?"

"Yes. I have to go back today. Leslie will take us to the airport. Bit of a rush, but don't worry about clothes—have a spending spree."

"You're not serious?"

"Oh, but I am. Quite serious. I left in the middle of important negotiations—coming to you was far more important. It still is. But other people are involved in this deal. I don't want to let them down."

"Oh Jack!" Kate did not try to disguise her dismay. "Couldn't it wait till next week? I need more time with you here."

Jack turned Kate to face him. "I promise it won't be for long. I can't bear us to be parted either. So—come with me, Kate." He searched her face.

"But I *can't*. Gloria and Jessie said they'd come over this morning to check everything through with me. I couldn't possibly just upsticks and go away after all they did for me yesterday—specially Gloria. Besides I must ring Janey Pulborough myself and Jo's expecting us for lunch."

"Joanna's not expecting me. I told her I'd have to go back to France this morning."

"Please don't go yet, Jack. I'll come like a shot next week."

Jack looked down at her, his expression inscrutable, while Kate battled with herself. Should she make a fuss, put his devotion on trial again and test his priorities? Did she want to submerge her life completely again in anyone else's, even his? Should she give up Midas?

Jack watched her struggle and then forestalled her.

"We're in similar boats now, aren't we, my dear love?" he said quietly. "We each have careers and commitments. It didn't seem to matter before, but I think it may matter now. It won't be easy for either of us."

"I'm so sorry, Jack." Kate felt a small thread of panic weave through her. She looked at him anxiously. "Do you understand?"

"Oh, I understand all right," he said. "The question is— do you? When you became involved in Midas you spread your wings for the first time. Now you must decide whether or not you still want to go on using them, which may sometimes mean flying solo."

"But do you think I'm right to try?" His verdict was desperately important to Kate. She longed for him to make up her mind for her.

"Ah," he said. "Only you can decide that." He kissed her gently on the mouth. "I'm not in the business of imposing my way of life on you, and you wouldn't want me for long if I turned into your tame pussy cat. I love you, Kate. I think you love me. We may both have to make compromises."

Kate telephoned Jane, who was very sympathetic about the work that had been wasted, but philosophical about the business.

"You've made a name for yourself now. Why don't you see if you could recruit more outworkers? I think it would pay us to have more help. Have a think."

Kate spent the rest of the morning with Gloria and Jessie. When she told them about Jack's return their delight was obvious. Kate, knowing how hard Gloria was battling to live with an aching void of her own, felt humbled by her generosity.

"I'm ever so pleased for you," Gloria said, her smile brilliant, but her eyes full of unshed tears. "It seemed such a waste when you two split up." She added: "My Jim and

I didn't have any choice about what happened to us, but you and Jack do.''

When Kate arrived at Longthorpe for lunch, Acer went wild with excitement.

"Jack gone back to Paris, then?" Joanna asked casually, but burning to know what had happened.

"He got me sussed, so he's flown back to France to finish his next takeover," said Kate dryly. "He asked me to go with him."

"And you wouldn't?"

"Not this time. I thought I should get things fixed here first."

"How's your patchwork, Mum?" asked Joanna. "Still stitching the bits together? I'm working on mine."

It was the first time Mike had played host to Kate at Longthorpe. Kate thought he was enjoying it. It gave her hope.

"I think I'll just pop up to Cecily," she said. "I must fill her in with all that's happened to me."

Cecily was snoozing. "That you, my darling?" she said as Kate bent to kiss her soft, creased cheek.

"It's me," said Kate, not sure which darling was being referred to.

"Oh, Kate—I thought it was Oliver. Is he coming soon?"

"No, Cecily. Oliver's not here," said Kate gently, bothered by this enquiry.

Cecily gave herself a little shake. "No, of course not. How silly of me. Funny—I could have sworn he was here earlier. I must have been dreaming. Have you come to tell me you've cooked lunch?"

"No, I've come over from the Observatory. Jo's cooking lunch." Kate was not sure if Cecily had fully woken up and had landed on the right spot yet. Cecily was normally so quick she was like the Red Queen in *Alice*, and usually had to run faster and faster in order to stay on the same spot.

"Oh, of course. How nice. Well, what have you been up to?"

"Do you remember Jack?" asked Kate cautiously.

"Really, Kate! I'm not senile yet—of course I do. What a silly question! None of us will forget that party in a hurry." Cecily had some tart things to say about Netta. She seemed to have woken up properly now and was her usual astringent self.

"Jack's come back to me," said Kate.

"Oh, darling! I'm so pleased. I always liked him better than your other stalker—poor, dull Gerald who can only talk about plumbing, pesticides, and peerages, when he's not banging on about killing things, that is."

This was the Cecily Kate knew and loved. She told her all about their misunderstanding and misery, their reconciliation and hopes for the future.

"Better stick to Jack now you've got him back," said Cecily, echoing Gloria.

"I mean to try. He'd have a job to get away from me a second time," said Kate. She produced photographs of Chloe and showed Cecily pictures of her latest greatgranddaughter.

"She looks much like any other baby, I see," said Cecily, but was pleased all the same.

"And what did you think of Harriet's father?" asked Kate.

"The monk? Not what one expected as Joanna's exlover, but I have to say I liked him. I told him that RC theory about Immaculate Contraception was a load of rubbish, and we had a good chat about the Vatican too. Father Paul was quite surprised at some of the things I know about the Pope." Kate's imagination boggled.

"Now I think I might have another quick snooze before lunch. Just fill up the nut thing for me and hand me my binoculars in case my robin comes, will you? I've almost got him to sit on my finger." So Kate put out more peanuts and promised to send Rupert up to fetch Cecily as soon as lunch was ready.

"See you in about ten minutes, Cecily. We'll give you a call."

"Thank you for coming up. I do miss you—you've been my sheet-anchor, Kate," said Cecily unexpectedly, and added sleepily: "Goodbye then, darling." Her eyelids drooped.

Kate's throat constricted. She felt choked with love for her often difficult mother-in-law.

There was noise and laughter coming from downstairs. Rupert and Tilly were playing "Hats Off" with Mike. Kate went through to the kitchen. Joanna was deftly chopping parsley to sprinkle on the mashed potato. Kate perched on the kitchen table and gossiped to her while she dished up; she thought how effortless Jo made cooking seem.

Rupert was dispatched to fetch Cecily while Joanna marshalled the rest of the family into the dining room. Tilly toyed with the idea of having one of her screaming attacks because they hadn't been able to finish the game, but after a warning look from her father decided it might be wiser to postpone a scene till a more propitious moment.

"Whatever can Rupert be doing?" asked Joanna irritably. "Tilly, do go and ring the gong really loudly." At that moment Rupert suddenly appeared looking very bothered.

"I can't make Granny-Cis wake up," he said. "I've been trying to push her deaf aid into her ear, but she still doesn't seem to hear me."

Kate and Joanna were up the stairs in a flash.

Cecily was sitting in her chair exactly as Kate had left her, still holding the binoculars on her lap. But she would never wake again. Her indomitable, contrary, loving spirit had gone elsewhere.

*   *   *

Kate telephoned Jack to tell him about Cecily.

"Of course you can't come to Paris now. I'm so very sorry, my darling—she was unique. I know you'll miss her terribly." Jack did not make the mistake of saying: "Oh well, you can't mourn. She'd had a good long innings— bound to be given out soon," as Gerald Brownlow said later when Joanna rang to tell him the news.

Jack decided not to come back to Ravelstoke till the funeral was over. He did not wish to intrude on the Rendlesham family at such a private time, and it hardly seemed a fitting moment to reactivate local speculation about his relationship with Kate. Though she agreed with him, Kate longed for his comforting presence during the following week.

Cecily had been much loved locally and at her funeral the church was crammed with friends from many different backgrounds who wished to pay their last respects. Everyone had their own particular Cecily story to tell. Harriet had helped Kate decorate the church.

"Let's not have anything too exotic," said Kate.

"It's a pity we can't have birds instead of flowers really," said Harriet, tears stinging her eyes. "Granny-Cis was a hedgerow person."

Together she and Kate covered the window sills with snowdrops embedded in moss, twined ivy round the pillars, and put some early catkins in the narrow-necked brass altar vases which Cecily had liked, scorning the more popular pedestals favoured by most volunteers on the church's flower-arrangement rota. Harriet found an old thrush's nest in the garden; she lined it with sheep's wool, filled it with the sugar almond eggs which her great-grandmother had always kept for visiting children, then balanced it on the ledge above the pew where Cecily had always sat.

The choir of Granby Abbey sang at the service and as the head chorister's soaring treble piped Mendelssohn's "Oh, for the Wings of a Dove" a good many people struggled with their emotions.

*   *   *

In the event, the reunion between Jack and Kate was delayed again. This time it was Jack's turn to telephone to postpone it. Sheila had done one of her unpredictable nosedives and Jack had been summoned back to New York by the doctors. No one had any idea what the outcome would be.

Kate was appalled at her own resentment. It had been one thing to accept Jack's absences on business back in the summer at the start of their relationship, one thing, now that she knew of Sheila's circumstances, to tell Jack that she would always want him to do the right thing about his wife. It was quite another to face the fact that because of her, he was liable to disappear back to America at a moment's notice. Kate wondered about the outcome too. She dared not examine her feelings about Sheila too closely.

Just before Jack had left for Paris he had taken Kate into the part of the store room where the garden tools were kept. Ironically everything there was bone dry. There were two packing cases against the wall. Jack had prised them open, and unwound yards of bubble packing.

"Something for you," he had said to Kate. "Or rather for us. I was going to give them to you after the Ravelstoke party. Hope you like them."

When he'd got all the packing off he revealed two lead unicorns. "You told me unicorns were symbols of magic," he said, "so I had them made. Perhaps now they'll always remind us of how very nearly we let our magic go. I told you magic was hard to recapture."

"Oh Jack, they're wonderful! I *love* them. They're you and me," said Kate.

Jack grinned. "Umm. Not sure which is which—we'll have to get hold of a unicorn sexer."

"I expect they're like guinea pigs and keep everything safely tucked away inside," she had said, laughing.

"How wise," said Jack.

The following week Frank and Josh set up the unicorns on either side of the gates. They lay facing each other, comfortably "couchant," on their pillars looking as if they had always been there.

Kate, leaning on the balustrade that ran round the tower, looked down at them now. Sheila had survived her crisis—yet again—and Jack had immediately flown back to England. He had just rung to say he was approaching Ravelstoke.

As Kate stood watching to see his car turn in at the gates of the Observatory, she ran a film of the last two years through her head. So much has happened to us all, she thought: loss and release, sadness and anxiety, the end of an era but the arrival of exciting new relationships and different resolves. At that moment she heard the triple toot on the horn that signalled Jack's arrival.

"I hope your magic is good and strong," said Kate to the unicorns.

Another delightful novel from
Rosamunde Pilcher's Bookshelf

A PRICE FOR EVERYTHING

MARY SHEEPSHANKS

Sonia Duntan has it all: a beautiful estate in the English
Countryside, a caring husband, four wonderful children,
and a burgeoning career as an artist. Yet she wants
more—and sees it in the form of the handsome and charming Simon Hadleigh. But Sonia may find out that sometimes the price of happiness it too high...

"*A Price for Everything* is linked, from start to finish, by
Mary Sheepshanks' humor and a rare sense of the ridiculous."

—From the introduction by Rosamunde Pilcher

A PRICE FOR EVERYTHING
Mary Sheepshanks
0-312-96478-1___$5.99 U.S.___$7.99 Can.